I could be yours.

Right. As if he'd ever in a million years be able to compete with the guy she'd just said she'd love forever. Besides, all his friend had wanted was for Levi to make sure Val was okay. He sincerely doubted falling for the woman had been part of his best friend's plan.

Then again...

Maybe it was time to set aside his loyalty to a dead man for a shot at something far bigger. Maybe, just maybe, this was his chance to be everything to Val, to her girls, that he couldn't have been before. Yes, it had to be her choice to move forward or not. But how could she make that choice if he didn't give her the option? And if the odds were stacked against him... tough.

Wouldn't be the first time.

* * *

WED IN THE WEST: New Mexico's the perfect place to finally find true love!

P9-DMO-261

Dear Reader,

What really makes someone a hero? How do we define *courage*? Those were the seeds that eventually blossomed into this story about a former soldier whose quiet courage not only stood him in good stead while deployed in a war zone, but back home as well, as he now struggles to make good on a promise he's not at all sure how to keep... A promise to a young, widowed mother who, with his help, finds the inner strength to not only overcome her past, but to fully embrace her new future, filled with hope and love.

Variations of Levi and Val's story play out every day, as soldiers return from war, and as widows—and widowers—call on reserves of strength they perhaps never knew were there, until eventually glimmers of joy pierce through the fog of pain and grief and loss. And, at least in some measure, happiness returns, even as those who didn't come home are still remembered and honored...and those who do return find peace in what so often is a new, and often unrecognizable, reality.

This story is for all those who have served, as well as for the families who support them, encourage them, love them.

Thank you.

Karen Templeton

A Soldier's Promise

Karen Templeton

HARLEQUIN® SPECIAL EDITION®

If you purchased this book without a cover you should be aware that this book is stolen property. It was reported as "unsold and destroyed" to the publisher, and neither the author nor the publisher has received any payment for this "stripped book."

Recycling programs
for this product may
not exist in your area

ISBN-13: 978-0-373-65939-5

A Soldier's Promise

Copyright © 2016 by Karen Templeton-Berger

All rights reserved. Except for use in any review, the reproduction or utilization of this work in whole or in part in any form by any electronic, mechanical or other means, now known or hereinafter invented, including xerography, photocopying and recording, or in any information storage or retrieval system, is forbidden without the written permission of the publisher, Harlequin Enterprises Limited, 225 Duncan Mill Road, Don Mills, Ontario M3B 3K9, Canada.

This is a work of fiction. Names, characters, places and incidents are either the product of the author's imagination or are used fictitiously, and any resemblance to actual persons, living or dead, business establishments, events or locales is entirely coincidental.

This edition published by arrangement with Harlequin Books S.A.

For questions and comments about the quality of this book, please contact us at CustomerService@Harlequin.com.

® and TM are trademarks of Harlequin Enterprises Limited or its corporate affiliates. Trademarks indicated with ® are registered in the United States Patent and Trademark Office, the Canadian Intellectual Property Office and in other countries.

Printed in U.S.A.

Karen Templeton is a recent inductee into the Romance Writers of America Hall of Fame. A three-time RITA® Award—winning author, she has written more than thirty novels for Harlequin and lives in New Mexico with two hideously spoiled cats. She has raised five sons and lived to tell the tale, and could not live without dark chocolate, mascara and Netflix.

Books by Karen Templeton

Harlequin Special Edition

Jersey Boys

Meant-to-Be Mom
Santa's Playbook
More Than She Expected
The Real Mr. Right

Summer Sisters

The Marriage Campaign
A Gift for All Seasons
The Doctor's Do-Over

The Fortunes of Texas: Whirlwind Romance

Fortune's Cinderella

Wed in the West

Husband Under Construction
Adding Up to Marriage
Welcome Home, Cowboy
A Marriage-Minded Man
Reining in the Rancher
A Mother's Wish

Visit the Author Profile page
at Harlequin.com for more titles.

To my oldest son, Christopher
Whose own service continues to bless.
Semper Fi, dude.

Chapter One

Sweat streamed down Levi Talbot's back as he sat in his pickup across the street, watching Valerie Lopez paint the window trim of a house he hadn't set foot in for… *Damn. Ten years, at least.*

She was even skinnier than he remembered, sharp shoulder blades shifting, bunching over the scoop of a white tank top that teased the waistband of her low-rise jeans. Her pale hair was still long, wadded on top of her head, pieces sticking out every which way. In a nearby play yard a dark-haired baby sat gnawing on a plastic toy, while her older sister lay on her belly on the mottled floorboards, quietly singing as she scribbled, bare feet swinging to and fro. Then the little girl shoved to her knees, thrusting the open coloring book toward her mother.

"Mama! I gave her hair like mine! See?"

Levi saw Val glance over, her smile gentle as she bent to get a better look. Chuckling softly, she fingered the girl's deep brown curls.

"A huge improvement, I'd say," she said. The child giggled, making Val smile even bigger, and Levi flinched.

How the hell was he supposed to do this? Whatever *this* was.

And why the hell had it never occurred to him he might actually have to make good on that dumb-ass promise he'd made to Tomas when they'd first enlisted?

A breeze lanced his damp shirt, making him shiver. Squinting in the bolt of sunlight glancing off the sharply angled tin roof, Levi frowned at the house, which seemed to frown right back at him. An uneasy cross between Victorian and log cabin, the house seemed to slump in on itself, like it was too tired to care anymore. Or had finally succumbed to its identity crisis. And slapping some paint over what was most likely rotting wood wasn't going to change that.

He could relate.

He waited for an SUV to pass—not much traffic on this stretch of Main Street, the last gasp of civilization before miles of nothing—before getting out of his truck, his boots crunching on asphalt chewed up even worse than usual after last winter's heavy snow. A hawk keened, annoyed, from a nearby piñon, whose branches tangled with the deep blue sky. From inside the house, a dog exploded into frenzied barking. Val and the child turned, the little girl's gaze more curious than concerned. Her mother's, however...

Yeah. Considering she hadn't exactly been a fan *before* he and Tommy had enlisted, Levi sincerely doubted that was about to change. Promise or no promise. In fact, what he saw in those blue eyes could only be described as... Well, *fierce* would work. *Pissed off* was more likely.

He stopped at the bottom step.

"Levi." Val hauled the baby out of her little cage, tucked her against her ribs. Close-up, she seemed even smaller, probably not even coming to his shoulders. He remembered, though, how her smile could light up the whole town. Not that she'd ever given him that smile. "Heard you were back."

He nodded, unsure of what came next. Hating that this puny little blonde was unnerving him more than driving supply trucks along dusty mountain roads that might or might not have been booby-trapped by the Taliban.

"Last week, yeah."

The baby grabbed hold of a hank of her mother's hair, tried to stuff it in her mouth. The older girl—seven, he thought—sidled closer; Val looped her arm around the girl's shoulders as dark eyes exactly like her father's regarded Levi with that same intense gaze. Had Val ever mentioned Levi to her daughter? Had Tommy?

"For good?" Val said.

"For now, anyway." The dog's barking grew more frantic. "So. These are your girls?"

Val shot him an are-you-nuts look, but she played along. "Yes. This is Josie," she said, giving the older girl's shoulders a quick squeeze. "And this is Risa."

Laughter in Spanish. Levi's heart knocked—Tommy had never even seen his second daughter.

"I'm sorry—"

"Don't," Val whispered, her eyes shiny.

"I couldn't get back at the time," Levi finished through a clogged throat, remembering his shock when he'd gotten the call from Tommy's dad. "I asked, but they said no."

Her face said it all: *And exactly what good would that have done?*

Along with: *You can leave now.* Except he couldn't. Because he'd made a promise. One he fully intended to keep.

Whether his best friend's widow was good with that idea or not.

* * *

Val'd figured she'd run into Levi eventually—his parents didn't live far, and there was only one halfway decent grocery store in town—but she hadn't counted on him actually seeking her out.

Of course, her rational side knew Levi Talbot wasn't responsible for her husband's death. That particular honor went to whoever had planted that roadside bomb near some godforsaken Afghani village with a name Val couldn't even pronounce. But if Levi hadn't joined the army six years ago, Val highly doubted that Tommy—who'd worshipped his best friend since high school for reasons Val had never understood—would've decided to enlist, too.

A thought that ripped open barely healed wounds all over again.

"Josie, why don't you go inside?" she quietly asked, smiling down at her daughter. At least this one might remember her daddy. Although considering how much he'd been gone…

"Mama?"

"Levi and I just need to talk alone for a sec, baby. And don't let the dog out, okay?"

Josie shot Levi a questioning look before shoving open the stubborn door and wriggling past the dog to get inside. Only after the door clicked closed did Val turn back to Levi, as muscled and tall as Tomas had been slight. All the Talbot boys were built like their father, tough and rough and full of surprising angles, like they'd been hastily hewn out of the mountains holding silent watch over sleepy Whispering Pines. Oh, yeah, Levi Talbot was one good-looking sonofagun, despite badly needing a shave and a half-grown-out buzz cut that wasn't doing him any favors—

"So you're living here now," Levi said. Carefully, like she was a horse who might spook. Val set Risa back in her play yard and handed her a toy, then crouched, gripping the top of the pen.

"Temporarily. Since Tommy's grandmother moved in with his folks, the family said we can stay as long as we need." She heard a creak behind her as he came up onto the porch.

"Big place for three people."

As in, way bigger than Val needed. Five bedrooms, three baths. Dark. Dreary. "Yeah. It is," she said, straightening in time to see Levi's gaze flick over the worn porch floorboards, the gap-toothed porch railings.

"Needs a lot of work."

Despite the situation, a smile pushed at Val's mouth. "Part of the deal was that I get it fixed up. So they can get top dollar when it goes on the market. After everything they've done for me, I couldn't exactly say no. Besides—" she almost smiled "—it would break Lita's heart if I wasn't here."

Levi's brows dipped. "They expect you to foot the bill?"

"Of course not. It's not my house, is it?"

He was staring at her. Not rudely, but intently, his muddy green eyes focused on her like lasers. Exactly like he used to do when they were younger, as though he couldn't figure her out. Or more likely, why his best friend would prefer her company to his. And damned if it didn't make her every bit as uneasy now as it did then—

"For pity's sake, Levi—why are you here?"

If her outburst threw him, he didn't let on. Although his Adam's apple definitely worked before he said, "Tommy was my closest friend, Val. I was best man at your wedding. Did you think I'd come home and not check on you?"

Risa began to fuss; Val picked her up again, pressing her lips into her curls, cool and soft against her hot face. "At least you got to come home," she murmured, then lifted her gaze to Levi's, the hurt in his eyes almost enough to make her feel like a bitch. Almost. Because there were days when her anger was about the only thing keeping her from losing it. That, and love for her daughters, she thought as Risa yawned, then plugged her thumb in her mouth and settled against Val's chest.

"And as you can see," she said, ignoring her stinging eyes, "I'm okay. So. We're good."

Levi did that staring thing again, his mouth stubborn-set, the earlier devastation in his eyes replaced by something else Val couldn't quite put a finger on but knew she didn't like.

"This place was a wreck fifteen years ago. I can only imagine what it's like now. Tommy's kids…" He paused, his nostrils flaring when he took a breath. "They deserve better than this." Another pause. "And so do you."

His words hit her. Hard. Not that people hadn't been kind since her return. But it'd been an uncomfortable kindness mostly, a ragtag collection of mumbled "sorries" and brief, awkward hugs, soon replaced by either gaping silence or a false cheeriness that made her want to scream. With Levi, though—it wasn't the same, that's all. Although it wouldn't be, would it?

"Thank you—"

"You can give me a list, if you want. Might as well start with this porch, though." He shifted his weight into the next plank over, making it squawk. "Some of these floorboards look pretty sketchy—"

"Levi."

He looked up, his brow creased. "Yeah?"

"Why?"

It was all she could think to say. Not enough, however, to provoke an answer.

"I'll be back in the morning," he said softly, then went down the steps and back across the street, where he got into a black pickup, slamming the door before taking off. Toward his parents' house, she imagined, where she'd heard via the grapevine he was staying.

Val rearranged the now sleeping baby in her arms and grabbed the wet paintbrush, then went back inside, where she dumped the brush into the chipped kitchen sink before hauling Risa upstairs to put her in her crib. This and Josie's room were the only ones she'd painted so far: a pale aqua in here, yellow in Josie's. The gouged pine floors still needed to be redone. Along with a dozen other projects that made Val's head hurt to think about.

Because the house *was* a wreck, the victim of decades of benign neglect and an old woman's failing eyesight. Yes, being so close to Tommy's parents was a blessing, and the family was being very generous in so many ways. But the idea of going through renovations on top of everything else…

All of which had sounded perfectly feasible when Angelita Lopez had promised the house to them two years ago, for when Tommy came back home.

A thought Val deliberately let linger, as though to toughen her heart. So when this one—she leaned over the crib to finger Risa's soft curls—asked about her daddy, Val would be able to speak with love, not pain. Less pain, anyway.

Risa flipped onto her back, arms splayed like she was making snow angels. A smile flickered across the baby's mouth, making Val smile in return, her heart swell. Because life, she sternly reminded herself, was about cherishing what you had, not regretting what you'd lost. About accepting the gifts that came your way. Even those that, at first glance, seemed more trouble than they were worth. Like this butt-ugly house.

Like, say, offers from the last man in the world you wanted to deal with right now—or ever—to help fix up said butt-ugly house.

Val sighed.

Back downstairs, she peeked into the cave-like living room, a hodgepodge of dull, dark wood and mismatched furniture pieces. Eyes glued to the TV screen, Josie sat cross-legged on the sofa, pointy elbows digging into scabbed bare knees. The hound stretched on the cushion beside her, dead to the world, chin and paws propped on the sofa's arm.

"Is he gone?" Josie asked.

"He is. Whatcha watching?" As if she didn't know.

"Elf."

Val smiled. "Again?"

The little girl shrugged. "I like it," she said, and Val's heart twisted. On his last leave—two Christmases ago—Tomas and Josie had watched the movie together a million times. Then Josie forgot about it…until she found the DVD when they unpacked.

"This was Daddy's favorite scene," her daughter said softly, and Val decided this was part of that toughening-up-her-heart thing. Although if a stupid movie helped her baby still feel connected to her father, she'd take it. Because Val knew those memories would fade, would be replaced by a whole life's worth of new ones. Oh, there'd be scraps left, of course, but they'd be as soft and faded as the ribbons from Val's wedding bouquet.

"Fried chicken okay for dinner?"

Josie nodded again, then pulled her knees up to her chin, her far-too-old gaze swinging to Val's.

"So that was Levi," Josie said, and Val nearly choked.

"It was. Did…Daddy talk to you about him?"

"Uh-huh," she said easily, her gaze returning to the TV. "He said if anything happened to him? Levi would take care of us."

Val could barely hear her own voice for the clanging inside her head. "When did Daddy say that?"

Josie shrugged. "Before he left. The last time. He said if he didn't come back, Levi would make sure we were okay. Because they were best friends, that Levi always had his back. That…" The little girl frowned, as though she was trying to remember, then smiled. "That, except for you, he trusted Levi more than anyone in the world."

Val dropped onto the edge of the craptastic armchair at right angles to the sofa, pressing her hand to her stomach as she rode out a new wave of anger. *What the hell were you* thinking, *Tommy?* To confide in Josie—who was only five at the time—rather than her…

Not to mention even suggest that he might not come back.

Val shut her eyes, breathing deeply. Funny how, with her background, Val had always considered herself a realist. Not a pessimist, exactly, but fully aware of how often things could go wrong. Tomas, though…he'd been the dreamer, the idealist, seeing silver linings where Val only saw clouds, giving her glimpses of shiny hope peeking through years of gloom and doom. No wonder she'd fallen in love with him. And consequently why, every time he left, she'd steeled herself against the possibility that he might not come home. Especially considering his particular job. "High risk" didn't even begin to cover it.

But little girls shouldn't have to worry about such things, or live in fear about what *might* happen. All she'd wanted—which Tomas knew—was to make a safe, secure life for her children. That her sweet, gentle husband had gone behind her back, undermining everything she'd fought so hard for—

"Mama? What's wrong?"

How about everything?

"I… I didn't know. About what Daddy said."

"You mad?"

She smiled—tightly—before holding out her arms. Josie

clumsily slid off the sofa to climb on Val's lap, where Val wrapped her up tight to lay her head in her daughter's springy hair, struggling to find the peace she'd once let herself believe was finally hers.

"I'm surprised, that's all."

"That Daddy didn't tell you?"

"Uh-huh."

Josie picked at the little knotted bracelet encircling Val's wrist, the one Tomas had given her when they'd first started going together, more than a dozen years ago now. It was grimy and frayed and borderline disgusting, and Val would never take it off.

"Daddy made me promise not to say anything. He said it was our secret. But that he wanted me to know it'd be okay." She leaned back to meet Val's eyes. "With Levi."

Yeah, well, somehow Val doubted that. For a boatload of reasons so knotted up in her head she doubted she'd ever straighten them out.

But she certainly didn't need to drag her little girl into the maelstrom of emotions Levi's appearance had provoked. However…she supposed she might as well let the man fix her porch, since those rotting floorboards gave her the willies, too, and it wasn't as if she could replace them herself. And the nearby ski resort had apparently hired every contractor, carpenter and handyman in a hundred-mile radius for a massive, and long-overdue, renovation.

So. A job she could give him. Anything else, though—

Holding her daughter even more tightly, Val reminded herself, again, to be grateful for what she still had—her beautiful daughters, Tommy's doting parents, a roof over their heads, even if it wasn't exactly hers. More than she ever thought she'd have, once upon a time.

And damned if she was about to let Levi Talbot screw that up.

* * *

Levi slammed shut the gate to his old pickup and piled high what he hoped was enough lumber to fix Val's porch. Yeah, he should've taken measurements, but that would've meant hanging around, that last "Why?" of hers buzzing around inside his head like a ticked-off bee. Not that it still didn't. But yesterday, with nothing separating him and Val but a few feet of hot resentment, he couldn't deal with the question and her eyes. Those eyes—they were surreal, a pale blue like pond ice reflecting the sky. Cold as that ice, too.

At least she hadn't told him to go to hell, he thought, as he headed out of the Lowe's parking lot. Not with her mouth, anyway. He only wished Tomas had been a little clearer about what he'd meant by "Take care of them, bro."

He turned off the main road leading to the ski resort onto the dinkier one that went on to Whispering Pines. At this altitude, early mornings were chilly even in May. Would've been a peaceful drive from Taos, too, if it hadn't been for the hard rock music pulsing through the cab, his head, driving out any and all wayward thoughts. Same music he'd listen to in the Sandbox, and for the same reason—to drown out that bizarre blend of boredom and constant anxiety nobody ever admitted to. At least not out loud.

He'd thought he'd known what he was getting into, that he was prepared, only to soon discover nobody and nothing could prepare you for reality. That reality, anyway. But he'd made a commitment, and he'd kept it. One of the few things he was apparently good at. God knew he'd done more than his fair share of dumb-ass stuff growing up, but he'd never, not once, gone back on his word. And damned if he was gonna start now.

Levi tapped the steering wheel in time to the beat as the road meandered through patches of ranch land, the occasional spurt of forest, backdropped by the mountains that provided Whispering Pines and other puny little northern New Mexico towns like it, both spring runoff and something resembling a viable economy. Differences were subtle—a new fence here, a fresh coat of paint on a house there. He should've found the continuity comforting. Instead, the sameness bugged him. Same way everybody expected him to somehow fit right back in, as if he were the same goofy twenty-two-year-old who'd joined up six years ago. Not that he knew for sure yet who he was, but for sure that clueless kid wasn't it.

The village was still half asleep, the tourist traps and art galleries and chichi restaurants on Main Street not yet ready to welcome the resort patrons curious enough to come down the mountain to investigate "real" New Mexico. Almost silently, the truck navigated the gentle roller coaster that was the town's main drag, past the sheriff's office and the elementary/middle school, the 7-Eleven and the Chevron station, the corner anchored by one bank and three churches. Rosa Munoz was out in front of the Catholic church, clipping lilacs, same as she'd been doing for as long as Levi could remember. Wearing the same sweater, too, from what Levi could tell.

Long before he reached the house, he spotted Val standing on the porch in a hoodie and jeans, clutching a mug in her hands. Like maybe she was waiting for him, although common sense told him that was dumb. He backed into the driveway, the top layer of cement eroded worse than the street in front of it. The dog—a good-size hound, he now saw—bounded up when he opened the door, baying loud enough to cause an avalanche. Still seated behind the wheel, Levi glanced down at the dog, then over to Val.

"You mind calling him off?"

"Don't worry—he doesn't bite. Hasn't yet, anyway."

Shaking his head, Levi got out, pushed past the still

barking dog and headed up the driveway…straight into Val's frown. Which he ignored. By now the damn dog was jumping around, occasionally shoving his cold nose into Levi's hand. "Uh…if you got him as a guard dog, you might want to see about getting your money back."

"*I* didn't get him at all. Tommy brought him home one day from some rescue place near the base. Scrawniest puppy I'd ever seen." Levi looked up. The frown was still there, but her eyes didn't seem quite as icy as before. "I didn't have the heart to say no. To him or the dog."

Levi looked back at the beast. Who'd planted his butt on the rough ground and was waving one paw at him, like he wanted to shake. Levi obliged. "What's his name?"

"Radar."

"Because Early Warning System would've been too obvious."

Val's mouth might've twitched. "Not to mention too hard for a toddler to say." Then she clamped her mouth shut, as if regretting her humorous slip.

"Where are the girls?"

"With their grandmother. Connie and Pete live closer to the school, and she takes care of the baby while I'm at the diner—"

"The diner?"

"Annie's Café. Part-time."

"You're waitressing?"

"I'm doing whatever it takes to keep sane. And we need to get a few things straight."

Levi propped one booted foot on the bottom step as a tremor shot up his spine. "Which would be?"

Val's cheeks went pink. He guessed not from the chill in the air. "This is strictly a business arrangement. Why you're here is…immaterial. As you duly noted yesterday, the house needs a lot of work. Work I can't do."

Levi decided to put the why-he-was-here comment on hold for a moment. "Because you weigh less than the dog?"

She smirked. "Because I don't know bubkes about fixing up houses. And I gather you do."

"Enough. Although if you've got serious electrical or plumbing issues, you'll need to call in a pro. I can change out fixtures and sh—stuff, but anything more than that—"

"Got it. But I'm hiring you. Meaning I expect to be given a bill for your work—"

"Not gonna happen."

"Then you're right. It isn't."

"You don't mean that."

A moment's hesitation preceded, "Yeah. I do. And, yes, I know what I just said—"

Levi held up one hand, cutting off the conversation before it got even stupider than it already was. He remembered Tommy's mentioning Val's stubbornness from time to time. His friend found it amusing, probably because he was crazy in love with the girl. Right now, Levi was more inclined toward annoyance. Pushing back his denim jacket to cram his hands into his front pockets, he frowned.

"You really hate me that much?"

Judging from her wide eyes, he'd shocked her. Good. Took a moment before she apparently found her voice. "What I do or don't feel about you has nothing to do with it. But when there aren't clear-cut expectations, things can get...weird."

"Agreed. Except since I doubt either of us would let it, not an issue. Besides..."

Damn. He could almost hear Tomas whispering in his ear, *Dude—you gotta be up front with her.*

"Okay...when you asked 'why' yesterday, the reason I didn't answer wasn't because I didn't have an answer. It was because... I couldn't find the words. Any that sounded right, at least..."

"You're here because Tommy asked you to keep an eye on me and the girls."

Levi started. "He told you?"

"No. Josie did. Yesterday, after you left."

"Hell."

"Yeah. Still haven't wrapped my head around the fact that he said something to our kid but not me. So I already know why you're here—"

"Because I made a promise, yeah. And I know you don't like me, or trust me, or whatever, so this is every bit as awkward and uncomfortable for me as it is you. Except the longer I think about it, the more I realize none of that matters. Because what *matters* is making sure my best friend's kids aren't living someplace that's gonna fall down around their ears. That here's something I can do to maybe make things better for somebody, to honor the one person who saw through my BS when we were kids, more than even my parents, my brothers. This is about…"

He felt his throat work. "About my debt to my best friend. One I fully intend to make good on. So it might make things a little easier if you'd get on board with that. Now. You want to pay for materials, I won't object. But my labor… It's my gift, okay? Because this is about what Tommy wanted. Not you, not me—Tommy. So deal."

That got a few more moments of the staring thing before Val released a short, humorless laugh. "Wow. Guess you found your words."

"Yeah, well, don't get used to it, I just used up at least three months' worth. So are we good?"

Another pause. "Except what are you supposed to live on?"

"Never mind about that. But here." He dug the rumpled Lowe's receipt out of his pocket, handed it over. What he kept to himself, though—for the moment, anyway—was that he knew how much the family had set aside for repairs, because he'd asked Pete Lopez the night before. Not nearly enough, if his hunch was correct about the extent of the work needed. Especially if she ended up having to call in pros. "Also," he said as she looked it over, "you don't need to stick around. I brought my own lunch. And the woods over there will work fine when nature calls." Her eyes shot to his; he shrugged. "I'm used to making do."

Shaking her head, she grabbed her purse off a table on the porch, stuffed the receipt inside. "The house is open, feel free to use the facilities—"

"You're very trusting."

"Don't read too much into it—there's absolutely nothing worth stealing. Unless you have a thing for Disney princesses. In which case, knock yourself out. I'll be back around three-thirty, after I pick up the girls. The dog can stay out front as long as his water dish is filled, but don't let him out back, since there's no fence. And no, I don't get it, either, why he won't leave the front yard but heeds the call of the wild the minute he hits the back deck."

Levi swallowed his smile. "Got it."

She started down the steps, only to turn around before she reached her car, a dinged-up Toyota RAV4 with a small American flag hanging limply from the antenna. "If you do a crap job on my porch? There will be hell to pay."

"Fair enough."

With a nod, she finished the short walk to her car, stripping out of the hoodie before getting in. And Levi couldn't help noticing how the sunlight kissed her hair, her slender shoulders…the shoulders, he knew, that had borne far more burdens than they should have. Not only recently, but before, when they were still in school and he'd hear the sniggering. Like it was somehow Val's fault her mother was the way she was, that her father had left them high and dry when she was a little kid.

No, he thought as she backed out of the drive, took off,

he didn't imagine trusting had ever come easy to Valerie Oswald. With damn good reason. By comparison he and Tomas had led charmed lives, with parents who loved them, were there for them, even if Levi's had sometimes been a little more *there* than he might've liked. But it hadn't been like that for Val, who must've figured it was simply easier to keep to herself than to either live a lie or apologize for her mother. Which naturally led everyone to think she was either stuck-up or weird.

Almost everyone, anyway, Levi thought, as he yanked a large toolbox out of the truck, grabbed a crowbar to start prying up the rotten floorboards. So how could the girl who'd worked so hard to overcome her past not look at Levi without being reminded of what she'd lost?

Clearly Tommy hadn't thought that part of his plan through.

With a grunt, he wrenched up the first board and tossed it out into the yard, chuckling when the dumb dog first scampered back, then growled at the board like it was a snake.

Which pretty much said it all, didn't it?

Chapter Two

Val shoved the last of the peach pies into the commercial-size freezer, then crossed to the stainless steel sink in the gleaming kitchen to wash her hands.

"All done?" AJ Phillips, who with his wife, Annie, had run Annie's Café for thirty years, called from the other side of the checkerboard-floored room, where he was molding a half-dozen meat loaves to bake for the dinner rush. On the massive gas stove simmered cauldrons of green chile stew and posole, although the fried chicken would happen later, closer to dinnertime. In any case, the kitchen already smelled like heaven. A New Mexican's version of it, anyway.

"Yep," Val called back, shaking water off her hands before grabbing a paper towel. "A dozen."

Grinning, the bald, dark-skinned man noisily shoved the trays in the oven. "My mouth's already watering," he said, and Val laughed.

It wasn't ideal, though, having to make the pies during the afternoon lull, then freeze them to bake the next morning. But between the kids and not having a health-department-approved kitchen—yet—this was the best she could do. And since nobody was complaining, neither would she. *Take that, Marie Callender,* she thought with a slight smile as she walked back out into the dining room, where the only customer was Charley Maestas, hunched over a probably cold cup of coffee at the counter. His part pit bull mutt, sporting a blue bandanna around his neck, lay on the floor beside him, still but alert, as if he knew he wasn't supposed to be inside. Although Annie said as far as she was concerned Loco was a service dog, and that was that.

Val squeezed the older man's shoulder, his vintage denim jacket worn soft, as she passed him on her way to the ladies'. "Hey, Charley—how's it going?"

Charley grunted his acknowledgment, his hand shaking as he lifted the heavy crockery mug to his mouth. The Iraq vet wasn't homeless, although the cabin on the town's outskirts next to his old cabinetmaking shop was no palace. But his graying beard was always neatly trimmed and his clothes clean, smelling of pine needles and menthol. She knew he'd served a couple of tours overseas with the National Guard, back before she and Tomas were married, that he'd been medically discharged when an IED went off close enough to inflict some brain damage of indeterminate severity. Some days were better than others, but according to Annie the poor guy would never be able to hold down a real job again. As it was, he often had trouble simply holding on to a thought.

"Can't complain, honey." He took a sip, swallowed, then turned droopy-lidded dark eyes to hers. "You?"

Val smiled, even though seeing him nearly every day was hard on her heart. And not only because he was a constant reminder of her own loss. She remembered him as a funny, sweet man who was crazy about kids—he and his wife, who'd passed away shortly before his last tour, had been childless—with a laugh that could be heard for what seemed like miles. Seeing him like this crushed her inside. Were the sacrifices really worth it? she wondered.

"I'm doing good, thanks. But seems to me you're missing something." She reached into the glass dessert case for the last piece of blueberry pie, which she set, with a fork, in front of the older man.

"Oh. I didn't—"

"It's too messy a piece to charge for. No, seriously, it looks like my dog sat on it." She smiled at his raspy chuckle; then he sobered, staring at the pie.

"He didn't really, did he?"

"No, Charley," she said gently. "I'm just pulling your leg. Because he would've snarfed it up long before he sat on it."

Charley chuckled again, the fork trembling when he picked it up. But the flicker of light in his eyes as he looked over at her, then back at the pie—a blob of flaky crust floating in a glistening, purple puddle—made Val's heart turn over in her chest. The same as it did each time they played out this little scenario, which was pretty much every day.

"You are an angel, girl," he said softly, releasing a blissful sigh as he took his first bite. "Some guy's gonna be damned lucky to get you."

Even as her face warmed, she smiled, ignoring his last comment. She'd told him about Tomas, more than once. Wasn't his fault the information didn't stick.

"It's only a piece of pie, Charley. No biggie." With another light squeeze to his arm she went on to the ladies' room, leaning heavily on the sink to gather her wits. Because to be honest, sometimes Val thought maybe it wouldn't be so bad, not remembering the stuff that hurt.

Except then it'd be like finding out for the first time over and over, wouldn't it? As awful as it was knowing she'd never see her children's father again, she couldn't imagine reliving that initial, searing, disbelieving pain. Whether she'd know she was reliving it or not.

And there went her hyperactive brain again, she thought on a sigh as she pushed away from the sink to go potty. Over the past several hours, between waiting tables and baking, she'd been too busy to think, thank goodness. Especially about how hiring Levi Talbot had left her feeling as if she'd sold her soul. And not only because she still wasn't sure she hadn't made a pact with the devil, but because as much as she wanted to stay angry that Levi had returned unscathed while her husband hadn't returned at all, the haunted look in the devil's green eyes told her he wasn't all that unscathed. Not on the inside.

And that could be a problem.

She flushed and went to wash her hands, grimacing at her reflection in the way-too-brightly-lit mirror. Like most men, Levi would probably bluster through whatever was behind that look, or pretend it didn't matter—Tomas had been a master at it—but Val was guessing Stuff Had Happened. Bad stuff. Which poked at that damned weak spot inside her that, despite everything she'd been through, she'd never been able to toughen up, or even ignore, no matter how badly she'd wanted to. Yeah, caring could be a bitch. The only saving grace was that she imagined the dude would appreciate her sympathy even less than she wanted to feel bad for him—

The door to the tiny bathroom smacked her in the butt as Annie pushed inside. "Sorry, honey—didn't know you were in here!" Her boss vanished into the stall, calling out as she tinkled, "You know the pies sold out today, right? Except for maybe a half-dozen slices, and I doubt they'll last until five-thirty."

"So I gathered. That's great."

"You're telling me."

The toilet roared behind her employer as she emerged to wash her own hands. As usual, half of Annie's salt-and-pepper hair had escaped its topknot, floating around her sun-weathered face as she grinned. "Especially since three people bought *whole* pies. Two cherries, an apple and a lemon meringue. One person bought two," she said to Val's brief frown, then cackled. "You're famous now, girl. In fact, Pam Davis—the Congregational pastor's wife?—said, thanks to you, she's given up baking. Although if her husband ever finds out, she'll have to kill me."

"My lips are sealed," Val said, smiling and tossing her rumpled paper towel into the trash before tugging a folded-up printout from her back pocket. She smoothed it out, then showed it to the woman who'd given Val her first job when she was fifteen, cleaning up after school and making sandwiches on the weekends—a job that had given her enough money to buy something new to wear now and then, to go on school field trips. Annie wasn't the only surrogate mother figure in Val's life, but she had been the first. Nor was this the first conversation they'd had in the diner's loo. Many tears had been shed in here over the years, a good many of them onto Annie's skinny shoulder. "You think the customers would go for this? With my own tweaks, of course."

Annie shook out her readers, hanging on their glittery chain, before wriggling the earpieces through her hair. "Dulce de Leche crème? Holy crap, you bet." She plucked off the glasses and let them drop, where they bungeed off her flat chest. "I'm thinking we're gonna give that Mary-anne Hopkins a run for her money. Especially since those cupcakes of hers she swears she bakes herself? I happen to know for a fact she gets 'em from some commercial outfit in Santa Fe. God alone knows what kind of preservatives and what-all they've got in 'em. So when can you get a sample pie to me? Please say tomorrow."

Val smiled. "I'll try. Depends on how the evening goes. Josie's been balking about doing her homework, so I may have to ride herd. Spring fever, I suppose. Only one more week of school, thank goodness."

Annie's light brown eyes went soft. "How's she doing?"

"Hard to tell," Val said on a sigh. "Most of the time she seems okay, but…she's too quiet. Too serious. She used to be—" she smiled "—gigglier."

"Give her time," Annie said gently, then laid a hand on Val's arm. "And how are *you* doing?"

"Getting by. Listening to hear what's next, I suppose."

The older woman pulled her into a hug, then released her, her hands still on her shoulders. "And that's all anyone can expect. Especially so soon. Although, for what's it's worth? I think you're doing a fabulous job. Those babies are lucky to have you."

"And I'm lucky to have *you*," Val said through her tight throat, adding, as Annie batted away the comment, "No, seriously. I'm…" She took a breath. "It's good to be home."

"Lord, I never thought I'd hear that come out of your mouth."

"Neither did I, Annie. Believe me."

After another hug, and a promise to bring her boss that new pie the next morning, Val left, blinking in the bright spring sunshine flooding the small town square— the brainchild of some enterprising, and optimistic, soul from who knew how many decades before. The native pines and aspens held their own, of course, but the poor maples struggled to thrive at this altitude, and in fact had been replaced more than once over the years.

Which could also be said, Val supposed as she got in her car, parked at an angle in front of the diner, of the town's inhabitants. Outsiders loved to visit but generally found the

small town stifling. There were exceptions, of course—
like plants, some nonnatives adapted better than others. AJ
and Annie, for instance, had landed here as newlyweds and
never left. And certainly not everyone born here stayed.
But most did. Or found themselves pulled back, for whatever reason. Because apparently those roots were harder
to kill than the aspens that cloaked the mountainsides in
a blaze of molten glory every fall.

After picking up Josie from school a few blocks away,
Val continued to her in-laws' to get the baby, gratitude
swelling for the hundredth time for Consuela Lopez's in-
sistence on watching her granddaughters whenever Val
needed. Even groggy, cranky ones, she thought as, with a
wail of displeasure, a sweaty Risa catapulted herself from
her grandmother's arms into Val's.

Underneath a colorful tunic, Connie's bosom jiggled
when she laughed. "Honestly, *reynita*…your mama will
think I've been pinching you!"

Shushing her screaming "little queen"—not that it
worked—Val smiled. Soft and round and all about the
hugs, the redhead-by-choice wouldn't have pinched an
ant if it was crawling on her, let alone her adored—and
only—grandchildren.

"She must've gotten too hot. It was chilly when she
went down for her nap, so I put a sweater on her. But it
warmed so quickly this afternoon! If I wanted hot, I'd
live in Cruces!" Her mother-in-law shuddered, the typical
reaction of most northern New Mexicans to the thought
of living in Las Cruces, three hundred miles to the south
near the Mexican border and a good twenty degrees
warmer than Whispering Pines. After being stationed
in the Bowels of Hell, Texas, Val could relate. "Josie,"
Connie now said, "go see what's out on the porch with
Gramma Lita! But just look, don't touch, okay?"

At Val's raised eyebrows after her daughter scampered

off, Connie sighed. "A mother cat and her kittens. Pete found them in the Dumpster behind the store. Can you imagine? Two babies, a tuxedo and a gray tabby. Almost weaned, I'm guessing. Adorable." Then she got that look. "I don't suppose…?"

"Forget it. The dog would think I'd brought him a snack."

"Aww, Radar's such a sweetie—"

"No."

Connie shrugged, then tromped over to the fridge for one of the baby's squeezie applesauce things. "There you go, sweetie… So I hear Levi Talbot's working over at the house?"

"Jeez, Connie—" Val readjusted the schlurping Two-Ton Tessie against her hip, then glared at her mother-in-law. "A breath between thoughts would be nice."

"Can't waste time. Josie could return at any second."

"Between Angelita and the kittens? I'll be lucky if I see her again before she's twenty. And yeah. Levi's back. But how did you know?"

"He came over last night. To catch up. To talk about the house."

"He was here?" Val's mouth tightened. "And you didn't think to give me a heads-up?"

Connie took a deep breath, and Val braced herself. Six months on they both might have had more of a handle on the waterworks, but the spigots weren't rusted shut by any means. And now, when Val saw her mother-in-law's eyes glisten, her own stung in response. Then the older woman sighed.

"Look… I know you had your issues with Levi," Connie said gently, then blew a short laugh through her nose. "Heaven knows, so did we. From time to time, anyway. The Talbots are good people, and were good parents, but Levi…"

"You don't have to tell me," Val said, hoping to hell she wasn't blushing. "Believe me."

"So we didn't understand, when Tomas took up with him, of all people. But you know what? Levi was the most loyal friend Tommy ever had. Sure, the boys pulled some boneheaded stunts—and even Tomas admitted that Levi spearheaded every one of them—but as heart-stopping as those stunts were, they also broke Tommy out of his shell. So all I'm saying is…be kind to Levi—"

"Mama! Look!" Josie ran into the kitchen, a squeaking black-and-white furball clutched to her chest, a pleading look in her eyes Val knew she was gonna have a helluva time resisting. She'd seen the same look in Tommy's eyes when he brought home Radar.

The same look but different—oh, so different—she'd seen in Levi's eyes the day before. That morning. The *I need something from you* look. And to ignore that look, to pretend it didn't affect her, only made her a big old meanie, didn't it?

Clearly, the entire world was conspiring against her.

"Look what I got, Levi!"

About to nail the last new plank on the porch floor, Levi glanced over to see Josie flying toward him, a loudly mewing something—not a skunk, then—cradled under her neck. And Radar, who'd been snoozing in the grass, surged to his feet to investigate the New Thing that had invaded his territory.

"Josie! Oh, jeez… No! Wait!" Val shrieked from the driveway as she tried to get the baby out of her car seat. "We need to introduce them slowly!"

Levi bolted down the steps before the child was traumatized for life. But even as he went to grab the dog's collar he noticed Radar's wagging tail…and that he'd plopped himself down in the gravel at Josie's feet to *awoo! awoo!*

at the kitten, now clutched even more tightly in a wide-eyed, clearly terrified, Josie's arms. Levi crouched beside the dog, curling his fingers around the collar, anyway.

"He just wants to be friends," Levi said gently, his gut twisting at how much the little girl looked like her daddy. "Why don't you let him sniff the kitty? It's okay, I've got him."

"You sure?"

"We had cats and dogs all the time when I was growing up on the ranch where my daddy worked. They're not natural enemies, no matter what people think. I promise— I won't let anything bad happen."

Josie shot him a look that rattled him as much as it warmed him. To be truthful, Levi was pretty much clueless about kids. Yeah, he was an uncle three times over, but he hardly knew his nephews, having been away for the better part of the past six years. And girls? They might as well be a whole different species.

So it made his heart swell when the kid sucked in a breath, nodded, then carefully lowered the kitty so the nutso dog could check him, or her, out. At the sound of gravel crunching, Levi glanced up to see Val with the baby, clearly holding her breath. And yet, if she'd let Josie have the kitten, deep down she must've believed it'd work out, right?

That, or the woman had balls of steel.

Radar nosed the kitten, then pulled back to bay at the poor little thing before resting his snout on his front paws. Waiting.

Levi chuckled. "Put the kitten down—let 'em get acquainted."

Josie glanced over at her mama, but Val only laughed. Nice sound, that laugh. "Go ahead. Levi's got it covered."

Now why those few words sparked such a feeling of confidence, Levi had no idea. Especially since it wasn't as if he was trying to prove anything to Val or win her approval. But there was a lot to be said for feeling like you were finally doing something right.

Slowly, Josie squatted and released the kitty, who arched and hopped back a whole six inches, hissing about as loudly as you'd expect something who weighed a pound to hiss. Encouraged, Radar inched closer to nose the kitten again, sending it tumbling backward. Tiny thing was *real* pissed by now, scrambling clumsily to its feet to charge the dog, smacking him squarely on his nose. Radar, being basically dumb as a rock, figured they were best buds now; he lifted his head again to let out a joyous bay, tail wagging the entire time.

By this time they were all laughing at the goings-on, particularly Josie, who scooped up her highly annoyed new pet. "That's enough, Radar!" she said sternly, then marched up the stairs and on inside, leaving the perplexed dog to jump up and run around in circles, nose to ground, wondering where his new friend went.

Still chuckling, Levi came up to Val and the baby. He got a whiff of something sweet, then another scent that reminded him of his mother's kitchen the day before Thanksgiving.

"You got her a kitten?"

"Not exactly. My father-in-law brought them home. Little girl, kittens…" She shrugged. "Thank God Connie had already called dibs on the second one, or I'd really be in trouble. And I'd seen Radar with cats before. Dog's an idiot, and doesn't know from boundaries, but I knew it'd be okay. Hoped, anyway. And Josie needs something to focus on."

Speaking of focusing, her gaze wandered to the porch. On a little gasp, she went closer, the baby clinging to her hip. "Oh. Wow. This is…impressive."

Levi stood behind her, getting another heady whiff of domesticity. "Thanks."

"I can't believe you finished it so fast."

"Wasn't that big a deal. The foundation was still okay, only needed the boards replaced. Whoever built this originally knew what they were doing."

"Still. It would've taken Tomas forever…" As if that thought had jump-started another one, her gaze jerked to his, an inch away from accusing. She hiked the baby higher on her hip, her voice soft but the anger underlying her words unmistakable. "How come you didn't tell me you'd gone to see Connie and Pete?"

"You're mad," Levi said, just as softly. Her cheek pressed against her mama's collarbone, the baby grinned up at him from around her thumb, and something squeezed inside Levi's chest.

"I'm sure as heck not happy," Val said, snapping him back to the moment. The baby leaned back to pat her face; Val grabbed her chubby little hand and kissed it before looking at Levi again. "If you wanted to know what the budget was, why not ask me? Why go to them?"

"First off, did you expect me *not* to go see them? And second, we got to talking about the house—"

"I have major issues with people not being up front with me, Levi. So as long as we're…working together, no sneaking around, no hiding stuff from me. Because if it's one thing I hate, it's surprises. Or having to wonder what's really going on in someone's head." She pulled a face. "Drives me batty."

"It was a judgment call, okay?" he said after a moment, guessing her strong reaction had little to do with the house. "Not to bog you down with details. Like the fact that this budget isn't going to go very far if you have to pay for labor. You're stressed, Val," he said when she glared at him. "More than you probably want to admit. So sue me for wanting to make things easier for you. Like I know Tommy would. Believe it or not, I'm trying my best *not* to be a jerk here."

Their gazes tangled for several moments before she sank onto the porch step, the baby still in her arms. Radar sauntered over to give kisses, and she smiled. Then sighed.

"Sorry," she mumbled.

"S'okay." Then he crossed his arms. "But you can't seriously expect me to share every single thing I'm thinking."

Another sigh preceded, "Not unless it pertains to me. Or my girls. Because I doubt either one of us really knows what the parameters are for…whatever this is. But as long as we're honest with each other, maybe it won't be quite as awkward?"

By rights, her request should've made him hugely uncomfortable. Because there was stuff lurking in his head he wasn't about to share with anyone, let alone someone in Val's situation. And yet at the same time he found her openness more of a relief than a threat. Especially considering some of the women he'd been with over the years. Might be nice, not having to work his ass off trying to figure out who this one really was.

Even if this situation was only a way to make good on his promise, since he didn't imagine Tomas would've expected it to be open-ended. Or that he and Val should become friends or anything. Besides that, she'd said her "rules" only applied to whatever affected her or the girls. Not what affected *him*.

"I suppose I can do that," he said.

Her lips curved. Barely. "So if I ask you something, you'll give me a truthful answer?"

Hell, he couldn't even answer *that* truthfully. But all he said was, "Long as you don't ask me if what you're wearing makes you look fat. 'Cause that dumb, I'm not."

He'd never noticed before the way her eyes crinkled

when she laughed. Made him feel good to make her laugh.
Not that it was much of a compensation for what'd happened. But since, aside from his handyman skills, it was
all he had—

"And you can ask me anything, too," she said.

"Deal." Although he wouldn't.

Because, again—that dumb, he wasn't.

Chapter Three

A short time later, Levi clacked the knocker on his oldest brother's front door, smiling at—over much excited barking—an equally excited "It's Uncle Levi!" coming from the other side. One of Zach's boys, probably. Although Josh was there, too; his twin's mud-spattered four-by-four was parked behind Zach's even dirtier Chevy pickup. Because around here, the filthiness of one's truck spoke directly to one's ballsiness. And that went for the women, too.

Speaking of ballsy...all three of them together for the first time in more than six years? *Should be interesting,* Levi mused as he took in the almost painfully cute front porch, attached to an equally adorable blue-and-white house, rosebush-choked picket fence and all. Next door stood a toned-down version, beige with black shutters, that housed Zach's veterinary practice and small-animal boarding facility. Although Levi gathered that a lot of the boarders ended up—

The door opened, and three little boys, a pair of Chihuahuas and one overly enthusiastic golden retriever all scrambled to get to Levi first.

—here.

"Guys, guys…" Laughing, Levi's fraternal twin made some lame attempt at untangling the exuberance before grabbing Levi in a back-pounding, bone-crushing man-hug. Then Josh held Levi apart, a thousand questions simmering in eyes the same murky green as Levi's, although his ten minutes' younger brother's hair was darker, straighter. Neater. Josh also stood a couple of inches shorter than Levi, a fact that had annoyed the hell out of Josh all through high school. Ten years later, though, what his twin lacked in height he'd more than made up for in rock-solid bulk. Which stood him in good stead, Levi supposed, for working with horses day in and day out.

"You look good," Josh said, grinning like crazy as he hauled his little boy up into his arms. Even a toddler, Josh'd been the sweet one, Levi the holy terror. He wondered how much that still held true.

"Thanks—"

Zach's two started messing with each other, making the dogs bark. From the kitchen, Zach called, "Cut it out! *Now!*" But not before the younger kid got in a final punch.

Ah, good times…

"Hey, Austin," Levi said over his chuckle. He'd only seen the little guy once before, as a toddler, although Josh had regularly sent pictures. "You don't remember me, huh?" The little boy shook his head, and Levi smiled. "How old are you?"

The little dude held up four fingers, then immediately tucked his hand back between him and his daddy. Who'd apparently had no issues with stepping up to bat when the boy's babymama decided to take a hike. Levi's heart cramped, thinking of Val, also the victim of a parent who hadn't stuck around.

"Wow. Big guy. Speaking of big..." Levi looked down at Zach's boys, who'd stopped wrassling with each other long enough to now give Levi matching intrigued looks. He pointed at the oldest, a gangly blond who was probably gonna spend some quality time with the orthodontist in coming years. "You're... Jeremy, right? You were this big—" Levi held his hand at hip height "—when I saw you last. But I've never met this little guy." He squatted to be eye level to his youngest nephew, redheaded and freckled and blue-eyed—like his mother, Levi thought with another cramp.

"That's Liam," Zach said, swiping his hands across his blue-jeaned butt as he came into the living room and Levi stood again. But instead of giving Levi a hug, his oldest brother extended his hand, like they were acquaintances meeting up at a business gathering. Taller than Levi, thinner, Zach had always been the most reserved of the four of them, even as a kid. But clearly he'd become even more so after his wife's death a couple of years before, the once ever-present, if quiet, spark of humor in his blue eyes faded to almost nothing behind his glasses. "Good to have you home."

"Glad to be here."

And he meant it. Even though he might not have, once upon a time, Levi realized as they crowded around Zach's beat-up dining room table for dinner, and his brothers' attempts to get spaghetti actually into their sons rather than on the table, floor and each other brought back a flood of memories...and the opportunity for reflection, since actual conversation was pointless.

Despite growing up with parents who were devoted to them and to each other, the four brothers had never been particularly close. As kids they'd all had radically different interests, temperaments, personalities. Still did, most likely. Josh was still the brawny one, and Zach had the brains. And Colin… Well, who knew about Colin, who'd fled Whispering Pines long before Levi. The idealist, their mother had said, her pride over her second born's accomplishments clearly conflicting with the pain of his rare sightings. And of course then there was Levi himself, still trying to figure out who he was, what he really wanted. How he fit into the big scheme of things.

Even so—the kids finished their meals in what seemed like two seconds flat, at which point their weary fathers released them into the wild—Levi sensed something had shifted since the last time they'd all been together. He wasn't entirely sure what. And, being guys, it was doubtful they'd actually talk about it. But like maybe whatever had kept them at such odds with each other as kids wasn't as much of an issue anymore.

"Beers?" Zach said, not even bothering to clean flung spaghetti off the front of his Henley shirt, although he did take a napkin to his glasses.

Calmly sweeping food mess from table to tiled floor— thrilling the dogs—Josh released a tired laugh. "You have to ask?"

Zach pointed to Levi, who nodded. His oldest brother disappeared, returning momentarily with three bottles of Coors, tossing two of them at his brothers before dropping back into his seat and tackling what had to be cold spaghetti. Clearly he did not care.

"This is really good, Zach," Levi said, and Zach snorted.

"Straight out of a jar, but thanks. No, mutt, that was it," he said to the retriever, sitting in rapt attention beside him. Sighing, the dog lumbered off to collapse in one of three dog beds on the other side of the room, the Chihuahuas prancing behind to snuggle up with him. The bigger dog didn't seem to mind. From the living room, somebody screamed. Josh cocked his head, waiting, lifting his beer in mock salute to his brother when there was no follow-up. Zach hoisted his in return.

"You guys look done in," Levi said, which got grunts—and exhausted grins—from both of them. Zach rubbed one eye underneath his glasses, then sagged back in his chair, his arms crossed over his chest as he chewed.

"Honestly? I can't remember *not* being tired. But it's just life, you know?" The last rays of the setting sun sliced across the table, making it hard to see his brother's eyes behind the lenses, but his smile had softened. "Either you deal with it or you go under. Speaking of which…" He leaned forward to scoop in another bite of spaghetti. "Dad says you're helping Val Lopez fix up her house?"

"Some, yeah. Although it's not her house, it's Tommy's grandmother's. The family's only letting her live there."

"For how long?" Josh asked.

Levi turned to his twin, seeing sympathy in his green eyes. Although they hadn't all hung out together much in high school—no mean feat with such a small class—Josh knew Tommy, of course. And Val. Levi doubted, however, his brother had been aware of everything, since he'd kept a pretty tight rein on his feelings. Not to mention his mouth. "As long as she needs."

"How's she doing?"

This from Zach, who knew more than anyone what it felt like to lose a spouse, especially long before you expected to.

"All right, I think." For a moment—if that—the thought flashed that his brother and Val should get together, do a miniature Brady Bunch thing with their kids. Or even Josh and Val, for that matter. Except hot on the heel of those thoughts came *Oh, hell, no.* Like a freaking sledgehammer.

"What about you guys?" he said. "How're you balancing it all?"

His brothers shrugged in unison. "Can't speak for doofus over there," Josh said, reaching for his beer, "but I don't know that I am. Doing my best, but…"

"Yeah," Zach said. "Same here. Especially juggling the child care situation. Mom helps when she can, absolutely, but since you never know when one of her clients might go into labor, that's not a sure thing. And Dad…"

Josh sighed, and Levi frowned.

"I thought he was okay?"

"Oh, he is," his twin said. "Doesn't mean he's up to herding three little boys under the age of seven. Hell, he didn't when *we* were little. No, seriously, Leev—can you remember him ever taking care of us on his own?"

"He used to take us fishing. And riding. And—"

"When we were older, yeah. Not when we were—" somebody bellowed "—this age. That honor, he left to Mom."

"So what do you do?"

Zach shrugged, his mouth pulled down at the corners. "There's a church day care, but it's only part-time. So we let 'em hang with us, when we can." He exchanged another glance with Josh. "Pawn 'em off on Gus, sometimes."

"Gus?" Levi belted a laugh. Gus Otero had been a fixture at the Vista Encantada—the ranch where he and his brothers had grown up—forever, first as a hand, then as the cook/housekeeper. Hell, the four of them had probably spent more time in Gus's kitchen than their own, and the tough old bird had never taken crap off any of them. But the man had to be nearly eighty by now.

"Don't laugh," Josh said. "I'd put my money on Gus before one of those fancy trained nannies any day. Even so…"

Josh took another gulp of his beer, then lowered his voice and said to Zach, "This isn't what either of us signed up for, is it?" A rhetorical question, apparently, since he didn't wait for a reply. Levi, however, noticed his older brother's deep frown as he stared at his bottle before Josh quickly added, "Don't get me wrong, Austin's the best thing that ever happened to me. Doesn't mean it's not a pain, trying to make the pieces fit. Or hard not to feel resentful, sometimes, that his mom didn't keep her part of the bargain."

Knowing that Josh had never been married to Austin's mother, it took Levi a moment to work up the nerve to ask, "So…it wasn't an accident?"

Josh barked out a laugh, then looked at Levi in a way he'd never done. "I know—when we were kids, you were always considered… Well, I don't want to say the *bad* one, but definitely the one more likely to get into trouble. So I did my level best not to. Then you left and maybe I didn't feel the need to compensate for your behavior anymore?" He took a swig of his beer. "And I may have gone a little nuts."

"A *little* nuts?" Zach muttered, and Josh shot him the evil eye. Then sighed.

"Okay, a lot nuts. Especially when it came to women. Not that there were dozens—"

"Which would be tricky," Zach put in, "considering where we live."

"Would you let me tell my story, for cripes' sake? Anyway. Then I met Austin's mother, and even though we were being careful…" Josh shrugged. "The thing is, though, I wasn't in love with her. Not even close. And frankly the thought of being somebody's daddy scared me to death. But the thought of Dad's reaction scared me more. So I asked her to marry me—"

"Like the good boy you always were," Zach said, half smiling.

"Shut up," Josh lobbed back, then returned his gaze to Levi. "She actually laughed. But she said she wanted to keep the baby. So we worked out this whole custody-sharing arrangement. Only…"

Josh linked his hands behind his head, his eyes on Austin, quietly building something out of blocks not ten feet away. "Only she left. Like, three years ago? Haven't heard a word from her since. And then *this* one…"

Whether because Josh's nod toward their oldest brother was met with a death glare, or because Austin came over to show off his Duplo masterpiece, Josh apparently changed his mind about whatever he was about to say. Instead he scooped his son into his lap, worry lines vanishing as he focused on his little boy. Then a minor crisis of some sort pulled Zach away from the table to tend to his crying youngest as Jeremy pled his innocence with all the fervor of a TV lawyer, leaving Levi feeling something for his brothers he'd never felt before. Admiration, maybe. Even… tenderness, if a guy was allowed to have such feelings for another dude. Let alone admit them.

For a woman, though, that was something else. Especially a woman dealing with the same issues as his brothers were. Trying to make the pieces fit, wasn't that what Josh had said?

"So how is it?" Josh said, jerking Levi out of his thoughts.

Levi frowned at his brother. Austin still sat on his lap, making soft explosion noises as he calmly, and repeatedly, smashed his creation against the tabletop. "How is what?"

"Seeing Val again." When Levi didn't answer right away, Josh chuckled. "Not exactly a secret, bro. How you felt, I mean."

So much for his brother being in the dark. "Do the others know?"

"Zach and Colin?" Josh shook his head, giving Austin's curls a quick kiss as the little boy slid off his lap and climbed into Levi's. "At that point, they didn't even want to acknowledge our existence. But you and I shared a room. Kinda hard to escape your moping."

"I did not—"

"Yeah. You did. And after Tommy and Val started going together…" Josh's head wagged. "So sad."

Levi's sigh stirred his nephew's curls, making the little boy slap his hand on top of his head, vigorously rubbing the spot like it stung.

"That tickles!"

"Sorry, dude," Levi said with a soft laugh, hoisting the slippery kid more securely onto his lap before meeting his brother's gaze again. "That was a long time ago."

"Yeah, it was. So?" When Levi didn't answer, Josh picked up his fork, dinging it softly against the side of his bowl for a moment before saying, "I have no idea what you've been through these past six years." The fork clanged back into the bowl before Josh folded his arms over his chest and met Levi's gaze again. "But I'm gonna guess it wasn't exactly a hayride. Then Tomas…" His cheeks puffed as he exhaled, shaking his head. "I'm just saying, you probably don't need any more complications right now."

Austin wriggled off Levi's lap to run back into the living room. Smiling slightly, Levi watched him for a moment, then looked back at his twin. "You're probably right," he said, taking another sip of his now-warm beer, which burned his throat as he swallowed. "Then again, who does? So what're the options? Run? Or deal? And you of all people," he said, nodding toward the living room, "should know what I'm talking about."

A long moment passed before Josh pushed out a half laugh. "Got me there," he said, then snagged Levi's gaze in his again. "Still. Be careful, okay?"

"Fully intend to," Levi said, tilting the bottle to his lips again, only to think if there was a quicker road to hell, he didn't know what it was.

That night, Val tucked Josie into the old twin bed that had once belonged to one of Tommy's aunts; the maplespindled headboard softly gleamed in the light from the bedside lamp. This was the smallest bedroom, one of three carved out of the steeply pitched attic sometime in the 1960s. But Josie had immediately laid claim to it, clearly taken with the skylight window with its unencumbered view of the night sky. Not to mention it was the perfect hideaway when, as Josie put it, her brain got too full and she needed to be alone to empty it.

Bending over to give Josie a kiss, Val smiled when a soft squeak alerted them to the kitten's arrival; a moment later the tiny thing clawed up onto the bed to snuggle against Josie's side, motor going full throttle.

Val sat on the bed's edge, reaching across her daughter to pet the kitten, who tried to nibble her fingers. She chuckled. "Looks like somebody's settling right in." Risa, bless her, had sacked out an hour ago and probably wouldn't be heard from again until the next morning. "You decide on a name yet?"

"I'm kinda waiting for her to tell me. Or him." Josie frowned. "How do you know whether it's a boy kitten or a girl kitten?"

"It'll be plain soon enough, trust me. In the meantime, maybe pick something that could go either way?"

"I guess, huh?" Radar plodded into the room to rest his muzzle on the bed, looking concerned. And confused. Because *he* had to sleep in his crate in the kitchen. The kitten all but stuck its tongue out at the dog before curling up even more tightly against Josie's hip. The little girl almost giggled, then looked up at Val with huge dark eyes.

"I like Levi. He's nice."

"He is," Val said. Sincerely even. Watching the man earlier as he patiently sorted out the dog and cat, how gentle he was with Josie, had definitely made her look at him in a different light. Maybe not a light she wanted to see him in, but nobody knew better than she that you don't always get a say in these things. So now she smiled and said, "And I think Daddy would have been glad you got to meet his best friend."

Petting the kitten, Josie frowned. "Was Levi your friend, too?"

"Not really, no," Val said, figuring it was only fair she live up to the mandate she'd given Levi. "Frankly, I thought he was kind of a goofball when we were younger. Although so was your daddy, so…"

Josie giggled again, with a little more oomph, then yawned. "Were you?"

"A goofball?" Val shook her head, then winnowed her fingers through Josie's waves. "I was much too busy being serious," she said, making a snooty face, which made Josie laugh again. One day, maybe, she'd tell her daughters about her own childhood, but that day was way off in the future. Right now it was about them, about the present, not the past. And certainly not about Val's past. "I'd like to think I've loosened up some since then, though."

"Well, I think you're just right," Josie said, and Val's chest ached. How was it possible that she somehow loved her babies more every day than she had the day before? And she prayed with all her heart that this one not lose sight of that amazing combination of sweetness and smarts and silliness that made her one incredible little kid.

"Well, I think you're just right, too," she said, giving her oldest daughter a hug and kiss. "You and Risa both."

The same as she'd believed Tomas was just right, she thought as she—and the reluctant hound—left the room, making sure the door wasn't closed all the way. Someone else who was sweet and smart and silly, who'd filled up a hole inside her she hadn't even known was there. Or at least wouldn't admit to. And she could still, even after all this time, remember when she first realized there this was someone who *got* her, someone she could trust without a moment's hesitation. She'd never doubted his love. Or believed he'd ever give her a reason to. The way he'd looked at her, with that mixture of gratitude and amazement—that had never changed. And that, she would miss for the rest of her life.

But she'd also thought she understood *him*, that they were on the same page about what they wanted, what their goals were. Except then—

Stop. Just...stop.

Pulling her hoodie closed against the evening chill, Val went back down to the cramped kitchen to make herself some hot chocolate, gather the ingredients to make this pie, the dog keeping her hopeful company. She poured milk into a mug and set it in the old microwave on the disgusting laminate counter, berating herself for letting her thoughts go down this path. Because she knew full well she'd only get sucked right back into the rabbit hole of hurt and depression she had to fight like hell not to go near, for the kids' sake.

But the nights were hard, silent and long and lonely, those thoughts whistling though her head like the wind in a cemetery.

The microwave beeped. She dumped Nesquik into the mug, swearing under her breath when half of it landed on the counter, the minor aggravation shoving her into the rabbit hole, anyway. And down she went, mad as hell but helpless to avoid it. Yes, her husband's work—work he loved and was *good* at—had been work that had saved probably countless lives. But it wasn't *fair*, that after everything she'd been through, everything she'd thought she'd finally won, that she'd had to spend so much of the past six years with her heart in her throat.

That he'd made her a widow before she was thirty.

Val shut her eyes, not only against the pain, but the frustration of not being able to get past it, to appreciate her husband's sacrifice. Dammit, everything Tomas did was for other people. Why couldn't she feel more proud of him? Why, no matter how hard she tried, couldn't she feel something more than that he'd abandoned them, broken his promise to *her*, to their children?

Hideous, selfish thoughts she didn't dare admit to anyone. Ever.

Radar nosed her hand; her eyes wet, she smiled down at that sweet face, a face she wouldn't even be looking at if Tomas hadn't rescued the dog. Much like he'd rescued Val. She couldn't imagine—didn't want to—what her life would have been like if he hadn't. She wouldn't have the girls, for one thing. Or his parents, who'd welcomed her as their own from the first time Tomas brought her home to meet them. And yet as grateful as she was for all of that—as in, her heart knew no bounds—none of it made up for what she'd lost.

For what—she took a sip of the hot chocolate, the taste cloying in her mouth—her husband's friendship with Levi Talbot had stolen from her.

And because the person she was the most honest with was herself, that was something she doubted she'd ever get over.

The haunted look in those murky green eyes notwithstanding.

Chapter Four

"That should do it," Levi said, testing the new kitchen faucet a couple of times to make sure it didn't leak. He turned to see Val standing beside him in a baggy T-shirt and even baggier jeans, arms crossed and bare mouth set, as usual. Behind her at the kitchen table Josie was drawing—the little girl tossed him a grin that punched him right in the heart—while Risa pushed and batted at things on her walker, making a helluva racket. And sprawled in the middle of the crappy linoleum floor was the dog, softly *whoop-whooping* in his sleep.

"Thanks," Val said, refusing to meet Levi's gaze. "Did you put the receipt in the can?"

"I did. And you don't have to keep asking—I'm a quicker study than you might think."

She might've smiled, but she still wouldn't look at him. So he glanced around the kitchen instead as he clunked and rattled his tools back in their metal box. In the past week, besides finishing up the porch, Levi had replaced a couple of the worst windows on the side of the house that got the most brutal winds, installed three new ceiling fans and changed out the disintegrating faucets. Except for the porch, all Band-Aid-type stuff until Val stopped dragging her feet about the more major projects. Like a sorely needed kitchen remodel. Hell, half the cabinets didn't even close anymore, and the laminate counters were completely worn through in places. However, since Val seemed loath to talk to him for more than a minute at a time, there was no telling when that—or anything else—might actually happen.

So he prodded. A skill he'd inherited from both his parents, apparently.

"You decide yet what kind of cabinets you want?"

He heard her sigh. "Keep going back and forth between white and cherry. Or maybe maple?"

"And the counters?"

"Butcher block. Or quartz." She pushed out another breath. "The family said it's up to me, but…" Levi glanced over to see her bony shoulders hitch. "What's the hurry, right?"

"Although you might as well take advantage of free labor as long as you can. Since I don't know how long I'm gonna be around."

Her brows, as pale as her hair, dipped. "I can afford to pay someone, Levi. I could afford to pay *you*. I've got my own money—"

"And you've got plenty better things to do with that money." Meaning Tommy's life insurance. As if there was any way in hell he'd take that. "Like put it away for the girls. For college or whatever. This is my gift, Val. To all of you. So let it go."

She paused. "And how long… I mean—"

"Until I'm done or you throw me out. Whichever comes first."

Pressing fingers into the base of her skull underneath her ponytail, she looked away again before offering another half-assed smile. "Well. Okay. Thanks."

"So I take it you're not throwing me out?"

"No. Not yet, anyway."

"Then we're good," he said, even though they weren't. Not by a long shot. He started toward the front door. The dog didn't even bother to get up. Lazy butt mutt. "But since we can't get going on the kitchen until you make a few decisions," he said, facing her, "I may as well start digging up those dead bushes out front on Monday. Maybe we could go over to the nursery, pick out something to replace them?"

"Oh, um…no, that's okay, I'll take the girls one afternoon. That'll save you some time, right?"

It was no skin off his nose whether they went to the nursery together or not. Especially since she was right, it would save time. But what rankled was how obvious she was being, that she didn't want to be around him.

No, what rankled was why he even gave a damn. But all he said was, "Sure, no problem," then called back down the hall, "Bye, Josie!"

"Bye, Levi! See you on Monday?"

"You bet," he said, then walked through the door, across the newly stained porch and out to his truck, feeling unaccountably pissed.

Again.

At first, Levi thought maybe her reluctance to move forward was because the house wasn't really hers. Except he eventually realized it wasn't the house she was avoiding talking *about* as much as it was him she was avoiding talking *to*. So he'd apparently imagined things thawing between them, when he'd made her laugh…when he'd thought he'd caught her looking at him like maybe he wasn't quite the slimeball she remembered.

Yeah, well, it wouldn't be the first time his imagination had played tricks on him. Not that she was snotty to him or anything, but she was cool. Careful. What he didn't get was why that bugged him. Especially since he couldn't remember the last time he'd given a rat's ass whether or not somebody approved of him. Even so, he wouldn't mind hearing that laugh again.

Being the cause of it.

Hell.

He pulled up in front of the nondescript ranch-style house his folks had been living in for the past year, a gift from Dad's old boss after his father's heart attack two years before forced him into early retirement. But the squat little house with its brown siding and white shutters seemed too small and plain to contain his parents' boisterous personalities. Too…ordinary. Heart attack or no, Levi doubted Dad would go gently into that good night. And for sure his mother never would, he thought with a soft laugh. But he supposed it would do.

His father was making sandwiches in the kitchen—bright, cheery, reasonably updated—when Levi got home, so he guessed Mom was on call. But since Billie Talbot had been a midwife ever since her boys had been old enough to fend for themselves, this was hardly the first time Dad had been left to his own devices.

Half smiling, Levi dumped his toolbox by the back door. "Dad. Really?"

Heavy white eyebrows raised, Sam Talbot turned toward Levi, a slice of bologna dangling from his fingers. He'd definitely lost weight after his scare, but the vestiges of a beer gut still hung over belted jeans. "What?"

"You could at least fire up the grill."

"Doc said I should avoid too much charbroiled meat."

"But bologna's okay?"

"It's chicken. Or turkey. One of those. Disgusting, but

at least on the approved list. Zach said you guys got together for dinner the other night?"

"We did."

"How'd it go?"

"It went fine." He chuckled at his father's side eye.
"We're all grown up now, Dad. We can be around each
for more than five minutes without coming to blows."

"Those boys of theirs…they're something else, aren't
they?"

"They are that."

Levi was grateful for the easy, ordinary conversation,
one that would've never happened a dozen years before. So
unlike that excruciatingly long stretch when he and his dad
never quite saw eye to eye. About anything. If Dad took one
side, Levi invariably latched on to the other. In fact, he'd
once heard his mother tell someone at church—laughing, at
least—that Levi had been born fighting the world. *Unlike
his brothers*, had been the unspoken addition to that sentence, who'd never seemed to struggle like Levi did to live
up to their father's high standards.

Not that Dad had ever actually said, "Why can't you be
more like them?" but Levi hadn't been blind to the frustration in those smoky-gray eyes. Problem was, he'd had
no idea how to do that. Hell, at that point he hadn't clue
one how to be himself—or what that even meant. Even
now he wasn't entirely sure if one of the reasons—among
many—he'd enlisted was to prove something to himself or
his dad, but considering how much better things were between them since Levi's return, he'd achieved his goal. He
and Dad might still be feeling their way with each other,
but he knew his father was proud of him.

Levi opened the fridge to get a beer—light, of course,
nothing else allowed in the house—spotting the defrosted,
already seasoned chicken breasts sitting on a plate, right
at eye level. Where, you know, even a man wouldn't miss

them. "There's chicken in here, ready to go. Real chicken, I mean. Why don't I cook 'em up for us—"

"And I swear if I eat one more piece of chicken I'll start clucking."

Levi looked over at the sandwich. Piled high with the fake bologna. "But…" He sighed. "Never mind," he said, then pulled out the plate of chicken. Although frankly he'd kill for a steak. Or a hamburger. But these days the animal protein offerings at Casa Talbot were limited to things with feathers or fins. Didn't seem fair to torment his father by bringing home something the poor man couldn't have. So pan-broiled chicken it was.

For the third time this week.

"So how're things progressing with the house?" Dad asked, sitting at the table with his sandwich and a glass of low-fat milk as, with much clanging and banging, Levi wrestled the cast-iron frying pan out of the stove's bottom drawer.

"Okay." He clunked the pan onto the gas burner. "Needs a boatload of work, though."

"I can imagine. Place was falling apart thirty years ago."

"You were inside it?"

"Oh, yeah." Dad took a bite of the sandwich, made a face and grabbed his milk glass. "Pete Lopez and I used to hang out some, when we were kids. When we could, anyway, when he wasn't working for his dad at the store and I wasn't out at the ranch with mine."

As usual, Levi heard the slight regret in his father's voice, that out of four sons only one had followed in the family tradition of working at the Vista. But the ranching bug had only bitten Josh, who'd taken over as foreman after his dad's retirement. Didn't take a genius to figure out his father hated that a single wonky organ—albeit an important one—had ripped away from him the one thing, outside his wife and sons, he most loved.

"Anyway," Dad was saying, "I spent a fair amount of time in that house. Big place. But dark. Gloomy."

"And free, for as long as Val likes. It'll be nice, once it's fixed up."

He could sense his father's gaze lasering into his back. He turned to the same frown that used to scare the bejesus out of all of them when they were kids.

"How's she doing?"

Even though he doubted either of his parents knew Val all that well—she'd only been over to the house a couple of times when they were kids, after Tommy'd started seeing her but before the bubble around them had set—his father's interest didn't really surprise him. That's just the way it was in small towns. With his dad, especially, who'd tried poking around Levi's head enough, after he got back, even if Levi wasn't about to give him full access.

"On the surface?" Levi now said, not wanting to think about Val. Unable to think about much else. "As well as could be expected, I suppose. Although she doesn't seem the type to go crying on people's shoulders, in any case."

"She always did strike me as a tough little thing."

"That's one way of putting it."

His dad was quiet for a moment, then said, "Her mother passed away four, five years ago now. Did she tell you?"

Levi turned back to the stove to flip the chicken sizzling away in the scant tablespoon of olive oil he'd poured into the pan. He supposed it wasn't surprising that she hadn't. Something they had in common, maybe, not being partial to exhuming the past. Examining it, dissecting it.

"No," he said, rearranging the chicken. "But Tommy mentioned it." At the beginning, even after their military careers took them in different directions, they'd kept up—emails, texts, the occasional phone call. Less and less, though, as time went on. Oddly, Levi remembered the text, partly because of its brevity. Only that Natalie Oswald had died, nothing more. "No reason, really, for Val to bring it up, though. I gathered there was no love lost there."

"And I imagine you'd be right." His sandwich done, his father crossed his arms high on his chest, frowning. "Your mother tried to make friends with her. Val's mother, I mean."

Levi twisted around. "You're joking."

Dad snorted a soft laugh through his nose. "Nope. Because that's your mother, determined to see the good in everybody. Or at least not get caught up in the gossip, which tends to get blown out of proportion. Especially in a town this small. Anyway, after Natalie got sick and that last boyfriend of hers took off, your mom and Tommy's mother took it on themselves to go out there now and again, to make sure she had what she needed or take her to the doctor's, whatever. Since there didn't seem to be anybody else. And I know Billie felt bad for Natalie, that her daughter wasn't around. Until she got to know the woman better and realized the gossips had missed half the story."

"Half the story?"

"What'd you hear, when you guys were in school? About Val's mother?"

"Not…nice things," he said, and Dad chuckled.

"It's okay, you can say it—that she was the town tramp. Not that it was anybody's business how she conducted her personal life. And *your* mother figured, that was all there was to it. Not pretty, but hardly a punishable offense. At least in this century.

"But as time went on, your mother began to understand why the boyfriends never stuck around. Even making allowances for how sick the woman was in her last months, she never seemed to appreciate anything anybody did for her. Instead she snapped and snarled and griped about everything. And your mom finally realized the illness hadn't made her mean—that's just the way she was. So can you imagine the childhood Valerie must've had? How tough she'd *had* to be to survive? And we don't even know what some of those men her mother brought home might've been like. Tomas ever say anything to you about it?"

His gut twisting, Levi shook his head. "Nothing beyond what everyone already knew. If Val said anything to him, he kept it to himself."

"Not surprised. He was a good boy."

"Yeah. He was."

"Which makes it even worse, that Valerie should finally find some peace, only to have it snatched away from her like that." Dad pushed out a breath. "It's the tough ones—the ones who keep their feelings all wadded up inside them—who're usually hurting the most. But if that hurt doesn't find a way out…" His father got up to put his plate and glass in the dishwasher. "Things have a way of exploding."

Something about the slight change in his father's tone made Levi clench his jaw. Keeping his gaze averted, he removed the chicken pieces from the pan to lay them on a plate by the stove. "And why are you telling me this?"

"Because since you've been back," Dad said behind him, "you haven't said ten words about your deployments."

Levi turned to find his dad leaning back against the counter, his arms crossed over his chest. "You didn't ask, either."

"Didn't want to pry."

"Then what's the problem? Because let's be honest, it wasn't like we were exactly best buds before I left. Right? Maybe…I simply didn't think you'd be all that interested. Crap," he muttered, giving his head a sharp shake. "That didn't come the way I meant—"

"Sure it did. But you're wrong. I've always been interested, Levi. I *love* you, dammit. I—" He took a moment. "I always have, whether you want to believe that or not," he said quietly, and Levi's gut cramped. If Dad had ever actually said that before, he couldn't remember. Except then he said, "Yeah, even when you were being a complete knucklehead," and Levi had to smile. "So I'm asking now. What went on over there?"

Feeling as if he'd been thrown a flaming curveball, Levi looked away. "You don't want to know. Trust me."

He heard his father sigh. "Yeah, I figured that'd be your response."

"It has nothing to do with you, Dad," Levi said, facing him again. "I swear. I don't like talking about it to anybody. Anyway, it's in the past, it's over and done with—"

"The past is never *over*, son. Not as long as we remember it. And before you say anything else—if you don't want to talk to me, or your mother, that's up to you. But I'm guessing you need to talk to somebody. Maybe somebody who's in as much pain as you are."

"I'm not—"

His father held up one hand, cutting him off. "You forget—we lived through your rebel phase. Barely, but we did. The only saving grace was that for all you nearly drove your mother and me crazy with your shenanigans, we could always see a spark of something that gave us hope, that eventually you'd channel all that energy into something worthwhile. But since you've been home..." His father sighed. "It's like you're *too* steady, if that makes any sense. Whatever happened over there, you need to deal with it. And I'm guessing if Tommy were here, he'd be the one you'd talk to."

Pain stabbed. "Well, he's not, is he?"

"No. But his widow is. She hasn't been through the same hell as I'm guessing you have, but she's been through hell, nonetheless. You two might be good for each other.

Which I'm guessing was the real purpose behind Tommy's request. Because he knew if anything happened, you'd both be hurting. And that nobody would understand your hurt better than each other."

Levi gawked at his father as if he'd announced he'd chatted with Jesus. Except, damned if the truth of his words didn't whisper through the buzzing in his head. Then he pushed out a soft, humorless laugh. "Except even if I were to accept your…theory, there's another major flaw in your reasoning. Which is why would she be even remotely interested in talking to me?"

"Meaning because of the knucklehead thing?"

Levi almost smiled. "Could be."

His father was quiet for a moment—never a good sign—before he said, "So why not tell her the truth? That you tried to talk Tommy out of enlisting?"

His appetite gone, Levi grabbed the plastic wrap out of a nearby cupboard, ripping off a length of the clingy film to stretch over the chicken. His parents had only heard the one conversation, of course, right after Levi had signed up and Tomas had come over—to the old house, on the ranch—to say he'd decided to enlist, too. His eyes bright with excitement, he'd gone on and on about how the military could change his life, make Val proud of him in ways that helping out at his father's store never would. Once she got used to the idea, that was. Levi's initial reaction—aside from the irritation that, once again, his friend was playing tagalong—had been to tell Tommy he was crazy, that Val was already plenty proud of him. So, yeah, maybe he should rethink this.

Except in the days that followed Tommy only became more enthusiastic about enlisting, and Levi eventually let it go. Because ultimately it wasn't his place, or business, to talk Tommy out of anything, was it? He was a grown man capable of making his own decisions. And of handling the ramifications of those decisions. If Val wasn't exactly on the same page, what on earth did that have to do with Levi?

Even so, regret that he *hadn't* tried harder bubbled like acid to the surface of his grief over Tommy's death, nearly devastating him. Now he looked at his father, shame still eating at his gut. That he couldn't tell his father, or Val, or anyone the truth only made the sizzling worse.

"And what good would that do, Dad? Either she'd think I was only trying to cover my own butt, or—far worse— she'd believe me. And how would that make him look, that he'd gone ahead with something that *everyone* tried to talk him out of? It would only wreck her even more than she is. I know it would."

"So you'd rather let her continue to—"

"Blame me, yeah. She worshipped Tommy, Dad," Levi said through a thick throat. "He was her savior. Even if I didn't know the entire story back when they first started going together, I knew that much. Like you said, after everything she's lost… I can't take that away from her, too."

"At least he died a hero."

"Doesn't make him any less dead, does it?"

Releasing another breath, Dad slowly wagged his head. "Ten years ago we couldn't get you to take responsibility for your own actions for love nor money. Now you're taking it for something that's not even remotely your fault? No, you listen to me—when Tomas asked you to make sure Val was okay…that was guilt talking, son. *His* guilt. For his own decision. It wasn't up to you to change his mind. It never was. But now, well, you accepted the burden he dumped on you—"

"Yes, I did. For my own reasons."

Their gazes butted for a long moment before his father pointed at him. "Then if you want to make good on that promise, there's a lot more that needs fixing than that *house*. Which isn't going to happen unless you get everything out in the open. And that's my last thought on the subject," Dad said, before going out on the back deck, probably to enjoy the sun's too-brief blaze of glory before it sank behind the mountains.

Leaving Levi—again—to wrestle with the truth of his father's words. Not to mention a dilemma the size of Texas. Because which *was* the better choice? To spare the woman any more pain? Or to abide by her own demand about being honest with each other?

He sighed so hard his chest hurt. Because truthfully? There was a big part of him that wanted to turn tail and run, like he would've done when he was younger. To make up some story, any story, that'd get him out of this predicament. Except the past six years of his life had done a pretty good job of slapping him upside the head with, yeah, that whole responsibility thing. Of manning up to a challenge instead of backing down from it.

Especially when the challenge went way beyond simply making good on a promise to his best friend. Oh, no. The challenge was how to really help Val without revealing truths that would only hurt her more.

Or change that look in her eyes from anger and resentment to…

To pity.

Of course, it wasn't like he'd been pining all these years for the girl who'd never been his, the girl he'd tried like hell to stop thinking about once Tomas had confessed he was sweet on her. But the truth was, the toughness and courage that had originally attracted him to the girl had only intensified in the woman…a woman obviously doing her best not to infect her children with her own anger and grief and loss issues. Hell, Val Lopez was frickin' amazing, the kind of woman any man would be proud to call his partner.

Any man but Levi, that is.

At this rate, he thought on a rough breath, he was gonna be able to rip out those dead bushes with his bare hands.

Sweatier than a race horse, and probably stinkier, Levi glanced up to find a wild-haired Josie sitting on the porch steps, the kitten in her lap, watching him dig up that shriveled up old lilac. He was beginning to get used to the staring, as well as the way she had of saying whatever was on her mind. Actually, in some ways it was a relief, letting her take the lead in the conversation, since what he knew about how to talk to little girls you could write on a Post-it note. One of those itty-bitty ones.

Like most little girls around here, she was more likely to wear jeans and boots than some froufrou tutu or whatever. Even if her T-shirt did have some glittery hot-pink design on it. Far as he could tell, Josie was her own person, nothing like either of her parents. As someone who'd been nothing like either of his, Levi could relate.

"Hey there, Miss Josie," he said, jabbing the point of the shovel into the stubborn taproot. "How are you today?"

A heavy sigh preceded, "Bored. I miss school." The kitten abandoned her lap to jump at a fly buzzing around the porch. "Mama says I'm not supposed to bother you."

"You're not."

"You sure?"

"I'm sure."

"Okay. Whatcha doing?"

Levi scrubbed his wrist across his sweaty forehead, then plucked at the front of the soaked T-shirt plastered to his chest. Even in the spring—and even though rogue snowstorms were not out of the question—the sun was hella hot at this altitude, and the bushes had been a pain to dig out. But at least he'd been grateful to see, once he started the excavation, that the foundation seemed to be in decent enough shape, thanks to some smart waterproofing efforts in the past.

He attacked the stubborn root again. "Digging up these bushes so we can plant the new ones you and your mama bought the other day." He grinned over at the child, sitting there with her pointy little chin in her hands, her elbows digging into her knees. "Wanna help?"

She sat up straighter, beaming. "Can I?"

Levi laughed. "Sorry, honey, I was only joking." At her disappointed expression, he gently added, "The shovel's way too heavy for you to lift, let alone dig with. Besides, you'd get all dirty."

"Oh, that's okay—these are my play clothes. And I'm not some little weenie wuss. Dirt doesn't bother me. At *all*."

And with that, he definitely saw her mama in her. Even to the way she pushed her shoulders back and crossed her arms over her ribs.

"Then tell you what—when I get around to planting the new stuff, you can definitely help me. How's that?"

"Deal." She plopped her chin in her hands again. Over in a pool of shade, the sleeping dog started *whooping* in his sleep. Josie giggled, then sighed. "I don't think Mama wants me talking to you."

Levi jerked his head up. "She tell you that?"

"Nuh-uh. But I can tell. 'Cause whenever I say something about you she gets this funny look on her face. Like this." With that, she flattened her mouth and squinched up her eyes in such a dead-on imitation of her mama Levi nearly laughed aloud.

He reached over to give the damn root a mighty tug. Nope. He went back to hacking at it. "I'm not surprised. Your mama and I..." His gaze flicked to the child's, then back to his task. "We weren't exactly best buds when we were kids."

"Oh, yeah. She said."

"She did?"

"Uh-huh. She said you were a goofball."

Levi chuckled. "*Idiot* is more like it."

"That's not a nice word."

"I wasn't a very nice person. Sometimes, anyway."

"Like, how? What did you do?"

Chuckling, Levi rammed the point of the shovel under the root ball, then put all his weight on it and rocked. "Nothing a sweet little girl like you needs to know about."

"You didn't—" Josie got very quiet "—hurt people, did you? Like beat them up and stuff?"

His cheeks got tight with his grin. This kid was something else. "Of course not. I wasn't bad. Exactly. I just got in trouble a lot. Did stuff I knew I wasn't supposed to do." Or rather, that nobody else would. No, he'd never hurt anyone. As big as he'd been, he'd never had to. But he'd sure as hell put the fear of God into a few people—

"Oh. Like the time Mama told me not to stand on the chair to get something out of the cupboard, but I did it anyway, only then it fell over and I banged my head? And broke the plate I was trying to get?"

The root ball finally gave way. *Eureka.* "Yeah. Like that." The mangled clump of roots and dirt tossed aside, Levi yanked up the hem of his army-issue T-shirt to wipe the sweat out of his eyes.

"Daddy said you were the funnest person he'd ever met—"

"Josefina Maria!" Val banged back the screen door, Risa propped on her hip. "What did I tell you about bothering Levi?"

"But I'm not!" she said, scrambling to her feet, wobbling for a moment in her boots. "Levi said!"

"She wasn't, Val," Levi said calmly. "And I liked the company."

"And he said I could help him plant the new bushes, too! Didn't you, Levi?"

"I sure did," he said. Only to add at Val's thunderous look, "But only if Mama says it's okay."

"Is it, Mama? Is it?"

"We'll see," Val said, then smiled for her daughter. "Now get upstairs and straighten out your room, little girl. Which I asked you to do three hours ago, so you can stop with the eye-rolling. Go on, now."

On another heavy sigh, the child shot what could only be described as a longing look in Levi's direction before snatching up the kitten and stomping into the house, the soft-close mechanism on the new screen door not even offering the satisfaction of slamming shut behind her.

Levi picked up the shovel again to start digging up the dirt around the last bush, a rangy euonymus that'd been ugly twenty years ago.

"You can trust me around your daughters, Val," he pushed out as he rammed the shovel into the rock-hard dirt. "No matter what you think of me, or what I was like then…" He glanced up into her startled expression. "I'm not gonna hurt your kids—"

"Levi! For God's sake! I know that—"

"Or say anything to them you wouldn't want me to say. I have added a few brain cells to my collection since we were kids."

She stared at him for a moment, then lowered Risa into her little play…cage…thing, waiting until the baby was happily beating a stuffed toy with something that made a mind-numbing racket before sitting on the edge of the steps a few feet away. As usual she was wearing beat-up jeans, a hoodie, a pair of those ugly-ass rubber shoes that made her look like a damn duck. Except the hoodie was soft and clingy, and her hair was soft and shiny, and her mouth was…

Doing that pressed-tight thing her daughter had just imitated so well.

"And I can't tell you how much it ticks me off that you would even think I'd think that," she said. "I know you wouldn't hurt the kids. Or say anything. But Josie…" She glanced up, even though Levi knew the girls' bedrooms were on the other side of the house. Providing, of course, Josie was actually in her room. "I don't want her getting all these…expectations. Because of what her father said to her. And I definitely don't want—" She looked down at her hands, tightly laced together in her lap, then back at Levi. "I don't need her looking at you and seeing something that's not there. I don't need her *liking* you. Especially not in a you-could-be-my-daddy kind of way."

Because clearly her mama wasn't about to see him that way, either. Not that this was a surprise. What was a surprise was her even considering the kid might.

"So, what? You afraid I'm gonna break her heart?"

"Quite possibly."

Anger spurted through him. "So I should stop being nice to her?"

"Of course not. Just not *too* nice."

Levi blew a short, dry laugh through his nose. "First off, that was the first real conversation Josie and I have had since I started coming over, so I think we've got some wiggle room between her and me being friends and her looking to me as her new daddy—"

"You don't understand. She barely saw her father. His skill… They couldn't simply send anybody over to do that job, could they? So he was away far more than he was home. Even when he was stateside, he spent more time at the training facilities than he did with us. She adored her father, but she kept feeling like he'd been stolen from her. It didn't matter so much at first, when she was tiny. But as she got older all she wanted was for him to stay home.

To stay with her. So I'm guessing she heard in that cocka-mamy promise he extracted from you—"

Frowning, Levi leaned heavily on the shovel. "That I would be his replacement?"

"I doubt her thought processes would label it as such—although knowing that kid, I wouldn't put it past her. But, yeah. Dammit, Levi—she's only now getting adjusted. She even aced school last semester. But it hasn't even been seven months since Tommy died. She may act like every-thing's fine, but I know how fragile she still is. So the last thing I want is for her to get attached only to get hurt all over again."

Levi let Val's words bounce around in his brain for a moment or two until they lined up right in front of his eyes, like a bunch of privates ready for inspection. Not that he doubted for a moment her wanting to avoid any more pain for her daughter. What mother wouldn't? But it wasn't only *Josie's* heart she was trying to protect, was it? Whether Val herself fully realized that or not.

Like she said, it'd only been a few months. Barely time for her to come to terms with being a widow, let alone move far enough past her grief to see a future. God, it still hurt like hell every time Levi thought about how he'd never see Tomas again, so he couldn't imagine what Val was going through, how she was holding it together for the kids. Sure, he'd made other friends in the army, some of 'em close. But not like Tommy.

Same way there'd been no one like Tomas in Val's life, either.

And most likely never would be again.

"And I would never, ever intentionally hurt another liv-ing soul," Levi said over the stab of pain. "Especially a child's. No matter what I might've been like at one time." He resumed digging, deciding it was the sun making the back of his head so hot. "I'm not that person anymore. So you can tell Josie..." He glanced over, then back at the stubborn ground. "Tell her the truth, if the subject comes up. That in all likelihood, I'm not going to be around forever."

"*Is* that the truth?"

Straightening again, Levi looked at her. "It's vague enough to probably keep my butt out of court." When she sort of laughed, he added, "Look—I don't know any more than you do what's going to happen down the road. Hell, I can't even see past next week. I'm here because, well, for one thing, I had no place else to go. And for another, yeah, because of that promise. But since it wasn't like Tommy was specific about what that entailed..."

He shrugged. "All I can do, all any of us can do right now, is play this by ear. Give ourselves some space to figure out what comes next." When she looked away, her jaw tight, he said, "I totally get what your issues are with me, Val. In your position, I'm sure I'd feel the same way. So all I want," he said when her gaze shifted back to his, "is a chance to make things up to you as best I can. Since I can't exactly go back and change what happened."

"I know that," she said softly.

"But do you believe it?" he asked, and her lips stretched into a tight smile.

"Working on it."

"Then that's all I ask. In the meantime it seems to me that if the two of us work together, we ought to be able to steer one seven-year-old away from fantasyland. *Without* having to resort to not being able to talk to each other on occasion."

"You really don't have a problem with that?"

"If you mean, do I know how to interact with little girls? Not a lot, no. But—"

His throat closed up, surprising him.

"What?" Val said, her voice surprisingly gentle.

"She's Tommy's, isn't she? To get a chance to know my best friend's kid…" Unable to finish his sentence, Levi shrugged. Then he hauled in a breath and pulled himself together. "Nothing says I can't be an uncle to the girls, right?"

"As long as you're around."

"Well…yeah."

After a long moment, Val sighed. "I guess that could work. As long as we make that perfectly clear to Josie."

"I'm good with that if you are."

She nodded, then got to her feet to scoop up her youngest daughter. "But fair warning—if you really want to get to know the kids, don't be surprised if I call on you to babysit."

"You're on," Levi said, releasing a long, slow breath after she went back inside.

Karma, he thought this was called, tackling the euonymus again.

Chapter Five

Over the next few weeks, spring finally edged into summer—with only one dusting of snow to keep it real—and the house, Val noted, began to look more like a home and less like the set from *Psycho*. Somebody's home, anyway. Now that school was out, both girls spent the time Val was at the diner with their grandmother, leaving Levi—as well as Radar and Skunk, the kitten—back at the house. And Val had to admit, as Josie burst out of the car to both snatch up her cat and prattle to Levi about her day, she'd grown used to seeing him there when they returned.

And not only because of the wonders he'd worked with the house and yard, but—even harder to admit—the wonders he'd wrought with, well, all of them. Despite her initial refusal to see Levi as anything but the loser who'd led Tomas down the primrose path—and then, later, into a war zone—his quiet steadiness and impeccable work ethic, as well as a gentle sense of humor that never targeted another human being, gradually chipped away at her resentment.

Not all of it, maybe, but enough that she finally had to acknowledge this was not the old Levi. At least, not the Levi she'd turned into some kind of monster in her head.

But mostly—as she stood at the car with the baby in her arms, watching Levi patiently listen to Josie's yammering—she realized it was how he'd gotten her older daughter really laughing again that made Val's heart swell with gratitude. Even as it cowered in terror—that something was happening here she had no control over. Something that was only going to bite them all in the butt—and sooner rather than later. Yes, both she and Levi had made it clear he was there only as an honorary uncle. But his obvious horror that she would even think him capable of hurting her children had touched something deep inside her, nudging at her own still sore—and lonely—heart, making her realize her fear of *Josie's* becoming attached was the least of her worries.

As if hearing her thoughts, Levi looked over, grinning. A grin that was maybe a mite too fuzzy around the edges. A grin accompanied by a brief flicker of something in his eyes that went beyond…whatever this was.

Yeah. Loneliness was a bitch. And what Levi saw, was thinking, when he saw her, she didn't want to know. Because what came to her mind when he grinned like that, was memories. Memories of another man whose sweet smile—a smile she'd never see again, except in pictures and dreams—could turn her into a puddle.

And she'd best remember that. Because, fine, so Levi Talbot wasn't so bad after all. In fact, she might even go so far as to say he was a good man. But if every time she looked at him, she remembered…

That wasn't good at all.

Like most men, Levi had no idea what a woman might be thinking at any given moment—hell, half the time he didn't know what they were really *saying*—but he definitely knew when they *were* thinking. Because a quiet woman was a thinking woman. Although, if he focused hard enough on a woman's expression, he could usually at least pick up on whether or not he should worry. Like if you looked outside and it was cloudy, it might rain or snow. And if it wasn't, it probably wouldn't.

But right now, watching Val holding the baby? The woman could be considering what to watch on TV that night or plotting his demise. No way of telling.

Which made what he was about to suggest even more fraught with danger. Granted, he'd been thinking it over ever since he'd stumbled across that old charcoal grill in the shed, which had cleaned up better than he'd expected. But he didn't want to spook her. Or overstep some boundary she'd set up in her head. And if he had a grain of sense he'd be grateful for whatever level of détente they'd reached. Because he was really enjoying getting to know Josie—and her sister, although since Risa didn't talk, there wasn't a lot to get to know yet—and working on the house was actually feeding something inside him he hadn't known was hungry.

It felt good simply being useful. Making somebody's life a little easier, maybe. Wanting to ease someone's burden for its own sake without thinking about what he might get out of it. It also helped him forget. Or at least, not remember so hard, or so often. So he told himself, this was enough.

That hearing a little girl's laughter was enough.

That seeing Val's smile—real smiles, not those stingy little things from before—was enough.

He didn't doubt that what he was about to propose—cooking up some steaks on the grill, maybe corn on the cob—was crazy. Like they actually had the kind of relationship where he could do that.

"Hey," he said as Val came up the walk. In her arms, Risa gnawed on her own fat little fist, glistening with baby slobber. Then she grinned at Levi, showing off the two tiny bottom teeth that had only popped out the week before. Was it weird that he hadn't held her yet? That he wasn't sure why he hadn't?

"Hey, yourself," Val said back, stray wisps of hair floating around her cheeks. Since it'd gotten warmer, she'd taken to wearing it up more often than not. Levi liked it better when it was loose, of course, but *up* definitely showed off her neck and cheekbones better; so there was that. Something like profound satisfaction gleamed in her pretty blue eyes. "Sold all fifteen pies today."

"Like this is a surprise?" he said, and she rolled those eyes, then smiled, making Levi's stomach jump.

"It's gratifying is what it is. Makes me think I could actually make a go of this baking thing."

"No doubt about it." While they'd yet to share an actual meal, she had pawned off leftover pie on him from time to time. Which, out of deference to his father who couldn't have such things, Levi had personally, and happily, disposed of. Woman made damn good pie. Definitely something to add to the plus column. If he were keeping tabs, that is.

"Thanks," she said softly, and Levi thought, *Now or never, dude.*

"Um…" Heat prickled his face before he cleared his throat. "You know that old grill I found? I was wondering what you'd think about firing it up tonight? Cooking some steaks. Because if I eat one more chicken breast or piece of tilapia I'm gonna lose it. Although I bought hot dogs, too, in case Josie would rather have them…"

Val had gone completely still, staring at him. Cripes, his heart was pounding so hard his sternum hurt.

"Of course," he said, playing it cool, "if you already have dinner plans—"

"No, no." Glancing down at the baby, Val grabbed Risa's slobbery little hand, wiping it on the front of her own shirt as Levi held his breath. "I suppose…" Her gaze lifted to his again. "I could make a salad, too?"

Levi wanted to kiss her. Not that the thought hadn't crossed his mind a time or six in the last little while— complete and total inappropriateness aside—but now the impulse was from absolute relief. And, okay, because she looked absolutely frickin' adorable standing there with the baby and those strands of hair messing with her face and baby drool glistening on the front of her shirt, like she was saying, *This is my life, dammit. Deal.* But mostly relief, that he hadn't come across like an ass.

He grinned, even as he realized his heart rate hadn't gone *less* off the charts. "A salad would be great."

"I think…um…there's a bag of charcoal in the shed, too."

"I know, I saw it."

Their gazes do-si-do'd for another second or two while Levi considered the wisdom of asking her why, when he guessed she didn't grill.

"Lugged the stupid thing all the way from Texas," she said. "Silly, right? Instead of leaving it with one of the other families on the base. But…"

And he could either ignore the elephant swaying from side to side between them, or acknowledge it and move on.

"Yeah, Tommy loved his grilling," he said quietly, and she smiled. Not a happy smile, no, but more of an *I can do this* smile.

"*Obsessed* is the word I think you're looking for. But I haven't had a grilled steak since…in a long time."

"Are you sure?"

"No. But yes. It'd be…lovely. And I'm starved. Thank you."

"Okay, then. Let me zip back to my parents' and get cleaned up, grab the steaks and franks, and I'll be back around five?"

"That'll be great."

But as he drove the short distance to his folks' house, Levi couldn't help but wonder if he'd made a mistake, forcing Val to face something she'd probably worked her butt off to forget. What if his lame attempt to make her happy only made things worse?

Then again, how often had playing it safe worked before?

Yeah. That's right. Never.

She could have said no.

Except…steak.

Grilled steak, perfuming the rapidly cooling evening with smoky sweetness. Even a half hour after they'd tossed the paper plates into the garbage and shoved leftovers into the decrepit fridge, the scent still hung in the air, clinging to their clothes, the dog's fur as he happily gnawed on a sturdy bone nearby. A bittersweet scent, reminding her of the one time in her life she'd been happy. Content.

Not exactly how she'd describe what she was feeling now.

"I'll clean the grill tomorrow," Levi said, dropping into a molded plastic chair next to Val, toothpick in mouth, long legs stretched out in front of him. He'd changed from his scuzzy work clothes into a clean pair of jeans and a lightweight plaid shirt. The same boots, though—around here "cowboy" was a state of mind more than an occupation. And six-foot-something Levi did the look proud.

Damn him.

He smelled good, too. Yes, even over the aroma of charred beef.

Double damn him.

"No hurry," Val said, looking away, wrapping her hoodie more tightly around her as she shucked off her ballet flats, pulling up her knees to plant her bare feet in the chilly seat of her own chair. She glanced at the baby monitor in her hand, even though there was no need. Risa had conked out right after they'd eaten, while her older sister was doing a good job of wearing her legs to nubs chasing the kitten around the yard.

"Yeah, but the longer the gunk sits, the harder it is to get off." Levi paused. "Thanks."

"For what? You cooked."

"For *letting* me cook. For you."

Val softly laughed, even though the tightening in the pit of her stomach wasn't particularly pleasant. Or due to her full tummy. She wasn't sure why Levi was still here, but it'd be rude to ask. And to be truthful she wasn't entirely ready for him to leave, although don't ask her why. Also, the words, "You can cook for me anytime," floated behind her eyes, but she didn't dare say them out loud. For a whole bunch of reasons.

Because it'd been a long time since she'd felt this... safe, she supposed it was. And wasn't that the craziest thing ever? No, not happy, and God knew a long way from *content*, but at least as if maybe the world had stopped spinning out of control, even if for only a moment. And that's all life was about, wasn't it? Moments. Flashes of joy—if you were lucky—connected by stretches of not-so-much.

Or, like now, vestibules of what's-next?

Those were the worst—those long, unsettling periods of not knowing. So go figure how she could feel unsettled and safe at the same time.

An owl hooted nearby, the sound mournful over the soothing, off-sync chirping of a dozen crickets holed up underneath the newly laid mulch in the flower beds. The growing season was ridiculously short, up this high. And even more ridiculously iffy, with snow possible even as late as May or as early as late September.

Iffy. The perfect word to describe her existence.

"Do I dare ask what you're thinking?"

Sighing, Val set the monitor on the table beside her, then tried to burrow herself farther into the hoodie by wrapping the hem around her cold toes. It'd been ages since anyone had asked her that. Like they really cared what her answer was, anyway. Because even with Connie and Pete, it was all about keeping up appearances, wasn't it? Acting stronger than she felt, so she wouldn't bring anybody else down with her.

But it was different with Levi. Who, for one thing, she suspected probably had a pretty good BS detector. And for another…well, if he couldn't take the truth, he didn't have to hang around, did he? Wasn't as if she had anything left to lose.

"About…moments," she finally said. "Being grateful for the good ones, getting through the bad ones—"

"Mama?" Breathing hard, Josie clomped up onto the deck in her almost-too-small boots, hanging on to the loudly purring kitten. "Can I go inside and watch my movie?"

"Not the whole thing—it's getting late. But sure. Get your jammies on first, though."

"No bath?"

Smiling, Val reached over to swing an arm around Josie's waist, tug her closer. She smelled of mustard and strawberries and hot little girl, and Val wished she could bottle it. "I think we can skip tonight. And did you thank Levi for the hot dogs?"

She gave him a big snaggletoothed grin. Her front baby teeth had taken their sweet time falling out; their permanent replacements seemed in no hurry, either. "Thanks, Levi. And thanks for cookin' 'em, too."

He chuckled. "You're welcome, honey." Then Val sucked in a breath when her daughter stomped over to throw one arm around his neck and kiss his cheek before running inside.

"And which is this?" Levi asked after the patio door slid closed behind her. Frowning, Val looked over. "You were talking about moments. Good and bad. So which is this? Tonight, I mean."

Val looked down at her toes, peeking out from underneath the hoodie. She used to paint them. Weird colors, like sky blue. Maybe one day she would again. The old bracelet itched; absently, she scratched her wrist. "Truthfully? A mix of both. Because…because as nice as it is to feel *almost* normal, the night, the smell of the grill…it also reminds me of Tommy. A lot."

There. She'd said it. Out loud. To another human being—that she missed her husband.

A long pause preceded, "Wasn't my intention to cause you any more pain."

"Oh, Levi…of course not. And I do appreciate the gesture. And the food. Really. I wouldn't have agreed to it otherwise. But…"

"I know. Believe me, I know."

Val sighed. "I try to stay upbeat. For the girls' sake. For Tommy's parents. They need to know—believe—I'm okay. But there are times when I don't think I'll every truly be okay again. Not completely."

"Yeah. Sucks, doesn't it?"

She almost laughed. "Truly."

At that, Levi leaned forward, planting his feet back under him to link his hands between his knees. "I do know there's nothing I can really do to make this better. To make up for what happened. I also take full responsibility for my part in it. But as long as we're being honest…"

He faced her, the pain etched in his features clearly visible even in the paltry light over the back door. "I don't think I'll ever really be okay again, either. I loved Tommy. More than I even knew until I realized I'd never see him or talk to him again. So I felt it, too, tonight. His absence. Not that I'm comparing his and my relationship with what the two of you shared. Obviously. But I can hardly remember when he wasn't part of my life. And coming back to Whispering Pines… Dammit, I can't go down a road or into a store or by the high school that I don't think I see that big old grin of his out of the corner of my eye. Think he's gonna come around the corner in that ridiculous lowrider he drove. You remember that monstrosity?" he said, half grinning when Val laughed in spite of herself. "Man," he said, shaking his head, "that was one ugly-ass car."

As in purple. *Iridescent* purple. With painted flames. Bumping up and down Main Street like it was having convulsions. Oh, yeah, she remembered it, all right. He'd sold it, right before they moved to Texas.

Levi chuckled. "But Tommy felt like such hot stuff when he was driving it, what could I say?"

Smiling, Val swiped at a tear trickling down her cheek. "I remember the first time he picked me up in that thing. I thought I was hallucinating. But you're right—he was so proud of it."

"Not nearly as proud, though," Levi said softly, "as when you said you'd go steady with him." He looked back into the night now swallowing up the weed-wacked excuse of a yard, those flower beds, the newly planted vegetable garden tucked into a back corner. All Levi's handiwork. "Your love, Val… That was the most important thing in the world to him. And I know he loved *you* like nobody's business. Because he told me, every chance he got." He slowly shook his head. "What you guys had was pretty damn special."

Levi pushed himself to his feet, reaching down to scratch the dog's ears when he sauntered over, tail wagging. "Tommy was one lucky sonofabitch. But so were you, because there was no better human being than Tomas Lopez. Maybe your marriage didn't last as long as it should've, but do you have any idea how many people would sell their souls for those memories?"

Tears stinging her eyes, Val stood as well, her arms crossed over her rib cage. Her shoes were right by her feet, but she didn't bother to slip them on. Instead she pushed herself up to grab Levi's shoulder, pull him down enough for her to kiss him on the cheek. He looked justifiably startled.

"What was that for?"

"To say thank you."

"For dinner?"

"For…helping me to remember. The good moments. Because nothing and nobody can take those away from me, can they?"

His hands in his pockets, Levi smiled. A soft smile, his lips barely curved. "No, ma'am. They sure can't."

He grabbed his denim jacket off the back of the chair, tucking it in the crook of his elbow rather than putting it on, despite the chill in the air. "You go on inside. It's getting cold. I'll see myself out." Then, with a slight nod, he left the deck, his boots clicking against the flagstone path leading around to the front of the house. Moments later, she heard his truck start, the engine purring as he drove off.

But Val didn't go inside right away, even though she did slip her shoes back on before her feet froze. Because she needed a think, and she couldn't do that properly with *Elf—*

yet again—blasting from the TV. What Levi had done was give her permission to grieve, for as long as she needed. To hang out in the past—to *remember*, dammit—until she was ready to deal with the present. Something she now realized she hadn't fully allowed herself to do, for fear of being a wallower.

Not that she needed his—or anyone's—permission. She was a big girl. It was her call how she handled her life. Even those aspects of it she rarely let anyone see. But all the same, he'd released her from a self-imposed prison, hadn't he?

Without asking, she thought with a start, or even suggesting, that she release him from his.

Val sharply turned toward the side yard where Levi had walked away, as if half expecting to see him there. Had it really made her feel better, holding him at least partly accountable for something that had obviously been Tomas's decision, and his alone? This was the man who'd driven around in a car so loud you could see it, let alone hear it, miles away. A man who didn't care what anybody else thought, who even laughed at the taunts, the gibes. How could Val have believed that Levi held any kind of real power over her husband?

Had she really been so jealous of their friendship?

Val shut her eyes, reeling slightly, both from that realization and the one that followed hot on its heels: That Levi could have easily pointed any or all of that out tonight. Made some attempt to save his own butt, absolving himself of any responsibility for what had happened.

But he hadn't. In fact, he'd done exactly the opposite, not only still shouldering at least some of the blame, but trying to salve her still-raw wounds by reminding her that what she and Tomas had shared would always be greater than what she'd lost. By making her fall in love with her husband all over again.

And in the process smashing to smithereens whatever vestiges of resentment she'd clung to so fiercely about her husband's best friend.

Damn him, damn him, damn *him.*

Chapter Six

His mother was in the living room when Levi got home, watching some dumb reality show. Brides picking out dresses or something. She paused the DVR, though, when Levi came to the door, leaning over to pat the nearby leather recliner. God love her, she'd saved the room from death by beige by adding bright area rugs and throws and wall hangings—many of them gifts from grateful clients—not to mention a forest of houseplants huddled in front of the picture window. Nothing matched, and heaven knew the place would never win any awards, but the longer Levi was there, the more he realized *home* was far more about what a person brought to it than what they put in it.

After he obeyed Mom's unspoken command, she glanced toward the door, then whispered, "You didn't by any chance bring me a piece of that steak, did you?"

"Crap. Sorry, we got to talking and I didn't even think about it. I'll remember next time—how's that? Where's Dad?"

"In the garage. Tinkering." One dark eyebrow lifted. "So there's gonna be a next time?"

Yeah, she would latch on to that. "Figure of speech, Mom. This is Val we're talking about, remember?"

Making a sound that was more grunt than sigh, his mother relaxed against the nest of pillows she'd made in the corner of the sofa, her bare feet tucked up by her hip. For a woman in her late fifties, she was still good-looking, Levi supposed, although not in a manufactured way. She rarely wore makeup, and midwives had no use for manicures. But even though her long, thick hair—usually worn in a braid—was mostly gray now, her skin was smooth and taut over high cheekbones, and deep brown eyes behind rimless glasses always sparkled with love and life and mischief. She could also rock a pair of formfitting jeans better than most women half her age. Although no way in hell would Levi tell her that.

"So dinner went okay?"

"I suppose. Yeah." Even if things did get a little heavy there at the end.

"If you want to talk about it—"

"Thanks, but no," he said, getting to his feet again.

"Didn't mean to sound nosy."

"Like hell," he said with a smile. "It's what you do. And, yeah, Dad told me about you and Val's mother, so I can probably guess where you're coming from with this. Even so, I doubt Val'd be down with the idea of me sharing our conversations with anybody else. Even you."

The corners of Mom's mouth curved. "So you sticking around or going back out?"

"Out. To walk off dinner." He smiled. "I'd almost forgotten how good red meat was."

"And that's just mean," his mother said on a sigh, looking back at the TV. "Enjoy."

"Thanks."

But before he got to the door, she leaned over the back of the sofa. "Levi?"

"Yeah?"

"I think you are one of the bravest people I know. No, I'm serious. And I don't only mean because of your military service." She pushed up her glasses. "Which I wouldn't know about, anyway, since you keep all of that to yourself, too."

"Mom—"

She held up one hand. "I know. Grown boys aren't partial to sharing with their mamas. But I also remember how you used to feel about that young woman." Levi's face warmed as ghosts from his past shuddered between them. Like he'd expected her to forget? "I also saw how you stepped aside for Tomas, after he told you how he felt about Val." Her eyes narrowed. "Never could decide if you were being honorable or stupid, but since that was one of the few decent things you did back then, it seemed best to let it go."

"I think that's called a backhanded compliment, Mom."

"And I meant every word of it. *And* if I'm not mistaken, you're not over her. Not by a long shot."

"You're nuts," Levi said gently, smiling.

"Common side effect of raising four boys. But I'm right, aren't I?"

Levi blew a breath through his nose. "And even if that were true, I'm not Tommy. And never will be."

"Which is why you're so brave," Mom said, her smile soft. "Not to mention selfless, doing all of this with no… expectations."

His face warmed. "I'm doing it because Tommy asked—"

"Bull. You're doing it because you're a good boy. And because you've got a thing for her, but mostly because you're a good boy."

"Mom."

She laughed. "Sorry. In my head you're still that too-tall kid about to ship out who didn't completely fill out his uniform. Gonna take me a while yet to wrap my head around the man who came back. But I can tell you I'm so frickin' proud of you I could pop."

Her words should have warmed him, made him feel better. Instead, all Levi could think of was everything she didn't know about him. Oh, sure, once he was in the service he'd been obedient to a fault, to the point where his parents wouldn't have recognized him. And most of the time that discipline and order had been good things, corralling a boatload of wayward tendencies. Making him grow up, and fast. But that obedience hadn't allowed much wiggle room, either, for things like judgment calls. He'd done what was expected of him, yeah. Didn't mean he was always proud of it. Like Val had said, life was made up of moments. And unfortunately the bad ones often had a way of eclipsing the good ones.

But his mother didn't need to know that, either. So all he did was grin and say, "You'll probably be a lot happier, though, when I get out of your hair, find a place of my own." He snorted. "Not to mention a life of my own."

"Please. You've been home, what? A month? There's no hurry."

"And like you said, I'm not a kid anymore—"

"You're twenty-eight," she said gently. "And goodness, I didn't even know I wanted to be a midwife until I was in my forties. The right thing will make itself clear. It always does. So give yourself a break. It's not as if you've been sitting on your butt the last six years doing nothing, right? Now go take your walk. We'll leave the door open for you."

Once outside, Levi filled his lungs with the clear night air, then started down the unpaved drive to the road leading back into the town proper, a trek of a couple of miles that hopefully would clear his head. Bring a little peace.

The thing about mothers—his, anyway—was not only their uncanny ability to make you say stuff you instantly regretted, but that whatever *they* said was more often dead-on right than not. Part of the problem when he'd been a kid was that life never seemed to move fast enough to suit him, which living in a town the size of an apple only made worse. Nine times out of ten, he'd gotten into trouble because he was bored. And now that he was back, that old impatience reared its sorry head, that he needed to get on with it... Except he had no clue what it was he was supposed to get on with. He'd hoped joining the army would help him find his purpose, only to realize he'd only postponed the very thing he now had to figure out.

Like what on earth he was supposed to do with his life.

Not to mention his feelings for Valerie Lopez. Feelings that, after tonight, he realized weren't *less* inappropriate than they'd been back then.

The blue-black night inhaled his sigh, as if whisking it away for safekeeping in the nearby Sangre de Cristo Mountains, like a herd of slumbering dinosaurs against the moonlit sky. Levi smiled, remembering the stories he and Tommy used to make up about them, when they were kids. From miles away came the long, lonely *whoo...whooooo* of a freight train. Levi told himself it was the sound of the train making him melancholy.

Not much traffic this time of night, except for the occasional car turning into Chico's, the only place besides the Circle K open past nine. He caught the twang of an amped guitar, the distorted sound of an overloud mike, boots thundering on the wooden floor. Laughter. He briefly considered going inside, having a beer, maybe sweet-talking a pretty girl into dancing with him.

Except there was only one pretty girl Levi wanted to dance with. Although he highly doubted she'd want to dance with him. Still, he let his mind wander again, just for a moment, imagining the feel of Val's waist against his palm, her soft hair tickling his chin. The scent of flowers and baby powder overriding the tang of hops and leather and fried food.

Blowing out a sound that was half laugh, half sigh, Levi kept on down the highway, hands in his jacket pockets, as the sounds from the tavern gave way to the chirps and squeaks of assorted night critters, the crunching of his boots against gravel.

And, yeah, his thoughts, zip-zapping around his brain like hyper bats. He welcomed them, though—unlike a lot of the guys he'd served with, whose usual method of dealing with the junk inside their head was to drown it out with loud music or video games. Booze. Drugs. Being alone, being *still*? Far too scary. Levi, though, had early on decided he'd rather face the suckers head-on, and on his own terms, than having them ambush him when he least expected it. Because they always did. Nobody could run, or hide, or pretend, forever. No matter how much they might want to.

Not that he was interested in sharing, and God knew there were plenty of times he wished the memories weren't part of him. But he'd gotten pretty good at telling them to go to hell.

Whether they were interested in listening to him was something else again.

The town was asleep, silent except for the buzzing of the fluorescents in the gas station. A couple of tourist types passed, hand in hand, softly chattering as they peered into the windows of this or that gallery or gift shop. Then he heard more laughter, this time from a clump of teenagers at the far end of the block, probably on their way to somebody's house, hoping to fend off the boredom before it ate them alive. Hard to believe that'd been him and Tomas barely a dozen years ago. Some things never changed.

And yet Levi felt strangely at peace and antsy at the same time, like when you know the presents are waiting for you under the Christmas tree but you're about to pop from not knowing what they are. The idea of staying here gave him the willies; the thought of leaving for good made his chest hurt. That whatever he did was totally up to him made him slightly dizzy.

Pushing out a breath, he plopped his butt on a park bench in the town's tiny square, only to nearly jump out of his skin when he heard shuffling behind him. He wheeled around, and the figure—a man, he could now tell, leading a stiff-legged dog on a leash—jerked back, as startled as Levi. Like Levi, he wore a worn denim jacket, jeans and cowboy boots, but his wiry beard and hair—held back by a sloppily tied bandanna—were heavily shot with gray.

Squinting, the guy inched closer, into a patch of god-awful yellowish light cast by a new halogen streetlamp—somebody's idea of improvement, no doubt. The dog yawned, then sat down to have a good scratch. "You're one of Sam Talbot's sons, huh?" he said a little too loudly. "The one who went into the army? Let's see… Levi, right?"

"Uh, yeah." Then he sucked in a breath. "Charley?"

The older man released a wheezy laugh, hopefully unaware of Levi's shock. Time hadn't done the man who'd given Levi his first job when he was seventeen any favors. Although a few years younger than his father, Charley Maestas looked at least ten, fifteen years older.

"Yep. They were talking, over at Annie's, about how you were home. Figured we'd run into each other eventually." He swayed for a moment, caught his balance. "You okay?"

Levi knew what he meant. Not all vets would ask, but they all thought it.

"Yeah." Because compared with so many, he was. Then he patted the space beside him on the bench, inviting Charley to join him. The pair crept over, sighing simultaneously as they sat, Charley on the bench, the dog on the pavement by his feet. Levi reached over to pet the beast's head. His stumpy tail wagging his butt, he gave Levi's hand a quick lick, then lay down with a groan and shut his eyes, as if it was all too much.

"What's his name?"

"What? Sorry, afraid you'll have to speak up, I don't hear so good these days."

Levi leaned closer, pointing to the dog. "His name?"

"Oh. Senor Loco." Charley chuckled. "Wandered into the yard one day, decided to stay. Mostly pitty, probably, but I swear he's the most laid-back pup I ever saw." Absently scratching his beard, Charley looked down at the dog for several seconds, then crossed his arms to squint at Levi. "I remember you boys, you and Tommy Lopez. How you two would help me and Gloria out from time with the yard and all like that. Or was it…?" Now he frowned at Levi, as though he was trying to get him into focus. "You used to work for me, too, didn't you?"

"I sure did. In fact, you taught me everything I know about woodworking and carpentry."

"Did I?" Charley snorted. "Maybe you can reteach me, then. 'Cause I don't remember squat." He tapped his temple with one finger. "Have a hard time these days, making the pieces fit. And I don't only mean the wood. But let's see… Tomas… Didn't he…didn't he marry the gal who makes the pies, over at Annie's? Or am I mixing her up with somebody else?"

"No, you're good." Charley curled a hand around his ear. Levi raised his voice. "Yeah, Tommy married Valerie Oswald. Right after you left on another deployment."

"That's what I thought. That Val…she is sweeter than her pies, and that's no lie. Her smile is like the sun coming up, you know?" He sighed, shaking his head, then turned to Levi. "So how is Tommy? Heard he enlisted the same time you did."

Crap. Levi had no way of telling, of course, whether Charley really didn't know or simply didn't remember, but either way the news was probably going to shake him. "I'm sorry...nobody told you?"

On a soft moan, Charley seemed to fold into himself. "He didn't make it home?"

Levi shook his head, even as a fresh wave of pain shunted through his chest. "No," he said softly. "He died in Afghanistan. Late last year."

"How?"

"An IED smarter than he was."

The older man breathed out a swear word in Spanish, then frowned again. "You know, now that I think about it, that sounds familiar. When— What did you say his wife's name was?"

"Valerie. Val."

"Yeah, yeah..." Mustache and beard became one as Charley's mouth flattened. Reaching up, he palmed his head, massaging it. "When she started working at Annie's, I must've asked then. You know, why she'd come back. Can't seem to hang on to anything these days. I think they said it's on account of a bomb going off close by. But if I don't remember it, did it really happen?"

Figuring that was a rhetorical question, Levi let it go. Then Charley blew another sigh through his nose. "That's too bad. He was a nice boy. Tomas. A really nice boy. He used to...he used to drive that purple car around, didn't he?"

Levi chuckled. "He certainly did," he said, and Charley laughed.

"You see? Some things, I remember just fine. Well, I won't keep you. It's time Loco and me got back home, anyway, see if there's anything good on TV. If I can remember where I put the…the…" He mimed clicking a controller, his agitation growing with each squeeze of his hand. "The damn thing you use to turn the TV off and on."

"The remote?"

"That's it. The remote."

With another exhale, Charley pushed himself to his feet, startling the dog awake. Ready to get back himself, Levi stood, as well. "You still live out by the Dairy Queen?"

"Yeah. Why?"

"Just wondered how you were getting home."

"Same way we got here. On our feet. We like to walk, Loco and me. It's the one thing we can still do. Right, boy?"

The dog didn't look up, but at the sound of his name his tail pumped once or twice. Charley chuckled, then stuck out his trembling hand, which Levi took, surprised at how firm Charley's shake was. "Us vets, we gotta stick together, you know?"

Levi surprised himself by pulling his old boss into a brief hug, patting his back a couple of times before letting him go. "Absolutely. And, hey—you need anything, anything at all, you let me know," he said, adding, when it occurred to him the dude probably didn't have a phone, "You can tell Val—she'll get me a message."

It seemed to take Charley a moment to focus; then he gave his head a sharp nod. "I tell Val if I need anything—she'll tell you."

"That's right."

Charley gave him a shaky thumbs-up, then ambled off. Hands shoved in his pockets, Levi watched man and dog trudge away, feeling a frown bite into the space between his brows. Obviously he'd been getting around for years without Levi's concern or assistance. There was no reason why tonight should be the night he didn't make it home. And it would've taken Levi longer to bring back the truck than it would have for Charley to get home on his own steam. If he'd even remembered to stay put and wait in the first place…

Levi blew out a breath. It wasn't up to him to take care of the whole world.

Even if sometimes it felt like it was.

"There's somebody here asking for you," Annie whispered the next afternoon as Val wiped down the stainless steel island in the restaurant's kitchen, redolent with the aroma of two dozen freshly baked pies cooling on racks on the island.

"Who?"

"If said, you might not want to go out there."

"And if you don't, I'm sure as hell not."

"Billie Talbot. Levi's mama?"

"I know who she is, Annie." Then she froze, staring through the open door. And, yep, there sat Levi's mother at the counter, giving her a little wave. Yay.

"Told you," Annie muttered.

"Shut up," Val mumbled back, brushed most of the flour and pie crust bits off the front of her apron—not a lot she could do about the cherry stains—plastered on a smile and marched through the door to meet her destiny. Or something. In a tentlike tunic and capris, her gray hair pulled back into a flowing ponytail, Levi's mom came around to fold Val into a hug, the parachute-like fabric practically swallowing her up. The woman wasn't that much taller than Val—maybe three or four inches—but she was definitely more substantial, and for a second Val feared for her bones.

Then Billie held her back, her eyes gone all soft, and Val thought, *Please, God, no…*

"Now, honey, I'm not even gonna try to make excuses for not coming to see you before this—"

"That's okay, I'm sure you're busy—"

"Not that busy. Honestly, I've been meaning to get over here and buy one of your pies for weeks now. Especially after the way Levi goes on and on about how good they are." Like Radar on a scent, she lifted her nose toward the kitchen. "And by the smell of things, my timing's perfect." Billie grinned, the skin around her eyes crinkling. "Or are they all already spoken for?"

Relief rolled through Val. Pies she could handle.

"No, not at all. But your husband...?"

"As long as it's not deep-fried, we're good. So what've you got?"

"Well, there's fruit—apple or cherry—or custard. Or meringue. Lemon or chocolate."

"Lemon meringue would be perfect." Billie lugged her leather shoulder bag around to dig inside it, pulling out her wallet. "It's Sam's and my anniversary today," she said, handing Annie—who'd reappeared like magic—her credit card. "We stopped giving each other presents years ago, but this will be a big treat for him. After thirty-five years, you learn to appreciate the little things."

And Val figured that was that. Except, even after Annie'd processed the charge and boxed up the pie, it was clear Billie was in no hurry to leave. And Val thought, *Hell*. Maybe she had never been close to the woman, but she knew the friendship between Levi and Tomas had bonded their mothers, as well. Meaning she'd most likely been the focus of at least a couple of recent conversations.

"So you're coming out to the Vista for the Fourth, right?"

Val blinked. Not that she didn't know what Billie was talking about—the big Fourth of July barbecue and fireworks shindig Granville Blake hosted for the town every year out on the ranch where Levi had grown up.

"I hadn't really thought about it."

"Well, you should. The kids would have a blast. Your older girl, especially. In the last few years we've made it more of a potluck, although Josh will still be in charge of the fireworks. Like his daddy always did." She chuckled. "In that respect, he never grew up. But then, I don't think men every really do." Billie winked. "You could bring a couple of pies, drum up more business."

Val laughed. "And you should've been in sales, yourself."

"So you'll come?"

"I'll...think about it."

Billie smiled. "I'll take it. Along with this," she said, hoisting the boxed pie. "And you know, if you ever need a babysitter, if I'm around and Connie and Pete aren't available, please feel free. Have Levi give you my number."

And, with another hug, she was gone.

"So you gonna go?" Annie said behind her, making her jump.

Val rolled her eyes, then went to retrieve her purse, Annie dogging her heels. As a kid, Val had never gone— her mother having declared they didn't need all those people looking down on them, by which of course she meant *her*. But once Val and Tomas became an item, they'd joined the festivities every summer, until he'd enlisted and she and Josie had moved away. That and the ranch's annual Christmas party were two of the town's biggest events, outside of the rodeo every September. But the memories—of Tommy's childlike delight at the fireworks, the way he'd held her close as they'd dance afterward...

"Maybe."

"Oh, come on—it'll be fun."

"Maybe."

"You are hopeless, you know that?"

"Probably."

Annie sighed, then handed her a quart of something hot and fragrant in a to-go bag.

"What's this?"

"Green chile stew. From AJ. Because you're too skinny, he says."

Tender pork. Chunks of potato and green chile, hominy and sweet red peppers and sautéed onions, all floating in a sauce guaranteed to clear your sinuses in five seconds flat. "And if I eat all this I definitely won't be."

"Then you can share."

"Right. Josie wouldn't touch this if it was the only food in the house."

"Not talking about Josie. Or the dog."

"Annie. Really?"

"What? Now go on, so it'll still be hot by the time you get home."

Uh-huh. The stuff would still be "hot" if it was frozen solid. But Val took the offering, its scent saturating the car on the short drive home, reminding her of the Lopezes' kitchen. Of sanctuary. Love. If she could even half approximate those feelings of security for her own kids, she'd be doing good.

Once out of the car, she followed the sounds of pounding out back, where a certain sweaty, shirtless, ripped dude in baggy camo pants was repeatedly ramming a posthole digger into the uncooperative dirt in the far right corner of what would be an actual backyard. She'd never seen the tattoos before, starkly simple but exquisite, one gripping his right biceps, another more elaborate number fanning across much of his upper back.

Speaking of *hot*. The bad boy was all grown up, God help her.

Which he'd better be, since until that moment she'd never realized how much of a buffer the girls had been between them.

Radar bounded over to greet her, regaling her with a dramatic aria about his day. Laughing, Val plopped in front of the dog, careful not to jostle the bag, laughing harder when he gave her kisses. Levi straightened, breathing hard. Glistening. Grinning. Funny, how Val'd thought she didn't find pretty boys all that appealing. Just goes to show.

Then she frowned. "How'd you get him to stay in the yard?"

"Electric fence. This one's to keep other things *out*. Um…you missing somebody?"

"Connie took the girls into Taos. To, in her words, pillage Walmart."

Levi chuckled, then lifted his head. "Am I imagining things, or is that green chile stew in that bag?"

"Jeebus. Your nose is better than the dog's."

His smile broadening, Levi crossed his hands over the top of the posthole digger, muscles bunching and shifting and such as he leaned into it. The heavy breathing had slowed down some, but not the glistening. Over the past few weeks his hair had gotten significantly longer, Val realized, framing his temples in damp curls, like those little cupids painted on fancy ceilings. Nothing innocent about those dudes, either.

"I do have a keen sense of smell," he said. "In fact, I've had the scent of green chile stew in my nostrils from the moment Annie called to say you were bringing me some."

"Bringing *you*…?" Val shut her eyes. And her mouth. Her ears caught the chuckle, though.

"Aw, you're not gonna make a liar out of poor Annie, are you?"

The kidding annoyed her. Warmed her. Confused her. Made her acutely aware not only of what she missed so badly it hurt but of what was standing right in front of her. Okay, thirty feet away. But still. In her frickin' *yard*.

She sure as heck was gonna make *something* out of

Annie. Soon as she figured out what. And how the hell did she have Levi's number, anyway? Still. Never let it be said that she couldn't be a gracious hostess.

"I suppose you're hungry."

"You suppose right. Give me a sec to hose off and I'll be right in."

"Oh. We could eat out here?"

There went that devilish grin again. "No, let's eat in the kitchen."

"Whatever." Val carted the food inside, where a whole mess of samples beckoned from the beat-up kitchen counter. Slabs of stone and squares of wood, paint chips and tiles in a dozen colors, gleaming like jewels against the blah of the drab, ancient laminate. Even a half-dozen types of pulls, everything from sleek and simple bronze to whimsical, wrought-iron curlicues.

Absently she set down the bag to finger a sheet of shiny glass mosaics, like little topazes. Or there was the white brick, too. Or maybe the subway tiles…?

"Just to get your juices flowing," Levi said behind her. *Right* behind her. As in, she could smell him, all damp and male and too damn close. Yeah, her juices were flowing, all right.

"Of course, if you don't like these, we can always go to Home Depot and you can choose whatever you like. But I thought this might be easier. So you wouldn't get overwhelmed with all the choices in the store."

And that right there was far worse than how good he smelled, or the way her sad, neglected lady parts were responding to his body heat. She could—and would—ignore her hormones' screeches in her ear, the thrum of sexual awareness making her slightly dizzy. But instead of impatience—the default setting for most men, it seemed—she only heard kindness. Genuine kindness. As if he genuinely cared. And not, she didn't think, about the state of her kitchen.

Well, crap.

But she smiled, anyway, even as she kept her gaze firmly fixed on the one cabinet finish that kept pulling her back, a not-quite white that would brighten up the small space considerably. "You tired of me dragging my feet?"

"No, ma'am. But I think you are." She shut her eyes against the gentleness, the truth, as his voice downshifted into a soft rumble. "I know you don't feel ready to tackle a kitchen remodel. But you also know this kitchen sucks, right?"

When she burped a little laugh, he moved beside her, picking up the curlicue pull and holding it up in front of the cabinet door. It was adorable and completely impractical and totally her. He was covered, after a fashion, in an army-issue T-shirt. "And you deserve a pretty kitchen. So I'm giving you a little goose in the right direction."

She knew he wouldn't touch her, that she was safe. From him, anyway. From her own thoughts, not so much. Until she'd met Tomas, she hadn't known what gentleness was. That teasing didn't have to hurt. Now she was beginning to see why this man and her husband had been such good friends, and for so long.

His gaze touched hers, eyebrows slightly lifted in question. Blushing, she looked away. "Some of this stuff looks expensive."

"Nope. Even if you chose the granite, or these pulls—" he waggled the curlicue "—you'd still be under budget. And there's another surprise—when I talked to Annie, she mentioned as how she and AJ were thinking of upgrading the restaurant's range. It's old, but she said it works just fine—"

"Are you kidding? It works perfectly. I've been doing most of my baking in it. And AJ keeps it immaculate—"

"So she said it's yours, if you want. It'd mean reworking the lower cabinets some, but I can do that—"

"Wait. They're giving me that range?"

"But only on the condition you get your butt in gear about the remodel." When Val blew out a sigh, Levi set down the pull, then slipped his hands in his pockets. "What's going through your head?"

"That there's way too many pushy people in my life?"

On a soft laugh, Levi dug into the bag for the stew, loosened the top and set it in the microwave. Sighing again, Val pulled a pair of bowls from the cupboard, wrestled open a battered drawer for a couple of spoons, a ladle. Then she remembered.

"Your mom came into the restaurant earlier."

"What? Why?"

"To buy a pie for your folks' anniversary dinner tonight."

"That's tonight? Damn, I guess it is." His forehead crunched. "My brothers and I should probably have done something for them, huh?"

The microwave dinged. Val carefully pulled out the container and set it on the old pine table taking up half the floor space, then grabbed two bottles of water from the fridge and a package of fresh tortillas.

"Sounded like she had things well in hand," Val said as Levi sat across from her and opened the container, releasing a spicy-scented burst of steam. He reached for her bowl, filling it before his. "Like, you know, they wanted to be alone?"

She almost laughed at the slight blush that bloomed in Levi's cheeks before the look he gave her stopped the laugh cold. "That near miss with Dad's heart scared the bejesus out of them both. So I imagine so. What kind of pie did she get?"

"Lemon meringue."

"Then at least if he goes, he'll go happy." A huge spoonful of the stew disappeared into his mouth before he said, "Your lemon meringue pie is the best I've ever had, no lie."

"You've also been eating army food for the past six years," Val said gently, adding, when his eyes shot to hers, "Tomas wouldn't talk about much, when he was home. But he bitched about the food constantly."

Levi stilled, then reached for a tortilla, which he slowly ripped into two before dunking a ragged edge in the stew. "Sometimes it wasn't so bad. When we weren't out in the field, anyway. Not particularly healthy, but if it stopped the hunger, we were good." He shoved the stew-soaked tortilla into his mouth. "Eating…it became all about filling your belly. Keeping yourself alive. Enjoyment ran a distant third."

"So I gathered."

Tension crackled between them for several seconds before Levi asked, not looking at her, "Did Tommy say much else? About his experiences, I mean."

She shook her head. "When he wasn't there, he *really* wasn't there. He didn't want to think about it, let alone talk about it."

"Yeah, that pretty much sums it up."

"But that's not really possible, is it? To not think about it?"

Another several seconds passed before Levi said, very softly, "I ran into Charley Maestas last night."

In other words, *Do not go there.*

So much for honesty.

Chapter Seven

Judging from how Val's eyes narrowed, Levi guessed his attempt at switching the subject hadn't gone over too well. But all she did was take a bite of her stew and say, "You did? Where?"

"In town. When I was out for a walk." He paused. "Does anyone actually look out for him?"

"I think we all do," she said, leaning back in her chair and fidgeting with her ponytail, which had slipped over her shoulder. One of her few nervous habits, Levi had noticed. Just like he'd noticed how she still wore that ratty old friendship bracelet Tommy'd given her way back when. "But we have to be sneaky about how we help him so we don't wound his pride. Like the way Annie and I pretend he's doing us a favor by eating the 'leftovers.'" Her mouth pulled flat for a moment before she sat up again, spooned in more stew. "The poor guy's already lost so much—his dignity is all he has left."

Something she could probably say about herself, Levi thought.

"I remember when he came back from Iraq that last time."

Val hesitated, then said, very softly, "And yet you enlisted, anyway."

Levi felt one side of his mouth kick up. "Weirdly, it was partly because of Charley that I did. I almost felt... I don't know. Like I wanted to pay homage to him. To finish what he started, maybe. Although there's no *finishing* any of it, is there? Not really. But what did I know back then?"

"And why else did you join?" When he frowned, she said, "You said *partly* because of Charley."

Levi paused, realizing that, once again, he didn't dare be entirely honest. "Because... I felt like I needed answers?" At her silence, he released a sigh. "I was doing okay, working with that cabinetmaker up in Questa, but... I can't explain it. Except that I felt incomplete."

"And did you find those answers?"

Too late, he realized she'd snagged his gaze in hers, the spoon in a death grip in her fingers. She was the one still looking for answers, about why her husband had voluntarily left her and their daughter to go fight a war she obviously believed wasn't his to fight. Answers he couldn't give her.

"Not really, no," he said. "Doesn't mean other people don't, though. Everybody has their own reason for enlisting. For serving. Take Charley," he said, gently steering the conversation back into more neutral territory. He hoped. "He didn't have to volunteer to deploy, especially at his age. But the Guard helped get a lot of our people home, you know."

"True. But—"

"And I'll bet Charley would say, if he was one of the drivers who helped get our soldiers safely out of there, his sacrifice was worth it. I knew Charley pretty well, remember. And I'm sure glory was the last thing on his mind. Getting the job done, however, probably wasn't."

Her gaze bored into his again. "Just like Tommy?"

"Just like Tommy," Levi said, as the stew bubbled in his gut. "Word was that he was damned good at what he did. Bomb disposal takes more than nerves of steel. It takes extraordinary skill—"

"Well aware of that, Levi."

He leaned closer to wrap his hand around hers, his heart aching at the pain in her eyes. "His work saved a helluva lot of lives, Val."

"Except his," she said, then puffed out a sigh. "I think about him every time I see Charley, you know. And I wonder, was any of it worth…that."

Another question he couldn't answer. If she'd even listen to him, anyway. Or anyone. So all he said was, "I know. Believe me."

Val looked at their linked hands. "Do you?" she said, then grimaced, her free hand fisting beside her bowl. "Of course you do, you were there, too… I'm sorry. I'm not always very rational these days."

"Understandable," Levi said, then let go. He bit off another chunk of tortilla. "So, I take it Charley lives alone? Or would you rather we not talk about him?"

"No, that's fine. And it's not like I can exactly escape the reminders, is it? Tommy's parents, the town…"

"Me," Levi said, and she pushed out a short laugh.

"Especially you. But the benefits of being home far outweigh, well, the other stuff. Family…it's something I never really had until Tommy came into my life. And I'd put out my right eye rather than take that away from the girls. I think it's the same for Charley. Yes, he lives alone. But he's not totally isolated. His neighbors ask him to help with little things, like keeping an eye out for the mail, stuff like that. So they can keep an eye on *him*."

"The memory thing, though." Levi shook his head. Like Val said, was it worth it? Lost limbs, memories, *lives*…

"I know. Breaks my heart. But apparently it hasn't gotten worse over the last few years. At least that." She sat back again, stretching out her arms on either side of her bowl, her fingers splaying as she frowned. Her wedding ring—a slim silver-and-turquoise band—was clearly too big, now. Levi wondered how she kept it on. "There might be services that would help, maybe in Santa Fe or Albuquerque. But since he couldn't possibly live there…" She shrugged, then folded her arms across her ribs, tucking her hands away. "Frankly, I think he's better off here, where at least he's with people who care. Where nobody will let him go homeless."

His chest aching, Levi thought about the women he'd dated, to use the term loosely. Before he joined the army he'd never really had a serious girlfriend. Because, for one thing, slim pickings. And for another… Well, that reason was sitting three feet away from him. And to be honest while he was in the service "dating" was more about occasional stress relief than working toward anything even remotely resembling forever. Not something he was particularly proud of, especially considering his parents' example. But at least he'd always been up front with any girl he took to bed, and if anyone ever had an issue with it, they never said anything. Not to him, anyway.

Except the life you choose when you're in your early twenties and not sure you're going to see your early thirties—and Levi had never been blind to the fact that going into a war zone could very well mean not coming *out*— wasn't necessarily the life you wanted when adulthood finally grabbed you by the throat and said, *You. Now.* Back then, he wasn't looking for compassion, or kindness, or anything much beyond looking and smelling good. But listening to Val now, hearing her voice shake as she talked about Charley, watching her eyes fill…

If only, he thought with a spurt of irritation that actually hurt.

"What about you?" he said, and puzzled eyes met his. "There's, you know, programs to help, um, surviving spouses?"

"Oh. Yeah. I was in one, for a while. Online." She shrugged. "I'm sure they're lifesavers for a lot of people, but some stuff I think a person has to work through alone, you know?"

Yeah. He did.

He got up from the table, holding out his hand for her bowl.

"You done?"

She nodded. "Thanks."

He carried their bowls over to the chewed-up ceramic sink, washed them out and set them into the drainer set over a towel on the counter.

"We are so getting you a dishwasher," he muttered, drying his hands on another towel, and she softly laughed.

"I never had one growing up. And the one in our apartment near the base kept going on the fritz. So no big deal?"

Something in her voice—a flatness, maybe—made him turn. Made him even madder, as though he couldn't figure out how to come up with a conversational topic that wouldn't upset her. Still seated, she was frowning slightly at her hands, folded in front of her on the table. A good, solid table Levi would love to get his hands on, bring it back to life.

Same as he'd like to do with her. With both him and her, frankly.

As if he had any idea how to do that.

"Val?"

She inhaled sharply, then gave him a bright smile. "Sorry. Slipped away for a moment. What were we talking about?"

"Dishwashers. As in, you're getting one whether you want it or not."

"Except…it wouldn't be for me, would it?" She got up as well, stretching her arms over her head before folding them across her stomach as she walked to the patio door. "I'm only borrowing the place, after all."

Like I've done with everything else.

The thought slugged Levi in the gut as hard as if she'd said the words out loud…that everything good in her life had been transient, a blip of happiness punctuating a long, long stretch of simply struggling not to go under. Not that he could hear a trace of self-pity in her voice, but he did hear resignation, that this was simply her lot in life. And on the heels of that thought came another—that, with the possible exception of his mother, Val was the strongest woman he'd ever met.

They heard the front door open, the pounding footsteps of an excited seven-year-old. A second later a grinning Josie burst into the kitchen with no less than three stuffed Walmart bags.

A second *before* Levi might've pulled Val into his arms. So, whew. Because for damn sure it wasn't *Levi's* arms Val wanted wrapped around her. Sure, he could build fences and replacing rotting porch floorboards and replace dying bushes…but he couldn't replace the only thing that mattered.

And he'd best remember that.

Honestly. There were enough pink and purple and turquoise duds piled on the kitchen table to outfit every second-grader in the state.

"You didn't have to do this, Connie," Val said, even

as, on the other side of the open patio door, she heard her oldest daughter jibber-jabbing away to Levi as he worked, as though unable to get her thoughts out of her head fast enough. "Really."

"Hey. I've been waiting a long time to buy little-girl clothes." On her lap, Risa let out a squeal, just because, then gave Val a slobbery grin. "So let an old woman live. Right, *reynita*?"

"Bah?" Risa said, pointing out the door. Her only "word" so far, but an amazingly versatile one.

"That's right, that's Uncle Levi," Connie said, her dark gaze sliding to Val. Full of meaning. Which was absurd since it wasn't as if her mother-in-law had caught them *doing* anything. "And somebody needs her diaper changed. Don't you, sweetie?"

Val stood, arms outstretched, but Connie shook her head, hefting herself—and the stinky, grinning baby— to her feet. "Nope, I've got this. You just sit here and admire the view."

"Really, Connie?"

Chuckling, her mother-in-law shuffled out of the room, and Val sighed. Because the woman was nothing if not perceptive. Meaning Val guessed she'd definitely picked up on something when she'd come in earlier.

A moment, Val was guessing.

A moment where she'd let down her guard, letting in verboten thoughts that kept creeping up on her no matter how often she told them to take a hike…a moment where she could feel Levi's mental pull like an actual physical thing. Or that could have been the loneliness talking. Hers, anyway. What was really going on inside his head, she had no idea. Partly because he clearly wasn't about to tell her, partly because she didn't want to know. Because *if* she knew, if he ever did open up to her…

The words *really, really bad* came to mind.

"There ya go, one much sweeter-smelling little girl," Connie said, returning to set Risa down on the not-exactly-pristine kitchen floor. Instantly the kid was on her hands and knees, flashing her frilled booty as she made fast tracks toward the only cupboard without a lock, where Val kept an assortment of things the kid could clang and bang to her heart's delight.

"So," Connie said, gathering her purse. "I assume you and the girls are going to the big doin's up at the ranch on the Fourth?"

"You're the second person to ask me that today." A half-dozen plastic containers tumbled onto the floor. Risa squealed and clapped her hands. "And the answer is I don't know."

"And you do not want the girls to be the only children in town who aren't there."

"So why don't you and Pete take them?"

"I think you know the answer to that."

Her eyes suddenly stinging, Val faced the open door, watching a giggling Josie with Levi, who was laughing, as well. Not from a strained politeness, the way a lot of adults might, but the kind of laugh guaranteed to get everybody around him laughing, too.

She remembered that laugh. Remembered, too, how often it led to shenanigans. Shenanigans that—in the early days, at least—had often involved Tommy. A laugh that still spelled trouble, but these days of an entirely different variety.

"And eight years ago, on the Fourth," Val said softly, "your son asked me to marry him, right before they started the fireworks."

"I remember."

Val sighed. "You know, I made a conscious decision to come back to Whispering Pines. It's where the girls belong, close to you and Pete. That doesn't mean I didn't have a lot of mixed feelings about it. Still do, even though I'm glad I'm here. The memories…"

Her mouth tight, she shook her head. "Mostly I can deal with them. But the ranch, on the Fourth." Her eyes burned.

On a soft moan, Connie wrapped her arm around Val's waist. "Which is exactly why you need to go. Not only for the girls' sake, but for yours—"

"I know, but—"

"Tommy's not coming back, honey," she said gently. "And no amount of wishing or praying or grieving's gonna change that… Oh, dear Lord," Connie said when Levi broke into some bizarre by-the-light-of-the-moon dance with the posthole digger, making Josie shriek with laughter and Connie chuckle. "That's exactly what he did with Tommy, you know."

"Levi danced for him?"

Her mother-in-law laughed again. "No. Brought him out of himself. Made Tommy more than he thought he could be." She paused. "And I'm thinking you need to let him dance for you, too."

"Connie, do not go there—"

"And where would that be? To maybe someplace where a young man might keep a young woman warm at night? From being lonely?"

"I can't believe you said that," Val said, pushing out a stingy little laugh. "And anyway, you do realize Levi's only here because of some dumb-ass promise he made to Tommy? Do I think he's changed? Maybe. But that doesn't mean…" She blew out a breath. "Jeez, Connie—it hasn't even been a year yet—"

"And opportunities don't always happen when we *think* we're ready, but when we *are* ready."

"That doesn't even make sense."

"Little about life does. And I'm giving notice—if you don't show up at the ranch? I will personally come and drag your skinny little ass there myself. Yeah, chew on that for a minute, missy."

Then her mother-in-law hustled her own not-so-skinny ass out of there, and Val blew out a long, long breath. Because Val wouldn't put it past Connie to make good on her threat.

All in the name of love, of course.

"Josie? Come on in, honey, before you talk the poor man's ear off!"

Levi glanced up as Josie let out a groaned "Aww…" before slogging off to obey her mama's call. And something to the set of Val's mouth, her posture, set off all kinds of alarms. His work done, anyway, Levi returned the digger to the shed, the dog keeping tabs to make sure he did it properly. Then, mopping off sweat with an old towel, he trekked back to the porch, where Val held Risa on her hip, her gaze fixed on him the way a woman does when she's trying to figure you out. Figure something out, anyway.

She gave the girl a quick one-armed hug, then said, "Take all those clothes Grandma bought to your room. We'll sort 'em out together after dinner."

"Did she show you what I wanna wear to the fireworks show?"

Levi saw Val's gaze shoot to the girl's. "No. But later, okay? Now git—go do what I said."

"She wasn't bothering me, Val," Levi said quietly after Josie huffed into the house. "Really." Frankly, he was getting pretty tired of repeating himself. In fact, the more he was around the kid, the more he *liked* being around her. Josie was the funniest thing going—although no surprise there, considering her dad's vehicle of choice. So he wished Val would get over whatever her issues were with him and her daughter, and simply let things be whatever they were going to be.

And he could only imagine the hell there'd be to pay if he actually said that out loud.

Val's mouth pulled flat. "And I said—"

"I know what you said. Although something tells me if she was thinking of terms of me being more than *Uncle* Levi, I'd know it. Josie doesn't strike me as somebody who plays her cards close to her chest."

At that, the tightness seemed to ease a little. "This is true—"

"Bah?" the baby said, pointing at Levi with a slimy finger.

Levi smiled. "Uncle Levi," he said, pressing a hand to his chest.

"Bah!" Risa squealed, clapping her hands and wriggling her nose, before hurtling herself out of Val's arms and toward Levi.

"Whoa, kiddo!" Levi said, laughing, catching the kid before she landed on her noggin.

His heart skipped a beat when she immediately settled against his damp chest with a satisfied, "Bah."

"Oh, jeez… I'm way too smelly to be holding a baby."

"That's okay. Give her time, and she'll smell a lot worse than you ever could."

Levi's gaze flicked to Val's. And, yep, two telltale red splotches gave her away. Calling her on it, though, would be highly ungentlemanly. He grinned for the slobbery baby, then bounced her until she belly laughed, making Levi laugh almost as hard.

"So…" Grinning, he turned to Val. "You all going out to the ranch for the Fourth?"

At that, the splotches practically glowed. Wasn't until he caught the pain, however, sharp as broken glass in those bright blue eyes, that he realized how deeply he'd put his foot in it. Because too late he remembered Tomas practically knocking down his door that Fourth of July all those years ago, his own eyes bright, his smile about to split his face in two.

"She said yes, bro! Holy hell, we're gonna get married!"

"Damn, Val… I'm sorry—"

"Why?" She reached for the baby, tucking Risa's soft curls under her chin. The way she mothered her girls… Man, that tugged at something deep inside Levi he didn't know could be tugged. Making him want things he'd had no idea he'd wanted. "Since clearly nobody else gives a rat's ass how I might feel about it."

Levi plowed his hands into his fatigues' pockets. "Well, I do. No, I forgot for a moment, and I really am sorry about that. But you know what? You don't want to go, just tell everybody else to back off. Whether you do or not, or why, is nobody's business but yours."

"But the girls…"

"Their grandparents can take 'em. Or mine. Or me, for that matter, if you trust me that far. But don't you dare let anybody push you around. Because believe me—I know how that goes."

It took a second for Levi's words to register. And more than the words, what was behind them. Because, once again, he was giving her permission to do what she felt was best for her. Instead of *telling* her what was best for her.

Pointing out, actually, that she didn't need anyone's permission to do—or not do—anything.

"Thank you," she said.

He looked surprised. "What for?"

"For backing me up."

"You mean, like friends are supposed to?"

She almost smiled. "Yeah."

He glanced away, squinting in the late-day sunlight clinging to the mountaintops, cloaking the yard—and the man in front of her—in a peachy gold, bronzing his damp skin, his curls. The T-shirt hugging his broad chest and shoulders. She hadn't realized how late it'd gotten.

Levi looked back, his eyes landing on the babbling baby slapping Val's chest. He smiled, then dug his keys out of his pocket.

"I'll be back tomorrow to set those posts. Josh said he'd come over to help string the fence, since he's got more experience than me. But as far as the kitchen goes…" His chest expanded with the force of his breath. "It occurs to me I was probably one of those people pushing you to make decisions before you were ready. If so, I apologize. God knows I never liked being pushed, so for me to do the same thing to you…" He shook his head. "So no rush. It's not like I'm going anywhere."

Then, with a nod, he walked around front to his truck, singing softly to himself. Wasn't until after she heard the roar of the truck's engine as he pulled away that his last words sank in, that he wasn't going anywhere. Words she should have found as reassuring as what he'd said about not letting other people push her around.

Instead, she felt as if the rug had been yanked out from underneath her all over again. Because the idea of him sticking around…

Bah.

Chapter Eight

"Mama!"

Val looked at her daughter, hands on hips as she stood in the master bedroom's doorway, shaking her head.

"What?"

Hands went out, all dramatic-like. "That's what you wear, like, every *day*. This is a *party*! You need to look *pretty*!"

Gee, thanks, kid, Val thought, as Risa—wobbling on her brand-new sparkly pink sneakers, fistfuls of hobnail bedspread clutched in her vice-like grip—screeched at the kitten trying to take a nap in the center of the bed. Val glanced at the baby, then the mildly pissed cat—whom Josie had finally named Skunk, of all things—before frowning at herself in the banged-up cheval mirror that'd seen who knew how many reflections over the years. Personally, she didn't see what was wrong with the outfit—jeans, a tank top, a cropped denim jacket for when it cooled off, later on. Dangly earrings. Because, hey. Like Josie said—*party*.

And the only pair of cowboy boots she owned, harking back from before she was married—the first thing she'd purchased with her own money. Deep red leather with, appropriately enough for the occasion, two blue and ivory stripes along the sides and matching stars across the instep.

Because, yes, she was going to the damn fireworks display out on the damn ranch. Not because anybody, or everybody, had bullied her into it, but because, dammit, the weenie wuss routine was not gonna cut it. Although she hadn't counted on being given a fashion critique by a seven-year-old. Who, Val had to admit, looked totes adorbs in a frilly little flowered dress and embroidered denim jacket and her own cowboy boots. New ones—because her feet *would* keep growing—that Connie had bought for her.

The cat yawned. The baby laughed. Val sighed. "And what would you suggest I wear?"

"A *dress*. Duh."

Now the dog wandered in, giving first Val, then Risa, a sniff before curling up into a ball under the window and immediately passing out.

"You do realize most of the women will be in jeans, right?"

"All I'm saying is that you can do better." And with that, her daughter marched to the piddly closet, rifled through Val's even more piddly wardrobe and pulled out the only dress she owned. From the *very* back of the closet. A dress she'd never worn. Never had the chance.

She knew she should've gotten rid of the damn thing.

"And you, young lady, were snooping."

Kid didn't even have the courtesy to look guilty. "You never said I couldn't," she said matter-of-factly, flipping the dress around like a saleswoman determined to score. The skirt softly flared, beckoning. "This is *so* pretty."

Yes, it was. A rare indulgence, ordered online on a whim. Although at least it had been half-off, so not a ter-

rible indulgence. And Val remembered, when she un-
wrapped it, her moan at how soft the fabric was. How,
after she slipped it on, she'd felt as if she were lying in
a field of wildflowers, blues and purples, reds and deep
pinks and white... How feminine the deep V neckline and
cinched waist and floaty skirt had made her feel.

How she'd imagined the look on Tommy's face when
he saw her in it.

Val held her breath, waiting for the ache. The sting of
tears. Something.

But...nothing. Not right now, anyway.

"Please try it on, Mama?"

Yeah, back in the Land of the Pushy People, all righty.
But how could she say no to her snoopy little girl, who'd
plopped down on the old stuffed chair in the corner of
the room with her chunky little sister on her lap, calmly
explaining to the baby that kitties didn't much like being
screeched at. So Val toed off the boots and wriggled out
of her jeans, her hair going all staticky when she tugged
off the top—Josie giggled—then slipped on the dress. It
floated over her body, weightlessly settling around her
bony hips and ribs. *Like a lover's sigh,* she thought, her
cheeks warming.

"Ohmigosh! You're so *beautiful*! Like a princess!"

The spell broken, Val laughed. "Not hardly," she said,
running a comb through her hair before tugging the boots
back on.

"You're gonna wear boots? With that dress?"

"Why not?" Val pointed to her daughter's feet. "You
are."

"But I'm a kid."

You were never a kid, Val thought, then said, "Well,
too bad. Because tonight I'm wearing cowboy boots with
my dress. And this," she added, slipping the jacket back
on and admiring her shabby chic country self in the mir-

ror. It'd been a long time since she'd worn her hair loose, too. She hadn't even realized how long it'd gotten, nearly to her waist in places. If she had a grain of sense she'd either put it up or at least braid it, but…no. Go big or go home and all that.

Grunting, Josie stood and came up beside her, the baby straddling her hip. Kid was a lot stronger than she looked. Like Val was herself, she thought before pulling them both close. One blonde, two brunettes, three rockin' chicks. "Do the Lopez girls rule, or what?"

Josie grinned, giving Val a glimpse of what she was going to look like in a few years. Also, heart palpitations. "Everybody there is so going to be looking at you!"

Yeah. *Just* what she wanted.

In the mirror, she saw Josie frown. "What are you doing?"

"It's a little chilly, don't you think?" she said, fastening most of the jacket's silver buttons, and her daughter released a you-are-hopeless sigh.

His cowboy hat angled against the sinking sun and a longneck dangling from his fingers, Levi propped the heel of one boot up against the massive gnarled trunk of a geriatric cottonwood, watching. Waiting. The air was already beginning to cool in the near-constant breeze rustling the bright green leaves, sending puffs of "cotton" floating across the front yard. More dirt than grass, pretty much like he remembered, but what grass there was was lush in the deep late-day shade.

From a half-dozen grills brought in for the occasion— and overseen by an equal number of people Levi didn't know—barbecue smoke tangoed with the cottony wisps, the scent reminding him of when he'd cooked up those steaks for Val and him a while back. The sun wouldn't set for a while, taking the wind with it. But once it did, it'd be a perfect night for fireworks. For other things, too, if one were inclined to let one's mind drift, like the smoke, in that direction.

Not that he was.

Never mind that, from the moment he'd heard Val and the kids were coming, he hadn't taken his eyes off the patch of pasture nearest the house, now chock-full of pickups and SUVs. None of 'em hers.

All around him folks milled about, yakking and laughing. Whispering Pines didn't seem so tiny once you got half the population jockeying for positions at the twenty-five-foot-long food table. And no wonder, considering the endless variety of dishes and casseroles on display, from pulled pork to steaming enchiladas, fried chicken and huge vats of spicy pinto beans, salads and rolls and every kind of dessert you could imagine.

And if the culinary delights weren't enough, the hacienda's massive flagstone porch took almost obscene advantage of the incredible view of the Sangre de Cristos, canopied by an endless sky with what people told him was a blazing tangle of purples and oranges and turquoises.

He took a swig of the beer, thinking how weird it was that this had been home for the first eighteen years of his life. How badly he'd wanted to escape. But whatever issues Levi might've had with wanting a different life from his father's, he doubted there was a more beautiful spot on earth. He smiled again, remembering that dinky two-bedroom house in town he and Tomas moved into after graduation, living the mighty fine bachelor life as only a pair of clueless nineteen-year-olds could.

Until Tomas and Val got married, anyway.

Good old Gus wandered over to stand under the tree with Levi, crossing his short arms high over his beach ball belly. Somebody's dog flounced over, carrying a stick in its mouth. Levi obliged.

"Seems like more people come every year, don' it?" the housekeeper said, his heavy northern New Mexican Spanish accent losing more end consonants as time went on. "Good thing I wen' back and bought more hamburger buns. Not to mention hamburgers."

At one time, the ranch had been all about steaks on the hoof. These days, however, it was a much leaner—and smaller—operation, the property's resources now devoted to breeding and training champion quarter horses. Even so, for a hundred years, maybe more, town and ranch had been inextricably connected, because Granville Blake—and his predecessors—had seen to it that they were.

Still focused on the makeshift parking lot, Levi smiled. "I remember when you and my mother did most of the cooking yourselves."

Gus snorted. "Those days, I don' miss. It was your mother, though, who put the bee in Mr. Gran's bonnet about turning it into a potluck. Except for the grilling, of course. They getting on okay?" he said, nodding at Levi's parents, chatting with Zach as he tried to keep tabs on two hyperexcited little boys. He hadn't seen his brothers much since that dinner—because even in small towns, folks got busy. But they talked. Texted. It was good.

"They are," Levi said, finally answering Gus's question. "I heard Dad's even riding again?"

"Yep, was out last week, in fact…"

But Levi barely heard Gus's comment, his gaze fixed on a certain old Toyota RAV4 that'd just pulled into the field. And behind that, the same Explorer Tomas learned to drive in more than fifteen years ago. A minute later, everyone disembarked from both vehicles, including Tommy's grandmother, her black dress shapeless as a garbage bag and nearly as shiny. Smiling, Pete Lopez tucked the old woman's hand in the crook of his arm before starting toward the house. Connie strapped Risa into a stroller, only to then fuss nonstop as the damn thing bumped and lurched over the uneven pasture.

But it was Val—hauling a half-dozen pie boxes as Josie bounced around, beside, in front of her, constantly yammering—who stole Levi's breath. The breeze snatched at her loose hair, filmy gold in the slanted sun, then at the hem of her dress, at total odds with the beat-up boots, her worn denim jacket. Then she looked up, her gaze catching in Levi's, and...

Damn.

Beside him, he heard Gus's low chuckle. "Gal looks like she could use some help," he said, walking away.

She wasn't the only one, Levi thought as he started toward the family, annoyed he couldn't reach her fast enough, half wanting to turn tail and get the hell out of there. Yes, even after all that waiting—

"Levi!" Her outfit similar to her mother's, Josie ran over, skinny arms and legs going in a dozen different directions. The arms stopped windmilling long enough to wrap around Levi's waist, allowing him a whiff of baby shampoo when her head briefly pressed into his stomach. Then she leaned back, grinning, and he thought no fireworks on earth could possibly rival the glittering in those dark eyes. Not to mention the explosions going on inside his head, at how this kid simply liked him for him. No judgment, no expectations.

She grinned, showing off the ridged beginnings of big-girl front teeth. "This is gonna be so much fun, huh?"

"That's the plan," he said, and she giggled. And for a moment, Tomas was right here, all that unbridled joy expressed in this elf-child with the sparkling eyes. His heart turning over in his chest, Levi hauled her into his arms, where she threw hers around his neck and kissed his cheek.

Hell. Yep, he was head over heels in love. And damned if those protective feelings didn't kick in, hard.

"See that man over there in the blue shirt?" he whispered into her curls. "With the bolo tie?"

"Uh-huh."

"That's Gus. He knew your daddy really well. Why don't you go on over, and he'll hook you up with the best food on the table."

Josie looked back at Val, who nodded.

"Okay," she said, sliding down Levi's leg as he lowered her to the ground before she took off. By now the others had caught up, Tomas's grandmother snagging his wrist in cool, trembling fingers before pulling him aside. A thousand wrinkles shifted when she smiled, although he caught the censure, too, in those dark eyes.

"You've been a bad boy," Angelita said in Spanish, her soft white curls like the old-fashioned spun-glass angel hair she'd put on her Christmas tree when Tommy and him were kids. "Not coming to see me." Then she wagged one of those skinny fingers at him, saying in English, "I should strip you of your honorary grandson status."

"And you'd have every right. I'm sorry—"

Lita winked. "And I'm sure you have better things to do than spend time with an old woman, no?" Her gaze slid to Val, crouched in front of the stroller as she tried to calm a fussy Risa, before coming to rest back on Levi. "I miss my Tomas so much," she said with a long sigh, and Levi gently tugged her to his side, like she used to do with him when he was a kid. Of course, she used to swat him, too, when he'd been naughty. Because sometimes love hurts, she used to say.

Wasn't that the truth?

"We all do," he said.

She sighed again, then motioned for him to lean down so she could kiss his cheek, only to make a face.

"You need to shave," she said, then toddled off to rejoin

the family…and Levi finally met Val's questioning gaze. And, oh, yeah, reached for the pies.

"Let me get those for you—"

"No, I'm good—"

"For godssake, Val," Connie said, grunting as she shoved the stroller over another bump on the ground. "Let the man help you!"

Levi grinned. Casually. Like his heart wasn't about to hammer right out of his chest, for reasons only partly influenced by how hot Val looked in that crazy getup. "You heard the woman. Hand 'em over."

With an eye-roll worthy of her daughter, Val complied. Only to then cross her arms as if she had no idea what to do with her hands. "Just so you know," she said so only he could hear, "I'm not here because anybody bullied me into it."

"Didn't think you were." He paused, partly to gather his thoughts, partly to get a stronger bead on her scent, something musky and flowery that had rattled those thoughts to begin with. "But I'm glad you are." He glanced down at her, walking beside him, her arms all tight against her ribs and a frown dug into her forehead, and he wished like hell he could make it better. "For Josie's sake, if nothing else. But for yours, too."

She didn't say anything for a second. Then, looking straight ahead, she said, "Why for me?"

"Same reason I'm here, I suppose. To nudge us both back to feeling normal again."

Another pause. "Thought you said that wasn't even possible."

"I think we owe it to Tommy to at least try, right?" They'd reached the veranda by now, where Levi shifted things around on the table's dessert end to make room for the pies. Trying not to read too much into her silence, he opened the first box, nearly falling over from the heady scent. "What are these?"

"Fruit, mostly," she said after a moment. "Since I knew they'd keep until dinner was over."

She let him finish setting the pies out on the table. Apple. Blueberry. Cherry. Peach, he thought. More than one person stopped to admire them, make Val promise to save them a slice. Smiling, she said she'd do her best, her voice as warm and friendly as usual but definitely subdued. Not that Levi blamed her. As hard as this was for him, it had to be a hundred times worse for her.

"Thanks," she said when the crowd thinned.

"No problem," Levi said, shoving the empty boxes underneath the table.

"No, I mean…"

Val huffed a breath, making him look at her. She'd unfolded her arms, only to stick her hands in her jacket pockets. Between the getup and the way the light played over her sharp features, she looked eighteen again. No, younger. Before Tommy, when she used to pile on defiance like some girls layered on makeup. And he realized it had been that defiance that had first snagged him all those years ago. Made him want to do something, anything, to mitigate whatever had put it there.

Still did.

She glanced out at all the people shuffling around in the yard, then back at him. "I mean, thanks for being okay with talking about Tommy."

"Why wouldn't I be?"

One side of her mouth lifted. Levi told himself the way her hair was floating around her shoulders wasn't distracting as hell. "Because everybody else… I don't know. I can't decide if they're afraid they'll lose it or I will."

As far as chinks went, it was pretty slim. But he'd take it. "His folks…?"

"The one exception," she said, averting her gaze again to skim her fingers on the edge of the table. "Even so, I can tell there's times when we're holding back. On both sides. You know what I was saying, about being honest?" A breath left her lungs. "I think the world of Tommy's parents. And I know I wouldn't've gotten through this without them. But…"

"But they're not exactly objective."

Another tiny smile pushed at her mouth. "How can I say everything I'm really thinking without causing them more pain?"

Levi glanced across the yard, where the Lopezes had staked out a claim underneath that old cottonwood, Connie spreading a blanket on the ground for them and the kids, Pete setting up a lawn chair for Tomas's grandma. The old lady leaned forward, smiling at Risa in her stroller, right as Connie looked over and caught Levi's gaze in hers. And he could see in her expression exactly what they were all thinking—that Tomas wasn't here. More to the point, that he *should* be. A lump rose in Levi's throat.

"And you think they don't know what's going on in your head? Whether you say it out loud or not? Tommy will always be part of our lives, Val," he said softly, nodding at Connie, who smiled back before returning her attention to her husband. Levi faced Val again. "So anytime you want to talk about him—or anything else, actually—I'm more than happy to listen."

At least that got a laugh out of her. "You better be careful or they'll revoke your membership in the Dude's Club."

He shrugged. "After listening to my army buddies bitch for hours on end, I'll take my chances. Now. How's about we get some grub before the locusts eat it all up—"

"The same goes, you know." Levi frowned down at her. The corners of her mouth lifted. Barely. "If you need an ear, I mean…" Her gaze darted away as she sucked in a breath. "Crap. What's he doing here?"

"Who?"

"Charley." She nodded toward the old vet making his way toward the table. "Annie said he came a couple of years ago, got totally freaked out by the fireworks. So she's been taking the cookout to him, afterward. How on earth did he even get here?"

Levi glanced down the table, where a grinning Charley was spooning baked beans onto his plate. His showing up wasn't even a question—the dude had his ways. But his guess was that the old soldier didn't remember about the fireworks. Or the effect they had on him. A lot of guys with PTSD didn't, until something happened to trigger the flashbacks. Levi had been one of the "lucky" ones, as far as that went—although he'd been close enough to a few explosions to scare the crap out of him when they'd happened, there hadn't been any real lasting effects. None that he could tell, anyway. Yeah, he had his issues, but fear of loud noises wasn't one of them.

"Maybe he's not planning on staying."

"Maybe. But…"

The concern in her voice twisted something inside him. "You're quite the mama hen, aren't you?" he said, and a short laugh bubbled from her chest, followed by a sigh.

"Everybody needs to know somebody cares about 'em," she said, still watching Charley. Then her eyes lifted to Levi's. "Don't you think?"

"Absolutely," he said quietly, then gave her shoulder a quick squeeze. "Go on back to your family. I'll keep an eye on him."

"You sure?"

At the incredulousness in her voice, his gaze sank to its knees in hers, smack-dab into a mixture of strength and pain and soul-deep kindness that shook him to his core. He smiled. "It's no big deal, Val—"

"Not to you, maybe. To him, though…"

"Hey," he said. "That man saved my butt, back when more than a few people wondered if it could be saved. The least I can do now is return the favor. And speaking of saving…" He pointed to the cherry pie. "That one." Then he started toward his old boss, thinking this was definitely not how he'd seen the evening panning out. But that slightly confused, if grateful, look on Val's face was definitely worth a slight change of plans.

And even that was more than he deserved.

It was something like Tommy would've done, Val mused some time later, the way Levi had given up part of himself to make sure somebody else was safe, taken care of.

Of course, between the crowd and needing to stick close to her chicks, she'd lost track of Levi and Charley shortly after that. But she'd occasionally catch glimpses of that beat-up old cowboy hat—yes, she could tell Levi's beat-up old cowboy hat apart from all the others, she had special powers like that—and since there hadn't been any set-tos that she was aware of, she assumed all had been well.

For Charley, anyway. Because as great as the food had been, and as hard as she'd smiled watching the girls' eyes and mouths go wide at the fireworks display, the more fun everyone else had, the wider the hole in her heart seemed to get.

A hole that, even if only for a moment, a tall man in a beat-up old cowboy hat had filled, like when he'd swung her daughter up into his arms, or volunteered to watch over a fellow vet who only half remembered who Levi— or anyone else—was.

A hole she had no business even thinking about letting anyone else fill. Because she'd learned her lesson about that, hadn't she—?

"You okay, *querida*?"

At her father-in-law's gentle voice, Val smiled. He'd temporarily commandeered Lita's lawn chair while Connie escorted the old woman to one of the nearby porta-potties. Now, on her knees as she gathered up everyone's paper plates and cups from dinner, Val smiled up at him. She imagined this is what Tommy would have looked like at fifty, handsome and silver haired, a little stockier than he should be. But with a smile that would have still melted her heart. Even though she understood her resistance, looking back it seemed silly how long it'd taken for her to accept Pedro Lopez as a real father figure in her life. As if this lovely man could hurt a fly. And she couldn't ask for a better grandfather to her girls.

"I'm fine," she said, looking up at the blue-black sky, pinpricked with a million stars softly glimmering through leftover tendrils of fireworks smoke. "I'm glad we came."

And she was, the hole in her heart notwithstanding. Because she'd faced down more than a few demons tonight, hadn't she? Okay, maybe she hadn't exactly vanquished them, but at least she wasn't off sucking her thumb in a corner, either. So she'd take that as a win.

"Good," Pete said, getting to his feet and hitching his belt underneath his belly, and Val smiled, knowing that was the end to the conversation.

If not the end to her swirling thoughts.

Way on the other side of the house, from the massive old barn that'd been original to the place a hundred years ago, came the screech of an amplifier system cranking up, a twang or two of an electric guitar. Because for some people the party wasn't anywhere near over. For *some* people, there was still dancing to be done, boot-scootin' and two-steppin', and hot-stuff cowboys kissing pretty girls—

"Everybody ready to go?" she said, standing so abruptly she stumbled. That'd been the plan, after all, getting the kids home and to bed after the fireworks. As it was Risa had conked out a half hour ago, and poor Josie, usually sawing logs by nine, was lurching around like a zombie.

"Oh, we're taking the girls back to our place," Connie said. "So you can stay and hang out with the other young people."

"And why would I do that?" Val said, thinking, *Other young people?* True, she had a ways to go before she collected Social Security, but compared with the *real* "young people" making tracks toward the barn, she felt like a long-buried pueblo artifact, brittle and dusty and faded.

"Because," Connie said, giving her a nudge as she folded up the blanket they'd been sitting on, "looks to me like somebody's come back for you."

"What?"

Val followed Connie's gaze. And sure enough, there was Levi, striding toward them, hatless and determined and grinning like a fool.

Of course, nothing said Levi's intentions—whatever those might be—even remotely lined up with Connie's active imagination. Or that Val couldn't plead exhaustion and worm her way out of whatever that look in his eyes—yeah, he was close enough now to see a definite glint to go along with the grin—meant. Because, really, hadn't she done enough demon banishing for one night?

Another electrified twang sliced through the cool, still, gunpowder-scented night, and Levi stopped a few feet away, his hands in his pockets, that stupid grin on his face, and Connie giggled.

And clear as day, she heard a voice in her head say,

Be honest—you wanna leave because you're tired? Or because you're scared?

You know, those damn demons could shut the hell up anytime now. Jeebus.

Chapter Nine

Levi still wasn't entirely sure what had prompted him to return after taking Charley home. What he'd expected to happen. For all he'd known the Lopezes would've been long gone, especially with two little girls and an old woman in tow.

He took the fact that they'd been still there as a sign. Of what, he wasn't sure. His own idiocy, most likely.

Because it wasn't like this was ever gonna go anywhere. Then again, he thought as the stomping and electrified music from the barn sucked Val and him in like moths to a flame, maybe that's what made it easier—knowing there were no expectations. Except, he hoped, seeing more of those smiles. Hearing that laugh. Easing something inside the woman walking beside him, her hands jammed in her jacket pockets, he'd never be able to fully ease inside himself. Of course, could be she was simply pissed that her in-laws had swooped off with her children like a pair of benevolent hawks, not even giving her a chance to protest.

"You mad?" he said, figuring he might as well get it out in the open instead of letting it fester for the rest of the evening.

Predictably enough, she sighed. "Not real fond of being ambushed."

"That what you think I'm doing?"

"I have no idea what you're doing. Connie and Pete, though…that's something else."

"You can leave anytime you like, you know."

"Heh. And did you notice Connie took my car? Because, she said, she didn't want to have to move the car seats." Her mouth screwed up. "Kind of a long walk back to town. So, yeah, I'm mad. But not at you."

"You sure about that?"

A beat or two passed before she shrugged. "All I want, all I've ever wanted, is to make my own choices. Within reason, I mean. Sure, there's times when your *only* choice is to deal with the crap life tosses at you, but you should at least have the opportunity to make your own decisions about how you deal with that crap, you know? I mean, jeez—I went from nobody giving a damn about me to people caring too much. A little balance would be nice."

Levi chuckled. "No such thing in a small town."

She sighed again, then shouted over the music, the general mayhem as they got closer to the barn. "I suppose you're right." Then she glanced over. "So what happened with Charley? He okay?"

Now who's caring too much? he wanted to say. But he wasn't that stupid. Somebody'd gotten a bonfire going, out in the dirt. The light flickered in her eyes, across her face. Val wasn't all soft and pretty in a conventional sense, but she had one of those faces you couldn't take your eyes off. He couldn't, anyway. And he was surprised to realize that if her hand had been where he could reach it, he would've taken it. Which was probably why it wasn't.

Nodding, Levi pushed his denim jacket aside to shove his own hands in his pockets. "Oh, yeah. He knew about the fireworks, but I couldn't talk him out of staying. So I steered us far enough away that I hoped it wouldn't be a problem. And he was good." He shrugged. "Maybe because he knew they were coming, so it wasn't a surprise… Where you going?"

Val'd hung a right toward the bonfire. Which felt pretty nice, actually, as the temperature dropped. She stood with her feet apart, hands stuffed in pockets. When he came up beside her, she said, "So it's not a problem for you?"

The genuine concern in her voice rippled through him. "Not like it is for some people," he said softly, focused on the writhing flames.

He felt her gaze on the side of his face, her unasked questions piercing his skull. Finally he lowered his eyes to hers, figuring he may as well answer one or two of them. "I'm okay, Val. Mostly, anyway. But when I was asked if I wanted to re-up, I had no trouble saying no."

She frowned again into the fire. "And that's all you're going to say, I take it."

"For now."

After a moment, she nodded, then sucked in a breath. "So. I guess we should do this," she said, backing away and heading toward the barn. Levi followed, grinning in spite of himself at the Western version of Cinderella's ball inside. God knew New Mexico wasn't entirely tumbleweeds and cowboy boots—in fact, most of it wasn't—but Whispering Pines had always taken great pride in its unapologetic Western vibes. And nowhere more than the Vista's Fourth of July bash.

The grin morphed into a chuckle. What the town lacked in size—or, let's face it, culture—was more than made up for in blatant over-the-topness. If nothing else, people around here knew how to have fun. Or at least how to make the most out of whatever fun there was to be had. Not that Levi could dance worth spit, but then, most of the people out there strutting their stuff couldn't, either.

At last, he had a reason to offer Val his hand. "Wanna dance?" he shouted, his smile dying at her expression when he glanced over—sadness, anger, determination, all balled up into something that broke his heart. He pushed his hand back into his pocket.

"Hey. You don't want to do this, I'm happy to take you home—"

"What I want," she said, chin jutting, "is a beer. Maybe two. *Then* I'll dance."

Okay, this wasn't good. Small as Val was, she probably had the tolerance of a gnat. Levi also guessed, judging from the weird light in her eyes—although that might've been from the lanterns strung up all over the barn—it'd been a while since she'd had to find out. "You sure?"

"About the dancing?"

"No. The drinking."

She huffed a sigh. "Oh, Lord…not you, too?"

"Me, too, what?"

"Telling me what I can or cannot do." That fierce little gaze zinged to his. "Not driving, no kids to take care of… If I want a beer, I can damn well have a beer."

"Yes, you can. Except you don't drink, do you?" When she glared at him again, he said, "Just pointing out the obvious."

Val looked back inside, at all those people having a grand old time, and Levi saw everything she was thinking right on her face. So it was no surprise when she said, "This is something I need to do. But no way am I gonna get through it without a little help. So come on."

She reached over to yank his hand out of his pocket and pulled him onto the makeshift dance floor, with a pit stop at one of the metal washtubs filled with ice and Coors. And behind the washtub, a stony-faced responsible adult, there to ensure that (1) no one under legit drinking age partook of the offerings, and (2) that no one *of* legit drinking age partook of more than they could handle. Or—

"He's driving," Val said, jerking a thumb in his direction before grabbing one of the beers.

—they were with a designated driver. Although one of the sheriff's deputies was probably out in the makeshift parking lot, anyway, making sure nobody got behind the wheel who shouldn't.

So he let her have her beer…and then another one, figuring this was one of those times when it's best to let the woman do things her own way, clean up the mess later. Yes, even if those messes were actual messes. After dealing with it plenty in the army, a little gal puke was hardly gonna put him off. Sure, maybe she thought she was relying on some liquid in an amber bottle to get her through this, but he was the one she was with. And not, say, one of any number of obviously willing candidates he'd been shooting death glares at for the past half hour. So, yeah.

Over the next little while, Levi discovered two things: That Valerie Lopez did indeed get drunk faster than a frat dude in a drinking game, and that she was the cutest drunk he'd ever seen. And God knew he'd seen his fair share of drunk women. Not all that much fun, truth be told. The slurring and hanging all over him and whatnot. But Val was not a slurrer. Or a hanger-on-er. Her eyes did sparkle more, though. And she actually giggled from time to time—

"Oooh" came out on a whooshed, hops-scented breath when the band started up with a line dance. They'd been sitting on a hay bale—well, she'd been sitting, perched atop the thing like a little kid, her short legs dangling— and now she clumsily clunked to the wooden floor and grabbed Levi's hand, this time tugging him into the crowd with a smile that arrowed right to his heart. Even if it wasn't for him.

Of course, the minute Levi got out on the floor he remembered that his feet had minds of their own. Tommy had been good at this stuff, he remembered. Not him. He could fake a two-step well enough, but this actually required some coordination. But damned if he didn't get caught up in the music and laughter, in watching Val's face glow in a way he hadn't seen in…well. A very long time. Yeah, she was drunk off her cute little ass, and she was probably going to wake up with one whopper of a headache. But right now, she was having a helluva good time. And who was he to begrudge her that?

Then, like somebody'd pulled a plug, the music slowed, and she was in his arms, all soft and sweet smelling and not exactly steady on her pins. Which, after they'd been swaying for a couple of minutes, her forehead pressed into his sternum, she even admitted, with a cute little hiccup.

"I might be a little…" She burped. "Dizzy."

Levi peered down at her, his breath teasing her hair, her scent teasing his…everything. "You gonna be sick?"

Still glued to his chest, she shook her head. Carefully. "Uh-uh. Long as I don't look up, anyway." She hiccupped again.

Chuckling, he slipped a hand to her waist and steered her toward the door. "Let's get you some fresh air, wild woman."

"'Kay."

They'd no sooner gotten outside when they ran into Gus, who clucked at Val like an old hen. "Somebody looks like she needs to go home—"

"No!" She gave her head a sharp shake, only to grab it like it might fly off her neck before peering back at the barn. "Not yet," she said softly, tears cresting in her eyes.

"I'll be good, I promise. Just don't make me go home yet. Please."

Gus snorted. "Go on up to the house, the back door's open. Coffee's in the cupboard to the right of the sink, right over the maker."

However, by the time they made the short trek to the house, the chilly night air had apparently cleared her head. At least enough that she appeared sober, although Levi seriously doubted she would've passed a Breathalyzer test.

"Gotta pee," she said the second they got inside, and he directed her to the hall bath right off the kitchen. Which, as he walked in, looked nearly the same as Levi remembered—dark wood cabinets, terra-cotta floors, brilliantly colored Mexican tile backsplash and counters. Off-white appliances, except for the dark blue six-burner stove. A hodge-podge of traditional New Mexican and 1990s cutting edge.

Behind him, Val's boot heels softly clopped against the tiled floor.

"Ooh…pretty."

He turned. "This your first time in the house?"

"Tommy never came without you, remember?"

And by an unspoken understanding, the three of them had never been together. Not here, anyway.

While Levi went about putting on a pot of coffee, Val leaned over the counter to inspect the tiles, hands fisted in her pockets. Then she straightened, looking around. "Actually, this is how I always pictured my own kitchen."

"Outdated by thirty years?"

She laughed. "Homey. With a history. And those tiles…" She reached out to skim her fingers across the bold hand-painted pattern. "I really love these. Like, more than I love chocolate. Which says a lot, believe me."

Levi leaned one hip against the counter edge, listening to the drip and hiss of the coffee trickling into the old-school carafe. "At least that's one mystery solved."

Val looked over, a slight crease between her brows. "Mystery?"

"Now I know why you've been dragging your feet about finishing the kitchen."

She blew a short laugh through her nose. "Maybe. Not that all those samples you showed me aren't pretty, but yeah. They're not…me."

When the pot was full, Levi poured two mugs and brought them over to the same six-foot-long pine table where he and his brothers often ended up doing their homework, usually under Gus's supervision, once their mother started delivering babies. "So let's rethink things," he said, sliding onto one of the benches. "It's not like we can't find a place or six that sells Mexican tiles around here."

"And—again—I can't exactly put my personal touch on a space I'm only babysitting, can I?"

Stirring sugar into his coffee, Levi looked up to see her still staring at the tiles with a wistful expression that tore him to pieces. Because once again, she didn't have free rein to make her own choice. Even about some stupid tiles. But before he could figure out what to say, she climbed over the bench to sit beside him, dumping three spoonsful of sugar into her own coffee.

"Thanks. And I don't mean for this." She jabbed her spoon toward the dark swirling liquid. "I mean for…indulging me, I suppose. Tonight. Although I may never live it down around town."

Levi smiled. "All anyone saw—if they even noticed, it was pretty crowded in there—was a gal having fun. Hardly a hanging offense." She snorted. "But you're welcome. I'm glad…" He frowned at his own coffee. "I'm glad you felt you could trust me enough to do that. That I wouldn't take advantage of you. Or something."

She actually laughed. "Seriously, Levi? You're surprised that I trust you?"

"Uh…yeah? I mean, considering our history and all. Right?"

She squeezed shut her eyes, then opened them again to blow out a breath. "Well, I do. Trust you."

He took a moment. "This is a new development, I take it?"

Her mouth twisted. "New…ish. You've been a good friend, Levi. And I don't have a lot of those. So thank you."

Levi stared at his hands, curled around the steaming mug, almost incapable of processing her sincerity. "You have no idea," he finally said, "how honored that makes me feel."

She took a sip of her coffee, then set down the mug, going very still. "Same goes," she said softly. "In fact… I owe you an apology."

"Now I know you're drunk," he said, and she laughed. But it was a sad sound, battering his heart all over again.

"Still drunk enough to let down the wall, maybe. But not so drunk that I don't know what I'm saying." Her eyes lifted to his. "You probably know I blamed you all these years for Tommy's going into the army."

"Kinda got that impression, yeah. But—"

"No, let me finish before the caffeine kicks in and I lose my nerve. All my life, people have left. Made promises they didn't keep. My parents, especially. Then Tommy showed up, and I thought—finally. Someone who'll actually stick around. So when he decided to enlist, I couldn't believe it. And I didn't want to believe it of him. That he'd leave me, just like everybody else. So since the thought of laying the blame at his feet nearly killed me, I shifted it to you."

"Since you already didn't like me and all."

One side of her mouth lifted. "You were definitely convenient. And then you came back, and…" She shrugged. "I wanted to be angry. I *needed* to be angry."

Without thinking, Levi reached for her hand. Which she let him take. "Except…" She exhaled. "Hanging on to a lie doesn't make it true. It only makes you look like an idiot." She stared at their linked hands. "Maybe your enlisting put the idea in Tommy's head to do the same thing, but it was his choice. A choice I doubt I'll ever completely understand, but blaming you for it…" She lifted her eyes to his. "That was wrong. And I apologize."

His brain locking up again, Levi let go of her hand to tug her to his side, his chest constricting when she laid her head on his shoulder. And it simply felt…right. For them, for this moment. Because he didn't have a whole lot of friends, either. And he could do far worse than having this woman fill that position.

"I could've done more, though," he said into her hair, "to talk him out of it—"

"No, Levi. You couldn't have. This was the dude who bought that god-awful purple car, remember? Jeez, Levi—the man gave up sex to serve his country."

"Um… I take it the coffee hasn't fully kicked in yet?"

"We were married, Levi. We had sex. *Good* sex. When he was around. Not gonna lie, I miss that." Yeah, definitely the beer still talking. Had to be. "But it was something Tommy felt he had to do," she went on. "And because of that choice, a lot of lives were saved." She pulled away, taking her warmth with her. "One of those things nobody warns you about falling for an honorable dude—"

"Thought I heard voices," said a gruff voice from the doorway, pushing both of them to their feet. A moment later Granville Blake came into the room, leaning heavily on a three-pronged cane. Levi started—the last time he'd seen his father's old employer the man had been as fit as any of his much younger hands, tall and proud and black haired, with light-colored eyes that could—and did—pierce straight through a person. And if it hadn't been for those eyes, Levi wouldn't have recognized him.

"Gus told me you were here." Stiffly, Granville walked toward them, his hand extended. "Welcome home, son."

Levi clasped the older man's hand, his chest constricting at how frail it felt. "Thank you, sir. I don't think you know Valerie Lopez? She married my friend Tomas."

"Ooh…" Granville's gaze turned to Val. "I'm so sorry, honey. *So* sorry. Yes, I remember Tomas quite well. Fine young man." Leaning heavily on the cane, he gave Val a sympathetic smile. "You getting on okay?"

"Yes. Thank you—"

"Wait. Valerie…your maiden name was Oswald, wasn't it?"

"It was, yes."

Granville sucked in a long breath, every line in his face deepening. "Knew your mother. Not well, but…" He cleared his throat, a slight flush sweeping across his pallid cheeks. "I was sorry to hear of her passing. Real sorry."

Even an idiot could've heard the subtext screaming underneath those words. And for damn sure Val obviously did. This time her "Thank you" was mumbled before she said, "It's getting late, I should really be getting back. But the party was great—thanks so much for hosting it…"

After a few more words with Granville, they left. The festivities were winding down, the only sounds the occasional slam of a truck door, tires bumping over dirt. A bellow of good-old-boy laughter. From a nearby barn, a horse nickered, the sound suspended in the chilled night air that cloaked them as they walked back to Levi's truck, Val with her arms pretzeled over her ribs.

"God, I could so use another beer right now."

"No, you couldn't."

"He slept with my mother, Levi." The darkness snatched at her words. Her anger.

"You don't know that."

"Don't I?"

"Okay," Levi said, knowing arguing would be pointless. Especially with a woman as ticked off as this one was. "But he's been a widower for a long time—"

"And we *all* know what my mother was. So no big deal, right?" Then she stopped dead in her tracks to lift her face to the clear, star-pricked black sky. His hands fisted in his jacket pockets, Levi had no idea what to do, what she wanted or needed from him. If anything. Except, maybe, simply his presence. Clearly his lot in life, he thought with a slight smile.

"Val?"

A breeze plucked at her hair, silver in the moonlight. "Why should I even care? Especially since it obviously happened years ago. When I wasn't even around. But damn…" A harsh laugh pushed from her lungs. "Sometimes I think the woman hooked up with every breathing male in a hundred-mile radius."

Unfortunately, he couldn't exactly refute her assumption. So instead he waited until she took his hand, then continued on to the truck. "And maybe, for a little while, she was able to offer a lonely man some solace."

"Solace? Clearly you never knew my mother."

"No, but I knew Granville Blake. And I remember when his wife died. How hard he took it."

Val was quiet for a moment. "They never had any kids?"

"One. A daughter. A little younger than Josh and me. Granville sent her to DC to live with her aunt and uncle when she was fourteen, fifteen, something like that."

"Why?" She sounded appalled.

"I have no idea. I know—it seemed crazy to us, too, that he'd send away his only child. Far as I know she hasn't been back in years. I'm guessing what you saw tonight was a lot of regret." He looked over at her. "So you might not want to take out your frustration on him."

"It's not him I'm frustrated with," she sighed out. "Obviously. And what my mother did after I left was her business. It just kicked a lot of memories back to life. That's all."

"You must've hated her."

On a sound that was half laugh, half sigh, Val picked her way across a network of braided cottonwood roots to plant her butt on a chewed-up swing that'd been dangling from that old tree for as long as Levi could remember. He feared for her safety, even though he doubted her weight even registered on the sturdy branch. He followed to stand in front of her, his thumbs hooked in the front pockets of his jeans.

"I'm guessing you're still not ready to go home?"

She gave him an almost apologetic smile. "It's funny. It's not as if there's anything there I'm trying to avoid. Except, maybe…" Her lips pursed. "The quiet."

"I can understand that."

"So you don't mind?"

"Not at all."

Tilting back her head, Val curled her fingers high on the ropes, looking up through a million heart-shaped leaves shivering in the gentle breeze, ghostly in the scant light reaching them from the house, the barns. "To answer your question…no, I didn't hate my mother. Although sometimes I think it would've been easier if I had. And God knows, I wanted to. Horrible as that sounds. But what I wanted more, was to simply feel important to her. To feel—" her gaze met his again, eerily clear in the shadowed light "—like I mattered. To her, to anybody. Seeing as how my father clearly didn't care, either."

Oddly, he knew she wasn't looking for pity. In fact,

she probably would've slugged him if he'd offered it. But he still felt compelled to say, "It must've been hard, when he left."

Val halfheartedly shoved off the ground; the swing wobbled, like it wasn't sure what it was supposed to do, before settling into a gentle rocking motion. "I was only five, so I don't remember much about it. Or him, for that matter. Except for a couple of vague impressions."

"Good, bad...?"

She shrugged. "Neither. Although not sure what difference that makes, since he's never tried to make contact."

"Not even once?"

"Nope. Although since my parents weren't married, maybe he never felt any real obligation...?"

"Plenty of men father children with women they're not married to, Val. Has nothing to do with how they feel about their kids."

"Not in this case. Frankly I've always wondered why he stuck around as long as he did. But whatever. Between that and my mother's always looking at me like she didn't understand why I was there..." Her fingers tightened around the ropes. "Nothing like being made to feel like a mistake nobody could figure out how to fix. So when Tommy came into my life..." She shrugged, her eyes glittering in the moonlight.

"He did make you feel like you mattered."

She smiled. "And then some. And that took guts, you know? In a town this small, hooking up with someone like me."

Anger spiking through him, Levi leaned against the tree's massive trunk. "You weren't your mother, Val."

"Tell that to the kids—and their parents—who judged me." Her mouth twisted. "Or assumed I was *exactly* like my mother."

Something hard and cold fisted in Levi's chest. The

sneers and snide comments had been bad enough. The close-minded judging. But something in her voice told him that hadn't been the end of it. "Who?"

Her eyes flashed to his, startled. Then she shook her head. "Not important."

"Like hell."

Sighing, she leaned her temple against her hand, fisted around the rope. "It wasn't anybody you would've known—he didn't live here. And this was before Tomas. I was lucky, if you can call it that. I got away before the worst happened."

He could barely breathe. "How old were you?"

"Thirteen? Fourteen?"

"Good God, Val. Did Tommy know?"

"No."

"Why the hell not?"

"Because for years I was too…ashamed? Confused? I honestly don't know. Then I guess I thought, why re-hash, relive, whatever, something I wanted to forget? It was enough that Tommy'd rescued me from what he did know about." She smiled. "That he loved me, baggage and all. And I will always love him for that. For seeing past all the stuff the other boys couldn't. Or wouldn't."

Through a wad of impossibly tangled thoughts, Levi waited out a surge of something he couldn't even define. Irritation, maybe, that he hadn't known? "But you're telling me now."

A slight smile touched her lips. "Yeah."

"Why?"

"Because…dunno. It's not so scary anymore?"

"The memory? Or the idea of telling someone?"

"Not sure. Both?"

"I'm so sorry—"

"For something that had nothing to do with you? Why? I never even told my mother," she said before he could answer her question. "Can you believe it? God, if my girls ever thought they couldn't tell me about *any*thing…" Her eyes glittered. "It would gut me, Levi. Absolutely *gut* me."

"I doubt you have anything to worry about on that score," he said, which got a little smile, even as he thought about how much he'd kept from his parents when he was younger. That undoubtedly there'd be times her girls would rather put their eyes out rather than share with their mother. But best not to go there. Instead, he veered onto a side road with, "Did you know my mother helped take care of yours, after she got sick?"

Val shook her head. "Natalie and I…well. We didn't have a whole lot to say to each other at that point."

"Did you even know?"

"No. And, yes, that's the truth."

"Did you think I wouldn't believe you?"

Her mouth thinned. "No matter what our relationship was—or wasn't—we were all each other had at that point. I can only imagine what some people must've thought, that I wasn't here to take care of her."

"And those people can go screw themselves," he said, and she almost laughed. "If she didn't tell you, I think that lets you off the hook. And seriously—according to my mother, yours was a bitch on wheels. Sorry—"

"No, sounds about right. There was a reason— several, actually—I stayed as far out of her radar as…" She yawned. "As possible. She knew about Josie, but…"

"The kid didn't need to be around that. And you were right to protect her." He hesitated. "Not to mention yourself. Her needs were met, as well as she'd let anybody meet them. And while God knows I may not have figured out much about life yet, I do know one thing—we're not responsible for anybody else's screwups. Our own, yeah. But not anyone else's. Damn, Val…"

He shoved his hands in his pockets again, not quite believing what he was about to say. But knowing he'd explode if he didn't. "You know the thing I most remember about you, from when we were kids?" Eyes glued to his, she shook her head. "Your dignity. The way you'd hold up your head high when you had to know the other kids were talking about you. Even though you were obviously going through a hell that nobody else had a clue about. Not really. But damned if you were going to let anybody else see it. Or let it poison you. And you could have, you know. And the way you cared about other people, even then…" He swallowed as he felt heat blaze across his face. Thank God it was dark. "There's a reason Tommy fell as hard as he did. Because you…you were something else. You still are."

Val stared at him for several seconds, which did nothing to help the blazing-face thing, then slowly smiled. "Holy crap, Levi," she said softly. "I…" She glanced away, pushing out a small laugh, before facing him again. "Wow…" Another yawn attacked, this one epic. She covered her mouth, then gripped the rope again. "I don't know what to say."

"Why do you have to say anything? It's true. But I think it's time we get you home before you fall off that swing."

She yawned again, then pushed out a tired laugh. "You might have a point."

A point she proved long before they got back to Whispering Pines, when, despite the coffee, she conked out in the car. She didn't exactly wake up when they reached her house, either, although she came to enough to murmur, "Where are we?" when he opened the passenger-side door. From inside, Radar went into overdrive, baying his fool head off.

"Your house."

Her eyes drifted shut again. "Not my house."

Levi reached inside, scooped her into his arms. She didn't protest. In fact, she looped her arms around his neck and snuggled right against his chest, and he thought, *Oh, hell*. "But that's definitely your dog."

Her head wagged again, her hair tickling his chin. "Not my dog, either," she mumbled. "Tommy's."

Beginning to see a pattern here, Levi carted her up the porch steps. She weighed, like, nothing. Behind the door, the dog went crazy. "How about the cat?"

"Josie's."

"Well, hell, woman..." He shifted to dig the keys out of her purse, unlock the door. "What *is* yours?"

"These," she said, lifting one foot. But not her head. "Boots are *allll* mine."

Chuckling over the sting to his heart, he carted her inside, kneeing aside the frantic dog before carrying her upstairs to her room. She was sawing logs again before he'd even lowered her to the bed. Carefully, he removed the boots, then dislodged a very miffed kitten to tug a fluffy throw off the chair, which he gently tucked around Val's delicate shoulders.

Then he stood back, half smiling as Skunk hopped up to curl into the space in front of her stomach and the dog climbed up to smash himself against her back, and he thought, *Me*.

I could be yours.

Right. As if he'd ever in a million years be able to compete with the guy she'd just said she'd love forever, for having the cojones to do what Levi hadn't. Besides, all Tomas had wanted was for Levi to make sure she was okay. He sincerely doubted falling for the woman had been part of his best friend's plan.

Then again...

Levi leaned over to place a soft kiss on Val's even softer cheek, then straightened, his hands in his pockets. A smile flickered across her lips, not unlike Risa's when she was dreaming, and Levi's heart started hammering in his chest.

Because there was no getting around it—for the first time in his life, he was in love.

As in, drowning.

So maybe it was time he find those cojones, setting aside his loyalty to a dead man for a shot at something far bigger. Maybe, just maybe, this was his chance to be everything to Val, to her girls, he *couldn't* have been before. Yes, it had to be her choice to move forward or not. But how could she make that choice if he didn't give her the option? And if the odds were stacked against him… tough. Wouldn't be the first time.

However, it was the first time that defying those odds made him feel as if he'd gotten hold of some bad booze. Hell, laying his life on the line was nothing compared with the prospect of offering his *heart*.

A floorboard squawked as Levi tiptoed out of the room, imagining his brothers laughing their fool heads off.

Chapter Ten

The sun was blasting through the open window when Val woke with a start the next morning, dry-mouthed and fuzzy-brained. To make matters worse, that fuzzy brain had way too much information to process at once, including, but not limited to, (1) she was still fully dressed; (2) her daughters were giggling like mad downstairs; and (3) since she could hear Levi as well, she was guessing he was the cause of the giggling.

Great.

She kneed the kitten aside—bad move, ouch—to peel off the throw so she could get to the bathroom before her bladder exploded, at which point a quick glance in the mottled mirror over the 1980s-era sink made her remember why she rarely wore makeup. Because raccoon eyes were not her friends. Also, if she was going to look—and feel—like a prime candidate for the walk of shame, shouldn't she at least have something to be ashamed *of*?

Something close to a chuckle burped from her chest. Oh, the irony.

Then it hit her, everything Levi had said, about…back then. About her being dignified and all that—a thought that brought a smile, considering at the moment she was about as dignified as roadkill. Add to that the look in his eyes, intense and searing and mad as hell, for her sake. The feel of him, holding her when they danced, when he carried her into the house, warm and solid and protective and, heaven help her, *alive*.

So alive.

Because, no, she hadn't been that drunk. Or sleepy.

Blood surged to her face, bringing her hand to her red-hot cheeks. Because only once before, had a man said or done anything to make her feel…special. Worthy.

As if she mattered.

And that man—the second one, not the first—was downstairs, right this very minute, making her children laugh. Also pancakes, if her nose was to be believed.

Val squeezed shut her hairy eyes. Granted, not hating him—anymore—was a good thing. As was forgiving him. Or rather, realizing she had nothing to forgive him for. But *liking* him…?

Being *attracted* to him…?

"Mama?"

Still leaning on the cultured marble sink—because she wasn't entirely sure she wouldn't fall over if she didn't—Val smiled in the mirror for her oldest child, all perky and adorable and grinning.

"Good morning, cutie," she said, and said child scurried over to wrap her arms around Val's waist. And then frown at her.

"You look funny. Are you sick?"

The thought crossed Val's feeble mind that this would be a great opportunity for an object lesson on the consequences of alcohol overindulgence. Except adolescence would come soon enough; why knock herself off the pedestal a minute before the kid would, anyway?

So all she said was, "I'm fine, sweetie. Just slept too hard is all." As in, like the dead, but let's not go there.

"Why are you still dressed?" Josie said, because *there* was exactly where a seven-year-old was going to go.

"I was too tired to undress." And somehow she left the question mark off the end of that sentence.

"Oh. Okay. Anyway… Levi's making pancakes."

"So I gathered." Wait. "When did Grandma drop you off?"

"A little while ago. Levi was already here. He said he spent the night."

"To *Grandma*?"

"Uh-huh. She got a real weird look on her face. And then she smiled. Like this." Josie demonstrated, giving Val the eeriest sensation of what her baby girl would look like in fifty years. And again, she was swamped with the unfairness of it all, that now her mother-in-law was probably thinking…

Sweet baby Jesus.

"So are you coming downstairs?"

"Not looking like this, I'm not. Give me ten minutes, okay?"

"Okay." Josie started to scamper away—honestly, the kid never walked if she could run, skip or hop—only to turn back around and say, "Levi makes really, really good pancakes."

Of course he did.

As promised, ten minutes later, showered and clothed and more or less in her right mind, Val ventured downstairs—carefully—where the dog rushed her, a blur of canine joy, only to rush back to Him Who Had the Food. Josie was at the kitchen table, prattling away about…something, while this big, sweet, handsome man held her baby against his hip as if he'd been doing this for years, giving Risa a step-by-step tutorial on how to flip pancakes as the kid gnawed on her own, happily getting soggy, crummy slobber all over Levi's shoulder.

Things were less bizarre when she *was* drunk.

"Mama's here!" Josie cried, and Risa clapped her gooey hands. Levi looked over, grinning, and for a second Val thought how easy it would be to buy into whatever Levi was selling. Although since he probably had no idea what that was, or that he was even selling it, she'd best be keeping her slightly hungover wits about her.

Especially since loneliness and grief—fading, yes, but by no means done with—blended with chronic disappointment made for really crappy soil to grow anything in. At least, anything that wasn't bound to eventually shrivel up and die.

"Mornin', Cinderella." Val grimaced, and he chuckled, and her hungover hormones got all shivery. "Coffee's on. Kids are fed. Would've made bacon but there wasn't any. And what's up with that?"

"Take it up with the food fairy," Val muttered, then gawked at the piled-high plate on the stove. "Exactly how many of those do you expect me to eat?"

"Figured you'd be hungry after last night," he said, not even trying to keep the innuendo out of his voice, and she was sorely tempted to grab the spatula from his hand and beat him over the head with it. However, having neither the energy to carry through nor the wherewithal to explain to Miss Big Eyes, she settled for sitting at the table and letting Levi wait on her.

Josie jumped up to run outside, taking the reluctant dog with her, and Levi lowered the babbling baby into her high chair.

"You have to strap her in—"

"Got it."

"And make sure her fingers are out of the way before you snap on the tray—" He shot her a *Seriously?* look, and she pressed her lips together.

"Okay, I'll shut up now."

"You do that," he said, handing the baby another pancake before setting a humongous plate of the same in front of Val, along with syrup and butter. And coffee, bless him. And damned if her eyes didn't go all stingy.

"What?" he said, sliding into the seat across from her.

Shaking her head, she smeared soft butter between each layer, then drowned the pancakes in syrup before the butter had fully melted, making little yellow islands in a glistening, gooey amber sea. The weird thing was, it wasn't as if nobody had ever made breakfast for her. Connie had, all the time, when she and the girls had lived with her and Pete. But before then, that honor had fallen to Tommy, initially when they were first married, then when he'd be home on leave. Because after everything she'd been through, he'd said, she deserved to be pampered.

But there was no need to mention that now. Really. Because maybe there was such a thing as being too honest. Levi needed to be appreciated for his own sake and his own deeds. Not because he reminded her of Tommy.

And certainly not because she was feeling especially... needy. Did she dream he'd kissed her on the cheek last night? Or had that really happened?

So she skirted his concern entirely by asking, "Why on earth did you stay?"

Chewing around a huge bite of pancakes, he shrugged. "Didn't like the idea of you being alone in the house at night."

"Never mind that I always am." He shrugged again, and she sighed. "You do realize that Connie probably jumped to all manner of conclusions."

"Since I was still sacked out on the sofa when she arrived, maybe not so much."

"Oh."

"Yeah. Oh. So no worries, sweet cheeks, your virtue is still untarnished."

She threw her coffee spoon at him. Risa squealed, delighted, clapping her hands as a chuckling Levi easily caught the spoon before handing it to the baby, then leaned over to touch his forehead to hers. Tears sprang to Val's eyes; she quickly blinked them away, chuckling when the baby lifted the spoon, triumphant.

"Bah?"

"Bah," Levi said, straightening. Grinning her evil baby grin, Risa curled in on herself, her prize clutched to her chest, and Levi laughed. Val smiled.

"You're really good with her. With both of them."

Straightening, he gave her an almost sheepish smile as the baby gleefully banged the spoon on her high chair tray. "I know. Surprised the heck out of me, too."

She took a bite of pancakes. They were freaking perfect. "You ever think about having kids of your own?"

"Before a few weeks ago?" Something bloomed in his eyes. Something she didn't want to think about too hard. "No."

Val lifted her coffee mug to her mouth, hoping her cheeks didn't look as red as they felt. "I'm so sorry you had to sleep on the sofa, it really sucks—"

"Considering I didn't exactly spend the last six years on a Sleep Number bed, I was good. You going into work today?"

"Yeah," she said, glancing at the kitchen clock. "Soon, actually. Since I couldn't bake yesterday, I have to go in early to get some pies done for the lunch rush. Which means I need to get the kids back to Connie's—"

"No worries, I've got 'em."

She blinked at him. "What? Why?"

"Why not?" He polished off his breakfast, stood to clear their plates.

"Because what do you know about taking care of a baby?"

He pointed to the obviously happy infant currently auditioning for lead drummer in a rock band, then carried the dishes to the sink. "You don't think I can handle it?"

"I..." She frowned. "Can you?"

"Yes," he said over the running water as he washed the dishes. "And if things get too crazy, I can always call Connie. She said," he said when Val opened her mouth to protest.

"Why?" she repeated, and Levi looked out the kitchen window for a long moment before turning back to her. And while she couldn't have defined what she saw in his eyes if her life depended on it, whatever it was reached right inside her and wrapped around her heart. And squeezed. Hard.

"Even if Tommy hadn't asked me to look out for you and the girls," he said, "I'd like to believe I would've, anyway. And now that I'm here..." He smiled down at the sticky-faced baby shrieking at the kitten who'd come into the kitchen, before meeting Val's gaze again. "I owe this much to him, to be whatever you all need me to be in your lives." His gaze touched hers. "And I do mean *whatever* you need me to be."

And what if I don't want you to do that?

The thought sliced through her like a samurai blade. Which it undoubtedly would have Levi, too, if she'd had it in her to give voice to it. But she was hardly going to slap the man's kindness in the face, was she? He meant well; she knew that. And it wasn't as if she wasn't grateful, because she was. Heart-achingly so. That didn't mean she wasn't also scared out of her gourd of losing everything she'd fought so hard for over the last little while, to trust her own decisions about what was best for her and the girls. Because if it was one thing she'd learned, it was that the only person she could truly count on was herself.

But now was not the time to lay all that out there, both because she needed to get her butt to work and because she'd put out her own eye before hurting Levi. So all she did was smile and say, "And I appreciate that. I really do," even as the hollowness of her own words made her inwardly wince. She got up from the table, scouring her hands down the backside of her jeans. "Lord, I didn't realize how late it was."

She jumped when Levi laid a hand on her shoulder, his touch so warm, so steady, searing through the thin fabric of her blouse. "Hey. I didn't mean to upset you—"

"You didn't—"

"And you're a lousy liar," he said, and her face flamed. And not only about being caught out. Because those hormones had sobered right up, boy, reminding her of that which she sorely missed. Including, apparently, her sanity.

Because oh, dear *Lord,* did she want to kiss him. Or have him kiss her. Whichever, whatever, didn't matter. Worse, though—since she clearly had a masochistic streak a mile wide—it was killing her not to ask him what he really wanted from her. With her.

Because if she did, then he'd have to answer. And whatever the answer was she already knew she'd have no idea what to do with it.

Because then she'd have to decide what she really wanted from *him.*

With him.

"Thanks for watching the kids," she mumbled, giving Risa a quick nuzzle and kiss before scurrying away, like the flustered coward she was.

* * *

Josie was lying on her back in the backyard, the sun hot on her closed eyelids, when suddenly it got darker.

"What on earth are you doing, little girl?"

The laughter in Levi's voice made her giggle before she opened her eyes to find him standing over her with Risa in his arms. He was so big, like a giant. *A lot bigger than Daddy,* she thought. Although truthfully she was remembering Daddy less and less these days. A thought that made her heart hurt.

"I like to lie in the sun and think about stuff."

"Sounds reasonable," Levi said, sitting beside her. He set Risa in the grass, although she immediately started crawling away. It was crazy, how fast she was on her hands and knees. But Radar, who'd been asleep beside Josie, jumped up and got in front of the baby, making sure she didn't go too far. Josie hugged her knees, her forehead squished.

"Where's Mama?"

"She went to work. So I'm staying with you guys until she gets back. If that's okay with you?"

"Oh. Yeah, sure." Josie picked off a piece of little plant with itty-bitty purple flowers on it. Mama said it was a weed, but it was still pretty. "Thank you for breakfast."

"You're welcome. Hey," Levi said, gently bumping shoulders. "What's going on?"

"Just thinking about Daddy."

"Ah."

She squinted up at Levi in the bright sun. "Do you mind if I talk about him?"

"Not at all. Why should I?"

"Because he was your best friend?"

"All the more reason to talk about him, right?"

"Yeah, that would be my take on it," she said on a sigh, wondering why Levi sounded like he was trying not to laugh. "But if I talk about him to Mama or Gramma, they go all weird on me. I mean, I can see they're trying not to, but that only makes it weirder. You know?"

"I do."

"So how come it doesn't bother you?"

Levi got real quiet, then said, "Because when I look at you and Risa, it's like your dad is right here. And that helps me not miss him so much."

"Huh." Josie thought about that for a moment. "So how come Mama and Gramma don't feel like that?"

"Couldn't tell you. Although I guess…it's all about perspective."

"What's that?"

"How a person looks at things. Not with their eyes, but with their minds. Your mom and your grandmother… maybe they only see what they're missing. I see what I *had*. The crazy times your dad and I used to have together. I'm not saying it doesn't hurt, knowing we won't ever be able to have any more of those crazy times, but remembering them…" He smiled. "It makes me feel very…rich."

"But what if you don't have those memories? Or at least, not a lot of them. And Risa…" She nodded at her sister, gurgling at the dog as she patted his back. "She never even met Daddy. So she *can't* remember him."

Levi leaned back on his elbow, his own forehead all crinkly. "I see your point."

"Yeah. Sucks."

He smiled again, then looked over at her. His eyes… They always made her feel safe. As if she didn't have to be afraid when he was around. "You know if there's any pictures of your dad?"

She thought. "I know Gramma has this big book with some. I'm not sure about Mom, though. Maybe on her phone?"

"And there's probably some on people's computers, too,"

Levi said. "So how's about we print out some of those pictures, then make an album for Risa? Then your mom and I, and your grandparents, could write down our memories of him to go along with the pictures. That way, your dad won't be forgotten."

"Really? We could do that?"

"Absolutely." Then Levi got a funny look on his face. "I know I said it'd be for Risa—and you, of course—but it might also be a good way to help your mom and your grandparents deal with your dad not being here anymore. To help them remember the good times." He grinned. "How funny your dad was. And how much he liked to *have* fun."

Josie wrapped her arms around her legs to lean her chin on her knees, thinking this over. "So if we do this, it might help Mama stop being so sad all the time?"

"Couldn't hurt to try, right?"

No, Josie thought. She didn't suppose it would. Then she made a face.

"Ew, Risa—you stink *so* bad!"

Levi laughed, and her baby sister grinned, her chin all shiny with drool. For somebody so cute, she sure could be gross. Then Levi got to his feet, swinging the baby up against his side, as if it didn't even bother him how yucky she smelled. "Oh, yeah, somebody definitely needs her pants changed," he said, then held out his hand to Josie. "Then let's go over to your grandma's, see about getting some of those pictures."

And Josie put her hand in his, and you know what? For the moment, things felt pretty okay. In fact, once they got inside and Levi took the baby upstairs to change her diaper, Josie went over to the DVD player and took out *Elf*. She'd watched it so much she could practically say all the words along with the characters. And she still loved it. But she thought maybe she didn't need it to remember Daddy anymore. Especially now that Levi was around.

Smiling, she carefully put the DVD back into its case and then on the shelf under the TV, where it would be safe.

It'd been slower than usual, which Val supposed wasn't all that surprising for the day after the Fourth. Even so, yesterday's shindig had netted her—and the diner—a few new customers, so the day wasn't a total loss. But by three the place was dead. Except for Charley, of course, in his usual spot at the end of the counter.

Val slid a piece of chocolate cream pie in front of him, warmth flooding her when his face lit up.

"For me?"

"Nobody else."

"She's spoiling you something rotten," Annie said good-naturedly as she swiped down the counter. Charley grinned around a mouthful of rich chocolate and whipped cream.

"And don't I know it."

"And what you probably don't know," Annie said to Val, "is that I had somebody from the ski resort in today asking if we—well, you—sold in bulk."

"The resort?"

"Yep. Apparently word's gotten out that we sell the best pies in northern New Mexico. So they want a piece of the action. Well, more than a piece. The gal said they could probably move several dozen whole pies a day during peak season."

"You're kidding?"

"Nope. And before you go off on some rant about loyalty or whatever…you'd be an idiot to turn up your nose at the opportunity. Unless you want to waitress for me the rest of your life? Yeah, that's what I thought. So, here." Annie dug into her pocket and handed Val a business card. "There's her number. Call her."

"And how on earth would I handle that kind of volume?"

"You give the idea to the universe, let the universe figure it out. Oh, customer…" Annie smiled for the slight graying man who'd come in clutching a brown cowboy hat in his hands. "Go on and take a seat anywhere. Want some coffee?"

"No, actually I'm looking for someone." Bandy-legged and slightly barrel-chested, the man had "rodeo rider" written all over him. Or one of the clowns maybe. In any case, Val'd never seen him before. Until pale blue eyes shot to hers, as a shy, almost frightened smile creased the man's sun-beaten face…and Val's heart shot into her throat.

"Valerie Ann?" the man said softly, gnarled fingers now strangling the hat's brim. "You probably don't recognize me—"

"No. I do," she said, impossible though that might seem.

The man's smile softened. Grew.

And once again, her world went sideways.

Chapter Eleven

Val couldn't remember when she'd determined that treating other people better than she'd been treated was her ticket out of her lousy childhood. Not that she hadn't had issues with people, for various reasons—like, say, Levi—but even as a kid she realized that returning cursing for cursing did nobody any favors. Especially herself. Maybe she had no control over the events of her life, but how she reacted to those events was entirely up to her. Mostly, anyway.

A fact she now reminded herself of as she sat in a back booth with her father, who looked every bit as awkward as she felt. God knows her first impulse had been to run, but something—Annie, most likely—had held her back. And thus far she couldn't decide whether being in shock made the encounter easier or harder. She only prayed it would be over soon.

She'd texted Levi to make sure it was okay if she was late. She didn't say why. Although what did it say about her sorry state of mind, that she half wished he was here with her, all calm and steady and rocklike? And right there was the problem, wasn't it?

"Why?" she now said, glaring at her hands folded in front of her on the table. Refusing to meet her father's eyes. Because no way was she getting sucked in. No. Damn. Way.

"Why am I here?" he asked. "Or why did I leave?"

At least he had the courage to come straight to the point. Meaning she needed to find enough to look at the man. "Take your pick."

"You have every right to be pissed off—"

"That's not even a question," she said, refusing to flinch at the guilt darkening his gaze.

He scrubbed his hand across his whiskery face, looking…worn-out. It occurred to Val she had no idea how old he actually was. Or even his last name, actually. "Surprising you like this probably wasn't the best move, but since I didn't know how else to contact you…it was one of those spur-of-the-moment things, you know? I was on my way north for a rodeo and… I can't explain it. It was like something pushed me back here, and then I found myself asking if anybody knew you. Guy up the street, he pointed me in the right direction." He smiled, revealing a missing incisor. "And here you are—"

"Right where I've been most of my life." Except for the years she'd been in Texas, when Tommy was in the service. But this man didn't need to know that. "So you could've put in an appearance anytime. And not only because 'something' prompted you to see if I was around, like some old high school classmate you decided to look up."

"Your mother…she didn't tell you? About what happened between us?"

"Natalie never mentioned you at all after you left."

Her father released a resigned sigh. "No surprise there,

I guess." His forehead creased. "You call her by her first name?"

"It worked for us." Val paused. "Do you even know she passed away?"

"No." A brief startled look was almost instantly replaced with what Val could only surmise was relief. "When?"

"Few years back. Cancer."

"I'm sorry to hear that—"

"Somehow I doubt it. Since you don't seem particularly bothered that she didn't talk about you."

"Considering how badly I screwed up? Why would she? I didn't... You need to know, Valerie, I didn't leave of my own accord. Your mother kicked me out." He cleared his throat. "Because she found out I was cheating on her."

Val almost laughed. "Oh, jeez—"

"I was a twenty-four-year-old asshole, Valerie. What the hell did I know about responsibility?"

Twenty-*four*? Which would have made him...nineteen when she was born. Seven years younger than her mother. Holy hell.

"That why you're not listed on my birth certificate?"

His mouth turned down at the corners. "That wasn't my choice—believe me."

Val sagged back in the booth, her arms crossed. "Are you even sure...?"

"That I'm your dad? Yeah. I took you into Albuquerque when you were a baby, had a paternity test done."

"Wow. Were they even that common back then?"

"Not like they are now, no. And, boy, was your mother mad when the test results landed in our mailbox. But..." His scruffy cheeks puffed when he released a breath. "I just wanted to be sure. Like you said."

To get away from the storm inside her head, Val looked out the window. At some point the absurdity of the encounter was going to hit her between the eyes, but for now shock numbed the anger. Somewhat, anyway.

"I found a picture," she said quietly, facing him again, "when I came back to clear out my mother's things. Of the two of you, with me as a toddler. Your name was on the back. Your first name, anyway. Otherwise I wouldn't have even known that much. The photo was mixed in with some other papers. I doubt she even remembered it was there—"

"It's McAdams."

"Pardon?"

"My last name. McAdams."

Val took a moment to process this before her forehead knotted. "You were really that young?"

Her father leaned sideways to pull his wallet out of his back pocket, which he flipped open to show her his driver's license. His hand shook, she noticed. Not badly, but way too much for a man only in his late forties. Craig Andrew McAdams, it said. The picture was recent. He wasn't smiling.

"I wasn't ready to be a father, to be honest," he said quietly, shifting again to replace the wallet. "But when Nat told me she was pregnant, I figured I should at least try. Shoot, I even offered to marry her. She was having none of it. Actually she wasn't even all that hot on us moving in together. And considering how bad things were between us, I should've probably listened to her."

"So you cheated on her."

His mouth tightened. "It was an impossible situation. We weren't getting along—at all—but there you were, and…" He shrugged, his eyes watering. "Like I said. I screwed up. With her, with you…everybody. But I did love you. And for more than five years, I gave it my best shot, I swear. As much as the sorry piece of crap I was understood how to do that."

"Only not enough to ever make contact again."

Craig glanced down at his scarred hands, then back at her. "There was more. I might've...been involved in a few things I shouldn't've been. Your mother used that as leverage."

"Things?"

"Drugs," he said, and Val shut her eyes, feeling as if she'd just stepped into an episode of *Breaking Bad*. "The cheating, I think Nat might've gotten over. Onetime thing, meant nothing. We'd had a fight..." He waved away the rest of the thought. "But the other stuff... I guess everybody has their line in the sand. That was hers. She said if I tried to contact you, she'd sic the cops on me. So my hands were tied. For what it's worth, I'm clean now. Have been for years."

"Glad to hear it."

Craig grimaced. "But by the time I'd gotten my head on straight, so much time had passed, I figured you'd probably forgotten me. Or didn't care."

"You're right. I didn't. Care, I mean." Or so she'd convinced herself.

"And the other?"

Val hesitated, glancing out the window before meeting his hopeful gaze again. "I didn't exactly remember you. How could I—I was so little when you left? But I never forgot you, either. Doesn't mean, however, that I'm even remotely interested in resurrecting a relationship you killed."

Her stomach quaking, Val pushed herself out of the booth. "Blame my mother all you want—and believe me, I understand where you're coming from on that—but everything happened as a consequence of decisions *you* made. And sorry, but excuses don't cut it. Because I was young, too, when I got married, had my first daughter. And trust me—nothing in heaven or on earth could've convinced me to abandon her. Yeah, you had a lot of crap to work through, I got it. But once you did..."

She swallowed past the knot in her throat. "You knew what my mother was like, but you never even tried to find out if I was okay. On what planet is that *loving* me? So thanks, but no thanks."

Several seconds passed before her father pushed out a heavy sigh. "So I guess checking to see if you're okay now doesn't really count?"

She thought of Levi, everything he'd done for her and the girls in the name of making sure they were okay, and her heart twisted in her chest. "What do you think?"

"It was a long shot," her father said quietly, then stood as well, grabbing his hat off the seat. "You're married, then? I mean, if I can at least ask that much?"

Oh, dear God—could this conversation get any worse? Val took a moment to steady her breathing. "Was. My husband…was killed. In Afghanistan. Last year."

What looked like genuine sympathy flooded faded eyes. "Oh, honey, I'm so sorry." Val nodded, unable to speak. "And you said, um, you have a daughter?"

"Two, actually. Josie is seven, Risa isn't a year yet."

"So you're raising them on your own?"

"Not entirely, no," she said and left it there.

Silence jittered between them for several seconds before her father dug his wallet out again, this time extracting a ratty-looking business card, which he handed to her. Along with his name and cell phone number was a picture of him in rodeo clown getup. Under other circumstances, Val might've smiled.

"What with everything you've been through," Craig said softly, "the last thing you needed was me butting back into your life right now. I'm more sorry about that than I can say. And God knows I don't deserve anything from you. Especially forgiveness. Because you're right. What happened between your mother and me was a long time ago, and at some point I should've at least tried to make things right between *you* and me. That I didn't…there's no excuse for that. So I'm just grateful…" He cleared his throat. "That at least I got to see you again. Talk to you for a minute. But you keep that card," he said, tapping it. "And if, at some point, it seems right to tell those girls of yours about me…"

He screwed his hat back on his head. "You were the sweetest little girl," he said, his mouth tilted in a soft smile. "And I bet your daughters are, too. Well…" He hesitated, then nodded. "You take care, sweetheart. Okay?"

Then he walked away, nodding at Charley before he left. Frozen to the spot, Val watched through the window as her father got into his pickup and drove off. And she wondered, briefly, if it would've been worse, when she was little, to actually see him go, rather than waking up to discover he'd already gone.

Because she hadn't been entirely truthful about not re-membering him. Not how he looked or sounded, maybe, but even now images played through, of sitting in his lap, of him carrying her piggyback. Of being hugged and kissed good-night.

Of feeling safe.

Annie slipped an arm around her waist. "How you doing, honey?"

"I have no idea," Val said, then left before she made more of a fool of herself than she already had. But the drive back to the house wasn't nearly long enough to sort out the million and one thoughts in her head. Except for two things that had become crystal clear in the space of the last few hours. One, that once again, a man was offer-ing to plug up that hole in her heart.

And two, that she'd be ten kinds of fool to let him do that.

Levi and Josie were cleaning up the kitchen table when he heard the front door open. A moment later, Val appeared, looking as though she'd just had a run-in with the devil himself. Levi's heart bolted into his throat as Josie looked up, grinning, apparently oblivious to the wretched look on her mother's face.

"Me and Levi are making an album for Risa all about Daddy. With pictures and everything. So we won't forget him. Come look!"

"Really?" Val said, her smile brittle even as she pulled the girl to her side, gently shuffling some of the photos laid out on the table with her other hand. Not that there was much to look at yet. But Connie had given them a whole bunch of pics from when Tommy had been a kid, so Levi and Josie had spent the past hour or so sorting through them, choosing which ones to put in the album. "What on earth made you think of doing this?"

"It was Levi's idea. And we're all gonna write stuff to go with the pictures. Him and me and Gramma and Grampa. And you, if you want. Gramma says she's got this special paper, it'll last for years and years. Cool, huh? Oh, and Levi said we can print pictures off the phone, too. Right?" She flashed him another grin, then picked up a photo of Tommy from when they were in high school. "This one's my favorite." Her forehead crinkled. "You remember how he used to smile like that?"

Val cleared her throat, her eyes shiny. "I sure do, sweetie," she said, then pulled her daughter closer to kiss the top of her head. Same as he'd seen her do a thousand times. But not like this. Not as though the only thing keeping her from losing it was the feel of her child in her arms—

"Mama! You're squishing me!"

"Sorry, baby," Val said with a slight laugh, then let go, shifting her watery gaze to Levi. "Thank you."

His face warmed. "I know I probably should've asked you first—"

"Not at all. This…" She glanced at the pictures again, then smiled for her daughter. "I'm only sorry I didn't come up with it myself," she said, and Josie giggled right as the doorbell rang. The kid jumped up from the chair.

"That's probably Luisa from school. She asked earlier if I could go over to her house to play until dinnertime. She lives right down the street, so is it okay?"

"Of course. Go on—have fun."

A minute later, the door slammed again, and Val dropped into the chair Josie'd been sitting in, her head in her hands, looking like all the air'd been sucked out of her. Levi's chest cramped.

"I just thought the album would be a good way for Josie to work through some of the stuff about her dad—"

"The album's a great idea," she breathed out, lifting her head but not looking at him.

"Val?"

"Is Risa asleep?"

Levi handed over the monitor; Val's expression as she looked at the tiny image of the sleeping baby nearly did him in. "She went down an hour ago. Josie says she usually sleeps until almost five?"

"Yeah." Her gaze shifted to the window. "My father showed up at the diner."

"Your…? You're kidding?"

"Nope." She pushed out a tight little laugh. "Surprise."

"And…not a good one, I take it."

"What do you think?"

What he thought was that the woman needed another shock like a hole in the head. Also, that she was holding in her emotions so tightly she was probably close to erupting. He held out his hand. "Come here."

Val frowned at his hand, then got up to wrench open the patio door and walk out onto the deck, clutching the monitor as Radar bounded up to her like she'd been gone for three years. Levi followed, not even trying to guess what was going on in her head as she lowered herself to the deck's steps, letting the dog lather her face in kisses for several seconds before gently pushing him away. Behind them, a storm softly rumbled on the plains, probably headed in their direction. *In more ways than one,* Levi guessed as Val picked up a stray branch and threw it for the dog.

He sat beside her, apprehension knifing through him. Because whatever she was about to say, he was pretty sure he wasn't going to like it.

Val hauled in a breath, inhaling Levi's scent, that calm strength that was the very reason why she had to get these thoughts out of her head. Because she at least owed him that much.

"As I was sitting in Annie's," she finally said, "listening to my father tell me how sorry he was for basically abandoning me, a lot of old junk roared back to the surface. Junk I thought I'd sorted through years ago. Apparently not."

Radar sauntered back, prize clamped between his jowls. Levi tugged the stick free, tossed it again. This time the dumb dog plopped down in the grass to gnaw on it.

"What kind of junk?" Levi said quietly. Patiently. Val hugged her knees, as if to steel herself against his kindness.

"If my mother ever held and cuddled me, I don't remember. I do vaguely remember my father being affectionate, but of course he left. And after that…well, there was that dirtbag who felt me up, but that doesn't count."

"I should hope not."

She pushed out a dry laugh, then sighed. "Tommy was the first guy I ever trusted, you know? First *person*, actually. That I could remember, anyway. And suddenly I was *happy*. Up to that point I'd survived, sure. Made the best of things and all that. But with Tommy... I felt as though I'd awakened from a bad dream. And, man, was reality sweet."

A rain-scented breeze shuddered the leaves, making a loose piece of hair tickle her nose; she shoved it behind her ear. "But we were so young when we got married. And I was so naive. So...underdone. But after all those years of deprivation—emotional, physical, all of it—I finally felt it was okay to let myself feel, well, *safe*, I suppose."

"Isn't that how it's supposed to work?"

"Maybe for some people, but..."

"Not only for some people, Val. For everybody."

His anger on her behalf made her smile. "Only..." A sigh escaped her lungs. "Only because Tommy was everything I'd never had, everything I thought I needed, I totally missed that I wasn't everything to *him*. And even worse..." She somehow met Levi's concerned gaze. "The problem was his love didn't make me less needy. It made me *more*."

"For crying out loud, Val, cut yourself some slack. You said yourself you guys were so young—"

"Which would be my point. It doesn't take a degree in psychology to figure out I just transferred that need for what I was missing to Tommy. Except looking to other people—even people who brought you out of hell—to make you whole and safe and loved...it's a trap. Yes, it is," she said when he glanced away, shaking his head. "I don't dare let myself turn back into that needy teenager, Levi. Cripes, even as I watched my father take off a little bit ago, all I wanted was for him to hold me. As if that would somehow make everything okay."

Thunder rumbled. The wind picked up, hard enough to loosen a few leaves. The dog abandoned the stick to chase them, barking.

"And why are you telling me this, Val?"

Oh, dear God... What she heard in those few words nearly shredded her. "Because," she said, her eyes stinging, "I walked in the house, and there you were, working on that album with my little girl, and I saw how happy she was…and the m-more you do for us the m-more I feel—" The rest of the sentence lodged in her throat. She swallowed it down. "And *then* you say all this stuff about being anything I need you to be, and…*dammit*. Everything I've worked so hard for this past little while… No!" Her hands flew up. *"Don't touch me!"*

Levi backed off, but Val couldn't bring herself to look at him, see the hurt in his eyes. And she felt like crap warmed over. Especially when he said, very softly, "You do realize you're not making a whole lot of sense, right?"

She nearly laughed, even as she wiped her eyes. Then she sighed. "What I'm trying to say is, I'm still that needy girl who just wants…connection."

Several seconds passed before he said, on a long breath, "I see."

"Do you?"

"We are talking about sex, right?" She nodded. "Then I get it." He scrubbed a hand across his face, then linked it with his other one between his knees. "But what *you* don't get…" He frowned into her eyes. "Is that what I'm feeling? It's is about a helluva lot more than that."

"Levi…don't…"

"Don't what? Let you know what I'm thinking? How I really feel? Hey, you want honesty, here it is. Hell, yeah, I want to make love to you. *With* you. But that's not all I want. Not by a long shot. I don't only want you in my bed, Val—I want you in my *life*. Because I'm *in love with you*. Yeah. Deal. God knows that's not at all what I expected to happen when I came back. But it did, so it's way past time I own it, you know? What you do with that information…" He glanced out at the yard, then back at her. "That's up to you."

Her heart hammering, Val looked away. Away from

those eyes so full of promises. Promises she didn't have the courage to accept. A tear trickled down her cheek.

"I can't be what you want, Levi," she said softly. "What you deserve. Not that…" Oh, Lord. "Not that I don't want to, but I can't."

"Why?" he said gently, and she thought her heart would shatter.

"Because until I saw my father a little bit ago, I didn't realize how far I still have to go. How much growing I still need to do. For the girls' sake, especially. And even being around you… I'm terrified of getting sucked in again, into believing you'd keep me safe. Because that doesn't last, does it? It's…illusion."

He was quiet for a long moment, then blew out a breath. "And there's nothing I can say to convince you—"

"Of what?" she said, making herself meet his gaze. "That you won't change your mind down the road? That you won't *die on me*?"

A couple of fat raindrops splatted in the dirt in front of them. Another few seconds passed before Levi stood, then pushed out a dry, humorless laugh. "And here my biggest worry was you'd think of me as a substitute for Tommy."

"Oh, for God's sake…" Val shoved to her feet, as well. "This isn't about you. Or Tommy. Or anybody else, including my dysfunctional parents. It's about me getting my head on straight. I'm *scared*, Levi. Petrified, actually. And if I can't go into something freely, *happily*, then…" Her eyes filled. "How fair would that be to you?"

Levi held her gaze for another long moment before, with a nod, he walked off the deck. Except, when he reached the yard, he turned, frowning. A second later he climbed the steps again to winnow his fingers through her hair and lower his mouth to hers, probably tasting in her kiss all the fear and doubt and desire and confusion she'd balled up into one holy mess. Then he broke the kiss to tuck her against his chest, where his heartbeat slammed against her ear.

"In the interest of full disclosure?" he whispered, his cheek in her hair. "You're the only woman I've ever loved."

Then he left, and Val collapsed in a blubbering heap on the deck, barely aware of Radar's worried nudges as he circled her, whining.

Chapter Twelve

Along with shorter days and chillier nights, August brought with it one of the soggiest monsoon seasons in recent memory—the main topic of conversation in a town close enough to the forest to fully appreciate the blessings of a wet summer. Much to be said for not having to worry about your house burning down. Or choking on fire smoke. This was also the month for shopping trips for school supplies and new clothes and gearing up for Josie's birthday in September. How was it possible Val's little girl was almost eight?

The lunch rush had been even more rushed than usual, although Val wasn't complaining. Keeping busy was also a blessing. As were her girls. What was hard were the nights, after the girls were in bed and the house was dead quiet, and the dog and cat were her only company. She told herself the normalcy, the predictability and constancy, was what she wanted. What she needed to heal. That this was the choice she'd made and she was good with it. Re-lieved, even.

Until she'd be sitting on her sofa, trying to watch TV, and the memory of that kiss would assault her like a mis-sile in some video game, and then she wasn't so sure.

Or, like now, when the crowd finally cleared enough for her to slip Charley his piece of pie—the gal up at the resort was still bugging her to sell to them, but since Val hadn't yet figured out how that'd work she kept putting her off—and she looked up to see Levi come through the door, toting a small cooler and a plastic shopping bag and grinning that grin of his that, let's face it, made everything quiver. Lord, spare her from the quivering. Worse, spare her from liking the man.

From missing him.

"Hey," he said softly, making a slow but deliberate bee-line for her as a million *What the hells?* exploded in her brain.

"Um…hey?" she said back, ignoring the quivering. It wasn't as if she hadn't seen him at all since that conversa-tion—and that kiss—but catching glimpses of him around town now and again was a whole lot different than his being practically a fixture in her house. Yeah, maybe the new Val knew she'd done the right thing, but the old Val—the whiny, needy Val—was sure she'd lost her mind.

She caught Annie giving her the eye—because she knew enough of the whole sordid tale to do that—before her boss turned her I-love-everybody grin on Levi.

"Hey, there, handsome. Sit anywhere you like—"

"Just came to see Val."

"Then she can sit with you. Yes, she can," she said to Val, and Levi chuckled.

"Now, Annie—you know she doesn't like to be pushed."

"Like that's gonna stop me? Ha!" Annie's saggy chins pleated when she lowered her head to glare at Val. "You wanna keep your job, girl?" She pointed to the booth. "Sit your skinny butt down and talk to the nice man."

Muttering, "A forest fire's got nothing on that woman," Val obeyed, only to smile at Levi's laugh.

"Man, I've missed that mouth," he said, clearly not realizing what he'd said as he plunked the cooler between them, stuffing the bag in the corner of the booth. Only then he met her gaze and winked, and she blushed and realized he'd probably never said anything by mistake in his life.

"What's in the cooler?" she said casually. As if it hadn't been weeks since they'd really seen each other, let alone had a normal conversation. As if her heart wasn't about to explode out of her chest. "Or maybe I shouldn't ask."

"Not a head, if that's what you're worried about. No, Josh and I went fishing this morning up at the ranch, caught a whole mess of trout. Thought you might like some. Don't worry, they're all cleaned, all you have to do is cook 'em up—" Then he frowned. "Do you even like trout?"

"Me? I love it. Josie probably won't touch it, but that only means more for me, right?" She hesitated. "Thank you."

"You're welcome. And it's all packed in ice. It'll be good for hours yet." Then he sucked in a breath. "So. How are you?"

What *was* the man about? "Good. You?"

His mouth tilted in a lazy grin. "You know, one of the problems with honest people is that they can't lie worth spit."

"Not to mention not knowing when to *leave* things lie." She swallowed. "Nothing's changed, Levi."

The smile softened. "Didn't figure it had. How're the kids?"

Val tucked her hands under the counter so he wouldn't

see how much they were shaking. "Um…they're great. Risa's trying so hard to walk—"

"You're kidding? Isn't that kind of young?"

"Eleven months. Not really. And Josie's gearing up for her birthday next month." Her cheeks heated. "She wants you to come."

"Wouldn't miss it." His eyes narrowed. "Unless Mama has an issue with that?"

Despite her flaming face—and sitting right next to the window, it wasn't as if he couldn't see—Val smiled and said, "Of course not—why would I?"

As it was, Josie asked nearly every day why they hadn't seen Levi, and when would they, and was there something wrong? And all Val could say was that he'd been busy, but she was sure they'd see him soon. Somehow, she doubted Josie was buying it.

"I have some news," Levi said quietly, jerking her back to the present.

"Oh?"

"Yeah. I've enrolled over at New Mexico Highlands for the next semester."

"What?" Was it surprising, how genuinely pleased she was? "That's wonderful! What in?"

He glanced at Charley reading a Louis L'Amour novel as he ate his pie, then back at Val before leaning over and lowering his voice. "Being around Charley, remembering my time in the service… I want to help. Somehow. Because I know what they've been through, right?" He straightened. "But I need to know *how* to help them. Besides just listening, I mean. And since Uncle Sam's good with paying my tuition…" He shrugged, then sighed. "Although it's been ten years since I did homework. And I wasn't exactly the best student. So it's kind of scary, frankly."

Val's eyes stung. "You'll do fine. Ohmigosh, I am so proud of you," she said softly, and the look on his face…

Oh, dear God. She could feel her resolve dissolving like sidewalk chalk in the rain. So good thing, then, he wouldn't be around much.

"You'll be living on campus, then?"

He frowned slightly. "Why? It's less than an hour from here."

"Not if you actually obey the speed limit, it isn't," she said, and he chuckled.

"I'm only on campus a couple days a week, two of my classes are online. So I'm not going anywhere."

"You're…staying in Whispering Pines."

The frown deepening, he looked at his folded hands, then back at her. "You know, when I got back home, I didn't know what the hell I wanted. What I was supposed to do with my life. So, yeah, I toyed with the idea of looking for something—although God knows what—'out there.' Turns out everything I need is right here. So… I bought a house."

"You what?" Clearly he wasn't giving her a chance to think too hard about that "everything I need" business. "Where?"

"That little adobe that went up for sale a couple of months ago, not far from Tommy's folks. Needs work, but I'm more than game."

Val knew the place. One of the rare real adobe homes in town. Cozy, was Realtor-speak for it. Lots of trees. Big yard. And "needs work" was a gross understatement.

"I wasn't, um, aware you were looking to buy a house."

His lips curved. "Meaning, how was I *able* to buy a house."

She blushed. "Well…yeah."

Levi glanced out the window for a moment, then back at her. "When our grandmother passed, years ago, she left each of us kids little nest eggs we couldn't touch until we were eighteen. Mr. Blake helped my father invest the money for us, in high-yield funds. What the others did with theirs, I have no idea. But I left mine alone. One of the few smart things I did back then, actually. Then I figured I might as well toss in a good chunk of my army wages, since it wasn't like I needed to spend them on much else. So the nest egg grew." He paused. "And I paid cash for the house."

"Wow. You have grown up."

Levi chuckled, then snapped his fingers. "Damn, don't know where my head is…" He reached for the bag, which he handed to her. "Happened to see this when I was out with Zach and his boys—thought immediately of you. Didn't have a clue about the size though, so I hope it's okay."

Giving him a puzzled look, Val removed the T-shirt from the bag and unfolded it, her eyes watering when she read what was on front.

I'm stronger than I thought.

The shirt was some hideous noncolor, and, yes, it was big enough to fit Levi, but…damn.

"Thank you," she whispered, fingering the lettering, then meeting his gaze. And his grin cracked her heart.

"You're welcome. Because it's true. Always has been." Then he got up, nudging the cooler toward her. "Enjoy the fish. Oh…and if you get a chance, maybe you could come by the house sometime, give me some ideas about what to do with it?"

"Me? You're the one with all the mad skills."

"Yeah, but I'm color-blind. Partially, anyway."

"You're kidding?"

"Nope. So's my dad. Josh dodged that particular bullet, but only because we're not identical. Anyway. Let me know when Josie's party is. I'll be there."

Val stayed in the booth after he left, clutching the soft shirt to her chest and staring at the cooler as if it were a crystal ball. Until Annie passed by and swatted her shoulder. "Customers," she said, and Val shook herself out of her stupor and got to her feet, only to run smack into Annie when she turned. "Also," her boss said, "you're an idiot."

"Love you, too," Val said, stuffing Levi's gifts under the counter before tromping over to table five to take their order, refusing to admit Annie might be right.

Josh's almost black brows practically collided as he glowered at the kitchen. Not that Levi blamed him. In the past week he'd done some painting and ripped up the tatty gold carpet, still flummoxed that people would cover the pretty pine floors. But the kitchen—while big and sunny— made the one in Tommy's grandmother's house look top of the line in comparison.

"Would somebody please tell me," his brother said, "how in the *hell* baby-poop green made it into the top ten colors of 1973?"

"Is that what color it is?" Levi said, reaching into the wobbly old fridge for a beer, handing one to his brother. "Green?"

"In a manner of speaking." Shuddering, Josh popped the tab before his eyes cut to Levi. "Val has no idea you bought the house with her in mind, does she?"

"Do I *look* like a man with a death wish?"

"You tell me. The woman rejected you, Levi—"

"What she rejected was a whole lotta crap from her past." He took a sip of his own beer. "Considering the mess *I* was? I can hardly blame her for that, can I?"

"I don't know, bro. Wouldn't it be better to just move on?"

"And why would I do that? When I'm right where I want to be?"

"Hoping some woman's gonna change her mind? Yeah, good luck with that."

He tilted the beer to his brother. "Hope's what makes the world go round. Look," he said when Josh shook his head, "the way I see it, my options are give up, press on or wait it out. So number three it is."

"I still think you're off your rocker."

"And you're entitled to your opinion. Doesn't mean I have to pay it any mind." Not that his brother was entirely wrong. Since even if he could eventually convince her he'd never walk out on her, he couldn't exactly guarantee he'd never die.

However. First things first.

One hand in his jeans' pocket, Levi shifted his weight against the counter. "Maybe I didn't go into the army for the best reasons, but it sure as hell made me grow. Learned more about myself in those six years than I had in the whole twenty-two before. Yeah, I still had—have—some fine-tuning to do, but by the time I got out I was at least beginning to get a handle on who I was, even if I still wasn't sure what I was supposed to *do*. Val never got that chance. She went from a borderline abusive situation into an early marriage, then became a mother soon after that…"

Frowning at the beer can, Levi huffed out a sigh. "The way I see it, this is her time to figure out who *she* is. What she really wants. So it's up to me to figure out the balance between being there for her and the girls and not getting in her face."

Josh crossed his arms. "Do you even know how she feels about you?"

He smirked. "Hell, I'm not even sure she knows how *she* feels about me. Not entirely. But I do know she's scared."

"Of what?"

"Best as I can figure out? Of letting herself be happy. Or at least, of trusting that it'll last."

"That's crazy."

"After what she's been through? Not as much as you might think."

"And do *you* really think she's worth the risk?"

"Do I honestly know if I'm doing the right thing? Not hardly. Maybe I am barking up the wrong tree. Except you know what? Once before, I gave up because…well, because I'd convinced myself I wasn't what she'd needed. Stakes are a helluva lot higher now. But what kind of choice am I giving her if I remove myself entirely from the equation? Kinda hard to convince her she can count on me if I'm not around to prove it. So I have to be patient."

"And I'm guessing she doesn't know about that, does she? That you had a thing for her way back when?"

"No."

"You think maybe you should tell her?"

"Why?"

His brother frowned at him for several seconds before blowing out a sigh. "I still don't get—"

"You don't see what I see, Josh. Yeah, she's doing a pretty hard-core battle with one big-ass bogeyman right now, but when she's not…" His jaw clenching, Levi glanced toward the kitchen window, then back at his brother. "You should see her with her kids. Tommy's parents. Hear how she worries about Charley. Woman's got a heart way too big for that little body. And if I could somehow get that heart to stop hurting…" He shrugged.

"And what if that never happens?"

Levi thought of that kiss. The look in her eyes when the kiss was over. When she spotted him in the diner the other day. Then again, he hadn't heard a peep from her since then. But the only way to be patient was to, you know, actually *be patient*.

"Then at least I'll know I tried," he said softly, before pushing himself away from the counter and out into the dining room, where all four walls were covered in nasty, peeling, Southwest geometric wallpaper that had nothing whatsoever to do with the baby-poop kitchen. He was guessing, anyway. "You any good at stripping wallpaper?"

"I have no idea."

"That makes two of us, then," Levi said, reaching up to tug at a curling corner. A whopping three inches came off in his hand.

"Let me guess," Josh said. "This is gonna take longer than you figured."

"Yeah, but it'll be worth it in the end."

"You hope," his brother muttered, and Levi was pretty sure they weren't talking about wallpaper anymore.

After a week, Val realized if she waited any longer to return the cooler she'd come across as either a lamebrain or a coward. Although at least taking the girls with her would prevent random pheromone/hormone interminglings between her and Levi. Or so she thought. Because soon as he opened his door—shirtless, damn him—she realized... nope. Not by a long shot.

Especially when he gave her—and the girls, let's be fair—one of those smiles that said there was nobody else he'd rather see.

"On our way to Connie and Pete's for dinner," Val said, her pulse banging in her throat. "Figured I might as well return the cooler while we're out."

"But you can come in for a minute? At least see the place?" This said while reaching for a babbly Risa with one hand, taking the cooler with the other.

"Um...sure. For a minute."

Mugging for the baby, Levi stood aside to let them in. Place looked like a bomb had gone off.

"Excuse the mess," he said, heading toward what she assumed was the kitchen. "Charley was over today helping me with the demo. We made real progress." He clunked the cooler on top of the counter. Which, along with the rest of the kitchen—except for the chewed-up dark cabinets—was kind of a slime green. "Although I don't suppose it looks like that to the casual observer. But the wall between the living and dining room? Had to go."

Still holding the baby, Levi smiled down at Josie, her forehead crimped as she surveyed the kitchen. The *huge* kitchen. With a *huge* window. And a skylight—

"Hey, kiddo. How's school?"

Her daughter grinned up at him. Her beaver-esque front teeth had finally finished their descent. Although at least they were straight. "It's only been a couple of days. But it's good. Second grade *rocks*. Mama says you're coming to my birthday?"

Levi turned that smile on Val, making her shiver underneath her sleeveless top, before focusing again on Josie. "I sure am. I remember when I turned eight, thinking *finally* I wasn't a little kid anymore."

"I know, right?" Then she slung her arms around Levi's waist to press her cheek into his stomach, her eyes squeezing shut. "I miss you, Levi."

Cupping the back of Josie's head with his free hand, Levi quietly said, "Miss you, too, little bit."

Just kill her now.

"Why don't you go check out the backyard?" he then said. "The previous owners left one of those play fort things."

"Cool!" Josie said, taking off through the French doors—*French doors!*—before Val even had a chance to yell at her to be careful.

"I already made sure it was safe," Levi said. "So my monkey nephews don't bust their heads or anything—"

"Bah!" Risa said, struggling to get out of Levi's arms.

"Nope, floor's not clean," Levi said, getting a firmer grip before pulling a box of graham crackers from a nearby cabinet. "This okay?"

"Go for it."

He handed the baby a quarter of a cracker; she happily settled in the crook of his elbow, gnawing. Somehow, Val tore away her gaze. "This kitchen sure is...green."

"See, I thought it was brown. So there you go."

"Some of that stuff you showed me for the other house would look good in here, I think."

"Actually, I was thinking of those Mexican tiles you liked. But you'd have to help me pick them so I don't end up with a bunch of weird colors."

"If it's only you living here, not sure what difference it would make. Unless you're thinking of resale value."

He got very quiet. The kind of quiet that makes a girl's heart pound. And makes her turn to watch her child playing outside. "Didn't buy the place to flip it," he said behind her. "Not planning on being the only one living here, either. Not forever, anyway. But in the meantime, seems to me this could be a real good setup for your pie business."

Val whipped around. Levi calmly handed the baby another piece of cracker.

"What?"

"Part of the reason I bought the house. Because of the kitchen. And don't worry, I already checked—got a list, in fact, of what we need to do in order to get it approved. Not easy, but definitely doable. Best news is, there's no limit on how much you can sell." He pointed to a space beside the sink. "Or how easy cleanup'll be with the top-of-the-line dishwasher that'll be right there. There's even plenty of room for AJ's stove, if you want. Or double ovens. Whatever would work best for you."

In the center of the room—right where, say, a good-size island might go—sat a pathetic Formica table and a couple of mismatched chairs. Onto one of these Val now sank, her emotions more tangled than Josie's hair after a restless night.

"Val? Look at me."

She finally did, sure that thunderbolts must be shooting out of her eyes.

"All I'm offering," he said gently, "is my kitchen. Since it seems a shame to waste such a big space on me maybe boiling a hot dog now and then. Making some toast—"

"Levi, I don't need—"

"You need a kitchen. I can give you a kitchen. Heck, maybe that's the only thing I can give you, to say…thanks."

"For what?"

He glanced out the window over the sink, then turned back to her. "You know the real reason Tommy joined the army?"

"Yes. Because he wanted me to feel proud of him."

"Yeah, but…it was more than that. Because he wanted to feel like he mattered, too. Like he had a purpose. I couldn't talk him out of it, no. But he told me that if *you'd* said no, he wouldn't've gone."

Her eyes filled. "And what right did I have to do that?"

Still holding the baby, Levi came closer to crouch in front of her; still gumming her cracker, the baby threw herself into Val's arms. "The truth?" he said gently. "You had every right. I'm not sure he ever knew how scared you were. Because you never let him see it, did you?"

Unable to speak, she wagged her head again. Levi smiled. "Of the two of you," he said softly, "I'm gonna say you were the braver one. So don't tell me you don't deserve something for that."

What the hell makes you think you deserve *anything, little girl? Like you're somebody special. Like you're better than your mama? Well, here's a news flash—you're not…*

Nausea roiled as the words oozed through her, oily and hot. Words she'd thought couldn't affect her anymore. As though trying to shake herself free from her mother's voice, Val shifted the baby to heave herself out of the chair.

"Meaning a kitchen?" she said, realizing looking at Levi made the nausea worse.

"Meaning a *future*," he said, standing as well to slug his fingers into his pockets. "One of your own making, finally. And maybe a little peace to go along with it?"

Peace? As if. Because when Val looked into those eyes, sure as hell *peaceful* was the last thing she felt.

Because sure as hell he was still offering a lot more than a kitchen.

And sure as hell she still wasn't sure which frightened her more—turning that offer down, or accepting it.

No, what scared the bejesus out of her was how much she *wanted* to accept it.

"Can I think about it?" she said, annoyed at how small her voice sounded.

"Absolutely. No rush." Levi touched her shoulder, forcing her to meet his gaze. "And no pressure, I swear. Totally up to you."

Nodding, she opened the glass-paned door, called Josie. "We're leaving, sweetie."

The kid came bouncing inside, out of breath and grinning. "C'n I come here again?"

"Anytime you like," Levi said.

Of course he would walk them outside, watching while Val strapped Risa into her stroller, then as they walked away, a hopping/skipping/bouncing Josie wriggling around to give him a last wave when they reached the sidewalk. Val, however, refused to look back, to see all those questions she couldn't answer in those kind, sexy eyes.

She was pretty sure she'd never be able to breathe properly again.

Levi slammed his hand against the gross laminate counter with enough force to make the coffeemaker rattle. *Idiot.*

Not that he hadn't meant what he'd said. All of it. But clearly he'd jumped the gun, hoping the past few weeks would've given her a little more perspective, stupidly taking encouragement from what he'd seen in her eyes, heard in her voice a week ago in the diner. Only, what he'd seen just now—leaking out from the edges of her bravado— was a woman every bit as stressed and rattled as any soldier returning from deployment. Or still in the middle of it, actually.

And dammit, he'd known better than to poke the bear of her stress, even in the guise of being helpful. Of *loving* her, of wanting to fix whatever was broken, *because* he loved her. Except judging from the look on her face, that fact that she hadn't even said goodbye…he'd blown it.

Releasing a harsh, lung-stinging breath, Levi could practically hear Josh's *told you so*.

Chapter Thirteen

"Okay," Connie said, stretching plastic wrap over the leftover enchiladas before sliding them into the fridge. "What's up?"

Val pushed out a sound that sounded more like a strangled cat than a laugh. "Why do you—"

"Because you barely touched your dinner. So unless you've been lying to me all these years about how much you love my enchiladas…" One eyebrow lifted.

Fortunately—or unfortunately, Val wasn't sure which—the girls were in the family room with their papa, watching some kids' movie. And Tommy's grandmother had excused herself to sit outside and watch the sunset, as she did every night. Leaving Val alone with her mother-in-law.

Who knew full well how much Val loved her enchiladas.

But before she could figure out what to say, Connie said, "So what's going on with you and Levi these days?"

Val stuck the last glass in the dishwasher, loaded it.

Turned it on. Stood for a moment, listening to the whoosh of water filling the machine.

Thought about that kitchen.

The half-naked man standing in the middle of it, holding her child, offering her...

So much.

Then Connie touched her arm and, yeah. Waterworks.

Muttering in Spanish, the older woman steered Val into the living room, a pristine testimonial to Southwest kitsch, making Val sit on the peach-and-aqua-patterned couch.

"Well?"

Val blew her nose. Sniffed. "Apparently a major reason Levi bought the house was so I could use the kitchen. For my pies."

"Gee, that'd make me cry, too."

She sniffed again. Skunk's sister jumped up on her lap, purring. "Yeah, well, this isn't only about his kitchen."

"Didn't figure it was," Connie said, clearly amused. "And does Levi know how you feel?"

"I didn't say—"

"*Querida*. Seriously?"

Groaning, Val sank back into the sofa's cushions, thinking about how, for so long, this had been her safe place when her own home hadn't been. That it didn't feel even remotely safe now. Especially when Connie said, "What are you so afraid of, sweetheart?"

The baby cat's fur was so soft, so soothing, under her fingers as Val stroked her, gathering her courage. Then she looked over at Connie, the patience and love she saw in her mother-in-law's eyes making hers sting. "Everybody thinks I was so...noble, I guess you'd call it. The proud military wife and all that. But the thing is, I hated it. Hated being left to raise Josie on my own, hated that... that Tommy yanked the *one* thing I'd wanted my entire life out from under m-me. And most of all, I hated that I felt so...so selfish. Like my m-mother."

"Oh, honey..." Connie practically jumped out of her chair to sit beside Val, wrapping an arm around her shoulders and squeezing, hard. "First off, do not ever let me hear you compare yourself to your mother again, you hear me? God rest her soul, but that woman's got some serious atoning to do wherever she is now. And second..." She sat back to gently stroke Val's hair away from her face. "If you really didn't want Tommy to go, why didn't you say something?"

"Because that *would* have been selfish—"

"Then call me selfish, too, because I felt exactly the same way. Sure, I was proud of him. Doesn't mean I wasn't mad as hell when he died. At him, at the army, at the bastard who planted that bomb. And I'm not seeing me getting over that anytime soon. But I'm not sure I understand what any of that has to do with you and Levi."

"Because maybe I *don't* deserve happiness. Maybe nobody *deserves* it, maybe happiness is totally random, this elusive thing that happens to some people and not others. I don't know. Here I've barely gotten my balance back after Tommy—"

"And you're scared of losing again."

Val took a moment, absorbing. Accepting the last piece of truth she hadn't wanted to face. "I don't think I could stand it. Not again. And Josie..."

"You're afraid Levi's going to leave you?"

"No." Val almost smiled. "*No.* But...stuff happens, doesn't it?"

"I see. So you've decided to let evil win?"

Val frowned at her mother-in-law. "I think it's more that I've decided to not give it that chance."

"And if that isn't the biggest load of crap I've ever heard, I don't know what is. Yeah, you're right. Happiness can be elusive. Seems like it, anyway. Which is why we've got to grab it when we find it, and then hang on with everything we've got. Doesn't matter how long the ride lasts, what matters is enjoying the hell out of it while we're on it. Because guess what? You do deserve to be happy. Just like everybody else on the planet. And would you deprive the girls of *their* shot at happiness? Of a *father*?"

"Dammit, Connie—do not guilt me—"

"So I'm guessing you don't know the whole story."

"What whole story?"

"That Levi loved you first."

"Excuse me?"

"Then you really had no idea that Levi had more or less appointed himself your guardian angel when you guys were still in school? That when he heard the other kids talking smack about you, he'd sometimes…intervene. That his mother got called to the principal's office more than once on your account."

"On my—"

"So Levi got something of a reputation as a hothead, even though I don't think he ever actually hurt anybody. Scared the pants off 'em a few times, though. But the thing is…if it hadn't been for Levi, I'm not sure Tommy would've given you a second look."

Her head was spinning. "And Tommy never…?"

Connie chuckled. "Sixteen-year-old boys aren't exactly known for their critical thinking skills. And Tommy told *us* that Levi said he was only sticking up for you because it was the right thing to do."

"Then why would you think there was anything more to it than that? It wasn't like Levi didn't have other girl-friends—"

"If you can call them that. And only after you and Tommy started going together. Not to mention Levi never put his butt on the line like that for anybody else. Think back, *querida*. Am I right?"

So she thought. And…hell. The woman was right. At this rate Val's head was going to explode.

Not to mention her heart.

"So Tommy really never knew?"

"That his best friend got out of his way to give him a chance with you? I really don't think he did."

"But why?"

"My guess? Because Levi believed being with him would've had exactly the opposite effect from what he was trying to defend you from. What with that hothead business and everything." Connie reached for her hand, holding it in both of hers. "But the result was…it gave us *you*." The older woman's eyes glittered. "The best daughter we could've asked for. Is it any wonder why we love Levi almost as much as we loved our own boy?"

Val slumped back against the sofa cushions, the sudden move dislodging the kitten, who gave her back paw a fast lick before streaking out of the room.

"Sweetheart," Connie said softly, "you're the one always on about choices. So don't you think you should have all the information possible to help you make those choices?"

Yeah, she knew that was gonna come back to chomp her on the butt someday. Her gaze slid to Connie's.

"So why didn't you tell me this sooner?"

"Because I was hoping you and Levi would've worked this out by now. Since you haven't…" Connie shrugged. "And so help me, God, do not tell me you feel like you'd be cheating on Tommy."

Despite her exploding head, Val had to laugh. "No. Well, okay, a little, maybe. But…"

She told her the condensed version of what she'd said to Levi, about how little physical affection she'd gotten as a child. And where that had led, with Tommy. And now, with Levi…

"I mean…am I just repeating history? How do I even know if this is real?"

"Man, you are one messed-up *chica*—you know that?"

"You're only now figuring this out?"

Connie chuckled. "Listen to me. What you had with Tommy, that was real. And I think you know it. Yes, despite all the garbage from your childhood. So why wouldn't this be real with Levi?"

"Because I'm one messed-up *chica*?"

"And what does that say about that young man, that in spite of that he hasn't given up on you? Not this time, anyway. Okay, so he had issues when he was younger. Issues that in large part stemmed from how he felt about *you*. Issues that made him the good man he is now. Do you really want to throw that away just because you're scared of what *might* happen? Is that what you want for your daughters, to be afraid to trust their hearts— *Dios mio*, what was that?"

What that was, was a very loud sneeze from a very small person.

Who, Val was guessing, had just gotten an earful.

Crap.

"Josie?" Mama called. "Get your little behind out here!"

Abuelita, who'd been hiding out in the hallway with Josie, held out her hand for Josie to take before slowly leading her into the living room. At the beginning, Josie'd only meant to come see what Mama and Gramma were doing, since Grampa had fallen asleep with the baby on his chest, and it was kind of a dumb movie, anyway. But something about their voices had made her stop, even though she knew she wasn't supposed to listen without them knowing she was there. Not that she understood everything they were saying, but she got most of it. All she knew, was that it sucked, almost never seeing Levi anymore, and that Mama was back to being sad all the time. And you know what? Josie was really, really tired of all the gloom and doom, like Mama would say. Seriously—

Mama's mouth dropped open. "Lita! You, too?"

"You should listen to Consuela," Abuelita said to Mama, like she didn't see how surprised she was. Or care, maybe. "Because I know you are not a fool." Still holding on real tight to Josie's hand, Abuelita bent over to lay her other hand on Mama's cheek. "What you are, little one, is brave. So brave." Abuelita smiled. "Like a warrior."

"That's right," Josie said, even though her knees were shaking a little. Mama didn't get mad a whole lot, but when she did…watch out. "You are." But instead of fussing at her, Mama's eyes got all wet.

"Oh, baby…" She pulled Josie into her lap, wrapping her up tight in her arms from behind as Abuelita kinda fell on the sofa to put her arm around Mama's shoulders. Across from them, Gramma looked like she was holding her breath.

"Blessings and fear," Josie heard Abuelita say, "are like light and darkness. They cannot live in the same place." Josie liked the sound of that, even if she didn't completely understand it. "So, *preciosa*," her great-grandmother said, "which will you choose?"

Mama got very still, holding Josie close. And it was like Josie could feel something change, in the room. In Mama. Especially when she blew out a breath that tickled Josie's curls.

"So, Lita," Mama said, very softly. "If I didn't want to stay in the house…?"

Abuelita laughed. "It was only there to use as long as you needed it. If you don't anymore…"

"But I never did finish up the kitchen—"

"That's what contractors are for," Gramma said, winking at Josie. Then she smiled at Mama. "Go, honey. Grab your future. Now. Before you chicken out."

"As if you'd let me."

"You got that right," Abuelita said, and all the grown-ups laughed.

Then everybody got real quiet for a long time, until Mama said, "Okay," on a great big breath, then gently slid Josie off her lap. Only then she turned her around and looked deep into her eyes, so it was like they were the only two people in the room. "Do you really like Levi, baby?"

"Are you kidding?" Josie said, wondering where on earth *that* question had come from. "I love him. He makes me feel…safe."

"Oh, yeah?" Mama said, her eyes getting all watery again.

"Yeah. And good." She giggled. "He's so funny."

Mama smiled. "Yes, he is. But he's not Daddy, you know."

Josie frowned. "Of course he isn't. He's Levi. Isn't that good enough?"

Blinking like a million times as she brushed curls off Josie's shoulder, Mama nodded. "Absolutely." Then she turned to Gramma. "The kids…?"

"Like you have to ask. Go, for God's sake." But after Mama picked up her purse and stuff, Josie thought of something.

"Mama?"

She turned back around. "Yeah, baby?"

"You know Daddy wants us to be happy, right?"

"Oh, jeez…" Mama grabbed Josie in a hug so hard it almost hurt, then held her face in her soft hands. "You have any idea how much I love you?"

Josie grinned. "Maybe," she said, and Mama laughed.

Then she was gone, and Josie let out a great big breath. Because this time, she was *sure* everything was going to be okay.

She could feel it in her heart.

* * *

A surprise thunderstorm had released its fury barely five minutes before Levi opened his door to a soaking-wet Val, her hair, clothes, everything, clinging like seaweed to her skin.

"I hope to hell you're alone," she said before he could find his voice, "because otherwise this could be awkward."

"Uh…" Slowly, his lips curved, even as his heart started beating like crazy. "Yeah."

"Good," she said, walking into his arms, rain pummeling the porch roof as he kissed her, over and over, half-afraid to stop. Like if he did he'd discover this was only a dream. Still, she had to be freezing in that clammy shirt.

So, in between mumbled explanations about the kids being with the Lopezes and her having stopped at the house to let the dog out and change, so she didn't have any place else she needed to be, he tugged her into the bedroom where he'd gotten a fire going in the kiva fireplace, tucked into the far corner. An air mattress, an old dresser… It wasn't much. But right now, the two of them and a fire and a mattress—it was enough.

Actually, what it was, was heaven.

Wasn't until he grabbed the shirt's hem that he realized what she was wearing. Damn thing hung to the middle of her thighs. "You're right—this is way too big."

"I'm thinking I might have to grow into it," she said, smiling, before she shivered, making her nipples poke at the damp fabric. With that, he tugged the soggy thing up and over her head, tossing it to one side, catching just enough of a glimpse of small, perfect breasts to get him hard before he wrapped her up in a towel he'd tossed on the mattress earlier. Then he kissed her again, one of those long, deep, kinda messy ones that went on forever, and she moaned and wrapped her hands around his neck to stand on tiptoe, and he remembered what she'd said, about liking sex, and he thought, *Well, all right*.

But…

"You sure?"

"Didn't come over to look at paint swatches. And, yes, I'm protected," she said, and like *that* they were both naked and on the bed, pretty much feasting on each other, the heat from the fire licking her dry as he licked her wet all over again.

"Oh, yes," she breathed, eyes closed, clutching the sheets. Toes probably curled, too, but he was too busy to check. Then he took things up a notch, and she laughed, and arched, and cried out—begged, actually—her hands now all tangled in his hair as he teased her some more, smiling to himself at her cute little noises, the change in her breathing as she got closer—

Then thunder cracked, loud enough to rattle the windows, and she shrieked, startled. Laughing, Levi shifted positions.

"Damn," she said, "now we have to start over."

"Not a problem," he said, placing a kiss on that delectable spot where neck meets shoulder. She shivered. And sighed. Especially when he started south again. Belly button. Hip bone. Lower. "Trust me," he said between kisses, "it'll be all the better for waiting."

"But you—"

"You complaining?"

"No, but—"

He hiked himself back up to palm her breast, flicking one thumb over that adorable little nipple. Her breathing hitched. He chuckled. "What can I say? I'm a giver. Now hush and let me give."

"Jeez, *fine*," she said, her eyes drifting closed, and the next few minutes were filled with a symphony of rain and thunder, the hiss and crackle of the fire, her moans and gasps and soft, sweet laughter...and then her cries as she sailed over the edge. But before the cries had even died out she'd flipped him on his back and taken him inside her, her messed-up, half-dry hair curtaining her shoulders, her breasts, glowing gold in the firelight.

Her lips, all puffy and red, curved slightly as she splayed warm, soft hands on his chest. "Hey. I'm a giver, too," she said, which was when Levi realized the glow was actually coming from someplace inside her. His eyes burning, he touched her hair, moving it off her shoulder to expose one breast. The nipple perked up, inviting. He tugged her closer, accepting.

"You kicked fear's ass?" he whispered around it.

"Working on it," she said, and he laid back down to hook her gaze in his, soft in the firelight. He threaded his fingers through her hair, afraid to say the words. Tears collected in the corners of her eyes.

"Same here," she murmured, bending to kiss him.

For a long time afterward they lay in silence underneath his comforter, wrapped in each other's arms and listening to their breathing, the dying fire's muffled hisses, the *plop-plop-plop* from dripping *canales* jutting out from the house's flat roof.

"I thought," Levi finally said, "when you left—"

"I know."

"So what happened?"

She softly laughed. "I was ganged up on."

"By?"

"Three generations of Lopez women. Lita. Connie. My own daughter." She softly chuckled. "I didn't stand a chance." Only then she sighed.

"That sounds ominous."

Val hitched onto one elbow to meet Levi's gaze, shiv-

ering a little when he stroked her bare back. "I'm here because I want to be—"

"Glad to hear it—"

"No, wait…" She palmed his chest, feeling his heart
beat. "I'm still sorting through a *lot* of junk in my head."

His gaze gentling so much it hurt, Levi sifted trembling
fingers through her hair. "It'd be weird if you weren't. But
we can work through it together. Okay?"

Nodding, she lay back down, reveling in his scent, his
feel. His solidity. "You know the real reason I didn't try to
stop Tommy from going into the army?" Her hand knotted
on Levi's chest. "I was scared to death if I didn't let him
go, I'd lose him, anyway. His love, I mean."

A second or two passed before Levi said, "That
wouldn't've happened."

"You don't know that. And for sure I didn't. Not then.
And even now…" She listened to that steady heartbeat
under her ear, drawing strength from it. "All my life," she
said quietly, "I thought if I could somehow be whoever
somebody wanted me to be, say whatever they wanted
to hear, they wouldn't leave. And not only did that not
work…" She waited out the sting of tears. "The only person I really lost was myself. *Not* a legacy I want to leave
to my girls."

Levi wrapped her up more tightly, kissed her temple.
"Good for you," he whispered, and she smiled, only to
sigh again.

"Yeah, well, I'm a work in progress. Maybe in some
ways I *am* stronger than I thought I was, but it's always
going to be a struggle for me to find that balance, I guess,
between supporting someone else and sticking up for myself. For *my* needs."

"And that right there is why I love you."

"Because I'm screwed up?"

That got a soft laugh. "Hell, who isn't? But not everyone has the cojones to admit it. Let alone—" his chest rose with his breath "—to *face* their fears. As far as legacies go, that's a pretty damned good one. However, since we're on the subject…"

At the change in his tone, Val shifted to meet his gaze. Still gentle but dead serious. "What I said, about Tommy being grateful for your support, was absolutely true. At the beginning, anyway. What I didn't say was that as time went on I think he began to question his decision. Only by then he didn't feel he could back out and save face."

"Save face? With whom?"

"You. So, see, he was as conflicted as you were. And he felt guilty as hell about it. Something even my dad picked up on."

Her brow puckered, Val watched the fire for several seconds, barely feeling Levi stroking her hair, her shoulder. "And since we weren't honest with each other…"

"Exactly."

Tears welled in her eyes. "So you think that's why he made you promise?"

"Maybe."

On a soft groan, Val sat up, tugging the comforter up over her breasts and wrapping her arms around her knees. "This has to be the strangest post-sex conversation ever."

Behind her, Levi quietly chuckled. "I somehow doubt that."

"Yeah, well, it's about to get stranger." She looked back over her shoulder at him. "Connie said you had a thing for me when we were in school. That you never told Tommy."

His fingers bumped down her spine. "I wasn't right for you, Val. Not then."

"So it's true?"

He nodded, and she laughed.

"What's so funny?"

"As it happens, I had a little crush on you, too. Before Tommy, obviously."

"You're kidding?"

"Nope. Until I realized you were way too much like the creeps my mother hooked up with."

"Oh, that's low," he said, then sighed. "Although not far from the truth."

"Actually," she said quietly, "it's about as far from the truth as it gets, apparently. Since according to Tommy's mother you regularly defended my honor."

His expression was priceless. "She told you that?"

"Yep. Oh, and then there's the small issue of you stepping aside for your best friend. What a jerk. Seriously."

Then she looked away again, hugging her knees more tightly. Several beats passed before Levi said, very softly, "Hey. You okay?"

She pushed out a little laugh. "I want to be—how's that? I really do want to move past the fear. Past…the past."

Levi sat up beside her, big and solid and *good*. "And I'd say you're well on your way," he whispered, kissing her shoulder. "You're safe now, honey. You can't lose me, not as long as I have breath. No matter what you say, or do, or think. Because there's no way I'm stepping aside this time, for anything or anybody. And I won't let you lose yourself."

She blinked back tears. "Promise?"

"Promise. Because what I saw back then was only a glimpse of who you are now. A woman who…" He swallowed. "A woman I'd be so damn proud to have by my side, I can't even tell you."

"Well, hell," she said.

"Yeah. Deal."

Way in the distance, the train whistle blew. Val snuggled closer, smiling when Levi draped an arm around her shoulders. Then his fingers closed around her left wrist. Oh, right.

"Where—"

"In my jewelry case. With my wedding ring." Which she'd taken off weeks ago, before it *fell* off. "Although I might let Josie put the bracelet in the album. If she wants to."

After a moment, she angled her head to look up at him again. "So why did you enlist?"

That got a soft laugh. "Your brain definitely works in strange ways."

"Believe it or not, there was a thread. The bracelet… Tommy…the army…you. Well?"

"I told you—"

"I know. But it keeps coming to me—" she kissed his hand "—that there's something more."

His fingers traced back and forth across her skin. "Because I was running away."

"From?"

He hesitated, then said, "Seeing how happy you and Tommy were."

"Oh, Levi…" Her heart cramped. "Really?"

"Crazy, right?"

"Probably," she said gently, leaning into him again. "Not to mention drastic."

"I needed to take my head someplace different," he said quietly. "Someplace I couldn't…" A breath left his lungs. "Wouldn't be tempted to think about you. As tempted, anyway. About what I'd let go. And, yes, I know what I said, every bit of which I believed at the time. Still do, to some extent. Didn't mean I didn't regret the hell out of it." He stroked her jaw, making her shiver. "I'd convinced myself I'd forgotten you. Biggest lie I've ever told myself. Because I've loved you since I was sixteen years old."

Enough to let her go, she thought, her eyes stinging.

Just as he'd loved both her *and* Tommy enough to get himself out of the way so they could find each other, when *each other* was exactly what they'd needed at the time. No matter what came later.

"And you had no idea what you were really getting into, did you? With the army, I mean."

He got very quiet again. "Not really, no."

"Was it hell?"

"Sometimes."

"Will you tell me about it someday?"

After a moment, he nodded. "Yes."

"Promise?"

"I'll try—how's that? Although…it wasn't all bad. I learned I had a lot more to offer than I thought. Like that I really get off on helping people."

"Ya think?"

He chuckled, then sighed. "I know *I* can't make you happy, Val. Or get rid of the fear for you. Only you can figure out how to do that. But I sure as hell want to be there when you do. Which I know you will, because you are one awesome lady."

"Oh, Levi…" Her eyes burning, Val palmed his cheek. "And you are one awesome dude." She smiled. "Well, now, anyway. According to Connie, it was touch and go for a while there."

Laughing, he shifted them so she was flat on her back again, kneeing her legs apart. About a million hormones released happy little sighs. "No doubt my parents would agree with you on that."

"Maybe we should stop talking about our parents now."

"Good point," he said and kissed her. And it was very good.

As in, off the charts.

Then she framed his face in her hands, smiling into his eyes. "You do realize the only other man I ever did this with, I married?"

His chuckle rumbled through all sorts of interesting places. "One helluva gauntlet you just threw down there."

"Yep. I want you in my life, too, Levi. And I know…" She swallowed. "I know Tommy would've wanted me to be happy. To be afraid of that—of taking chances— isn't exactly honoring the man who was all about taking chances, is it?"

"No," Levi said softly. "It isn't. One thing, though…" His face went all stern. "Whatever choices we make, about anything, we make together. None of this suffer in silence crap. Unless the other person willingly concedes to the other. Like, say, on wall colors. 'Cause even if I could see them, I probably wouldn't care." When she laughed, he said, "And if you don't like the house? Consider it sold. We can pick out something together."

Her eyes pricked. "But you love it—"

"More than you? Not a chance. Sweetheart," he said so gently she teared up all over again, "the only thing that matters to me about the house, *any* house, is whether you and the girls are in it with me. That it's someplace where the past can't hurt you anymore. Although that would be tricky, since it's gonna have to get through me first."

Aching for him, Val linked her hands around the back of his neck. "And would that be you picking up that gauntlet?"

His gaze softened. "Shoot, I caught that thing before it even hit the ground. I know this is crazy, but…marry me, Val. Whenever you're ready—no rush. But even before that, let me be whatever I can be for you. For those little girls. Because I love them every bit as much as I love you—"

"Yes," she whispered. "To all of it. Because I love you, too, you big goof."

The look in his eyes slayed her. "Say that again."

"I love you." She touched her forehead to his. "I *love* you." Smiling, he kissed her nose. "Thank you."

"Anytime."

Then he grinned, that same wicked grin that used to make her roll her eyes, that always meant he was up to no good. Now, however, what she saw behind that grin was a man who knew what he was about…a man who would love her girls every bit as much as Tommy had. And who would never let them forget their father. How could she *not* love this man? How could she not trust him?

Or more to the point, trust that being with him would make her the best *herself* she could be?

"So," Levi said, his hand sliding down over her waist, her hip, "should we seal the deal?"

"Sounds like a plan," she said, smiling, embracing her future with her whole heart.

Epilogue

"Josie! Stay where we can see you! And don't get too close to the water!"

Not much more than a speck in the distance, the girl waved to them from the riverbank as Radar barked his own reply. Levi smiled—what with the water being friskier than usual after the latest storm, he couldn't half blame Val for the mama bear routine. But still. They weren't talking the Amazon.

"You sure this is the spot?" Strapped to his back, Risa babbled away. To what, God only knew.

"Enough." Val glanced up at the small mobile home park, at the half-dozen dingy trailers hugging the bluff. The second stop on their little field trip on this cloudy morning. She squinted out toward the river, then pointed, her eyes lighting up. "That's it—that's the outcropping."

Pushing through a clot of overgrown salt cedars hugging the river's edge, Val stopped a yard or so from the water. Above them, a mature cottonwood lazily embraced the patchy sky, glowing against the somber clouds. He knew it was supposed to be green, but since he didn't really know what *green* was, he had no choice but to accept its beauty as he saw it. And that was just fine with him.

"My mother wasn't exactly a big fan of nature," Val said quietly over the gurgling river, hugging closed a heavyweight hoodie. "But I remember her bringing me here in the evenings during the summer, when I was little. Especially after my father left. And she'd go out there—" she nodded toward the flat rocks several yards out from the shore "—and just...stand there, looking up at the sky."

"Praying?"

"I somehow doubt it. But I think she found peace. As much as she could, anyway."

"You want me to wait here?"

"Please? Keep an eye on Josie?"

"Sure."

Carefully, she navigated the slippery rocks until she came to the biggest, flattest one. Then she took a moment, her eyes closed, before opening the small cardboard box to dump the ashes into the swirling current, and Levi's chest cramped.

The past week had been a whirlwind of planning and talking and, yes, lovemaking...and more talking. So much talking, sorting through their thoughts and feelings as much as their things. Much to his relief, Josie had been thrilled at the idea of Levi's becoming her stepdaddy, although she hadn't yet decided what she should call him. He'd reassured her it was completely up to her. So far, Dad seemed to be winning. Since, she'd said, she was already too big for "daddy," and anyway, that's what she'd called Tommy, so...

He doubted she had any idea how pleased he was.

And he and Val had decided to forgo a big wedding in favor of a quick—and cheaper—one, to be held out at the ranch in the next month or so, before it got too cold. Instead they decided to concentrate on fixing up the house, getting the kitchen up to snuff so she could have her pie business in full swing by the start of ski season. Honestly, he didn't think he'd ever met a more focused human being…or, now, a happier one. Except, perhaps, for himself.

But after dinner the other night at Lita's house—which, with her blessing, would go on the market as soon as she and girls moved in with him after the wedding—Val had said that as much as she was all about looking forward, she still needed to tidy up a few things from her past.

So they'd started by taking the girls to see where she'd grown up. The lot was surprisingly pretty, surrounded by pines and aspens with a pretty decent mountain view. None of the disintegrating mobile homes were occupied, though, and a For Sale sign proclaimed the owner's intention. Levi imagined he'd get a pretty penny for the lot.

Val had walked up to the trailer through foot-high weeds, looking up at it as she laid her hand on the pock-marked siding. There'd been no discernible expression on her face, except maybe of relief. As though the memories had finally lost their hold over her.

He'd no idea, either, she'd had her mother's ashes. He could only imagine how freeing that must've been, too, finally letting them go. But what Val said—and what had touched him so deeply—was that, actually, it was her *mother* she was freeing, from all the hurt and nega-tive thoughts Val had been carting around inside her own head for so long.

She came back up onto the bank with the empty car-ton, folded flat.

"Any plans for that?"

"Dunno." She frowned at it, then smiled. "It's biode-gradable, though, so…maybe shred it, use it as mulch for a rosebush at the house?"

"Sounds good."

Josie and the dog ran toward them, both panting. "Can we get lunch now? I'm *starving*."

Val chuckled. "In a minute, baby. Okay?"

"'Kay," the kid said, flashing a grin at Levi as she bounded off again, arms flailing, and he loved her so much it hurt. Releasing a breathy laugh, Val looked out at the water, determinedly chugging south. "Thought I'd call my father a little later."

"You don't have to do everything at once, you know. There's no rush."

"No, it feels right. And I want him to meet you. And his granddaughters."

"You sure?"

She paused, then said, "Whether he'll ever be a real part of my life again, I have no idea. But I'd like him to know that you are." Her eyes lifted to his, the light in their pale depths turning him inside out. "Thank you for not giving up on me. On us."

Levi wrapped an arm around her shoulders, pulling her close. "Wasn't even a possibility."

And it hadn't been, he realized, from the moment he'd seen her again. Because that purpose he'd been looking for? She and the girls were it. His whole reason for returning to Whispering Pines. And definitely his reason for staying there, he thought as Josie ran back and he hauled her up into his arms.

"Levi! For heaven's sake," Val said, laughing. "You've already carrying the baby!"

"It's okay," he said, grinning into Josie's eyes. "I can handle it."

Linking her hands behind his neck, Josie grinned back at him, then leaned close to whisper, "You kept your promise, huh? To Daddy?"

His eyes stinging, Levi kissed the top of her head.

"You bet," he whispered back just as the clouds parted. And call him crazy, but Levi could have sworn he felt his friend's smile in the sunbeam that washed over them—

"Ohmigosh, Levi! Look! Across the river!"

Levi squinted at where Val was pointing, catching a glimpse of a bright purple lowrider bumping along the road on the other side, playing peekaboo with the trees.

Laughing, his arms—and heart—full, Levi looked up at the sky and winked.

* * * * *

COMING NEXT MONTH FROM

HARLEQUIN®

SPECIAL EDITION

Available February 16, 2016

#2461 "I DO"...TAKE TWO!
Three Coins in the Fountain
by Merline Lovelace
On a trip to Italy, Kate Westbrook makes a wish at the Trevi Fountain—to create a future *without* her soon-to-be-ex, Travis! But Cupid has other plans for these two, and true love might just be in their future.

#2462 FORTUNE'S SECRET HUSBAND
The Fortunes of Texas: All Fortune's Children
by Karen Rose Smith
Proper Brit Lucie Fortune Chesterfield had a whirlwind teenage marriage to Chase Parker, but that was long over—or so she thought. Until her secret husband shows up at her door...with a big surprise!

#2463 BACK IN THE SADDLE
Wed in the West
by Karen Templeton
When widower Zach Talbot agrees to help Mallory Keyes find a horse for her son, he falls for the paralyzed former actress. But can the veterinarian and the beauty both give love a second chance?

#2464 A BABY AND A BETROTHAL
Crimson, Colorado
by Michelle Major
Katie Garrity is on a mission to find her perfect match—only to be surprised by her own pregnancy! When her first crush, Noah Crawford, comes back to town, will they get a chance at a love neither expected?

#2465 FROM DARE TO DUE DATE
Sugar Falls, Idaho
by Christy Jeffries
When dancer Mia Palinski has one magical night with Dr. Garrett McCormick, she winds up pregnant. Both of them aren't looking for love, but a baby changes everything. Can a single dance create a forever family?

#2466 A COWBOY IN THE KITCHEN
Hurley's Homestyle Kitchen
by Meg Maxwell
Single dad West Montgomery is doing his best to be Mr. Mom for his daughter. He's even taking cooking classes with beautiful chef Annabel Hurley. But West and his little girl might be the secret ingredient for her perfect recipe to forever.

**YOU CAN FIND MORE INFORMATION ON UPCOMING HARLEQUIN® TITLES,
FREE EXCERPTS AND MORE AT WWW.HARLEQUIN.COM.**

HSECNM0216

REQUEST YOUR FREE BOOKS!
2 FREE NOVELS PLUS 2 FREE GIFTS!

H HARLEQUIN®

SPECIAL EDITION

Life, Love & Family

YES! Please send me 2 FREE Harlequin® Special Edition novels and my 2 FREE gifts (gifts are worth about $10). After receiving them, if I don't wish to receive any more books, I can return the shipping statement marked "cancel." If I don't cancel, I will receive 6 brand-new novels every month and be billed just $4.74 per book in the U.S. or $5.49 per book in Canada. That's a savings of at least 12% off the cover price! It's quite a bargain! Shipping and handling is just 50¢ per book in the U.S. and 75¢ per book in Canada.* I understand that accepting the 2 free books and gifts places me under no obligation to buy anything. I can always return a shipment and cancel at any time. Even if I never buy another book, the two free books and gifts are mine to keep forever.

235/335 HDN GH3Z

Name _____ (PLEASE PRINT) _____

Address _____ Apt. # _____

City _____ State/Prov. _____ Zip/Postal Code _____

Signature (if under 18, a parent or guardian must sign)

Mail to the **Reader Service**:
IN U.S.A.: P.O. Box 1867, Buffalo, NY 14240-1867
IN CANADA: P.O. Box 609, Fort Erie, Ontario L2A 5X3

Want to try two free books from another line?
Call 1-800-873-8635 or visit www.ReaderService.com.

* Terms and prices subject to change without notice. Prices do not include applicable taxes. Sales tax applicable in N.Y. Canadian residents will be charged applicable taxes. Offer not valid in Quebec. This offer is limited to one order per household. Not valid for current subscribers to Harlequin Special Edition books. All orders subject to credit approval. Credit or debit balances in a customer's account(s) may be offset by any other outstanding balance owed by or to the customer. Please allow 4 to 6 weeks for delivery. Offer available while quantities last.

Your Privacy—The Reader Service is committed to protecting your privacy. Our Privacy Policy is available online at www.ReaderService.com or upon request from the Reader Service.

We make a portion of our mailing list available to reputable third parties that offer products we believe may interest you. If you prefer that we not exchange your name with third parties, or if you wish to clarify or modify your communication preferences, please visit us at www.ReaderService.com/consumerschoice or write to us at Reader Service Preference Service, P.O. Box 9062, Buffalo, NY 14240-9062. Include your complete name and address.

HSE15

SPECIAL EXCERPT FROM

SPECIAL EDITION

*All Kate Westbrook wants to do on her trip to Italy
is to get over her soon-to-be ex-husband. But then
irresistible Air Force pilot Travis shows up in Rome!
When Travis offers to whisk her off for one last
adventure, can Kate resist the man who still holds the
key to her heart?*

*Read on for a sneak preview of
"I DO"...TAKE TWO!*
by *Merline Lovelace*,
the first book in her new miniseries,
THREE COINS IN THE FOUNTAIN.

Travis had heard the words come out of his mouth and
been as stunned as the two men he'd come to know so well
in recent weeks. Yet as soon as his brain had processed
the audio signals, he'd recognized their unshakable truth.
If trading his Air Force flight suit for one with an EAS
patch on it would win Kate back, he'd make the change
today.

"So what do you think?" he asked her. "Again, your
first no-frills, no-holds-barred gut reaction?"

"I won't lie," she admitted slowly, reluctantly. "My
head, my heart, my gut all leaped for joy."

He started for her, elation pumping through his veins.
The hand she slapped against his chest to stop him made
only a tiny dent in his fierce joy.

"Wait, Trav! This is too big a decision to make without talking it over. Let's…let's use this time together to make sure it's what you really want."

"I'm sure. Now."

"Well, I'm not." Her brown eyes showed an agony of doubt. "The military's been your whole life up to now."

"Wrong." He laid his hand over hers, felt the warmth of her palm against his sternum. "You came first, Katydid. Before the uniform, before the wings, before the head rush and stomach-twisting responsibilities of being part of a crew. I let those get in the way the past few years. That won't happen again."

The doubt was still there in her eyes, swimming in a pool of indecision. He needed to back off, Travis conceded. Give her a few days to accept what was now a done deal in his mind.

"Okay," he said with a sense of rightness he hadn't felt in longer than he could remember, "we'll head up to Venice. Let Ellis's proposal percolate for a day or two."

And then, he vowed, they would conduct a virtual burning of the divorce decree before he took his wife to bed.

Don't miss
"I DO"…TAKE TWO!
by USA TODAY *bestselling author Merline Lovelace,*
available March 2016 wherever
Harlequin® Special Edition books and ebooks are sold.

www.Harlequin.com

Copyright © 2016 by Merline Lovelace

HSEEXP0216

Turn your love of reading into
rewards you'll love with

Harlequin My Rewards

**Join for FREE today at
www.HarlequinMyRewards.com**

Earn **FREE BOOKS** of your choice.

Experience **EXCLUSIVE OFFERS** and contests.

Enjoy **BOOK RECOMMENDATIONS**
selected just for you.

PLUS! Sign up now
and get **500** points
right away!

Earn
FREE
REWARDS
HarlequinMyRewards.com
Join
Today!

MYR16R

Love the Harlequin book you just read?

Your opinion matters.

Review this book on your favorite book site, review site, blog or your own social media properties and share your opinion with other readers!

Be sure to connect with us at:
Harlequin.com/Newsletters
Facebook.com/HarlequinBooks
Twitter.com/HarlequinBooks

HREVIEWS

THE
SPELLS BIBLE

THE
SPELLS BIBLE
THE DEFINITIVE GUIDE TO CHARMS AND ENCHANTMENTS

Ann-Marie Gallagher

WALKING STICK PRESS
Cincinnati, Ohio

First published in the U.K. in 2003
by Godsfield Press Ltd,
Laurel House, Station Approach, Alresford,
Hampshire SO24 9JH, U.K.

www.godsfieldpress.com

Distributed to the trade markets in North America by
Walking Stick Press, an imprint of F+W Publications, Inc.
4700 East Galbraith Road, Cincinnati, OH 45236
Tel: 1-800-289-0963

10 9 8 7 6 5 4 3 2

Copyright © 2003 Godsfield Press
Text copyright © 2003 Ann-Marie Gallagher

Designed and produced for Godsfield Press
by The Bridgewater Book Company

Photography: Mike Hemsley at Walter Gardiner Photography
Senior designer: John Grain
Project editor: Sarah Doughty
Designer: Jane Lanaway
Prop-buyer: Claire Shanahan
Model: Genevieve Appleby

All rights reserved. No part of this publication may be reproduced,
stored in a retrieval system, or transmitted in any form or by any
means, electronic, mechanical, photocopying, recording, or
otherwise.

Ann-Marie Gallagher asserts the moral right to be identified as
the author of this work.

Printed and bound in China

ISBN 1-58297-244-3

CONTENTS

PART 1

BEFORE YOU BEGIN

INTRODUCTION TO THE SPELLS BIBLE

The craft of magic is making something of a comeback—not that it ever went entirely away—and the resurgent public interest in myth and magic shows no signs of abating. It may seem odd that in the age of technology people are still intrigued by ancient traditions and beliefs and interested in casting spells. There are many theories for this renewed interest, all with their particular attractions, but it is likely that growing concern for the environment, our diets, and our lifestyles have generated a similar concern about a spiritual vacuum that is not answered by established religions. This has led to a search for meaning that has taken many people beyond the church or temple door to ask themselves new questions about our place in the cosmos.

Exploring spirituality outside of the strictures of organized religion can be extremely liberating, but it can be quite scary, too. For this reason, many people look for inspiration to the old ways and ask what our ancestors believed and did.

To the delighted surprise of many of us, there is a whole history of spirituality and magic just waiting to be discovered. Embedded in folklore, superstition, and tales of gods and goddesses are clues to the importance of magic in the life of our forebears. We know, from spells inscribed on cave walls or sheets of lead found in sacred wells, that our ancestors practiced and believed in the efficacy of magic. We know that they lived closer to nature and respected and utilized the natural energies and forces they found within and around them. You will find within this spell book many references to the traditions behind some of the ingredients, tools, and techniques of spell work, and hopefully you will yourself contribute to its many customs as you become confident enough to design spells of your own!

What can you expect to find in the *Spells Bible*? Well, with spells for love, passion, work, career, health, beauty, and protection, all key life concerns are catered to. Moreover, as you will see, there are generally a number of spells to choose from, each approaching similar circumstances from a different angle. This enables the reader to select the spell that most nearly addresses the specific need in question. All of the spells

spells designed to coincide with the ancient festivals that mark the wheel of the year.

Reading through the *Spells Bible* should also be something of an education in itself. It is designed as a directory, with easily identifiable sections with background information and guidance, making it easy to dip into it at need, but it also contains kernels of ancient wisdom and magical knowledge. If you read through the introductory texts for each spell, you will find discussed within them elements of folk and magical lore as well as the origins and meanings of certain magical customs and traditions. In addition, within the spells themselves, you will find descriptions of magical techniques from all around the world and practical lessons in the principles of magic.

This book is a veritable Aladdin's Cave of magical information covering history, customs, symbolism, and magical correspondences within the texts accompanying the spells. Between its covers you will discover a range of charms and enchantments using chants, talismans, amulets, poppets, fith-faths, herbs, incenses, candles, cords, and many other unexpected ingredients. If any of these are unfamiliar to you, both the

carry brief explanations and advice, making it simpler to match the spell to the occasion. In addition, there are magical workings for banishing or binding—designed to prevent harm—as well as divination spells through which you will be able to discern and act on life patterns revealed within spell work. The importance of the natural rhythms and energies of nature are also recognized here, and there is a section of seasonal introductory section of this book and the texts of the spells themselves offer clear explanations and guidance to their uses. The accounts of magical practices offered within this *Spells Bible* should also go some way toward discounting some of the more ignorant assumptions about wax figures and large pins that have found their way into popular culture through the distorting lens of Hollywood and the uninformed scribblings in sensationalist novels!

Welcome, then, to the *Spells Bible*, your comprehensive guide to spells for all areas of your life. Whatever your need, you are sure to find a choice of charms and enchantments within

these pages to answer it. Here you will find a blend of the ancient and modern, all flavored with the customs and traditions of magical crafts from around the world, set in a directory that lists the purposes, timing, and background to each spell. Within the pages that follow, you will discover a world of knowledge and ideas that can, ultimately, guide you toward developing your own very individual magical strengths.

Materials for charms and enchantments

WORKING WITH MAGIC
ETHICS, ATTITUDE, AND PRACTICALITIES

Before attempting any spell work, it is important that you first grasp certain principles regarding the use of magic and your attitude toward it. The attitude with which you approach magical work is the key to its success and has a bearing on your development as a magician. In case you are tempted to pass over this section, let me add that failure to do the basic work described here will result in wasted effort as far as spell casting goes. Further, you may find yourself in a pickle if you ignore the advice offered.

Don't worry, you are not going to be given a heavy lecture on the abuse of magical power; as you will come to realize while you progress in your work,

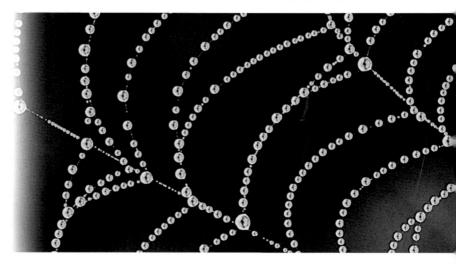

it is not in the nature of magic to accommodate misuse in the way often depicted in films and literature. However, magic operates in such a way that you do need to be sure that the changes you are seeking to make are truly for the good of all concerned.

One way of describing magic is as connection. Imagine, if you can, that all things in the world are connected by invisible threads, all of which join up as a series of webs. All of these webs in turn are connected with each other, making a multi-dimensional pattern that describes all life. As large as this web is, it is so delicate that an event on one part of the web affects the whole. This is because the matter from which it is made is spirit, which in the magical tradition behind most of the spells in this book is known as the *fifth element*. When we work rituals or do spells, we are weaving new patterns into this great spirit web, and these interventions need to be considered in the context of the whole. In short, the questions we need to ask ourselves prior to spell work are those that ensure that we respect the well-being of the whole web—not just the part of it that we inhabit. On the whole, this isn't such a bad way of approaching everyday life!

There are certain questions you need to ask before "casting off." First of all, be practical; consider whether you really need to be casting a spell at all. Magic should never be used as an alternative to material action—this just wastes everybody's time, enables people to avoid facing reality, and feeds whatever delusions they may be harboring that their problems can be solved with no effort on their part.

Secondly, ask yourself what is really needed. Nine times out of ten, someone asking for a love spell actually needs help in another area of their life. Some people, for example, believe that finding a partner will resolve their lack of confidence; others assume that meeting someone will make them happy with their lives. What they are asking for may not actually be what they need; commonly, what is needed is counseling or healing and thereby some work and effort on their part to build their inner resources and self-esteem. A spell for their self-esteem can be very empowering and complement the practical steps that are actually being taken, but what will be utterly wasted on them at this point in their lives is a love spell—"Do I really need to cast a spell?" and "What is really needed?"—if you ask

yourself these two questions before proceeding with spell work, you won't go far wrong. There are, however, a number of other issues that you need to take into consideration in your magical work, and these are related to the difference between what people think magic is and how magic actually does work.

There are laws of magic in the same way there are laws of physics, and while some of these are pretty obvious, others are less so and will be discovered as you progress in the craft. One of the most

common pieces of magical lore quoted at beginners is something called the Law of Threefold Return. Although some magicians take this very literally as an absolute, cast-in-stone natural law, it is more accurate to say that it refers to a belief that whatever we send out into the universe comes back to us, multiplied by three. Acceptance of this law has been important to some witches and magicians in their attempts to dispel fears about the "dangers" of what they do. There is absolutely no point, it is

reasoned, for witches or magicians to send out a "curse" when they know that such an action would simply rebound on them multiplied by three. It makes much more sense, or so the theory goes, to send out blessings and cast spells to do good, as magic will ensure that these are likewise multiplied and sent back to us. It is a nice theory, and it has performed some good public relations work for us magical folk, but it is not a law. It is actually a spiritual principle that has been taken rather too literally.

When we claim that what we send out we get back, we are probably right. If we all did good deeds, then they would be repaid in kind at some point. Similarly, it is observable that destructive behavior engenders an increase in negative conduct, rather than otherwise—hence sayings such as "Violence begets violence" or, more biblically, "He who lives by the sword shall die by the sword." The trouble is that this is not a hard-and-fast magical law. When somebody is behaving in a damaging way, they are doing themselves damage in that they are failing to grow psychologically and spiritually, and ultimately this will rebound on them. However, this is not the same as having what you send out revisited upon you three times. The knowledge that someone is restricting their spiritual development, furthermore, is no consolation for those suffering as a result of their appalling behavior. The fact is that though we may feel that wrongdoers harm themselves in the end, this does not add up to a specific law whereby all damage is visited upon them in kind three times over.

Reference to cause and effect, however, is highly relevant to magical ethics. Just as we need to be careful about what we deal out in terms of our everyday behavior, we need also to take note of our magical actions. This means that the changes we seek need to be weighed carefully, both in the context of our own lives and the lives of others.

It is not possible, for example, to change another person's free will by magic; neither should it be an aspiration to do so. A person who attempts to subject the will of another to their own,

eventually finds themselves rendered indecisive, confused, and easily misguided—for the reason that the lack in them that drove them to demand obedience from another will simply be magnified. This reflects a general law that bending magic toward selfish purposes will not have the effect the magician intends; rather, it will focus on and emphasize their own shortcomings.

This raises another general law observed in magic—that of the magnifying properties of the magical circle. Most spell work takes place within a magical circle—a space where the energy raised from spell casting is contained until it is ripe to be released into the cosmos to go about its business. Whatever you bring with you is magnified and brought to your attention until you deal with it. If you cast a spell that is about greed, lust, or obsession, this will simply amplify the flaw in yourself that initiated such a need, until you deal with it.

All in all, the ethics of magic are practical and based largely on common sense. If you enter the circle of magic with an attitude of respect for yourself and respect for others, you will find success and enrichment.

SPELL WORK
RANGE AND TYPES OF SPELL, MAGICAL TECHNIQUES, TOOLS, AND INGREDIENTS

Each of the spells in the directory section offers a brief explanation of its purpose, the ingredients required, the symbolism deployed, and the appropriate timing to work with. They also supply brief descriptions of the techniques employed, and as you read through the different sections, you will inevitably accumulate a working knowledge of magical tools and techniques.

Magic has survived through the ages because a good magician can improvise and find resources all around them. This is reflected in the large number of spells in this book that use everyday objects. Others use more arcane materials— specific herbs and incenses—for their established properties, in keeping with traditional correspondences. The majority of spells in this volume arise from a tradition of sympathetic magic, a system that uses symbols to represent the people, objects, and intents of the spell. Many of the ingredients, tools, and techniques used are adaptable to a

variety of uses and purposes. When you develop more confidence as a seasoned magician, you will no doubt test their flexibility yourself.

Sympathetic magic is very straightforward. In addition to its system of transference, which symbolizes "like with like," it also draws on a range of other symbolic systems. One such example is the use made of the phases of the moon. Although there are physical energies at work at different times—

evident from tides and animal and plant responses—there is an element of symbolism attached to lunar phases. The waxing, or growing moon, for example, is seen to favor spells for growth, increase, and attraction. The waning, or shrinking moon, on the other hand, symbolizes decay, banishment, and repulsion. The dark moon, known more conventionally as the new moon, favors new projects, building protection, and disposal. The full moon is symbolically linked with reflection, illusion, revelation, and wholeness.

Other symbolic correspondences include the days of the week, linked to planetary influences which themselves represent different aspects of human existence. Monday is linked with the mysterious powers of the moon, and favors dreams, psychic activity, and money. Tuesday is the day of Mars, the fierce planet of courage, will, and defense. Wednesday is ruled by Mercury, the planet of communications, while Thursday is the day of Jupiter, the generous and expansive luck planet. Friday is dedicated to Venus, planet of love and harmony. Saturday is dedicated to ringed Saturn, the disciplinarian, and Sunday to the sun, bringer of joy and success.

An important system used here in magic is that of the five sacred elements: earth, air, fire, water, and spirit. Their symbolic correspondences cover all matters of human existence. Earth represents the material world and our need for shelter, food, and physical health. Air is the element of communication, memory, ideas, and learning. Water is associated with love, healing, and dreams, while fire symbolizes courage, willpower, and inspiration. Spirit, the fifth sacred element, is the element of connection and transformation. It oversees birth, communion, and death, as well as the realm of magic.

In addition to these symbolic systems, the spells occasionally refer to gods and goddesses. Where they are invoked in this book, there is generally an explanation of why their influence is considered significant, except in cases where a figure is generally well known.

The spells in this book are divided into sections that reflect key life concerns, but across these dividing lines, many of the spells share common techniques. One of the most common techniques used is that of making a declaration of intent. This is usually announced at the opening of the ritual—when the first candle is lit, for example. Speaking the declaration aloud has a dual purpose: to knock on the doors of your subconscious in order to awaken your latent magical abilities; and to focus your attentions on the energies you are invoking.

Raising energy to empower the spells in this book is generally achieved through chanting, concentration, or visualization. In some of the spells, the means of energizing are obvious from the directions, for example, where the words to a chant are provided or where guidance is given on how to visualize

outcomes. In other spells, you are being asked to focus all your concentration on the spell. When your confidence grows, you may consider exercising other techniques, such as dance, drumming, or trance.

Whereas chanting is pretty straightforward, visualization needs a little practice, and it is a good idea to "rehearse" beforehand using relaxation techniques such as breathing slowly, stilling your thoughts, and sitting quietly for a short length of time. If you are considered a bit of a daydreamer, it is likely that you are already a natural!

The tool kit of magic is pretty simple. Although some magical systems insist on a complex specification of swords, wands, and cords, the tools used in this book are very basic. Traditionally, magicians have a wand or a knife to direct their energies, but it is not expected that you have a dedicated tool of this type. Most of the tools required for the spells in this book can also be described as ingredients—candles, cords, herbs, oil burners, charcoal disks, incense, and so on.

The best guideline to follow in any spell work is to keep it simple. The rules for the spells found here are uncomplicated. Allow the candles to burn down in safety unless otherwise directed. You do not need new element candles for each spell. When you are asked to keep something "safe," this means that you do not dispose of it or return it to its usual use until what you have asked for has been achieved.

Juniper berries

Rosemary

Mugwort

21

SEASONS AND FESTIVALS
CELEBRATING AND TUNING INTO THE NATURAL RHYTHMS OF MAGIC

Many of us who work frequently with magic consider it a natural part of life that comes from within us and from our surrounding environment. Our understanding of our place in the world and in the cosmos is our spirituality, so working magic, for us, is a spiritual practice. The way we attune to the energies we find around us is also part of that practice, and the more closely we work with and try to understand the rhythms of nature, the more we develop magically and spiritually.

In order to become acquainted with the natural energies we draw on for spells and rituals, we need first to become acquainted with the tides and seasons of the earth. The correlation between the phases of the moon and spell work is generally well known. However, the most intuitive and gifted magicians know that, in order to work with earth energies, we need to assimilate the planetary rhythms of continuity and change. This involves learning about the

seasons of the earth, attuning ourselves to our passage through the solar system, and experiencing the changes around us independently of the calendar that hangs in the kitchen or the office. Approaching the changing seasons experientially and learning about the old traditions associated with them is the best way of beginning to understand the nature of magic, which comes from the world around us.

The wheel of the year, as seen from the magical traditions in the West, is divided into eight festivals, all linked to the natural flow of the seasons and astronomical events. These festivals are sometimes depicted as eight spokes in the wheel of the year, and this is a quite useful image to hold on to, if this is new to you. Strictly speaking, there is no beginning and no end to the year, even though different cultural traditions have at some point nominated one or two of them as candidates for the title of "New Year." Because they observe the natural

YULE/WINTER SOLSTICE
DECEMBER 21–22

IMBOLC
FEBRUARY 1–2

EOSTRE/VERNAL EQUINOX
MARCH 21–22

SAMHAIN
OCTOBER 31–NOVEMBER 1

BELTAINE
APRIL 30–MAY 1

MABON/AUTUMN EQUINOX
SEPTEMBER 21–22

LAMMAS/LUGHNASADH
JULY 31–AUGUST 1

LITHA/SUMMER SOLSTICE
JUNE 21–22

rhythms of nature rather than the dates on the Gregorian calendar, beginnings and endings are seen as integral parts of the festivals, which are themselves seen as interlinked with each other. The festivals are a mixture of solar events—solstices and equinoxes—and fire festivals from Celtic and Nordic cultures. The four solar festivals occur on the day of the astronomical event in question: Yule, the shortest day, or winter solstice, usually on December 21 or 22; Litha, the longest day, or summer solstice, on June 21 or 22; Eostre, the

23

vernal equinox, on or around March 21; and Mabon, the autumnal equinox, on or around September 21. These are interspersed with the fire festivals—so called because of the custom of setting bonfires at these dates: Imbolc, "ewe's milk," falls at the beginning of February when the first snowdrops appear; Beltaine, or May Day, occurs around May 1, or when the May blossom appears; Lammas, or Lughnasadh, comes at the beginning of August with the grain harvest; and Samhain, "first frosts," the feast of the ancestors, on or around the end of October.

There are a number of customs connected with the eight seasonal festivals, and you will find on pages 206–255 a number of spells that are particularly relevant to their celebration. Each spell is accompanied by an explanation, but it is useful to know something of the framework that guides them.

Yule is an ancient festival, taking its name from an Old Norse word thought to mean "wheel." From the alignment of several prehistoric stone monuments in England, Scotland, Wales, and Ireland, it is clear that our ancestors considered the winter solstice an important part of the ritual year. We know that it was being celebrated in the fourth century C.E., as records from that era state that the Christian church expressly declared December 25 as Christ's birthday in order to persuade Christians participating in the pagan midwinter festival to commemorate the Nativity instead! On the shortest day, darkness triumphs over light. At the same time, however, we know that thereafter the hours of daylight will increase, and so the sun is "reborn." In some quarters, the winter solstice is called "sun return" to emphasize the promise of lighter days to come. Although at this time solar

energies are at an ebb, Yule is still seen as a festival of light, hope, and promise. At this time many of us feel the lack of light and warmth, and we gather together to brighten up the long, dreary winter nights. Some of us even feel the need to hibernate—thus the common occurrence in the Northern Hemisphere of the winter blues, or "seasonal affective disorder." This is a time to go into the dark and seek the potential that lies within us. For magicians seeking to tune into the cycle of the seasons, this is the time to meditate, work on our creative potential, and take note of our dreams, which at this time of year are deeper, richer, and more vivid. It is also a time to take note of what is around us, and to note the passage of the moon and the bright points of the winter stars and planets. Yule is a season of contemplation and the search for power within.

Imbolc, when the snowdrops emerge in Europe at the end of January, comes at the time when lambs are born. This festival marks the thawing of the earth in preparation for planting and crop sowing. A Celtic fire festival, Imbolc is sometimes known as the festival of Brigid, a much beloved Celtic fire and healing goddess. Brigid has the reputation of being fiercely protective of women, children, and newborn animals, so this is seen as a time of justice. It is also a time of renewal, when the winter loosens its grip on the earth and sets the rivers and streams awash with the melted snows. Daylight is of noticeably greater length now, and just as Brigid is invoked as a midwife to the newborn lambs, Imbolc is seen as the midwife to the spring.

This is the time to witness the earth awakening and feel the energies around us gearing up toward the surge of life that characterizes spring and early summer. Imbolc is the season for beginning to look outward again after the long nights of winter, which means that it is a good time to consider "spring cleaning" our own lives in anticipation of the season to come.

Eostre marks another astronomical event—the spring equinox, when day and night are of equal length and in perfect balance. Thereafter, the hours of daylight will outstrip those of darkness until the summer solstice, when the sun will triumph altogether on the longest day. Eostre is sacred to a fertility goddess of that same name. Her totem is the

hare, and we see in depictions of Easter bunnies and the giving of chocolate eggs remnants of old fertility rites. Now the sap is rising, the earth is green again, and the hours of light are set to increase. Themes of balance, fertility, and growth run through the festival of Eostre, and this is a good time to think about balance in our lives and our potential for growth, and to tap into the rush of natural energy around us. This is a good time of year to meditate with your back to a tree and to try to feel the life rising through its roots, trunk, and branches. Eostre is also known as the Festival of Trees—this is a good time to acquaint yourself with traditions, customs, and magical knowledge associated with trees.

Beltaine, celebrated when blossoms deck the May tree or from sundown on the eve of May I, is another fertility festival. It marks the beginning of summer and is the time of the Green Man and Woman, Jack in the Green, Robin Hood, and Marian. Now the spirits of the greenwood are abroad, and the veil between the world of humans and the Celtic otherworld, the land of the sidhe or "fairy people," is at its thinnest. Beltaine is a time of rampant sensuality. For this reason, over the centuries its celebration has been discouraged by the more puritanical Christian churches. Celebrated with the use of phallic and yonic symbols such as the Maypole and the wreaths of flowers that crown it, May Day festivities are accompanied by the images of sexuality that are a testimony to its origins as a fertility festival. The people's defiance of prohibitions against celebrating Beltaine mark this festival with a tradition of disobeying authority. May Day is also used to celebrate workers' rights and is increasingly a signal for the people to protest on the streets of Western cities.

Beltaine is a time to communicate with the spirits of the greenwood, to make promises and pledges, and to honor your sensuality.

Corn dolly

Litha, the summer solstice, celebrates the triumph of the hours of daylight over the hours of darkness. The longest day is greeted in parts of the British Isles at stone circles, on hillsides, or at other significant sacred prehistoric sites, by crowds of people who camp out overnight to keep vigil together for the rising sun. This is a time when you can draw strength and energy from the triumphant sun—Sol Invicta—and concentrate on your outgoing energies. This is a time of year to get out into the open air, meet new people, and learn new things about the world. It is a perfect time to go camping away from city lights, where you can sit out and appreciate the beauty of the night sky. With the better weather, it may also be possible for you to travel to the sea or other large expanses of water and there attune to the energies of the waters—the origin of all life.

Lammas or Lughnasadh marks the bringing in of the grain harvest. It has many traditions associated with it, particularly relating to corn dollies and casting out evil. At this time, when the wheat is separated from the chaff, we can focus on things in our own lives that need casting aside and also celebrate our personal harvest. It is a good time to ensure that the blessings we have are shared and to ensure that the bounty of the harvest returns to us at this time next year. This festival has ancient precedents and customs, and it is good to know that many of our ancestors' concerns are reflected in our own. For the magician, this is the time to tap into the fruitfulness of the season and listen to the spirits of the land.

Mabon, the equinox in the fall, marks the time of perfect balance between light and darkness. At this festival, however, the balance turns thereafter in favor of the darkness, and so there is a certain sadness attached to it as we say goodbye to the best of the summer. In the wheel of the year, Mabon is in the west—the place of the sunset and, for our ancestors, the direction the soul traveled after death. It is the time when we go into the dark, and we remember the many myths around the world that account for the time of darkness and barrenness of winter on the earth. It is a time to travel into the darkness with some of these characters in order to find wisdom and truth and to obtain arcane knowledge. It is also a good time to cast aside sorrow and place the past where it belongs—behind us.

Samhain, sometimes described as the Celtic New Year, marks the time of the first frosts and the descent into the dark days of winter. We commemorate the dead at this point of the year's turning and honor the ancestors. Now the veil between the world of the living and the world of the dead is thin, and the spirits of the dead are invited to visit with us. Samhain is considered an auspicious time for divination, and at this time of year our dreams become more vivid and telling. This season provides an opportunity to explore our developing psychic abilities and a space in which to consider our own mortality. The mysterious forces around at this time of the year remind us of the mysteries of life and death and our connection thereby with every other living thing. It is a time to consider the nature of death and to question our beliefs.

Becoming attuned to the rhythms and tides of the earth as we travel the solar system is a brilliant way of developing our own magical abilities. If you work through the solar cycle, noting the phases of the moon and the planets, you are already on your way to becoming one of "the wise" and adept at using the power you find within and around you.

SACRED SPACES
CREATING AND RECOGNIZING SPIRITUAL SPACE

Space that we create for the purpose of spiritual activity is sacred. Within this space, we may come to recognize our place in the universe and acknowledge certain truths about the human condition. We may even develop an understanding about what some people refer to as "divinity." Or we may practice the sacred art of magic—sacred because it draws on spiritual knowledge in order to effect change.

Creating sacred space is simple, but it requires concentration, clarity of purpose, and an ability to withstand the mental and physical distractions of your particular circumstances. You can create a space for meditation or spell work within your own home without having a room set aside for that specific purpose. This involves claiming a physical space in your home for the duration of the spell and later returning that room to its original purpose. For many of us, clearing the physical space is the easy part. But psychological debris is sometimes a little

harder to shift, and this will take practice. In time, and when you have undertaken the tasks described in this section several times over, switching to ritual mode inside your head will seem as easy as preparing the physical space in your home.

The most natural shape of a sacred space is a circle, and this has been used for centuries as a boundary—and for protection—for the casting of spells by magicians. Casting a circle is very straightforward. If you are working at home, choose a room in which you will

not be disturbed for the duration of your task; usually this will mean at least one hour. Clear a space in the center of your room, so that you can sit comfortably on the floor in the center of it. Place four candles—one yellow, one red, one blue, and one green, all in secure holders safely away from fire hazards around the room—in directions that roughly equate with east for yellow, south for red, west for blue, and north for green. These candles represent four of the five sacred elements: air, fire, water, and earth. In the center, you should place a purple candle in a secure holder, representing spirit, the fifth magical element.

Most magicians like to psychically "cleanse" the space before a circle is properly cast, and this means purifying water and blessing salt, then mixing the two, and sprinkling this around the room. All you have to do is to place your hand over half a wineglass or vessel of water, then visualize any energy that the water may have absorbed as dark smoke coming out of the glass, and declare: "I exorcise thee, o creature of water." Now place your hand on the salt and bless it, saying: "Blessings be upon this creature of salt." Place the salt into the water and stir, then sprinkle it around the room clockwise.

Wand

Using a wand, a knife, or your forefinger, and beginning at the east, move clockwise, or deosil ("sunwise"), around the room; "describe" a circle of light in the air all around it. This should move outward to encompass the whole room. Draw energy from the earth up through your feet, through your trunk, and down your arms into your wand, knife, or forefinger. When you have completed this circle, you should declare it cast. For example: "I conjure thee, o circle of power, that thou be a boundary and a protection for this space between the worlds."

When the circle is cast, the elements should be invoked. Some people like to visualize these as humanoid and see them in angelic or god or goddess form. Others prefer to visualize the raw energy of the elements. Whatever your inclination, it is important to acknowledge the elements when you are building the circle. When we invoke the elements, this does not mean that we summon the mighty forces represented by them to that particular spot for an

hour or so—rather it means that we call up their meaning within ourselves. Externally, we acknowledge their presence in all things and symbolize and unify that presence for the duration of the circle in the appropriate direction. It is best to keep the wording of any declaration very simple. Beginning in the east, welcome the element of air; then move around the circle deosil, hailing the elements appropriate to the direction and adjusting the following wording for each as appropriate: "In the east, the element of air, you are honored in this sacred circle." When you have welcomed the outer elements, move to the center and welcome the element of spirit. You should light the candle for each element when you have welcomed it in, saying: "Hail and welcome."

When your spell or ritual is completed, move around the circle counterclockwise, or *widdershins*, to close it, blowing out the candles in reverse order, beginning with earth and ending with spirit.

It is customary to move deosil within the circle at all times. There are occasional exceptions—for example, when casting some banishing spells— but generally this tradition should be observed. You should not walk through the boundaries of the circle or leave this sacred space for the duration of your ritual, unless an emergency occurs which necessitates disruption. This helps to keep the focus and concentration necessary for magical undertakings and contains the power raised within the circle until you are ready to release it.

Circles of standing stones, ditches, and earthworks have been found in many Neolithic sacred sites and are thought to symbolize the mysterious cycle of life, death, and rebirth, as celebrated by the ancients. In magic, when we talk about work in the circle, we actually mean very much the same thing as our ancestors did when they chose to build their monuments—that all circles are one great circle, and that the nature of all existence is cyclical.

Describing a circle

MAKING AN ALTAR
A FOCAL POINT FOR MAGICAL WORK AND SPIRITUAL GROWTH

It is possible to build altars—focal points of spiritual contemplation—almost anywhere. An altar can be as simple as a space set apart, in your home or place of work or study, in which you can place objects that are special or sacred to you. Alternatively, it can be more elaborate, with candles, pictures, figures, or symbols representing a deity, natural element, or moon phase with which you have a particular affinity. The loveliest altars can be built in gardens, using rocks, wood, and natural materials. If you need to be relatively discreet about your magical and spiritual interests, altars that are out in the open can be passed off as garden décor, while the indoor variety can be officially listed as a place where you keep things that you don't want moved. If you are lucky enough to have a whole room

set aside for meditation and magical work, you can afford to dedicate some of this space to constructing an altar, to provide a focus for your circle work and your spiritual development.

Many magicians like to have this focal point while they are doing circle work. Some prefer to have a table in the center of the circle, while others choose to place one in the north of the circle, a direction particularly sacred to pagans and witches.

This type of altar is generally set up for the duration of the circle, then dismantled, and the objects are packed away carefully until the next one. It is very much an individual taste as to what is included on an altar of this kind, but there are general guidelines as to what you might include.

Athame

It is usual to represent the five sacred elements present on the altar during circle work. Traditionally, incense represents air; an athame (a witch's knife), a candle, or an oil lamp represents fire; a chalice or cup represents water; and a pentacle (a five-pointed star) set in stone or wood represents earth. The magician's cords or measure (cords measuring the exact height and the measurement around the heart and head) represent spirit. The first four of these are considered to be traditional tools of witchcraft, even though in practice it is more common for magicians to use a wand, an athame, or their own hands to direct energy during spell casting. Other element symbols can serve just as well, and some people like to have a feather for air, a flame of any kind for fire, a shell for water, a potted plant for earth, and a crystal for spirit.

What really matters is that the symbols you choose are meaningful to you and bring to mind the nature of the five sacred elements, all of which are drawn on in magic. Symbols of the sun and moon are quite common, too, and can be found in candlesticks or small statues. Planetary and zodiac symbols are also quite popular, though these tend to appear on hangings or altar cloths. Gods and goddesses, if included at all, are depicted in framed pictures, small statues, or in totem form. For example, my favorite representation of Athena, the goddess of wisdom, is a carved wooden owl that I own.

One or two candles are usually in place, in addition to any other candles used in the circle. Their color is generally representative of the ritual being undertaken during any particular circle.

Symbols of the sun and moon

This may be influenced by the season (if celebrating one of the eight festivals), the type of spell that is being cast, or the phase of the moon that is being marked. Many magicians use the altar as a power point and as a center for spell work. It is not necessary to carry out spells on an altar in order to make them successful, but if this aids concentration, which many magicians feel it does, then it is a good idea to build this into your working practices. If at all possible, it is useful to have an altar that you can leave set up following circle work, as this can provide a place where you can leave magical items undisturbed.

Altars can play a part in our spiritual development outside of the context of spell casting, too. A small, personal space specifically dedicated to contemplation and spiritual expression can invoke

Representing the elements

powerful responses and its importance should never be underrated. The simple act of lighting a candle in memory of someone at your own altar can engender more spiritual meaning than an entire requiem performed in a cathedral. Remember—a personal altar is pertinent to your own spiritual path and to the meanings you attribute to whatever you may wish to include.

Creating an altar of your own can be immensely empowering and indeed this should be regarded as integral to your spiritual, as well as your magical, growth. Consider setting aside some space in your home or your garden in order to build your own personal sacred site.

You will be joining a long ancestral line of magicians who have, through the ages, built altars for both sacred and magical purposes! Your altar is a space dedicated to what *you* hold sacred.

39

PART 2

THE SPELL DIRECTORY

HOW TO USE THE SPELL DIRECTORY

The following section of the book, from pages 46–383, contains 150 spells. They have all been placed in sections according to their key themes. The titles of each section are generally self-explanatory, but you are nonetheless advised to read the introduction to the section very carefully to ensure that you are looking in the right place for the right spell.

Once you have identified the spell that seems most suited to your purpose, read through the opening text of the spell carefully, and check the advice under the section titled "Purpose." The "Background" section will offer useful counsel and sometimes include a little of the history or meaning of the symbols or ingredients used. It is important that you read this guidance thoroughly, as your understanding of their purpose contributes toward the energy raised within your spell work. The intent with which you cast a spell is crucial to its working and so is your understanding of its key components.

The ideal "Timing" for each spell is given just below the section that offers some background. This will refer to the moon phase, considered important in magic, and sometimes the most

auspicious day, with some reference made to the planetary influence at work. You are advised to take the advice regarding timing seriously—particularly when it comes to the difference between waxing and waning phases of the moon, which are used for very different purposes. Where a spell refers to the dark moon, this means the phase that astronomers term the new moon. The full moon and half-moon phases are often logged in diaries or on calendars. Many daily national newspapers list the dates of the new, full, and quarter phases of the moon, so until you tune into the rhythms of the moon more instinctively, you should be guided by charts and lists of this type.

As a rough guide, in the Northern Hemisphere a waxing moon is one that is growing from the right side and filling up toward the left. A waning moon shrinks from the right toward the left. You can identify the waxing or waning phase by observing on which side the circular outline of the moon appears. If the regular curve is on the right, this is a waxing (growing) moon; if on the left, this is a waning (shrinking) moon. A waxing half-moon, therefore, is lit on the right-hand side, while a waning half-moon is lit on the left-hand side.

All spells, apart from those that specifically indicate otherwise, should be cast within a circle in accordance with instructions set out on pages 32–35. If you are lacking the correct number or color of candles to cast a full circle, you should be prepared to improvise. This may mean, at a pinch, gathering together a few tea-lights in jars and situating them at the appropriate point of the circle in place of the standard yellow, red, blue, green, and purple candles.

If there are other reasons why you cannot prepare a circle in the way described—for example, if your mobility is impaired either permanently or temporarily then directions to walk around the circle can be safely ignored, and you can visualize the casting of the circle instead. This is not difficult—it simply involves directing the energy you raise with the power of your mind rather than with the power of your feet and arms. The circle will be just as cast as one that has been walked around and directed through an athame or a finger!

You will notice that some of the spells incorporate the use of essential oils. These are very powerful and should be used with a carrier oil when being applied directly to the body, because they could cause irritation. They should not be used during pregnancy or by anybody with hypertension. If you have any serious medical condition, consult a medical advisor before exposing yourself to any of these oils. They are therapeutic, used in the appropriate context, but may be dangerous if used in the presence of people with certain medical conditions.

All candles used as part of a spell should be placed in secure holders and, unless the spell specifically advises otherwise, allowed to burn down in safety, meaning under supervision. This does not apply to the element candles; these can be extinguished at the end of the circle and used again and again. Ensure that all candles are placed away from drafts and drapes or flammable materials. It is advisable to keep a home fire extinguisher in the room in case of any accidents.

Incense sticks and cones should be placed in safe holders that have a "catchment area" in which secreted hot ash can burn out safely. Charcoal disks can be placed in fireproof dishes or censers, but orb censers, which can be swung to distribute the perfume, should be avoided because they often cause accidents. Be aware that whereas sticks and cones cool off quickly, disks take a little longer and should be treated with caution when clearing up.

Many of the ingredients required for the spells are easily obtainable. Remember that some of the herbs used in the spells are toxic and care should be taken in the home to keep them away from children and pets. If you have trouble tracking down some herbs and incense gums, you can order these by mail from suppliers advertised in specialist magazines or order them over the Internet.

With only one exception—and that is made clear in the directions—the spells in the following sections are specifically designed for those who do not have a good deal of magical experience. Cast them with respect and love, and magic will be kind to you.

LOVE AND
PASSION SPELLS

INTRODUCTION TO LOVE AND PASSION SPELLS

Spells for love are probably the most frequently requested in a magician's repertoire. The extent and regularity of demands for love spells are testimony to the emphasis that many of us place on partnerships and the need to feel attractive. There are a wide range and variety of spells in existence, both traditional and modern, which focus on romance and passion. The fact that some of these spells have quite ancient antecedents confirms that love is a perennial concern of humans. It is poignant, and perhaps comforting, to think that this obsession with love gives us common cause with our ancestors who lived thousands of years ago.

In the following pages you will find spells that cover a range of situations. There are spells to enhance and increase your powers of attraction, to signal that you are ready for a new lover to come into your life, or to gain the notice of one to whom you are attracted. Magical recipes for love are not just about new romances, either. This section contains

spells to revive passion, aid communication, and secure harmony within existing relationships. If your current relationship is stuck in a rut, there are plenty of magical recipes here to pep up your love life!

If you feel unsure whether you need a love spell or something else, you could always consult the Health, Beauty, and Well-being section (pages 134–177) for a spell to help build self-esteem or attain inner harmony. Sometimes working on yourself in this way can help you to make important decisions about what you want from a relationship in the future. Remember—loving and accepting ourselves bestows the kind of confidence that makes us attractive as partners.

Before you delve into this section, however, a word of advice is in order. The stereotypical view of love magic is that it will cause the object of your desire to fall hopelessly and inextricably in love with you. This view could not be more mistaken. You cannot change the free will of another by magic. Should you attempt to, it would simply misfire. If you try to use magic to enforce your will, you are failing to advance yourself spiritually, and magic works on the level of spiritual development. In love magic, it is positive action that attains positive outcomes!

ROSE PETAL SPELL
TO SUMMON TRUE LOVE

PURPOSE   To help those who are single and ready for true love. It will send out the magical message that you are now ready to settle down with the right person.

BACKGROUND   Roses have long been symbols of love and physical attraction, their beautiful scent often captured in perfume formulas to create a romantic and erotic ambience. Red roses, in particular, carry the symbolism of true love and passion—essential ingredients in a lasting, loving relationship. In the lexicon of magic and pagan spirituality, roses are sacred to Venus, the ancient Roman goddess of love and sexual passion, and her powerful influence is an essential element of this enchantment.

This spell draws on the ancient symbolism of the rose in order to signal your willingness to welcome a worthy and true lover into your life. In order to ensure that everything does "come up roses" for you, be sure to choose roses with lots of petals, as this spell uses them to create a path of love to lead your true love to your door—and beyond.

HOW TO CAST THE SPELL

TIMING Cast this spell on a waxing moon to draw true love toward you. The best day for this spell is Friday, day of Venus. Work after sunset.

CASTING THE SPELL

1 Cast a circle in accordance with the guidelines on pages 32–35, visualizing a circle that surrounds your entire home.

2 Light the red candle, saying:
Bright Venus, bless this circle well.
Honor and empower my spell.

3 Taking the wineglass in your left hand, hold your right hand palm down over the water, saying:
This water, blessed in purity is blessed by the goddess.
Blessed by me and charged to draw true love to me.
Sprinkle the water over the rose petals, saying:
May the love I receive be as pure as my intent.

4 Take out three petals, and take the remainder in the bowl to your front door. Trail the petals to lead from the doorstep to your bed.

YOU WILL NEED

One red candle, 6–8"/15–20 cm in length

Matches or a lighter

One quarter wineglass of pure spring water

Petals from six red roses, placed in a bowl

One fine sewing needle

One 48"/120 cm length of fine red cotton sewing thread

5 Double-threading the needle, pierce the remaining three petals at their base to form a rose-petal pendant and necklace. Wear it overnight, then keep it under your pillow for one lunar month.

6 Thereafter, place your rose petal charm into a natural water source, and await the appearance of your true love.

CHERRY STONE SPELL
TO ATTRACT A NEW LOVER

PURPOSE To help those looking for a new lover. It sends the signal that you are ready, willing, and able to embark on a new romance.

BACKGROUND The association of cherries with magic and divination goes back a long way. The custom among single people of counting out cherry stones to find out when and if they will marry is still widespread today. In addition, the old children's rhyme "Tinker, Tailor, Soldier, Sailor, Rich Man, Poor Man, Beggar Man, Thief" originally accompanied the counting out of cherry stones as a way of predicting the future. Both practices echo the ancient custom of casting stones or bones for divination purposes.

HOW TO CAST THE SPELL

YOU WILL NEED

One white candle, 6–8"/15–20 cm in length

One red candle, 6–8"/15–20 cm in length

Matches or a lighter

Nine ripe red cherries

One glass of white wine

One teaspoon of clear honey

One 4"/10 cm square piece of red cloth

One 24"/60 cm length of thin cord or twine

TIMING Best cast on a waxing moon, to draw your object toward you. Avoid Saturday, when restrictive Saturn rules. Work after sunset.

CASTING THE SPELL

1 Cast a circle in accordance with the guidelines on pages 32–35.

2 Light the white candle, saying:
Firm of purpose, pure intent.
The same be said of [he/she] who's sent.
Light the red candle, saying:
Passion's fire, heart that's true.
This guiding light I send to you.

In the days before mass-produced cosmetics, staining the lips with cherries was a way to accentuate your attractiveness. This spell carries a little of that association with it.

In magical terms, the cherry also symbolizes partnership, fruitfulness, and a glowing future. This symbolism is so well established that in some cultures another way of saying that life is good is to claim that "life is a bowl of cherries." In this spell the cherry stones represent the qualities your future lover will bring with them, so you will need to keep the stones safe to ensure a romance in your future!

3 Now eat the cherries, and spit the stones into the wine, reciting one of the following words for each stone you spit:
Beauty, Sweetness, Vigor, Youth, Faith, Loyalty, Passion, Truth, Love.

4 Stir the honey into the wine, saying:
Sweetness draw you to me
Love intoxicate thee.

Sip the mixture until only the cherry stones remain.

5 Place the stones in the center of the red cloth, and tie it into a pouch with the cord.

6 Hang the pouch over your bed until your new lover joins you there; then bury the cherry stones in your garden to ensure that love will grow.

APHRODITE'S TALISMAN SPELL
TO INCREASE YOUR POWERS OF ATTRACTION

PURPOSE   To help those who wish to attract the notice of potential lovers.

BACKGROUND   In magic, a talisman is a charm that is charged with the magical potential to perform a particular task. Here, the aim is to magnify the attraction of the wearer in order to gain the attention of potential lovers. In order to charge the talisman successfully in this way, you are asked to concentrate on your most engaging attributes. These qualities may be physical: appealing eyes or lovely hair, for example. They may be

personality traits such as a good sense of humor or a cheerful nature. Anything that you can identify in yourself as an attractive quality is a valid attribute to focus on when working this spell.

One of the symbols used in this spell is sacred to Aphrodite, the Greek goddess of love, counterpart of the Roman Venus. The symbol (a circle with a conjoined cross at the bottom) is still used in astronomy and astrology to symbolize the planet Venus, the celestial body associated with love deities for thousands of years.

HOW TO CAST THE SPELL

TIMING Work on a waxing moon, preferably close to the full moon, and if possible on a Friday, which is sacred to Venus. Avoid Saturday—Saturn's day.

CASTING THE SPELL

1 Cast a circle in accordance with the guidelines on pages 32–35.

2 Light the incense first; then light the candle, saying:

I invoke thee, star of the evening
Rising in beauty from the sea
Shine on the beauty within me.

3 Using the point of the nail, inscribe the sign for Aphrodite on one side of the copper disk. On the other side inscribe your first initial.

4 Hold the disk between your palms, envisaging your most attractive attributes, and charge the talisman by chanting the following at least nine times:

As the serpent sheds her skin
Shines the beauty that's within.

5 Show the talisman to the four elements—air, earth, fire, and water. Pass it through the incense smoke; pass it through the candle flame; sprinkle it with water; and breathe hard on it.

 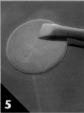

YOU WILL NEED

One stick of ylang-ylang incense

One green candle, 6–8"/15–20 cm in length

Matches or a lighter

One sharp nail

One small copper disk, perforated for wearing

One teaspoon of spring water

One 24"/60 cm length of fine cord for wearing

6 By the time the "serpent" of the rhyme—the green candle—has shed its skin by burning down, the talisman will be ready to wear by attaching the cord.

MAGIC MIRROR SPELL
TO VISIT A LOVER IN DREAMS

PURPOSE   To draw your lover's thoughts to you or, to send comfort when apart.

BACKGROUND   Mirrors have a special place in magical lore, and they are used
in many traditions the world over. Their ability to reflect three dimensions on a flat
surface, and to magnify and distort, has earned them the reputation of being powerful
amplifiers of magical energy.

There is an old superstition that the mirror has the mystical ability to hold our
"soul" in the reflection it provides. In this spell you will send your own reflection—
to enter the dreams of the person whose thoughts you wish to turn toward you.

HOW TO CAST THE SPELL

YOU WILL NEED

One jasmine incense stick or cone

One white or silver candle, 6–8"/15–20 cm
in length

Matches or a lighter

One mirror, full or half-length, covered
with a black cloth

One large bowl of spring water

TIMING Best carried out at full moon, after
dark. Any day will suffice, with Monday
(moon day) being the most auspicious.

CASTING THE SPELL

1 Cast a circle in accordance with the
guidelines on pages 32–35.

2 Light the incense.

3 Light the candle, saying:
I call upon the powers of the full moon
Sun's light reflected in the night sky
To empower my spell and carry my likeness
To light my lover's dreams in the darkness.

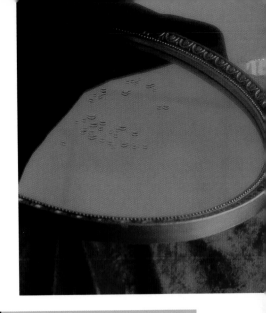

This "thought form" has a limited life span and purpose, so don't worry that you will be sending out a likeness of yourself to take on a life of its own or that you are abandoning a piece of your soul!

To cast this spell is to set out on something of a psychic adventure; you can use it to comfort an absent lover or to ascertain, by their reaction to their dreams, how serious they are about your relationship. Mirror magic can bring you closer to your beloved but should not be used once a relationship is broken.

4 Uncover the mirror, and concentrate on fixing your reflected image in your mind's eye.

5 Sprinkle a little water from the bowl onto your mirror image, saying:
I name thee [insert name of choice— not your own].
Then, speaking to your reflection, raise your arms and intone the following:
[Name], I give you life for one moon only To go to [lover's name] in [his/her] dreams To put them in mind of me So mote it be.

6 Cover the mirror immediately and snuff out the candle.

WATER WISH
A POWERFUL REQUEST FOR LOVE TO COME INTO YOUR LIFE

PURPOSE To help those who are serious about a new love match.

BACKGROUND Of the five sacred elements, water is the one most associated with love. In the material sense, water is one of the most powerful forces on the planet. It has the ability to sustain life or engulf it. Little wonder, then, that its magical reputation is built on its twin properties of subtlety and power. Deep, loving relationships draw on both qualities, and love, it can be argued, shares water's claim to being among the most powerful energies in the world.

The element of water symbolizes our emotional self and the subconscious and is often invoked for psychic work and dreaming. In magic, to wish on water is to invoke all of the delicate nuances and powerful attributes of its material and its symbolic meaning. Those who go to water to look for love should brace themselves for a surprisingly powerful response—one that may creep in quietly like lapping lakeside water but carry the emotional force of a tsunami!

This spell work is performed outdoors by a body of natural water, be it ocean, sea, river, or lake.

HOW TO CAST THE SPELL

YOU WILL NEED

One ripe apple

One penknife

One thick embroidery needle

One teaspoon of sugar

One blue candle of any type

TIMING Test this spell on a waxing moon, on Monday, in honor of the moon, queen of tides. If the water is tidal, cast when the tide is incoming and near turning.

CASTING THE SPELL

1 Find a safe, private place by the waterside.

2 Breathe deeply, relax, and center yourself.

3 Cut the apple in half horizontally to reveal the five-pointed star at its core. Cupping one half in each hand, look out on the water, and intone the following nine times:

> *By the water in my blood*
> *By the rivers of the earth*
> *By the tides of the moon*
> *Bring me one who knows my worth.*

4 Put aside the half-apple in your right hand, and on the other inscribe an equilateral downward pointing triangle (the symbol for water), the letters of your first name, and the shape of a waxing crescent moon, using the needle.

5 Pour on half a teaspoon of sugar, and cast it as far into the water as you can. Place the remaining sugar on the other half-apple, and eat it.

6 Once home, light the blue candle to honor your wish. Allow the candle to burn down safely.

LOVE OIL
A BLEND TO ATTRACT POTENTIAL LOVERS

PURPOSE   To help those who are looking for loving fun as well as those who are looking for romance with a touch of spice.

BACKGROUND   Most seasoned magicians become aware, at some point in their careers, of legends concerning oil blends that attract the most reluctant of suitors and turn the shyest wallflower wanton. Such oils remain myth rather than reality. However, certain fragrance blends have observably positive effects on the mood and state of mind of those who are exposed to them.

HOW TO CAST THE SPELL

YOU WILL NEED

One red candle, 6–8"/15–20 cm in length

One blue candle, 6–8"/15–20 cm in length

Matches or a lighter

Thirty drops of almond carrier oil

Four drops each of cinnamon, geranium, and orange essential oils

One teaspoon of water

One oil burner with tea-light

One sterile oil bottle with a lid

Four sterile droppers

TIMING Cast on a waxing moon to attract attention, on any day of the week. Friday, day of the love planet Venus, is the most powerful.

CASTING THE SPELL

1 Cast a circle in accordance with the guidelines on pages 32–35.

2 Light the red candle, then the blue candle, saying:

I invoke the spirit of water
I invoke the spirit of fire
To turn interest to attraction
And attraction to desire
An' it harm none.

This is useful to note in the case of wishing to attract romantic attention, as some essential oils are noted for helping fancy turn into love. Blending oils that promote emotional engagement with those that invoke sensuality can have some interesting results. The blend employed in this case carries some powerfully evocative qualities. In this spell, cinnamon, associated with the sun, is used to fire up the passions, while geranium, which emits powerful love-vibes, is deployed to attract affection. Essential oil of orange is used to attract love—and to make the wearer delectable.

3 Using a different dropper for each oil, place five drops of almond and three drops each of cinnamon, geranium, and orange, along with the water, into the oil burner dish.

4 Place thirty drops of almond oil into the empty bottle. Add to this one drop each of cinnamon, geranium, and orange; stir and seal.

5 Light the burner. Breathing in the fragrance, sit in the center of the circle, then envisage an attractive figure walking toward you and see yourself opening your arms in welcome.

6 When you are ready, dab some oil from the bottle on your pulse points, and extinguish the burner flame. Wear the blend daily until it is all used.

SNAKESKIN SPELL
TO ENHANCE THE LIBIDO AND PEP UP YOUR LOVE LIFE

PURPOSE To revive a decreased libido and to send out sexual vibes to appropriate interested parties. It is suitable for those already in a relationship and for those who are actively seeking passionate liaisons.

BACKGROUND Snakeskin is among the more arcane of magical ingredients recommended in this book. Traditionally, it has been used in spells and charms to promote sexual potency. Apart from the obvious phallic symbolism of the snake, there is also an ancient symbolic connection between serpents and female sexuality, so this magical charm is suitable for both sexes.

   The skin shedded by a serpent carries powerful spiritual connotations. In particular, the ability of the snake to renew its appearance and to slough off the old, spent skin

represents transformation and vigor. This is directly relevant to the aims of the spell: to reenergize, and thus transform, your libido so that your sexually charged attractions encourage the amorous attentions of a present or prospective lover.

   Sometimes sloughed snakeskin is found in the wild, but if you are a city-dweller, you may be able to strike a deal with a local pet store in order to obtain one.

HOW TO CAST THE SPELL

TIMING Test this spell on an early waxing crescent moon for maximum effect. Any day of the week is suitable, but Tuesday, day of energetic Mars, is favored.

CASTING THE SPELL

1 Cast a circle in accordance with the guidelines on pages 32–35.

2 Light the incense, then the candle, saying:

I light this fire
To honor the snake
That gifted its skin
For passion's sake.

3 Open the snakeskin out, and spoon the nutmeg, pepper, chili, and soil into the middle.

4 Roll the snakeskin into a packet to contain the ingredients, and fasten it crosswise with the ribbon.

5 Hold the snakeskin packet out toward the candle flame, and sprinkle the ash onto it, saying:

Out of the ashes
Comes a fire
Out of the serpent
Comes desire.

YOU WILL NEED

One vanilla incense cone or stick

One red candle, 6–8"/15–20 cm in length

Matches or a lighter

One shed snakeskin

One 24"/60 cm length of thin red ribbon

One teaspoon of nutmeg

One teaspoon of diced red pepper

One teaspoon of chili powder

One teaspoon of fresh soil

One pinch of ashes from an open fire

6 Place the snakeskin charm under your pillow, where it should stay for one moon cycle; then bury it in earth.

CATNIP SPELL
TO ATTRACT AND PROMOTE PLAYFULNESS AND PASSION

PURPOSE   To encourage a partner to exercise their imagination in bed. Ideal for those in established relationships wishing to spice up their love life.

BACKGROUND   The plant *Nepeta cataria*, better known as catmint or catnip, is noted for the amazing effect it has on domestic cats. Magical correspondences for catnip include the element of water and the planet Venus— both associated in magic with love. This association, along with the wild effect it has on the most sedate of pets, makes it ideal for turning your lover from an absolute pussycat into a tiger. A few teaspoons of the chopped, dried herb sewn into a cloth sachet soon has puss frolicking and rolling about the floor in ecstasy. The aim in this spell is to get your lover to do the same by loosening up some inhibitions and letting their amorous imagination run riot!

Catnip is sacred to Bast, the Egyptian cat goddess, hence the invocation to her at the beginning of this spell.

HOW TO CAST THE SPELL

YOU WILL NEED

One oil burner with a tea-light

Nine drops of ylang-ylang essential oil

One teaspoon of water

One green candle, 6–8"/15–20 cm
in length

One red candle, 6–8"/15–20 cm in length

Matches or a lighter

Two tablespoons of dried catnip

Two 3"/7.5 cm square pieces of
cheesecloth

One 30"/75 cm length of red thread

One sewing needle

TIMING Spell casting should coincide with
a waxing or full moon and take place on
Friday, day of Venus and of Freya, a Norse
goddess who rides in a chariot pulled
by cats.

CASTING THE SPELL

1 Cast a circle in accordance with the
guidelines on pages 32–35.

2 Put the essential oil and water in the
oil burner. Light the tea-light, then the
candles, saying:

I call upon Bast, lady of cats
To witness, bless, and empower
   my charm.

3 Place the catnip
in your right palm,
and cover it with
your left. Visualize
yourself and your
lover making love
in a way that you
would like them to
initiate. Hold onto
the feeling that this
evokes, and direct
that energy into
the catnip.

4 Place the catnip
in the center of one
of the cheesecloth
pieces, and place
the other on top.
Sew all of the edges
together firmly with the thread doubled,
and fasten off.

5 Pass the catnip sachet through the oil
burner's steam nine times and then over
the candles dedicated to Bast.

6 Keep the sachet in the bed you
share with your lover for at least one
moon cycle.

PURPLE CANDLE SPELL
FOR RED-HOT PASSION

PURPOSE To help those who desire a passionate encounter without the need for a long-lasting relationship. It is most suitable for confident singles who are not looking for commitment.

BACKGROUND Traditionally, the color purple is said to raise energy vibrations and magnify the power raised during the casting of a spell. In magical terms, it is seen as the color of spirit, the fifth sacred element, which represents connection. This spell seeks to obtain connection of the more physical kind and so draws on the earthier aspects represented by this hue as well as the powerful vibes it sends out.

 HOW TO CAST THE SPELL

YOU WILL NEED

Sixty drops of grapeseed oil

Three drops each of patchouli and ylang-ylang essential oils

Three sterile droppers

One sterile oil bottle

One purple candle, 6–8"/15–20 cm in length

Matches or a lighter

One open lily or orchid flower head

One acorn, the cup intact

One small drawstring pouch

TIMING Cast on any day of the week, after dark and after moonrise on the night before the full moon.

CASTING THE SPELL

1 Perform this spell naked.

2 Cast a circle in accordance with the guidelines on pages 32–35.

3 Using separate droppers for each oil, place the amounts in the empty bottle, and stir. Anoint with a little oil, in the following order, your thighs, lower abdomen, breasts, and throat.

The Purple Candle Spell has achieved a certain notoriety among magicians, due to its erotic effects. The version included here is the most straightforward and should be treated with respect. Some magicians disapprove of spells to attain sexual gratification, but then the same people also disapprove of sexual gratification outside of a committed relationship. This magician takes the view that sexual desire is a need as natural as hunger or thirst, so the only warning here is to be sure that this is what you want, and to act responsibly; and needless to say, with safety in mind.

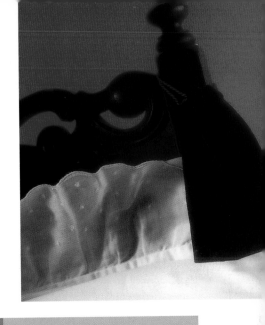

4 Smear the candle with oil, avoiding the wick, beginning at the bottom with upward strokes, then from top to bottom, stopping halfway. Repeat three times.

5 Kneeling, anoint the flower and acorn, saying:

As I anoint thee now with oil
Thou shalt anoint me with thy pleasure
Draw unto me with sweet desire
And taste a passion without measure.

6 Light the candle, and leave it to burn down completely. Seal the flower and acorn in the pouch. Hang it on your bedpost until your wish has come to pass; then bury it in the earth.

FAITH BRACELET
TO SEAL A LOVE PLEDGE

PURPOSE To help lovers who wish to endorse a declaration of fidelity magically.

BACKGROUND Berries are traditional ingredients of love pledges, perhaps because they bear both the nourishment of fruit and the seed of future fruition. In this spell, the berries cover and effectively "house" a blood pledge, while bringing their own magical properties into play to make it fully effective. If you are squeamish about obtaining blood, then you and your partner can use saliva— although this is not as romantic as the version outlined below! Use sterile needles and take care not to let any wounds or abrasions (including the pinprick you make for this spell) come into contact with a partner's blood, for health and safety reasons.

Here, holly berries are used to represent fidelity; juniper berries protect your pledge; and mistletoe's fertility connection enables your relationship to grow. Placed together in this way, these berries signify a serious commitment to be faithful and loyal to to each other, and accepting of positive change.

HOW TO CAST THE SPELL

YOU WILL NEED

Three sterile fine sewing needles

Ten each of dried holly, juniper, and mistletoe berries

One 30"/75 cm length of black thread

One white candle, 6–8"/15–20 cm in length

One red candle, 6–8"/15–20 cm in length

One green candle, 6–8"/15–20 cm in length

Matches or a lighter

One pot with a lid, for needle disposal

Two adhesive dressings

TIMING Cast on a waxing or full moon, on Saturday, day of serious-minded Saturn.

CASTING THE SPELL

1 Cast a circle in accordance with the guidelines on pages 32–35.

2 Say together:
We are present in this circle
To seal our love and commitment
To each other
May vows made here
Hold for one year.

3 Thread a needle, doubling the thread and fastening it with a large knot. Using another needle, prick your thumb, then

squeeze out a drop of blood and smear it onto the thread. Dress the "wound," and dispose of the needle used to extract blood immediately.

4 Get your partner to do the same, using the other sterile needle onto another part of the thread, avoiding the blood placed there by you.

5 Sew five holly berries each onto the thread, and light the white candle, saying:
That we keep faith.
Do the same with the juniper berries, and light the red candle, saying:
That faith holds true.
Repeat the process with the mistletoe berries, and light the green candle, saying:
That love flourishes under this pledge.

6 Tie the berries into a circle and fasten it off, then hang it over your hearth for a year and a day.

CHILI PEPPER SPELL
TO REVIVE PASSION IN A RELATIONSHIP

PURPOSE To help when passion has faded in an otherwise loving and committed relationship.

BACKGROUND Occasionally, magical symbolism is very literal, and this spell is one where the theory matches the reality in a very immediate and palpable way! Chili peppers are noted for their hot taste as well as their ability to heat up physically those who dine on them. This makes them ideal ingredients for a spell that seeks to put the heat back into a relationship where passion has cooled of late.

HOW TO CAST THE SPELL

YOU WILL NEED

One cinnamon incense cone or stick in a holder

One red candle, 6–8"/15–20 cm in length

Matches or a lighter

Six red and two green fresh chili peppers

One strand of your partner's hair

One 12"/30 cm length of fine red ribbon

One 36"/90 cm length of florist wire

One sharp kitchen knife

Scissors, to cut wire

TIMING Cast on a waxing moon, on Friday to bring Venus's love of pleasure into play, or alternatively, on Tuesday to invoke the impulsive energy of Mars.

CASTING THE SPELL

1 Cast a circle in accordance with the guidelines on pages 32–35.

2 Light the incense, then the candle, saying:
Element of fire
Raise [his/her] desire
Flame grow longer
Heat grow stronger.

70

Here, green and red chili peppers represent different aspects of passion—respectively, sexual desire within the individual and passion for the other partner. The chilies that remain once the charm is completed should be used to prepare a spicy dish for your lover—for example a lively chili or hot curry—as an overture, perhaps, to a romantic evening! At any rate, this spell should certainly pep up your love life.

Take care not to get any chili juice near your eyes or any other delicate membranes, as the burning can be very painful.

3 With the knife, make a slit on the side of a green chili. Place your partner's hair inside, and reseal the chili, binding it with the ribbon—this is the "torso."

4 Thread five red chilies with florist wire, leaving 1 inch/2.5 cm of wire protruding at one end of each. Thread the beribboned chili using two lengths of wire, which should join at the thin end and emerge separately at the thicker end—this is for the "legs."

5 Join the four red chili "limbs" to the torso, and select the fattest red chili to secure as a "head." Hold your doll before the candle flame to energize it.

6 Keep the doll under your bed until passion is restored. Cook the remainder of the chili peppers in a spicy dish for your lover.

CLADDAGH SPELL
TO SECURE PEACE AND CONCORD IN A RELATIONSHIP

PURPOSE   To bring peace and harmony to a loving relationship that occasionally strays into stormy and volatile territory.

BACKGROUND   The tradition of the claddagh is quite well known. It is the symbol of two hands clasped around a heart, and with a crown, denoting friendship and loving understanding. This symbol, which originated in Ireland, is often seen in items of jewelry, especially rings, and both lovers and friends buy them for each other. In many cultures, clasping hands represents the end of enmity, or assurance that friendly approaches are being made, as in the custom of the handshake. In this spell, the clasped hands signal the desire to bring peace to a relationship undergoing a difficult period.

Before casting this spell, it is important that you give some thought to why a relationship is becoming unsettled. If your partner is displaying signs of a dangerous and violent temper, magic is not going to resolve this problem for you. Seek help and advice, and get out before it is too late. If this is not the case, and you find that you are simply touchy with each other, perhaps some relationship counseling will help—as will this spell.

HOW TO CAST THE SPELL

TIMING Put this spell to the test at the full moon, on any day of the week.

CASTING THE SPELL

1 Cast a circle in accordance with the guidelines on pages 32–35.

2 Light the candle, saying:
Blessed be the full moon
And the high tide
Enmity washed away
Harmony washed in.

3 Place your right palm down on one sheet of paper, and use the pen to outline it on the page. Now draw an outline, freehand, of what you think the outline of your partner's left hand looks like, and write their initial on the palm.

4 Placing your right palm on your imprint and your left on your partner's, chant the following nine times:
Let there be peace and harmony
As I will it, so mote it be.

5 Clasp your own hands together, palm to palm, saying:
May what I have in my hands take root.
Place the two outlines palm to palm, and fold them five times.

YOU WILL NEED

One pale blue candle, 6–8"/15–20 cm in length

Matches or a lighter

One ink pen with black ink

Two 8"/20 cm square pieces of plain white paper

One large potato

One sharp kitchen knife

One 24"/60 cm length of fine red cord

6 Cut the potato in half and scoop it out, then replace the insides with the folded paper. Bind the halves together with the cord, and bury them in earth immediately.

CHAIN SPELL
TO AID COMMUNICATION IN A RELATIONSHIP

PURPOSE To encourage partners in a relationship to be more open and communicative with each other.

BACKGROUND An easy flow of communication is important in any relationship. Difficulties in this direction can lead to misunderstandings, which in turn may cause arguments or bad feeling. Having a partner who is clearly troubled, but unable to communicate their worries, can also be upsetting. This spell calls on the element of air to encourage the openness and clarity that is found in good, strong relationships.

HOW TO CAST THE SPELL

YOU WILL NEED

One cone or stick of lavender incense

One yellow candle, 6–8"/15–20 cm in length

Matches or a lighter

One feather quill pen

One bottle of green ink

One package of paper chain decorations

TIMING Work on a waxing moon to bring ease of communication, on a Wednesday, sacred to Mercury the messenger.

CASTING THE SPELL

1 Cast a circle in accordance with the guidelines on pages 32–35.

2 Light the incense, then the candle, saying:
Element of air, carry my prayer.

3 With the quill pen, write your name on one side of a paper chain strip and your partner's name on one side of another paper chain strip.

In this spell a symbol of air doubles as a practical magical tool: a feather made into a writing quill, with the use of a sharp knife and a little experimentation. Practice first on a few feathers, and rehearse your quill-writing skills before casting the spell.

The "paper chains" used here are thin paper strips, with adhesive at one end, that you thread through each preceding link to form a chain. If you cannot obtain ready-made "paper chains," you should use plain paper strips approximately 4" x 1"/10 cm x 2.5 cm, and glue in place of adhesive.

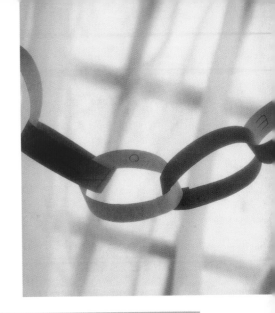

4 Using one side of the paper only, one word to a strip, write the following seven separate strips: *Speak, Listen, Look, Touch, Give, Receive, Trust*. Allow them to dry. Fasten the strip with your name into a loop with the writing side inward.

5 Thread through the seven strips in the order outlined above, fastening them into links to make a chain. To the final strip, link the strip bearing your partner's name.

6 Hang the paper chain over the window of the room in which you spend the most waking time together, so that the light coming in shines on your paper chain.

SHOE CHARM SPELL
TO GAIN THE NOTICE OF SOMEONE TO WHOM YOU ARE ATTRACTED

PURPOSE To obtain the attention of someone who has taken your fancy.

BACKGROUND This is one of the rare love-related spells in this book that is designed to work on a specific person. As already stated, you cannot make someone fall in love with you, and as a rule spells for attraction should not be aimed at a particular person. However, the ethical rules of magic are not being disregarded here, as this charm is designed, not to attract someone to you, but to grab their attention and so offer them the chance of regarding you as a potential partner.

The Shoe Charm is a very old magical device, based on herbal and floral lore and sympathetic magic. You are expected to gather the ingredients by hand for this spell, and it helps if you, or an understanding friend, have a garden. Otherwise a quick visit to a garden center will enable you to buy the various potted varieties of the stipulated flowers and herbs.

HOW TO CAST THE SPELL

YOU WILL NEED

One white candle, 6–8"/15–20 cm
in length

Matches or a lighter

Two mint leaves

Petals from two pansy flowers

Two borage leaves

Two sprigs of marjoram

One small earthenware bowl

TIMING Work on an early waxing moon to
draw attention to you, on any day but a
Saturday.

CASTING THE SPELL

1 Cast a circle in accordance with the
guidelines on pages 32–35.

2 Light the white candle, saying:
I invoke the lady of the moon
To make me shine in [name of
person]'s eyes
I invoke the evening star
To form me in beauty before [her/him]
I invoke the morning sun
To warm [name]'s heart toward me
I invoke this holy flame
To light [her/his] way to me
So mote it be.

3 Place the mint into the earthenware
bowl, saying:
Draw [her/his] eyes to my presence.
Add the pansy petals, saying:
Ease [her/his] heart when I am near.
Put in the borage, saying:
An [he/she] like me, give [her/him]
courage.
Add the marjoram, saying:
Joy to [her/him] that holds me dear.

4 Place the bowl and ingredients in open
moonlight for one hour.

5 Secrete the ingredients inside your
shoes the next time you are with the
object of your affection. Wear them until
the day after the full moon.

6 If they have not expressed interest
within one moon cycle, cease to consider
them as a potential love interest.

CRYSTAL SPELL
TO HELP YOU CHOOSE BETWEEN LOVERS

PURPOSE To help you come to a decision when there is more than one suitor, and it is time to make your choice.

BACKGROUND If there are two people contending to share your life, deciding which is the better prospective partner can be tough going. We often take a liking to different people for different reasons, all of which can be equally valid as far as our emotions are concerned. This can make it hard to decide which relationship to keep and which to let go.

   In truth, you already know the solution to the problem, and this lies deep within your subconscious. After casting the spell, the answer will reveal itself to you in your dreams, which often hold clues to the inner wisdom that is there to guide us whenever we are prepared to listen.

   The tumbled stones you are asked to use are available in many rock and crystal stores and New Age outlets. You are asked to select a stone for each of your two suitors, matching their properties or appearance to the qualities of the person they are chosen to represent.

HOW TO CAST THE SPELL

TIMING Cast this spell as near to the first crescent of the waxing moon as possible, on any day of the week.

CASTING THE SPELL

1 Cast a circle in accordance with the guidelines on pages 32–35.

2 Light the incense and the candle.

3 Close your eyes, and taking your time, imagine walking downstream in a small, shallow river which gradually gets deeper and flows more strongly. When the river is above your head, swim underwater toward its source. When the waters are completely dark, open your eyes.

4 Take the rose quartz, and place it in the goblet, saying:

May my heart know my heart.

Place one of the other stones into the goblet, saying:

My heart knows [name of suitor].

Repeat this with the other stone.

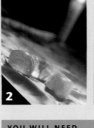

YOU WILL NEED

One jasmine cone or incense stick

One blue candle, 6–8"/15–20 cm in length

Matches or a lighter

One small tumbled rose quartz

One goblet, chalice, or wine glass

Two tumbled stones to represent your suitors

One bottle of fresh spring water

5 Fill the goblet with springwater. Before bedtime, drink half the water. Keep it at your bedside until the day after the full moon, after which pour away the water and secrete the stones under your pillow. The answer will come in your dreams within a month.

PILLOW CHARM
TO DREAM OF YOUR TRUE LOVE

PURPOSE To catch a glimpse of your true love in your dreams.

BACKGROUND There are many old spells and charms whose object is to reveal the identity of your true love. Additionally, there are a number of interesting folk beliefs concerning actions to be taken at propitious times of year, superstitions that are distortions of earlier magical wisdom. Among some of these are kernels of magical knowledge gifted to us by our ancestors. This spell, which will reveal your true love to you, draws on this ancestral knowledge.

 ## HOW TO CAST THE SPELL

YOU WILL NEED

One pale blue or silver candle, 6–8"/15–20 cm in length

Matches or a lighter

One half-length mirror

One ripe and flawless apple

One sharp black-handled knife

One black cloth to cover the mirror

Mortar and pestle

Two 3"/7.5 cm square pieces of cheesecloth stitched together on three sides

One 8"/20 cm length of fine blue ribbon

TIMING The spell is cast in two parts, the first to take place on the day of the dark moon at true midnight (exactly between sunset and sunrise), the second to take place at true midnight on the night of the full moon.

CASTING THE SPELL
PART ONE

1 Cast a circle in accordance with the guidelines on pages 32–35.

2 Light the candle; then address your reflection in the mirror thus:

Placed out of moonlight but in the mirror's seeming
Reflect my true love's secrets into my dreaming.

The means by which you will "see" your true love is in dreams. Our dreams frequently offer hints about our life's journey, clues which, when pieced together, provide vital information as to the correct path to take. This magical working will prompt dreams in which symbols, puns, and maybe even literal images will serve to reveal the identity of your true love. If these do not point to someone you presently know, then they will help you to recognize your true love when that person does appear. Keep watching the horizon!

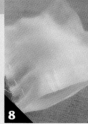

3 Peel the apple in one continuous piece; then, looking into the mirror, toss it over your shoulder.

4 Cover the mirror and extinguish the candle, then place the apple to dry near a source of heat.

PART TWO

5 Cast a circle in accordance with the guidelines on pages 32–35.

6 Light the candle.

7 Using the mortar and pestle, grind down the dried apple peel.

8 Place it in the cheesecloth bag. Tie the bag with the ribbon, and place it under your pillow. Make careful note of unusual dreams over the following two weeks.

LOVE SACHET
TO DRAW LOVE AND AFFECTION TOWARD YOU

PURPOSE   To help those who feel the need of love and support around them, whether from a lover, family, or friends.

BACKGROUND   Just as there are many forms of love, there are many different types of love spell. This one is geared toward drawing love and affection toward you from a variety of sources, including relatives, friends, or colleagues. We all need to feel loved, especially at times when we are not feeling as strong or confident as we would wish to. This touch of magic encourages people around you to let you know you are

HOW TO CAST THE SPELL

YOU WILL NEED

Two teaspoons of water

Six drops of geranium essential oil

One oil burner with a tea-light

Matches or a lighter

One pink candle, 6–8"/15–20 cm in length

Three drops of rose water and violet water

Cheesecloth bag 2"/5 cm square

One small piece of absorbent cotton

Six pink rose petals

Six hyacinth flower heads

One teaspoon of dried orris root

One 30"/75 cm length of fine black cord

TIMING Perform this spell on a waxing moon to draw affection, and on a Friday, sacred to love deities.

CASTING THE SPELL

1 Cast a circle in accordance with the guidelines on pages 32–35.

2 Place the water and geranium oil in the burner dish and light it.

3 Light the candle, saying:
Loving spirits, heed me
When the need is near me
Smother all affliction
With heartfelt affection.

held in affection. It also works by encouraging you to love yourself, something you may have forgotten to do if you have been too busy or too blue to remember. The Love Sachet is stocked with ingredients traditionally associated with love and affection, including violet and rose. Whilst roses are more popularly associated with love, violets draw forth amity. Rose water is an acceptable substitute for the prohibitively expensive rose absolut and is available from many herbalists and general stores. Similarly, violet water is often more easily available than violet essential oil.

4 Drop the rose water and violet water onto the absorbent cotton, and place it in the cheesecloth bag. Add to it the rose petals, the hyacinth, and the orris powder.

5 Holding the sachet between your palms, intone the following chant to charge it with power and energy:

> All will be well
> All will be well
> All is completed
> Under love's spell.

Experienced magicians will feel the energies peak, but if you are new to circle work, ensure that the chant is repeated at least twenty-one times.

6 Fasten the bag with the cord, and make it into a pendant. Wear your love sachet about your person at all times.

LOVE PHILTER
A LOVE POTION TO ENHANCE YOUR POWERS OF ATTRACTION

PURPOSE To help those who are single and wish to make themselves attractive to others.

BACKGROUND The stereotypical—and inaccurate—concept of a love philter is of a mysterious and potent liquid that is slipped into another person's drink in order to bedazzle them. This love potion is drunk by the person who wishes to become more attractive. Drinking it activates your most attractive qualities, and when these are emphasized, you are naturally more attractive to others. It is also chock-full of healthy, wholesome ingredients, which variously offer a vitamin boost or aid the digestion, so even if it doesn't exactly turn you into a smoldering Morgan le Fay type, it has the added bonus of lending youa healthy glow!

The word *philter* simply denotes "a magical liquid," and this spell creates a tea brewed from magical ingredients. Prior to casting the circle, you may need to grind the whole dried mint leaves and the dried apple pieces yourself. The base for the philter is blended in the circle and empowered by the spell work you do within it, but should be drunk once a day until the mixture is all gone.

HOW TO CAST THE SPELL

YOU WILL NEED

One green candle, 6–8"/15–20 cm in length

One white candle, 6–8"/15–20 cm in length

Matches or a lighter

Mortar and pestle

Three heaping tablespoons of ground dried mint

Three heaping tablespoons of ground dried apple

One tablespoon of dried marjoram

One tablespoon of rose petals

One large box or chest for holding tea

TIMING Cast this spell between a waxing half-moon and full moon, on any day except Saturday.

CASTING THE SPELL

1 Cast a circle in accordance with the guidelines on pages 32–35.

2 Light the green candle, saying:
For that which is without.
Light the white candle, saying:
For that which is within.

3 Grind all the listed ingredients together, chanting as you do:
Everything that I am I will be
Everything changes from within me.

4 Place the blend in the caddy and seal it. Then, holding it in both hands, close your eyes and visualize yourself entering a room directly opposite a full-length mirror. See yourself as others might see you: bright, attractive, with a kind smile, nice eyes, and so on.

5 When the vision is fixed in your mind, open the caddy, and on your next out-breath, breathe the power of that vision into the mixture. Seal it immediately.

6 When you wish to have a cup of tea, pour 8 fl oz/225 ml of boiling water onto two teaspoons of the mixture, and leave it to brew; then pour it through a strainer, and add honey to taste.

HERBAL RING CHARM
TO DISCOVER IF A LOVER IS DECEITFUL

PURPOSE   To uncover a lover's deceit.

BACKGROUND   When we have cause to doubt someone in whom we have placed our trust, it is easy to fantasize about a foolproof method of discovering the truth. But in spite of the invention of lie detector machines and "truth serums," there is no guarantee that what a person tells us is genuine. In love, this uncertainty can be torment, as we risk a great deal emotionally when we make ourselves vulnerable and

HOW TO CAST THE SPELL

YOU WILL NEED

One censer with a charcoal disk

Matches or a lighter

Frankincense grains

One black candle, 6–8"/15–20 cm in length

Three sewing needles

One white candle, 6–8"/15–20 cm in length

One white tea-light

One large bundle of lady's mantle

One large bundle of yarrow

A long length of blue woolen yarn

TIMING Cast this spell on the day of the dark moon, after sunset. This spell takes some time, so you will need to ensure privacy for at least 2–3 hours.

CASTING THE SPELL

1 Cast a circle in accordance with the guidelines on pages 32–35.

2 Light the charcoal disk, and sprinkle on frankincense. Light the black candle.

3 Heat the point of a needle in the flame, and stick the point into the side of the white candle, ½ in/1 cm from the wick, saying:
   Truth.

trust someone. This spell is designed to help the truth to come to light and is based on a very old charm traditionally applied to uncover a wrongdoer.

It is a powerful spell, and all the consequences of magical misuse apply. Cast it inappropriately and it will bring out truths about yourself that you may not be happy to have uncovered. So use this spell only in need and where you have genuine reason to seek its aid. On a practical note, if you are having doubts early in a relationship, this may be a signal to end it.

Repeat with a second needle, spacing it away from the first, saying:
Proof.
Repeat with the third needle, saying:
Right.
Light the white candle, saying:
Light.

Using the first needle that falls, inscribe on the tea-light the rune daeg—two even triangles with one point touching.

4 Place the herbs in a ring approximately 12"/30 cm in diameter around the tea-light, and light the candle, saying:
Fire lies under stone
Truth lies under bone.

5 When the rune is no longer visible, using the wool, gather the herbs into a ringed garland 4"/10 cm in diameter.

6 Hang the ring in a window so that it casts a shadow in the room. The truth will come to light within a moon cycle.

GARLAND SPELL
TO KEEP LOVE EVERGREEN

PURPOSE To bless a strong relationship and to keep it fresh.

BACKGROUND The symbolism of plants is frequently drawn on in magic, and no wonder, as some of the first magical—and medical—ingredients known to humans were found growing in the ground around us. In nineteenth-century England, there was a concerted effort to collect and compile a comprehensive list of the symbolic language of flowers, and this included some genuinely ancient meanings. However, the magical associations and properties of some plants have been known for a great deal longer, and this is true of the plants used in this spell.

In the vocabulary of plants, holly represents fidelity, ivy constancy, and yew endurance. Holly, or *tinne* as it is known in Gaelic, is also a protective herb and is said to guard against bad temper—a bonus for the well-being of any relationship! Ivy, or gort, encourages cooperation and mutual aid, while yew, or ioho, promotes the resilience and growth a relationship needs to endure through life's many changes.

This magical blessing garland is ideal to offer as an anniversary gift to a couple who have been together for some time.

HOW TO CAST THE SPELL

TIMING This spell should be cast on a waxing moon, and on a Friday, the day sacred to Venus, friend of lovers.

CASTING THE SPELL

1 Cast a circle in accordance with the guidelines on pages 32–35.

2 Light the candle, saying:
I light a candle to shine upon
This deed
That the light of the evening star
Shine upon [names of couple].

3 Divide the holly, ivy, and yew into smaller sprigs, and insert them stem first into the oasis, intertwining all three in a regular pattern.

4 When the oasis is completely invisible and the garland is covered in greenery, place it before the candle.

5 Hold the glass of water in your left hand, and cover it with your right hand, with the palm downward, saying:
I bless and consecrate this water
To bestow life and love
Wherever it flows.

6 Sprinkle a few drops of water over the greenery; then pour the rest onto the oasis to be absorbed by it and by the plants.

YOU WILL NEED

One green candle, 6–8"/15–20 cm in length

Matches or a lighter

One large bunch of holly (preferably with red berries)

One large bunch of ivy sprigs

Several large sprays of yew

One green oasis florist ring, 7–9"/17.5–22.5 cm in diameter

One wineglass of spring water

CAREER AND
WORK SPELLS

INTRODUCTION TO CAREER AND WORK SPELLS

The enormous range and scope of spells concerning career and work can be seen in the variety found in the following pages. If you browse through the twenty spells in this section, you will notice that "career and work" are interpreted to include issues having to do with enterprises and initiatives as well as employment. Education and preparation for advancement in the workplace are also covered, as is communication—one of the most important aspects of education, qualification, work, career, promotion, and enterprise. Although paid work is a fairly recent idea in human history, having the means to ensure shelter and sustenance is not, and so many older spells and traditions lend themselves well to employment matters.

Among the spells in this section you will find magical workings to find gainful employment, to obtain promotion, and to remove obstacles in your career path. Others found here are designed to enhance your workplace or educative abilities, and so you will find spells with an emphasis on confidence and courage,

the ability to concentrate, and verbal and written communication skills. For those seeking help and guidance, there are charms to attract a mentor and to draw attention to your work and ideas.

The atmosphere in the workplace and at school or college is important to work and study. A little magic can aid in achieving harmony in your working environment. Communication—so important in work and education situations—can be improved by deploying any one of several spells in this section. There is also help at hand in the form of protective magic, if you find you are being blocked in your progress, or if an atmosphere of negativity pervades your workplace or classroom.

If you do experience difficulties in your workplace, school, or college, and it is due to bullying or discrimination, you should seek advice and take the appropriate action. Magic can help in various workplace situations, as you can see from the extensive list in this section, but plain common sense travels along the same lines and you can achieve much in a practical way, too.

Spells in this section are powerful and potent workings based on ancient traditions and magical knowledge. They are, however, also flexible and can be applied in a variety of contemporary work, career, or study contexts. Because of this, they can justifiably claim to be ancient and modern both in concept and application!

TYR AMULET
TO GAIN EMPLOYMENT

PURPOSE
For those wishing to find paid employment of all kinds.

BACKGROUND
In the language of the sacred runes, *tyr* represents "success and victory in a quest." It is the rune of the Norse god known as Tiw, a mighty warrior and a good entity to have on your side in times of adversity. In the 24-rune alphabet, tyr is the first of the eight runes over which Tiw is said to preside, and so brings with it all the blessings of energy, determination, and steadfastness associated with him. Invoking the magical properties of this rune will strengthen the resolve and resourcefulness you need to ensure that your search for gainful employment is successful.

You will notice from the illustration that tyr resembles an arrow; this emphasizes the importance of having a clear target in mind when seeking a job. It also denotes shelter, indicating that this spell is invoked for need rather than greed and is thus more likely to bring material success if it is used in this spirit.

HOW TO CAST THE SPELL

TIMING Test this spell on a waxing moon to draw your target closer. Wednesday, day of communications and planet Mercury, is best, with Tuesday, named for the god Tiw, as a close second choice.

CASTING THE SPELL

1 Cast a circle in accordance with the guidelines on pages 32–35.

2 Light the candle, saying:
Spirit of sure victory
Look well and kindly upon me.

3 Hold the pebble firmly between your palms, and visualize yourself looking happy, setting off to work, and having money in your wallet or pocket.

4 When you are ready, take a deep breath, and breathe onto the stone, envisaging all that you have just wished for yourself going into the stone, and say:
By my breath
I charge thee.

5 Paint onto its flat surface the rune tyr. Leave this to dry next to the candle.

6 The next day, pop the pebble into your coat or pants pocket, and carry it with you wherever you go. When your object is achieved, cast the pebble into the nearest natural water source.

YOU WILL NEED

One yellow candle, about 6–8"/15–20 cm in length, if casting on a Wednesday
or
One red candle, about 6–8"/15–20 cm in length, if casting on a Tuesday

Matches or a lighter

One small pebble with a flat surface— light enough and small enough to carry in a coat or pants pocket

One small pot tube of oil-paint

One fine model paint-brush

SOLAR CROSS CHARM
TO FIND THE CORRECT CAREER PATH

PURPOSE To aid decision-making in planning for your career.

BACKGROUND Deciding on your future occupation, or mapping your progression in your chosen career, can be difficult. After you have spoken to your friends, family, colleagues, and career advisor, the next step is yours alone. But which direction should you take?

When you are drowning in information, help, and advice and can progress no farther, it is time for inner knowledge to take over! This spell activates that wisdom by applying tradition to a thoroughly modern context.

The mark inscribed on this charm is an ancient symbol that has nothing to do with the more recent influence of Christianity. The solar cross, as it is known, is characterized by arms of equal length. As well as its solar associations, this sign represents the meeting of the spiritual and earthly planes of existence. The equality of length and intersection of the lines are a visual example of the magical maxim "as above, so below". This spell draws on both meanings and adds a third—the tradition of reaching a crossroads—in order to promote your inner awareness of the direction you should take.

HOW TO CAST THE SPELL

YOU WILL NEED

One censer with a charcoal disk

A mix of myrrh, benzoin, and cinnamon incense

One gold, yellow, or orange candle, 6–8"/15–20 cm in length

Matches or a lighter

One thumbnail-size ball of self-hardening hobby clay

One dull knife

One 30"/75 cm length of fine black cord

TIMING Cast this spell on a dark moon— also known as the new moon—which favors new projects and beginnings. Any day will suffice, but Sunday, with its solar associations, is most favorable.

CASTING THE SPELL

1 Cast a circle in accordance with the guidelines on pages 32–35.

2 Light the charcoal, and sprinkle on incense.

3 Light the candle, saying:
Eternal sun
Lamp of the universe
Shine upon and bless my pathway
Light my way forward.

4 Roll the clay between your palms, and flatten it into a round disk. Take the knife, and make an imprint of a solar cross on one side. Use the knifepoint to drill a hole at the top, on the vertical cross shaft.

5 Holding this disk in the incense smoke, visualize yourself at a crossroads at midnight. Hold this image for as long as you can; then set the disk aside to dry.

6 When the disk is hardened, thread it with the cord, and wear it until you have made your decision. The answer will come to you within one lunar month.

BLACK PEPPER SPELL
TO AID CONCENTRATION IN INTERVIEWS OR EXAMS

PURPOSE To enhance concentration levels when studying or preparing for exams or interviews—and to help to retain focus for the event itself.

BACKGROUND A lot can hang on a test, exam, or interview, but the associated pressure can make it hard to concentrate. This ritual bestows the ability to focus during periods of preparation and study and can even help you stay calm and centered on the great day itself.

Aromatherapy is a well-established alternative treatment which uses olfactory or fragrance signatures to stimulate nerve endings that carry messages to the brain. The volatile oils used by practitioners are also absorbed into the bloodstream via inhalation. This spell harnesses the powerful properties of black pepper essential oil to give your concentration levels a wake-up call.

Black pepper, or *Piper nigrum,* is a renowned stimulant. It is also a muscle relaxant, which makes it ideal as an aid to study and to keeping some of the physical symptoms of anxiety at bay when under pressure in an examination or interview situation. Think carefully before using it near bedtime, especially if you have trouble sleeping. Its aphrodisiac qualities may be of benefit, but not if you are looking for rest!

HOW TO CAST THE SPELL

YOU WILL NEED

One yellow candle, 6–8"/15–20 cm
in length

Matches or a lighter

Two teaspoons of water

One oil burner with a tea-light

One bottle of black pepper (*Piper nigrum*)
essential oil

One ounce of dried juniper berries

One 7"/17.5 cm square piece of cheesecloth

TIMING Use on a waxing moon. Saturday,
day of disciplinarian Saturn, is best.

CASTING THE SPELL

1 Cast a circle in accordance with the
guidelines on pages 32–35.

2 Light the candle, saying:
   I summon the element of air
   To bring me clarity of purpose
   To aid me in my firm intent
   And help to keep my mind in focus.

3 Place the water in the oil burner dish,
and light the tea-light.

4 Hold the bottle of black pepper oil
between your palms, and focus on your
goal. Place six drops of oil into the oil
burner dish.

5 Place the berries in the center of the
cheesecloth, and add six drops of oil; then
tie the opposite corners together to
secure it.

6 Hang this pouch in your study area.
Use oil in the burner whenever you are
studying and immediately prior to the
exam or interview.

SIGIL SPELL
TO AID WITH INTERVIEW SUCCESS

PURPOSE To obtain a successful outcome to an interview.

BACKGROUND A sigil is "a compound symbol containing all the separate symbols, or letters, that form the name of the thing it represents." The traditional way of forming a sigil is to leave out all vowels, write the consonants in cubic letters, and superimpose them on each other. The resulting symbol embodies what is named in a powerfully concentrated form.

In this spell, you construct a sigil to signify victory in order to obtain a successful outcome to an interview. A successful outcome is one that is right for you and that

---

HOW TO CAST THE SPELL

YOU WILL NEED

One yellow or white candle,
6–8"/15–20 cm in length

Matches or a lighter

One ink pen

One bottle of green ink

One 4"/10 cm square piece of thick
drawing paper

TIMING Cast this spell on a waxing moon
to bring success, and on a Sunday, sacred
to the wholesome rays and blessings of Sol.

benefits all concerned. This interpretation builds in a safeguard to ensure that your interests are protected in ways that are not always immediately obvious. It may, for example, prevent you from getting a job that is wrong for you.

Spells to help you in interview situations are not going to be of the least use if you are unprepared or unqualified for the job or promotion to which you aspire. Remember, then, that the Sigil Spell is designed to give you the edge *in addition to* your preparedness and appropriateness for the situation you seek.

CASTING THE SPELL

1 Cast a circle in accordance with the guidelines on pages 32–35.

2 Light the candle.

3 Dip the nib of the pen into the ink, and in the center of the paper inscribe the letters *V, C, T,* and *R* in squared script, one on top of the other.

4 Write the following three phrases, one to a line, to form an equilateral triangle around the sigil you have formed:

Auxilio ab alta
Sol victorioso
Sol omnipotens.
Light the candle, and dry the ink by the heat of the flame.

5 Fold the paper in half, then in quarter, saying:
Victory be mine
Fortune be kind.

6 Carry your sigil with you to your interview.

IRON SPELL
TO PROMOTE CONFIDENCE AND COURAGE FOR INTERVIEWS AND EXAMS

PURPOSE   To help those who suffer from debilitating nervousness in interview or exam situations.

BACKGROUND   Examinations and interviews can reduce the most sensible and well-prepared person to jelly. The Iron Spell is designed to bestow the confidence and courage to help the most nervous candidate acquit themselves with calm assurance.

Iron is a proverbial symbol for bravery and endurance in the face of adversity; we even use phrases such as "iron-willed" or "nerves of steel" to describe someone with

HOW TO CAST THE SPELL

YOU WILL NEED

Two teaspoons of water

Two drops of basil essential oil

Two drops of borage essential oil

One oil burner with a tea-light

Matches or a lighter

One red candle, 6–8"/15–20 cm in length

Approximately two tablespoons of fine sand

One saucer

One 6"/15 cm iron nail

TIMING Cast this spell on a waxing moon to draw courage. Tuesday, sacred to Mars, is the best day on which to cast this powerfully affirmative spell.

CASTING THE SPELL

1 Cast a circle in accordance with the guidelines on pages 32–35.

2 Place the water and oil in the oil burner dish, and light the tea-light.

3 Light the candle, saying:
Spear of Mars
Pierce timidity
Iron sword
Check humility.

admirable resources of steadfastness. In the tradition of alchemy, iron is the metal of Mars and a symbol of willpower and determination. Here, it is used to support magically the steadfastness and poise required to perform to the best of your abilities in a high-pressure situation. The form of the iron used will also help you to "nail" the problem of those pesky, undermining nerves.

This spell can be repeated as often as you please. Because it doubles as a form of self-affirmation, it has a powerful cumulative affect that is very beneficial to those who suffer from nervousness.

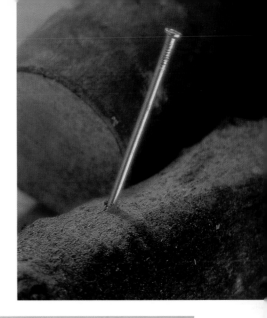

4 Place the sand in the saucer, and level the surface. Using the nail point, write the word "FEAR" in the sand. Shake the sand to obliterate the letters. Next, draw an *X* encircled.

5 When the candle has burned completely down, take the sand outdoors, and cast it into the wind.

6 Carry the nail with you in your pocket in the days leading to the interview. On the day of the interview, drive the nail partway into a piece of wood near your hearth.

ARROW SPELL
TO OBTAIN PROMOTION

PURPOSE To help those seeking to get ahead in their careers—including those who are planning to move from one job or line of work to another.

BACKGROUND Many of us experience a feeling of stagnation in our working lives from time to time, particularly if we feel that our career has ground to a halt. This spell is designed to light the fuse of your career so that it can take off in a satisfactory direction. Primarily a ritual to obtain promotion, it is also useful for those who wish to leave their present position and progress into work that is more rewarding financially, psychologically, or spiritually.

HOW TO CAST THE SPELL

YOU WILL NEED

Two teaspoons of water

Three drops of basil essential oil

Three drops of mint essential oil

One oil burner with a tea-light

Matches or a lighter

One red candle, 6–8"/15–20 cm in length

One yellow candle, 6–8"/15–20 cm in length

One sheet of paper approximately 10" x 3"/25 cm x 7.5 cm

One pen with red ink

Two paper clips

TIMING This spell should be cast on a waxing moon to attract your target ever nearer, with Tuesday, ruled by go-getting Mars, as the most auspicious day.

It may interest you to know that arrows have been used in magic from ancient times. Arrowheads were sometimes carried in pouches as amulets of protection, and there is even a branch of divination—belomancy—that uses the direction in which arrows fall as a means of prediction. Here, the arrow is used to signify the forward direction in which your future lies. Folding the paper on which it is drawn—to bring the end of the arrow close to its point—symbolizes the speed with which you wish to attain your target. May your journey take you somewhere wonderful.

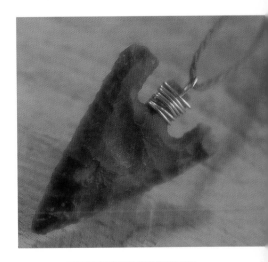

CASTING THE SPELL

1 Cast a circle in accordance with the guidelines on pages 32–35.

2 Place the water and oil in the oil burner dish, and light the tea-light.

3 Light the red candle, saying:
Great Mars, launch this arrow well.
Light the yellow candle, saying:
Swift Mercury, direct this spell.

4 With the longest side horizontal, draw on the paper an arrow pointing right.

5 Fold the paper into a concertina, so that the arrow is foreshortened, its point close to its end. Fasten it with paper clips.

6 Hold this between both palms and concentrate on your target, then chant the following six times:
Wind of change
Carry me forward
Flight of arrows
Carry me onward.
Keep the folded paper in a safe place.

DANDELION CHARM
TO GET YOURSELF NOTICED AT WORK OR AT SCHOOL OR COLLEGE

PURPOSE To help those who get overlooked at work. It is designed to help them attract notice, make friends, and gain popularity.

BACKGROUND Dandelions, or *Taraxacum officinale,* have a wonderful history of herbal and magical traditions associated with them. Sometimes called "wet-the-beds," they have diuretic properties that are well known to herbalists, as are the highly nutritious and detoxifying properties of their leaves. Among the magical traditions is the belief that the yellow flowers, if rubbed all over the naked body, have the power to ensure that a person thus anointed will make friends wherever they go. This conviction probably arose from the dandelion's reputation as a flower of the fairies, who have the ability to bestow the "gift of the gab."

This charm is for those who feel overlooked in the workplace or classroom. It helps them to attract the notice of colleagues and employers so that they can really shine for others to see. If this applies to you, getting into the habit of drinking dandelion tea following this spell will aid your confidence. This is because dandelion dispels emotional blockages and can release the resentment and hurts that boil away under the surface. In this respect, dandelions are truly food for thought.

HOW TO CAST THE SPELL

TIMING Perform this spell on a waxing moon to attract notice, and on a Sunday, day of the blessings of the sun.

CASTING THE SPELL

1 Perform this circle naked.

2 Cast a circle in accordance with the guidelines on pages 32–35. Light the tea-light.

3 Cupping the dandelions in your hand, visualize a recent incident in which you were overlooked but wished to be noticed. Mentally re-create the scene, this time with a more positive outcome.

4 Place the dandelions in the cheesecloth. Add the lemon balm and six drops of oil. Fasten the cloth into a pouch, using the ribbon.

5 Light both candles, saying:
Power of the sun
Caress me
Flower of the sun
Now bless me.
Rub the cheesecloth sachet over your body, avoiding your eyes and other delicate parts.

6 Carry the sachet in the workplace. At home use six drops of oil in your bath, for each subsequent bath, until it is all gone.

YOU WILL NEED

One tea-light

Matches or a lighter

Six fresh yellow dandelion heads

One handful of dried lemon balm leaves

Six drops of melissa oil diluted in sixty drops of almond carrier oil

One 6"/15 cm square piece of cheesecloth

One 12"/30 cm length of yellow ribbon

Two yellow candles, 6–8"/15–20 cm in length

SESAME SPELL
TO REMOVE OBSTACLES TO YOUR CAREER

PURPOSE To help those who feel blocked in their efforts to progress in their career.

BACKGROUND If you have been trying to get ahead in your career, but have been frustrated by obstacles that spring up in your way, this spell is just the one for you. It works by releasing the potential that is being blocked, and it does this in a rather dramatic fashion that emphasizes the spell's aim—which is to blast through opposition! Using sesame seeds, which symbolize discovery and openings, will aid you in your cause.

HOW TO CAST THE SPELL

YOU WILL NEED

Twelve sesame seeds

Water

One ice tray with twelve compartments

One bunch of dried white sage

Matches or a lighter

One fireproof dish

One black candle, 6–8"/15–20 cm in length

Two teaspoons of sesame oil

One bunch of dried garden weeds

Dry wood and kindling

TIMING This working should be performed on a waning moon to destroy obstacles, and on a Saturday, day of Saturn the banisher.

CASTING THE SPELL

Prior to the spell, freeze one sesame seed per cube in an ice tray.

1 Cast a circle in accordance with the guidelines on pages 32–35.

2 Light the sage leaves, and allow them to smolder. Use the smoke to cense the circle clockwise. Place the leaves in the fireproof dish.

This element of the spell will involve using a balefire, which is a "fire made for magical purposes," so you will need to work outdoors for the second part of the spell. The fire should be composed of the usual fuel—dry wood and kindling—but do not be tempted to add anything artificial to it, such as gasoline or charcoal lighter. The magical ingredients to be cast into the fire as part of this spell will require a well-established blaze in order to ignite or disperse appropriately. You should therefore ensure that the fire is at its peak temperature before throwing these in.

3 Anoint the candle with sesame oil, using upward strokes, avoiding the wick. Place the candle in the holder, and light it, saying:

> Destroyer of barriers
> Purify this flame
> Turn it to thy work
> No hindrance remain.

4 Close the circle, and carry the ice tray, weeds, sage, and lit candle outside. Use the black candle to light the fire. Once the fire is at peak temperature, cast on the weeds, saying:

> Away, all that chokes
> Disappear in smoke.

Cast the ice cubes into the fire separately; these should evaporate instantly.

5 Circle the fire counterclockwise with sage smoke three times. Cast the sage into the fire.

6 Allow the candle to burn down completely in safety.

FIRESTONE SPELL
TO BRING INSPIRATION TO YOUR WORK

PURPOSE To seek inspiration in a work or study situation.

BACKGROUND You may have heard the saying that inspiration often "strikes like lightning." This spell takes that very literally and calls on the powers of Oya, a great African goddess, who is associated with lightning storms. She is certainly deemed a fierce goddess, so any boon that she brings, when invoked, is difficult to ignore!

In order to find the ingredients for this spell, you may need to go out into your garden or to a local park or green space. This is so that you can find a stone that has been out in the heat of the sun. The stone should be small enough to slip into a pocket or purse and smooth enough to close into your palm. It should also have at least one flattened side so that you can paint on a small symbol during the casting of the spell. Use your instincts— if a stone feels good when you hold it, it is obviously the one for you.

The paint for this spell should be available from most hobby or model craft stores.

HOW TO CAST THE SPELL

TIMING Cast on a waxing moon to invite inspiration, on any day of the week apart from Saturday, day of restrictive Saturn.

CASTING THE SPELL

1 Light the charcoal disk, and blend the frankincense with the oils.

2 Cast a circle in accordance with the guidelines on pages 32–35.

3 Sprinkle the incense blend onto the hot charcoal disk.

4 Light the candle, saying:
Oya, I invoke you
Lady of the lightning stroke
Lady of the sudden fire
May it strike as I desire.

5 Paint onto the stone a vertical zigzag of lightning surrounded by the outline of a flame. Pass the stone through the incense smoke, then through the heat of the candle flame. Hold it in your cupped hands, saying:
I seek inspiration
In the name of Oya
And by all of her names
Known and unknown.

YOU WILL NEED

One charcoal disk in a censer or in a fireproof dish

Matches or a lighter

One teaspoon of frankincense

Three drops of ginger essential oil

Six drops of cinnamon essential oil

One red candle, 6–8"/15–20 cm in length

One stone

One fine artist's paintbrush

One tube of copper oil paint

One can of clear varnish

6 Visualize lightning striking the stone, and imagine that energy passing into it. Close the circle. When the paint is dry, seal the symbol with clear varnish. Whenever you seek inspiration, summon it by clasping the stone.

SILVER CANDLE SPELL
TO AID QUICK-WITTEDNESS IN STUDY AND IN THE WORKPLACE

PURPOSE To help you gather your wits together more quickly in study and in the workplace.

BACKGROUND In a world of information overload, it is crucial to be able to function by making prompt decisions and by selecting and absorbing essential information quickly. Busy lifestyles call for speed in such matters, so keeping our wits about us is just as important now as it was when our ancestors took risks to gather the right herbs and fruits while avoiding large predatory animals! This spell will aid your wits in study or work situations.

HOW TO CAST THE SPELL

YOU WILL NEED

One silver candle, 6–8"/15–20 cm in length

Matches or a lighter

One 6" x 6"/15 cm x 15 cm square piece of yellow paper

One pen with black ink

One tube of hobby glue, with a fine-holed applicator

One tube of loose silver glitter

TIMING Perform this spell on a waxing moon to attract quick-wittedness, and on a Wednesday in honor of Mercury, patron of this spell.

CASTING THE SPELL

1 Cast a circle in accordance with the guidelines on pages 32–35.

2 Light the candle, saying:
   Silver-heeled Mercury
   Lend me your swift aid
   Let my head judge quickly
   Gift my wits with speed.

This spell calls on Mercury, the swift messenger of the gods. The metal mercury, named for the divine messenger, is also known as quicksilver, "quick" meaning "live." It is noted for its mutable qualities, such as expanding and shrinking at different temperatures and flowing to fit the shape of the space it is poured into. This quality of mutability is just as relevant to this spell, as is the reputation of Mercury as the patron of swift communication. We need to remain adaptable and flexible in the fast-changing world of work and study in order to soak up, select, and assess the information we are expected to act on.

3 In each corner of the paper, draw the sign for Mercury (similar to the symbol for Venus, with "horns" on the top of the circle).

4 Beginning from the center of the page, draw with a line of glue an outwardly increasing spiral. Keeping the flow of glue constant, turn the line back on itself to trace an inward-moving spiral.

5 Pour the silver glitter onto the paper. Wait a few seconds; then pour the excess glitter away. Allow the glue to dry completely in the light of the candle.

6 Hang this silver spiral, representing Mercury and swift thought, in the place where you do most of your thinking.

AIR INCENSE SPELL
TO COMMUNICATE YOUR IDEAS AT WORK OR IN CLASS

PURPOSE To ensure that your ideas are carried at work or in class.

BACKGROUND In magic, the element of air is closely associated with communication. In this spell, designed to help your ideas take wing in the workplace or classroom, the magical association between incense and the air element is put into action. Incense not only produces smoke, making the physical element of air momentarily visible, it also distributes perfumes, which are perceived via the sense of scent—a sense very much associated with air.

HOW TO CAST THE SPELL

YOU WILL NEED

One charcoal disk in a fireproof dish

One yellow candle, 6–8"/15–20 cm in length

Matches or a lighter

Two teaspoons of benzoin granules

One teaspoon of pine needles

One teaspoon of dried lavender

Mortar and pestle

Three drops of pine essential oil

Three drops of lavender essential oil

TIMING Be sure to cast your spell on a waxing moon to encourage a flow of communication, and on a Wednesday, day of Mercury.

CASTING THE SPELL

1 Cast a circle in accordance with the guidelines on pages 32–35.

2 Visualize a bright silver circle surrounding the ritual area.

3 Light the charcoal disk, then the candle, saying:

I invoke the element of air
To witness and empower my spell.

The ingredients used in this air incense recipe carry symbolic properties, as well as the physiological benefits. Lavender, sacred to the communication planet Mercury, is an excellent relaxant when inhaled, rendering those who breathe it both eloquent and receptive to ideas. Benzoin, symbolically associated with air in herbal or incense tables, carries a resonance that works positively in work or class. Pine is an air-related tree in terms of symbolism, and its scent initiates levels of awareness that make bystanders alert to conventional *and* subliminal messages.

4 Place all dry ingredients in the mortar bowl, and grind to a fine consistency, chanting:
Flower of Hermes
Leaf of pine
Carry my words
Let them be heard.
Blend in the oils.

5 Sprinkle a little incense onto the glowing disk. Closing your eyes, imagine your words darting through the air, powered by feathers. Visualize positive reactions from those with influence and those whose respect you wish to win.

6 Place the remaining incense in an airtight bag for future use in communication spells. When you wish for an all-round boost of power, wear the incense in a pouch around your neck.

OWL CHARM
TO ENHANCE YOUR WRITING ABILITIES

PURPOSE To boost your writing skills and help your written communications flow more smoothly and impact more effectively.

BACKGROUND These days, in addition to "paper" qualifications, we are often required to have a number of additional skills. Employers and educators agree that abilities such as interpersonal skills and the capacity to take responsibility or to be self-managing are crucial qualities for successful students and workers. Foremost among the many skills we are now required to attain are communication skills—and this means confidence and competence in written, as well as spoken, communication.

This spell invokes the blessing of Athene, the Greek goddess of wisdom, learning, and communication—and the patron of writing. Her totem is the owl—an archetypal symbol of wisdom—and the gift of writing well is sometimes dubbed the "owl gift." You will need to obtain an owl feather for the charm. This should be naturally shed, so you may need to visit a bird center or sanctuary and ask the staff to help.

If you are genuinely worried about poor writing skills, you can register for a basic writing skills class at your local college. This spell will aid your learning process and help you to concentrate on written tasks generally.

HOW TO CAST THE SPELL

TIMING Cast this spell on a waxing moon to increase your writing powers, and on a Wednesday, day of Mercury.

CASTING THE SPELL

1 Cast a circle in accordance with the guidelines on pages 32–35.

2 Light each candle in turn, saying:
This flame I light in honor of wisdom
This flame I light in honor of learning
This flame I light in honor of the owl gift
May each be mine
In time.

3 Holding the feather in your writing hand and the stone in the other, envisage your written work gaining the approval of your teachers or employers.

4 Hold the feather out in front of the candles, and say:
Athene, you know my thoughts
Help me bring them to paper.
Do the same with the stone, saying:
Athene, you know my wishes
Help me to bring them to pass.

5 Place the stone in the pouch, and fasten it. Wind the thread around the base of the feather, and fasten it securely to the outside of the pouch.

YOU WILL NEED

Three yellow candles, 6–8"/15–20 cm in length

Matches or a lighter

One owl feather

One smooth thumbnail-size white stone

One small brown drawstring pouch

One 30"/75 cm length of thick brown embroidery thread

One 30"/75 cm length of fine cord or thong

6 Attach the cord, and hang the charm in the room where you do most of your writing.

CLARY SAGE SPELL
TO AID VERBAL COMMUNICATION

PURPOSE   To bestow the gift of clear and persuasive speech.

BACKGROUND   This is the magical equivalent of the Blarney stone—a magical stone in Ireland which, if kissed, is said to impart the "gift of the gab," or the ability to charm with words. Clary sage, or *Salvia sclarea*, the main ingredient of the spell, is said to confer wisdom as well as the gift of clarity, both important ingredients in the power of clear and persuasive speech. Used as an herbal remedy, it enhances confidence and aids perception.

The power of good speakers was recognized by many ancient cultures, particularly in those traditions whose survival depended on the skills of storytellers, bards, priests, and priestesses. The Celts particularly prized the skills of speech, and the power attributed to skilled speakers is evident from legends that claim St. Patrick magically struck dumb the pagan priests and counselors of the people he was sent to convert to Christianity. The ability to always speak fair words and to charm any company is also said to be the gift of the fairies, or the "good folk." The endurance of such beliefs signifies the importance in which eloquence is still held in some traditions.

Blarney Castle

HOW TO CAST THE SPELL

TIMING This charm is best performed on a waxing moon for increase, and on a Monday, day of the Moon.

CASTING THE SPELL

1 Cast a circle in accordance with the guidelines on pages 32–35.

2 Light the charcoal disk and candle, saying:

Power of the old ones
The high ones
The low ones
Power of the moon
Bestow fair speech
An it harm none.

3 Sprinkle sandalwood onto the charcoal disk, and add three clary sage leaves saying:
This I offer to the old ones.

4 Bind three leaves together with thread, and place them beneath the candle, saying:
This I offer to the moon.

5 Place three leaves in a cup and pour on a teaspoon of honey. Then fill it with boiling water, saying:
This I offer to myself.
When the drink is cool enough, drink it straight down, and bury the leaves in soil outside your home.

YOU WILL NEED

One charcoal disk in a fireproof dish
One silver or white candle, 6–8"/15–20 cm in length
Matches or a lighter
White sandalwood incense
Nine clary sage leaves
One 18"/45 cm length of black sewing thread
One teaspoon of honey
One cup/250 ml of boiling water

6 At the next full moon, take the bound leaves outside. Offer them up to the moon, kiss them, then cast them into a natural water source as soon after as possible.

HARMONY OIL SPELL
FOR HARMONY IN THE WORKPLACE

PURPOSE To aid in creating a harmonious atmosphere in the workplace, particularly if colleagues are involved in conflict.

BACKGROUND When our surrounding work environment is out of balance, we tend to get out of balance, too, and our home life as well as our work can suffer. This is particularly the case when the quarrels of colleagues get out of hand and others are dragged in, often involuntarily. Even if you are wise enough to keep out of such disputes, you are still likely to be affected by the ensuing hostile atmosphere and therefore justified in taking magical measures to restore harmony.

 HOW TO CAST THE SPELL

YOU WILL NEED
One green candle, 6–8"/15–20 cm in length
Matches or a lighter
Five elder leaves
Five drops of sandalwood essential oil
Five drops of camomile essential oil
Five drops of ylang-ylang essential oil
Four sterile droppers
One sterile oil bottle
One 4" x 8"/10 cm x 20 cm piece of cheesecloth, sewn into a sachet
One 12"/30 cm length of white thread
One needle

TIMING Blend on a waxing moon for maximum impact, and on a Friday, day of harmony planet Venus.

CASTING THE SPELL

1 Cast a circle in accordance with the guidelines on pages 32–35.

2 Light the candle. Hold the elder leaves before the flame, saying:
   Elder for protection
   Love to lend direction.

The magical potion brewed in this spell is intended to smooth things over and restore some equilibrium on the work front. You and your co-workers will benefit from its beneficial aromatherapeutic effects—so everybody wins! However, if there is real bullying involved in the quarrel, advise the party concerned to seek help from personnel or from their union. This spell will still help calm things down, but magic helps those who are grounded and resourceful, so ensure practical measures are sought where appropriate. Remember to tend your pot plant once the spell is cast.

3 Place five drops of sandalwood oil into the sterile bottle, saying:
Away negativity.
Add five drops of camomile oil, saying:
Forward with harmony.
Add five drops of ylang-ylang oil, saying:
Quarrel mend peacefully.

4 Place three drops of the blended oil onto each of the five elder leaves. Sew one leaf into the cheesecloth sachet.

5 Hide one leaf at each of the four corners of your workplace, and carry the sachet with you at all times to spread the harmony around.

6 Once the atmosphere calms, bury all five leaves beneath a potted plant, which should remain in the workplace.

WARNING A medical condition or pregnancy can be adversely affected by the oils in this recipe.

ASH CIRCLE SPELL
TO GUARD YOU FROM THE ENVY OR SPITE OF A CO-WORKER

PURPOSE   To provide protection against a troublemaker in the workplace.

BACKGROUND   The unpleasant behavior of a colleague, particularly when it is difficult to prove or pin down, can make work hell. This spell is designed both to defend you from spite and to cause their plans to misfire.

The protective nature of an ash circle is well known to seasoned magicians. Cinders and ash from a hearth fire symbolize, in concentrated form, the protection of fire and the shelter of hearth. In this spell, there are two ash circles—one representing the present situation, and one representing an improved future situation. These draw, respectively, on the inherently protective qualities of ash and on ash as a condenser. This latter aspect comes from the notion that a burned item condenses, and thus concentrates, the power of whatever the item symbolizes. For example, if you burn an effigy of a spiteful person, the resultant ash contains and represents their spite in concentrated form. The way that the ash is then acted on will be what happens to the behavior it represents— in this case, you literally blow it away!

A final word: magic works on the basis of common sense and resourcefulness. If you are being victimized, get advice and support prior to casting this spell.

122

HOW TO CAST THE SPELL

TIMING Cast on a waning moon to banish bad behavior. Saturday, dedicated to Saturn the disciplinarian, is best.

CASTING THE SPELL

1 Cast a circle in accordance with the guidelines on pages 32–35. Light both candles.

2 Hold up the quartz, and say:
  I name thee [your name].
Place the quartz on the upturned mirror.

3 Draw a likeness of the troublemaker on one sheet of paper. Set the paper alight using the black candle, and place it in the pot. Sprinkle the ashes in a circle around the stone, saying:

  Evil to fail
  Good to prevail
  Go thee hence and
  Get thee gone!
Blow the ashes away.

4 Draw an eye on the second sheet of paper. Set it aflame using the white candle. Place it in the pot.

5 Sprinkle the ashes from the pot in a circle on the floor. Step into it, and say:

  As I stand in this circle now
  May I ever be protected so.

6 Place the stone in the pouch, then fasten it and keep it safe.

YOU WILL NEED

One white candle, 6–8"/15–20 cm in length
One black candle, 6–8"/15–20 cm in length
Matches or a lighter
One small tumbled quartz
One small mirror
One pencil
Two sheets of paper
One fireproof pot
One small drawstring pouch

TAROT SPELL
TO ATTRACT A HELPFUL ADVISOR AND PATRON IN YOUR WORK

PURPOSE To help you obtain a mentor and patron in your work.

BACKGROUND The voice of experience is always worth listening to, and gaining the counsel and interest of an experienced or influential person in your place of work can be extremely useful. This spell helps you to draw the notice of an appropriately helpful mentor and patron toward you by using the age-old wisdom of the tarot.

In all tarot decks, the cards most associated with advisors are the court cards depicting the Kings and Queens of Cups, Wands, Swords, and Pentacles. Prior to spell

HOW TO CAST THE SPELL

YOU WILL NEED

One oil burner with a tea-light

Two teaspoons of water

Six drops of heliotrope essential oil

One deep blue candle, 6–8"/15–20 cm in length

Matches or a lighter

One tarot card

One sprig of chickweed, or *Stellaria media*

One small free-standing mirror

TIMING Test this spell on a waxing moon to draw your advisor, and on a Thursday, ruled by generous Jupiter.

CASTING THE SPELL

1 Cast a circle in accordance with the guidelines on pages 32–35.

2 Light the oil burner, placing the water and oil in the dish.

3 Light the candle, saying:
   Good Jupiter, I invoke thee
   Bring fair advice to me.

4 Choose a card. Stand your card against the mirror, with both facing toward you.

casting, select an appropriate advisor from the list below, choosing a queen for a female advisor or a king for a male:

King or Queen of Pentacles—both offer good advice on financial matters.

King or Queen of Cups—both offer creative ideas and advice, particularly in the areas of art, the sciences, and travel.

King or Queen of Wands—both aid communication, particularly in teaching, journalism, or in commercial situations.

King or Queen of Swords—both are incisive and perceptive and offer excellent advice in the areas of law and insurance, and in career advancement generally.

4

5 Pass the chickweed through the rising aroma from the oil burner, saying:

Bring fair words.

Now pass it through the heat of the candle flame, saying:

Bring fair counsel.

Lay the chickweed in front of the card, saying:

Generous counselor and wise
Look to me with friendly eyes
Before another moon is past
Seek me out to give advice.

6 Keep the card in front of the mirror for one moon cycle, or until the right advisor appears.

IVY SPELL
TO PROCURE SUCCESS IN A NEW BUSINESS OR ENTERPRISE

PURPOSE To protect a new business or enterprise and thereby procure its future success.

BACKGROUND This spell offers a blessing and protection for a new business and a boost to improve its chances of future success. It uses ivy, known to the Celts as *gort*, which is associated with protection and endurance, both of which will benefit a brand-new enterprise. Ivy is fast growing, as well as tenacious, and has the ability to find its way over and around obstacles. Any project blessed by the power of ivy is sure to find such qualities useful.

Although setting up your own enterprise can be exciting, it can also feel pretty scary—particularly when you are set to stand or fall by your own actions. Trading in employee status for self-employment offers the chance to make your own way in the world, but it brings with it responsibilities and risks that you may not have encountered head-on in your previous working life. At the same time as this spell works to protect and advance your new project, it also works to erase worries and steady the nerves of the proud new owner/manager! In order to maximize this particular benefit, burn juniper berries every night for seven nights prior to the full moon, and secure a twist of ivy to place around your bedpost.

HOW TO CAST THE SPELL

TIMING Work on a waxing moon to attract success and build protection and endurance, and on a Thursday, day of fortuitous Jupiter.

CASTING THE SPELL

1 Cast a circle in accordance with the guidelines on pages 32–55.

2 Light the charcoal disk, then the blue candle, saying:
> *Fortuna, mother of fortune*
> *Smile upon your child.*

Light the green candle, saying:
> *Erce, mother of evergreens*
> *Smile upon my venture.*

3 Burn the juniper berries on the disk.

4 Pass the twig of mountain ash (rowan) through the scented smoke, saying:
> *Steadfast and pure*
> *Hold fast and endure.*

5 Twist the ivy around the stick, bottom to top and back again, and pass it through the incense smoke again, saying:
> *Semper, semper, semper.*

6 Place the entwined twig in front of the candles, and using both hands, direct the incense toward your heart, saying:
> *Guard and protect me; I harm none.*

YOU WILL NEED

One charcoal disk in a fireproof dish

One deep blue candle, 6–8"/15–20 cm in length

One green candle, 6–8"/15–20 cm in length

Matches or a lighter

Two teaspoons of dried juniper berries

One 8"/20 cm forked twig of mountain ash (rowan)

One long twist of wild ivy, approximately 24"/60 cm in length

MAGNET SPELL
TO DRAW CUSTOMERS TO A BUSINESS OR ENTERPRISE

PURPOSE To draw customers toward a new business. To be used in need, not greed.

BACKGROUND It can be immensely disappointing, indeed, damaging, when the goods or services you offer remain unused through lack of customer interest. This spell works to drum up interest to gain the notice of potential paying customers in order to get them through the door—literally or metaphorically. The rest, of course, is up to you and your goods and services, but as many failed businessmen and women will testify, half the battle is getting people to the point of seeing what is being offered.

 HOW TO CAST THE SPELL

YOU WILL NEED

Two teaspoons of water

Three drops of lavender essential oil

One oil burner with a tea-light

Matches or a lighter

One needle

Five white tea-lights

One 6" x 6"/15 cm x 15 cm square piece of yellow paper

One small magnet

One teaspoon of honey

One spider's web

TIMING Perform this spell early in the waxing moon cycle, and on a Wednesday, ruled by commercial patron Mercury.

CASTING THE SPELL

1 Cast a circle in accordance with the guidelines on pages 32–35.

2 Place the water and oil in the oil burner dish, and light it.

3 Inscribe with a needle on the surface of each tea-light a matchstick humanoid figure.

4 Place the tea-lights in a circle on a heatproof surface, around the paper.

This spell works on the basis of age-old metaphors and symbols. Everybody recognizes the symbolism of drawing bees to a honey pot, and this is the effect that you wish to have on potential customers. Similarly, the proverbial properties of a spider's web in catching prey and the attraction of magnets are well known. Here, all three are used to catch the curiosity of the public, although presumably you will not be "preying" on customers but offering goods and services from which they will benefit—and from which you will make a living.

Place the magnet on the paper, saying:
I draw you forth
By the power of the north.
Place a teaspoon of honey on the magnet, saying:

I draw your money
As bees fly to honey.
Place the web on the honey, saying:
Stick close by
As the web to the fly.

5 Light all five tea-lights, saying:
By this bright light
And Mercury's might
By iron, web, and sting
I draw you to this ring.

6 When all have burned down, fold the ingredients into the paper, and hide it in your place of business.

BROOMSTICK SPELL
FOR ENSURING COMMERCE AND PROSPERITY FOR YOUR BUSINESS

PURPOSE To bring prosperity blessings for an established business.

BACKGROUND The broomstick is the archetypal symbol of witchcraft and abounds in Hollywood B-movies as well as in historical depictions of witchery. Its association with witches is interesting, as traditionally the symbol of the broom has functioned more to define boundaries than to depict flight. In the days before sidewalks and asphalt roads, the broom tracks and sweep patterns left on the ground around your home marked out your territory. The broomstick was often left by the front door to indicate when the inhabitant was at home, or away.

In this spell, the broomstick is used as a blessing on the boundaries of your business, in the hope that it will continue to take flight unimpeded. The elements of air and earth are called to empower your enterprise with the commercial viability and stability it needs to continue.

You will need to purchase a broomstick for this spell. These are generally easy to obtain from reputable garden centers. Once the spell is cast, the broomstick should be placed inside the room above the lintel of the door through which customers access your premises.

HOW TO CAST THE SPELL

YOU WILL NEED

One charcoal disk in a fireproof dish

Matches or a lighter

One teaspoon of benzoin granules

One teaspoon of chopped basil

One green candle, 6–8"/15–20 cm in length

One yellow candle, 6–8"/15–20 cm in length

One broomstick

One large bunch of fresh rosemary

Two yards of natural twine

One 12"/30 cm length of freshly strung dried juniper berries

Six drops of mint essential oil

TIMING Work this charm on a waxing moon for growth, and on a Wednesday, ruled by the king of commerce, Mercury.

CASTING THE SPELL

1 Cast a circle in accordance with the guidelines on pages 32–35.

2 Light the charcoal disk, and sprinkle on the benzoin and basil.

3 Light the green candle, saying:
Earth, witness this spell.
Light the yellow candle, saying:
Air, carry it well.

4 Tie the rosemary around the band fastening the handle to the brush, wrapping the twine around until it is completely used, chanting as you do:
Born of earth
Carried in air
Increase worth
Away with care.
Fasten it off; then tie the strung juniper berries around the twine.

5 Anoint the handle and brush with the mint oil; then pass the broomstick over the incense smoke three times, saying:
Once I invest thee
Twice I impress thee
Thrice I then bless thee.

6 Keep this broomstick charm over the doorway of your business premises.

SUNBURST TALISMAN SPELL
TO REVIVE THE FORTUNES OF AN AILING ENTERPRISE

PURPOSE To aid a failing enterprise.

BACKGROUND It can be distressing to see that a business you have built from nothing, with a lot of hard work, is failing. Sometimes projects fail because they were not well thought through, publicized, or supported financially. Other times, an enterprise can take a dive because of circumstances entirely beyond your control. If the latter applies to you, and you have taken all possible practical steps to ensure the continuation of your business, then this spell can give it just the edge it needs to survive.

In magic, as in many divinatory systems such as the tarot, the sun represents joy, happiness, and success. The symbol of the sunburst, a central disk with a zigzag penumbra surrounding it, was used by many ancient peoples to denote divine blessing. We recognize the significance of the sun's blessing in sayings such as "fortune shines upon them" when describing somebody's luck or success in their endeavors.

The Sunburst Talisman is designed to attract the blessing of the sun and all its associated powers to save your business. If successful, you should ensure that a small portion of all earnings from that business in the future is dedicated to those less fortunate than yourself.

HOW TO CAST THE SPELL

TIMING The talisman should be made on a waxing moon to favor increase, and on a Sunday, ruled by the sun.

CASTING THE SPELL

1 Cast a circle in accordance with the guidelines on pages 32–35.

2 Light the charcoal, and sprinkle on the frankincense. Light the candle, saying:
I call upon the infinite sun
To shine upon this
*   enterprise/shop/business.*

3 Cover the clay disk with the foil; then inscribe on it with the dull pencil the shape of a sunburst.

4 In the center of the sunburst, draw a dot, and around this write the words:
Bel, Sol, Salve.

5 Blend the benzoin, cinnamon, and saltpeter in the mortar, and throw them onto the charcoal disk, repeating the words you have written on the disk. Pass the talisman through the incense smoke.

6 Hang the talisman from the highest central point inside your business premises.

YOU WILL NEED

One charcoal disk in a fireproof dish
Matches or a lighter
One teaspoon of frankincense
One orange or gold candle, 6–8"/15–20 cm in length
One circular clay disk prepared with a hole through it
Gold-colored foil to cover the disk
One dull pencil
One pinch of benzoin
One pinch of cinnamon
One pinch of saltpeter
Mortar and pestle
One 30"/75 cm length of fine cord

HEALTH, BEAUTY, AND WELL-BEING SPELLS

INTRODUCTION TO HEALTH, BEAUTY, AND WELL-BEING SPELLS

Each of the categories covered in this section is interpreted broadly in order to encompass the many senses in which health, beauty, and well-being are perceived. Health is seen here as a positive and whole state of physical and mental existence—not simply the absence of pain. Similarly, the concept of well-being incorporates our own sense of inner peace and balance. Beauty, the most subjective of ideals, is interpreted here as going beyond a social or cultural sense of perfection to embrace alternative notions of physical and spiritual beauty.

Taken together, the interpretations of health, beauty, and well-being offered in this section have, arguably, more validity than the sometimes arbitrary and limited senses in which they are so commonly defined. Perhaps this is because magic does not have a spending budget that curtails cures, a vested interest in making women anxious about their bodies, or a tendency to overload participants with anxiety, beyond that of getting enough space and privacy to practice!

Some of the spells for physical healing in this section have a very worthy lineage; our ancient ancestors used magic to heal or disperse sickness or disease. For millennia prior to the professionalization of medicine and surgery, healers had extensive anatomical and herbal knowledge, which was often blended with folk magic and religion. Many healing spells have been preserved in the annals of folk beliefs, having been passed from the hands of the old village or country practitioners known as cunning men and wisewomen into the hands of collectors of folk customs and other curiosities. Other spells have passed from generation to generation—often from mother to daughter—surviving as "superstitions" or "old wives' tales"—tellingly, an epithet that links such knowledge with the aforesaid wisewomen. As well as spells

to ease physical symptoms, you will find magical recipes to overcome emotional pain, ease grief, and work against a sorrowful disposition. This is because health and well-being are so much more than simply being able to function. Ridding yourself of unhealthy habits and attaining physical and mental balance are important elements of both. The quality of beauty, both physical and spiritual, is intimately connected with self-esteem, health, and inner peace—which in turn are key elements of well-being. Thus, in this section, you will find that the spells and their objectives all flow into each another with the ease that you would expect in a tradition that encourages holism and wholesomeness.

HEALING STONE SPELL
FOR HEALING PHYSICAL AILMENTS

PURPOSE To heal a variety of physical problems.

BACKGROUND This spell is taken from a very old tradition in sympathetic magic, based on the idea that sickness or blight can be transferred to another, or to an inanimate object. In less enlightened times, an ailment might be symbolically transferred to a living animal; one old charm to cure warts, for example, included instructions to rub them on a toad, which was then weighted down and drowned in a pond.

You will be happy to learn that although this spell acts in line with the ancient principles of symbolic transference, it does not resort to such cruelty. Rather, it employs an ingredient that is not harmed during the making of the spell—a stone. Using an inanimate object is not a second-rate option; the power of stones and crystals and other earth-based objects was well known to our ancestors, and many old transference spells mention the use of specific types of stones or pebbles.

Prior to working this charm, you will need to find a smooth, white, oval-shaped pebble that fits snugly in the palm of your hand. It should be shaped naturally by water or weather, so you are likely to need an expedition to the sea, or to a river or lakeside.

HOW TO CAST THE SPELL

TIMING This spell should be cast on a
waning moon to take ailments away, and
on a Monday, day of the mysterious moon.

CASTING THE SPELL

1 Cast a circle in accordance with the
guidelines on pages 32–35.

2 Visualize a white circle encompassing
the entire room.

3 Using the nail, score an X-shaped cross
onto the surface of the tea-light, with the
wick at the intersection of the X, saying:

Ill things are scored out
And sickness brought to rout.

4 Light the candle, then fold the cheesecloth in half and sew up the sides with
double thread to form an open pouch.

5 Rub the pebble on the part of the body
that is troubling you, visualizing what you
wish to expel as black smoke drawing
from your body into the stone, while
repeating the following:

The waning moon
Shall shrink to bone
And take with her
What's in this stone.

6 When you are done, place the pebble in
the pouch and tie it firmly with the cord,
then cast it into the deepest local natural
water source.

YOU WILL NEED

One sharp iron nail

One white tea-light

Matches or a lighter

One 4" x 8"/10 cm x 20 cm strip
of cheesecloth

One sewing needle

One 24"/60 cm length of white sewing
thread

One white, naturally oval-shaped pebble

One 9"/22.5 cm length of fine black cord

HEART CHALICE SPELL
TO INCREASE SELF-ESTEEM

PURPOSE To build self-esteem.

BACKGROUND The pressures of modern fashions and ever-changing ideas of physical perfection can make it difficult for us to appreciate what we have and who we are. This spell is the perfect antidote to the type of thinking that sees beauty and worth in the looks of the exceptional few; it will help you to focus on the beauty and value of your looks, your personality, your spirit.

The symbolism of the chalice is ultimately bound up with many of the legends of northern and western Europe, the quest for the Holy Grail being a more recent, Christianized version of a cup representing healing and spiritual quest. In the *Mabinogion*—the book of ancient Welsh spiritual traditions and stories—a magical cauldron is associated with the gift of renewal. In Western magical traditions the chalice represents the magical healing qualities of water and the accompanying correspondence of that element—love.

The chalice of this spell is a cup of healing *and* love, as building self-esteem is really about coming to love yourself and healing the damage caused by distorted social values.

HOW TO CAST THE SPELL

YOU WILL NEED

One stick of frankincense in a secure holder

One green candle, 6–8"/15–20 cm in length

One pale blue candle, 6–8"/15–20 cm in length

Matches or a lighter

One sharp tack

One clean copper disk

One wineglass or goblet

One red rosebud

One sprig of rosemary

Apple juice, 3 fl oz/85 ml

Natural spring water, 3 fl oz/85 ml

TIMING Work on a waxing moon to enhance feelings of self-worth, and on Friday, day of loving and harmonious Venus, after moonrise.

CASTING THE SPELL

1 Cast a circle in accordance with the guidelines on p. 32–35.

2 Light the incense and the green and blue candles.

3 Using the tack, inscribe the initial of your first name and a heart symbol on the copper disk.

4 Place it in your chalice, saying:
  By that which I hold dear.
Add the rosebud, saying:
  By that which I love best.
Add the rosemary, saying:
  By that which I value.
Pour on the apple juice and water, saying:
  By what is sweet
  By what is pure.
Hold the chalice in both hands before the candles, and say:
  May I hold myself dear
  May I love myself well
  May I be that which I value.

5 Leave the chalice undisturbed in the open in moonlight for an hour; then drink the potion.

6 Bury the disk, rosebud, and rosemary beneath a beloved plant in your garden or in a nearby green space.

FOUR WINDS SPELL
TO PROMOTE HARMONIOUS LIVING

PURPOSE To bring harmony and balance into all areas of your life.

BACKGROUND This charm calls on the power of the four winds to bring balance into all areas of your life. It does not guarantee protection against all of life's crises but works toward a balance in your life that enables you to deal with them as they arrive.

There are many traditions concerning control of the winds, many of them associated with witches, who were accused at the height of the witchcraft persecutions in Europe of conjuring up storms in order to cause shipwrecks and ruin crops. One of the methods by which witches were said to summon high winds was by "knotting" them into a cloth or cord.

Of these superstitious tales, only the account of knotting in magical work comes anywhere near the truth; witches have used knotting as a means of sealing a spell for time out of memory—though not to unleash bad weather. In the making of this charm, you will be using a technique that is truly ancient.

HOW TO CAST THE SPELL

TIMING Cast on a waxing half-moon—the day of the week is immaterial, as the moon phase must take precedence.

CASTING THE SPELL

1 Cast a circle in accordance with the guidelines on pages 32–35.

2 Place the water, salt, incense, and tea-light at equidistant points around the circle. Light the charcoal disk and the tea-light; then light the candles, saying:

I stand between the darkness and the light.

3 Tie four knots at equidistant points along the cord, one after each of the following lines:

I invoke the east wind, by my breath
I invoke the south wind, by my body's heat
I invoke the west wind, by the water in
   my blood
I invoke the north wind, by my flesh
   and bones.

4 Bury it in salt, saying:
I show you to earth.
Soak it in water, saying:
I show you to water.
Pass it through the incense smoke, saying:
I show you to air.

5 Pass it through heat from the tea-light, saying:
I show you to fire.

YOU WILL NEED

One bowl of water

One bowl of salt

One pinch of frankincense

One tea-light in a holder

One charcoal disk in a fireproof dish

One black candle, 6–8"/15–20 cm
in length

One white candle, 6–8"/15–20 cm
in length

Matches or a lighter

One 24"/60 cm length of pale blue
silken cord

6 Hold the cord up, and declare:
May all around me balanced be
Whenever the four winds blow on me
May I retain true harmony
Blessed and so mote it be!
Keep the cord safe.

143

PEACE INCANTATION SPELL
TO ATTAIN TRANQUILLITY AND INNER PEACE

PURPOSE To help those wishing to achieve a sense of inner peace.

BACKGROUND All of us experience troubles from time to time, and we are better equipped for dealing with them when we have inner resources of calm and tranquillity. Sometimes this is easier said than done, as attaining peace within requires patience, persistence, and determination. This spell goes a long way toward touching a place of inner calm—and can be repeated as often as needed. Your sense of peace will increase each time you use it.

 ## HOW TO CAST THE SPELL

YOU WILL NEED

Thirteen white candles of varying heights

Matches or a lighter

One charcoal disk in a fireproof dish

Two tablespoons of incense blended from equal parts sandalwood, camomile, and myrrh and six drops of apple essential oil

One small handbell

TIMING The night of the full moon, on any day of the week, is ideal for casting this spell.

CASTING THE SPELL

1 Place the candles in a circle around the area in which you are working. Cast a circle in accordance with the guidelines on pages 32–35.

2 Light the charcoal disk and sprinkle on the incense.

3 Beginning in the east of the circle and moving clockwise, light all the candles. Sit in the center of the circle, and slow your breathing until you feel calm. Say aloud:

> *Iris, goddess of peace*
> *Aid me in my quest.*

The practice of chanting is a very ancient technique, one found in many world religions. One theory holds that chanting occupies the logical left-hand brain, enabling the right-hand brain, allegedly the more spiritual center, to come to the fore. Certainly the rhythm and act of chanting can alter our levels of consciousness and promote different states of being. Repetition can be very soothing, and although you can go back into the circle as often as you wish to cast the whole spell, you will find that using the Peace Incantation outside of the circle is also very strengthening.

4 Ring the bell to signal that you are ready to begin.

5 Chant the following, finding as you chant a pattern of notes to match the rhythm of the words:

Air flows within me and around me
Air flows around me and within
Life flows within me and around me
Life flows around me and within.
Continue to work your way through the five elements—air, fire, water, earth, spirit—and end with the following lines:
Peace flows within me and around me
Peace flows around me and within.

6 Repeat this entire incantation nine times; then ring the bell to signal the end of your chant.

CANDLE THORN SPELL
TO PROMOTE MENTAL HEALTH AND HYGIENE

PURPOSE   To help drive away nagging worries and mental "clutter."

BACKGROUND   At a time when stress is a major health problem in industrialized countries, finding a way to drive worries away is somewhat of a health priority! Part of maintaining a healthy mental state is the ability to wash away the worries that hang on long after we are able to do anything about them. This is particularly the case at the end of a working day or on the weekend when work-connected worries continue to nag, even when we are not in a position to tackle them head-on. If this happens to you, then this spell could help you take the sting out of the most irritating of anxiety states.

It is not difficult to see where the symbolism for this spell comes from—if a person is a constant nuisance or worry to us, we say they are a "thorn in the side." Here, more abstract worries are represented by the thorns that are pressed into the side of a candle. As the candle burns down, the worries are released, leaving you with a clearer head and the ability to shuck such burdens from your shoulders more effectively in the future.

HOW TO CAST THE SPELL

YOU WILL NEED

One charcoal disk in a fireproof dish

Matches or a lighter

One tablespoon of dried juniper berries

One pale blue candle, 6–8"/15–20 cm in length

One black candle, 6–8"/15–20 cm in length

Sufficient rose thorns to represent each of your worries

5

TIMING Work on a waning moon to take worries away, on any day of the week.

CASTING THE SPELL

1 Cast a circle in accordance with the guidelines on pages 32–35.

2 Light the charcoal; sprinkle on some juniper berries.

3 Light the blue candle.

4 Hold the black candle between your palms, and closing your eyes, concentrate on the anxiety that besets you; envisage it as a dark cloud drawing out of you and going into the candle.

5 Hold the black candle over the heat of the blue candle flame to soften the sides. Pick up the thorns, ready to press them into the softened wax, naming them as you do, for example:

> *I baptize thee [anxiety over money/worries belonging to the office, etc.]*

6 When you are satisfied that you have covered all the anxieties, light the black candle, saying:

> *As you burn,*
> *You will release*
> *Anxiety*
> *Which hence shall cease*
> *As you burn*
> *The thorns shall slough*
> *All worries*
> *Then shall be cast off.*

BOTTLE SPELL
TO ENCOURAGE FEELINGS OF WELL-BEING

PURPOSE To promote a sense of well-being.

BACKGROUND A sense of well-being comes both from enjoying general good health and from a sense of wholeness that comes from within. Sometimes it is possible, with a little magic, to begin the task of bringing your life, health, and work into balance by starting off with a sense of well-being.

This spell is designed to kick start your plans to balance your life more effectively by drawing on the powers of the sun—the traditional patron of good health and fortune. It centers on achieving a sense of well-being, through which you can explore those parts of your life and health that need to be brought into balance or that simply need tending to. If you are intent on neglecting some aspects of your health or lifestyle, be warned that casting a spell alone will not compensate. The sense of well-being achieved via this charm is but a taste of what can be accomplished with patience, thought, and effort.

HOW TO CAST THE SPELL

YOU WILL NEED

Two teaspoons of water

Six drops of cinnamon essential oil

One oil burner with a tea-light

Matches or a lighter

One orange or gold candle, 6–8"/15–20 cm in length

One marigold flower head

One wineglass

Pure water, 2 fl oz/50 ml

One sterile bottle with a lid and dropper

TIMING Cast this spell during the daytime, on a waxing moon and on a Sunday, day of the munificent sun.

CASTING THE SPELL

1 Cast a circle in accordance with the guidelines on pages 32–35.

2 Place the water and oil into the oil burner dish, and light it.

3 Light the orange candle, saying:
May the sun's Eternal power
Found within this gentle flower
Grant me good health from this hour.
The flower, or candle-flame, should be held up to greet the four cardinal directions, then brought back to the center.

4 Place the marigold in the wineglass, and pour on the water. Take it outside to allow the sun to shine on its contents. Return with it to the circle, and pour it into the bottle.

5 Place three drops of the water on your tongue, saying:
That which I seek
So might it speak.
Now anoint your eyelids with the water, saying:
That I would know
I will understand so.
Anoint your ears with the water, saying:
That I would receive
So might I achieve.
Anoint your forehead, saying:
That wisdom come near
Let it begin here.

6 Keep the bottle in a safe place, and use the water any time you wish to feel the power of the sun.

DAWNTIDE SPELL
TO ACHIEVE BEAUTY

PURPOSE To bring out the beauty in you.

BACKGROUND Perceptions of what is
beautiful are notoriously subjective, differ from
culture to culture, and change over time. What is
thought beautiful in one era is often thought
unattractive in another, and what is deemed the
epitome of beauty in one culture may be
disregarded in another, or even considered ugly!
There is no such thing, in short, as a universal
measure of physical beauty.

If you wish to bring out your most attractive
features and draw out your inner beauty, this is
just the spell for you. Based on a very old custom,
it requires access to grass uncontaminated by
crop spraying or chemicals, in order to gather pure
morning dew. It is best performed in the summer,
from May onward, at sunrise, so you will need to
get up and out early for this one!

This spell is, unusually, performed in the open
air, so you will need to ensure privacy. Given the
time of day when you will be out and about, this
shouldn't be too difficult. Please give some
thought to your safety, too, and take a friend
along if at all possible.

HOW TO CAST THE SPELL

YOU WILL NEED

One shortened green candle, in a jar

Matches or a lighter

A grass meadow, full of dew in the morning!

TIMING Work at dawn on a waxing moon, between May I and August 31, and on any day but Saturday.

CASTING THE SPELL

1 In place of casting a circle in the usual way, work out your position by the sun; as you bow, respectively, to the east, south, west, and north, speak the line appropriate to the direction, as follows:

In the east, I honor the element of air
In the south, I honor the element of fire
In the west, I honor the element of water
In the north, I honor the element of earth.

2 Then, facing the rising sun, say:
At the center of all, I honor the element
of spirit.

3 Light the green candle, saying:
I call upon the spirit of this green field
And the essence of nature
To reflect in me your glory and
natural beauty.

4 Gathering dew from the grass with both hands, bathe your face with it.

5 Repeat this action nine times, each time reciting the words above.

6 Blow out the candle, and take it home to re-light at sundown; allow it to burn out completely.

HEALING CAULDRON SPELL
TO HELP HEAL GRIEF AND EMOTIONAL PAIN

PURPOSE To bring closure to grief and emotional pain.

BACKGROUND Without wishing to sound morbid or pessimistic, it seems reasonable to say that grief and emotional pain are part of human experience. Indeed, some may argue that if we do not give ourselves the time and space for these emotions, we cannot grow and mature. When the time for grief and pain is past, it is healthy to let these feelings go. This is not always easy, and some cultures acknowledge this by providing rituals to mark the end of mourning.

Death is not the only situation that causes us to grieve—the end of a happy time or the breakup of a relationship can also cause deep distress. The healthy way to deal with grief is to take time to express it, remember the person or time we have lost, then move on and grow from that experience. If moving away from grief is difficult, and you are finding it hard to let go of painful feelings because they have become a habit rather than a healthy way of dealing with loss, this ritual will help you to move on.

152

HOW TO CAST THE SPELL

YOU WILL NEED

One black candle, 6–8"/15–20 cm
in length

Matches or a lighter

One copper or bronze-colored coin

One large metal cauldron or rounded
ceramic pot

One small, dark, rounded pebble

One teaspoon of water

Two trowelfuls of soil or potting soil

Red wine or grape juice, 4 fl oz/125 ml

TIMING Cast this spell on a waning moon
to carry grief out with the tide, on any day
of the week, with Saturday, day of Saturn
the banisher, the most favorable.

CASTING THE SPELL

1 Cast a circle in accordance with the
guidelines on pages 32–35.

2 Light the candle, saying:
Light upon grief
Cast out all pain
Tears to be lost
Happiness gained.

3 Place the coin in the cauldron, saying:
Ties are now rent
Anger is spent.
Now place in the pebble, saying:
Banished the frown
Weighing me down.
Pour in the water, saying:
Hence the last
Teardrop passed.

4 Cover these with the soil or potting
soil; then raise the glass of wine, saying:
A toast to sorrows gone
That will not come again.

5 Drink half, and pour the remainder
onto the soil, saying:
The earth to soak up
The last of this cup.

6 Stand the cauldron by the candle
until it is completely burned down. Then
remove it and keep it in a hidden place for
one moon cycle. Then bury the soil and
its contents after dark, away from
your home.

BALEFIRE SPELL
TO DESTROY WORRIES

PURPOSE To send your worries up in smoke.

BACKGROUND If you need a dramatic way to get rid of troubles that are hanging over you, you are looking at the right spell. Rather than fend off worries, this spell destroys the ones that are already bothering you. Needless to say, the spell does not sort out all of your problems for you but works by ritually naming and burning them in a magical fire, known as a balefire.

 ## HOW TO CAST THE SPELL

YOU WILL NEED

One large bundle of dry wood

One tea-light in a lantern or jar

Matches or a lighter

One ink pen, with red ink

Sufficient slips of paper to represent each worry

One large bundle of dry weeds

One large bundle of dry yarrow

Dried orange peel from five oranges

TIMING After dark, on a waning moon, on any day—warn your neighbors to get their washing in from the yard, as the fire will create a good deal of smoke!

CASTING THE SPELL

1 Put together and light a bonfire using dry wood outdoors.

2 Visualize a circle of white light all around the bonfire and the area in which you will be working.

A balefire is any fire made for magical purposes and therefore eminently suited for burning ingredients assembled for a spell. The destruction of what is named in a magical circle is a very powerful act, and you gain the most benefit from this spell if you keep it simple. Try to name your worries by summing them up in a single word. If it is a troublesome person, just write their name. Don't worry—you won't be harming them. It is the intent that counts here, and the intention of this spell is to obliterate the worries, *not* the person who causes them (however tempting).

3 Light the tea-light, and by its light, write your worries, one on each paper slip.

4 Throw the weeds on the fire, saying:
   By this bane, I root you out.
Throw on the yarrow, saying:
   By this boon, I cancel.
Naming each worry as you do so, throw the slips of paper in one by one, and watch them burn.
Cast in the orange peel, saying:
   Troubles begone
   Sweetness anon.

5 Stay outdoors until the fire is completely burned down.

6 Remove the ashes, and bury them away from the house.

WEDJAT EYE CHARM
TO KEEP ANXIETY AT BAY

PURPOSE To exorcise anxiety and keep it away.

BACKGROUND Wedjat Eye is the healed eye of the Egyptian god Horus, said in ancient mythologies to represent the powers of the moon. It has long been used as a protective charm, if worn as an amulet about the body or drawn on the outside of your home. In this spell the Wedjat Eye is used to raise the power to protect against evil from others, be that evil envy, wishing ill, or other ill feeling. Before this power can be effectively invoked, however, it is necessary to dispel all causes of anxiety from your life.

 HOW TO CAST THE SPELL

YOU WILL NEED

One large white plate

One fine artist's brush

One tube of black oil paint

One charcoal disk in a fireproof dish

One teaspoon of frankincense gum anointed with honey and geranium essential oil

One black candle, 6–8"/15–20 cm in length

One silver candle, 6–8"/15–20 cm in length

Matches or a lighter

One small, plain tea-plate (or flat dessert-plate)

TIMING This working should be performed on the dark of the moon, on any day of the week, after dark.

CASTING THE SPELL

1 Prior to the circle, and allowing enough time for the paint to dry, paint the following words onto the inside of the plate:

Every evil word, every evil speech, every evil slander, every evil thought, every evil plot, every evil fright, every evil quarrel, every evil plan, every evil thing, every evil dream, every evil slumber.

This is achieved symbolically by using an Egyptian spell, dating back approximately four thousand years.

In order to perform this charm, you should find an expendable plate on which to paint the words prescribed for the spell, as you will need to smash it immediately after the words are spoken in the circle. You will also need to purchase a plate-hanging bracket for the hanging of the Wedjat Eye amulet onto the outside of your home. Prior to casting the spell, it would be wise, provided your health will allow it, to fast during the day.

4 Light the black candle, and speak the words on the plate aloud. Smash the plate immediately after you finish speaking.

5 Light the silver candle, and paint the Wedjat Eye, on the center of the tea-plate (dessert plate).

2 Cast a circle in accordance with the guidelines on pages 32–35.

3 Light the charcoal disk, and burn the incense.

6 Allow it to dry; then hang it on the outside of your building to protect you from anxiety. Bury the broken plate deep in the earth, away from your home.

OUROBORUS SPELL
TO AID PHYSICAL BALANCE

PURPOSE To achieve physical balance and thereby pave the way to good health.

BACKGROUND This spell is based on an ancient principle that makes good sense for us today, the principle prescribing "moderation in all things" as the basis for sound health. This is not just a warning about excess, but a positive encouragement to ensure that we are balanced in all essentials, and that no one physical desire or need should overrule the well-being of our other physical requirements.

 HOW TO CAST THE SPELL

YOU WILL NEED

One charcoal disk in a fireproof dish

Matches or a lighter

Benzoin granules

One black candle, 6–8"/15–20 cm in length

One white candle, 6–8"/15–20 cm in length

One pen with green ink

One 1" x ½"/2.5 cm x 1 cm strip of paper

Nine 18"/45 cm lengths of thick-stranded cotton embroidery thread, three each of black, red, and white

One 18"/45 cm length of thick-stranded gray cotton embroidery thread

TIMING This should be cast on a waxing half-moon to draw positive balance. Any day of the week is suitable, with Monday being especially powerful.

CASTING THE SPELL

1 Cast a circle in accordance with the guidelines on pages 32–35.

2 Light the charcoal, and sprinkle on benzoin.

3 Place the black candle to the left of the white candle, and light both, saying:
Hermes, magus of the eternal
Grant this boon
Of perfect elemental balance.

The symbol used in this spell is that of the ouroborus, the "serpent that swallows its own tail." It is an ancient alchemical sign that represents oneness, wholeness, and the nature of universal balance. There is a well-established link, throughout the Near East and northern and western Europe, between snakes and healing, as they have evolved as an image of earth wisdom. Brigid, an Irish goddess associated with healing wells, is closely associated with serpents, as are many other goddesses of the healing arts.

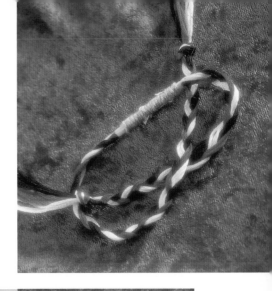

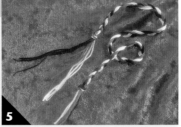

4 Using the pen, draw on the strip of paper the symbol of the ouroborus—the curved serpent swallowing its own tail.

5 When the ink has dried, pass the paper through the incense smoke. Place it to one side, and tie and braid a wristband to fit your left wrist from the black, red, and white threads.

6 Prior to tying this onto your wrist, roll the strip of paper with the ouroborus inscribed on it around the bracelet, and cover it by rolling the gray thread over it until it is completely used up; then fasten it firmly. Wear your ouroborus bracelet until it falls off.

SUNFLOWER SPELL
TO ENCOURAGE A HAPPY DISPOSITION

PURPOSE   To invoke happiness.

BACKGROUND   The secret of true happiness differs according to whom you ask and where they are in their lives. Those who have walked the earth for many years and who have meditated greatly on the matter may claim that happiness lies in finding peace within. People who have suffered, or witnessed suffering through privation, claim with equal validity that happiness resides within the simple things needed for physical and spiritual survival: food, warmth, clothing, shelter, freedom, companionship, and love. Most often, the secret of true happiness lies within those who ask the question.

This spell is based on the power of our friend the sun to generate warmth, health, and joy on the earth. The powers of Sol can sometimes be found concentrated in certain herbs and plants, and perhaps nowhere more so than in the seeds of the sunflower. Nutritionally speaking, sunflower seeds contain a concentrated property of sunlight—they are a good source of vitamin D. Vitamin D aids calcium absorption and helps regulate our metabolism. Since sunflowers in magical tradition represent the powers of the sun, the seeds carry in concentrated form Sol's ability to bestow health and happiness.

HOW TO CAST THE SPELL

YOU WILL NEED

One charcoal disk in a fireproof dish

Matches or a lighter

Frankincense

One orange candle, 6–8"/15–20 cm in length

Fifteen sunflower seeds

One small pouch with a drawstring mouth

One 26"/65 cm length of thong or fine cord

TIMING Work on a waxing moon to attract happiness, and on a Sunday, ruled by glorious Sol.

CASTING THE SPELL

1 Cast a circle in accordance with the guidelines on pages 32–35.

2 Light the charcoal disk, and burn the frankincense. Light the candle, saying:

> *Sol Invictus*
> *You are honored here*
> *Shine your blessings*
> *Upon your child.*

3 Take five sunflower seeds and cup them in your left hand, then raise your right hand, saying:

> *Your power*
> *To pass to me.*

Eat the seeds.

4 Take five more sunflower seeds and place them in the pouch, saying:

> *Your strength to*
> *Abide with me.*

Fasten the pouch, attach it to the cord, and place it around your neck, saying:

> *Happiness reside within me*
> *Happiness reside around me.*

5 Carry the incense around the circle *deosil* (clockwise) three times. Bow your head to the candle flame, saying:

> *Sol Invictus*
> *Blessed be*
> *May I give*
> *As I receive.*

6 Plant the remaining five seeds in the spring, approximately ¼"/5 mm below the surface of finely tilled soil.

161

LAVENDER SPELL
TO AID RESTFUL SLEEP

PURPOSE To aid relaxed and untroubled sleep.

BACKGROUND Lavender is known as one of the great universals among scented herbs. Noted for its antiseptic qualities, its essential oil is also wonderful for curing headaches, healing scalds, and treating eczema and other troublesome skin conditions. It is a great relaxant and often used in dream pillows—sachets stuffed with soporific herbs to aid restful and natural sleep. Drops of the essential oil, either placed in a warm bath before bedtime or placed on a pillowcase, are used to bring on drowsiness.

HOW TO CAST THE SPELL

YOU WILL NEED

One lavender-scented pillar candle, any size

Matches or a lighter

One white candle, 6–8"/15–20 cm in length

One pliable whip of willow of a length to fit over a person if it is hooped

One 36"/90 cm length of strong twine

One large bunch of dried camomile

One large bunch of dried lavender

One roll of florist twine

TIMING Work on a waxing moon to bring rest, and on any day of the week save Saturday, ruled by restrictive Saturn.

CASTING THE SPELL

1 Cast a circle in accordance with the guidelines on pages 32–35.

2 Light the lavender-scented candle, and carry it around the space deosil (clockwise) to scent it.

3 Light the white candle, saying:
The purity of light
Guide the way to gentle sleep
Hence may I be known
For the peace that I keep.

This spell uses a magical technique that has a venerable history in the annals of magical practice. It requires a hoop to be passed over the entire body of the person for whom the spell is being cast. The technique of passing someone through an opening or hole is very old—ancient holed standing stones have long been used for the purpose of blessing those passed through them. The flower hoop used in this spell has a similar principle—that once one has passed through a sacred space, its passing is irreversible, and so the blessing is sealed.

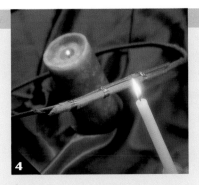

4 Bend the willow into a hoop, and fasten it firmly using the strong twine. Fasten the camomile and lavender onto it with florist's twine until the willow is entirely covered by the dried flowers.

5 Hold up the hoop vertically before the white candle, saying:

Through this circle
I will pass
On the road to
Morpheus
So my spell for sleep
Is blessed.

Pass the hoop over your entire body, head to toe, and step out of it.

6 Hang the hoop above your bed.

SPIDER SPELL
TO BRING HAPPY DREAMS

PURPOSE   To bring happy, wholesome dreams.

BACKGROUND   Native American dream catchers act as nets, letting good dreams through the net but catching and holding bad dreams at bay—until the morning light melts them away. But different types of nets can be used for different purposes, and in this spell a spider's web is used to catch happy dreams to nourish your imagination and grace your nights.

This spell is inspired by the magical and spiritual symbolism of the spider, which has at times been falsely associated with evil and deceit. In fact, many cultures honor the spider as a symbol of creativity and spirit energy. In Western magical traditions, their webs are likened to the patterns of magic, spirit, and connection. The spider is a truly amazing creature, and its weaving abilities are proverbial. Wonderful webs which join leaf to concrete, gateposts to trees—nature to the built environment— announce the turning of dreaming's tides. After the equinox in September, we pass into the darker days and so into our more creative selves, which are often revealed through the rich and vivid dreams we experience at this time of year.

HOW TO CAST THE SPELL

YOU WILL NEED

One oil burner with a tea-light

Two teaspoons of water

Six drops of poppy essential oil

Matches or a lighter

One white candle, 6–8"/15–20 cm
in length

One small nugget of pyrite (fool's gold)

One spider's web

One white drawstring pouch

One 24"/60 cm length of thin white
ribbon

4

TIMING To be cast on a waxing moon, with
Monday, dedicated to the moon, who rules
our dreams, as the most auspicious day.

CASTING THE SPELL

1 Cast a circle in accordance with the
guidelines on pages 32–35.

2 Light the tea-light, placing the water
and poppy oil in the oil burner.

3 Light the white candle, saying:
Lady of the moon
Grandmother spider
Weave your magic
Into my dreams.

4 Wrap the pyrite nugget inside the
spider's web, and place it in the pouch.

5 Fasten it firmly halfway down the
length of ribbon. Then, enclosing the
pouch in your cupped hands, chant the
following over again for the space of at
least sixty heartbeats:
Grandmother spider
Weave your threads
Wrap all beauty
In your web.

6 Hang the pouch over your bedpost
or above your bed. Every night until
the next full moon, touch your hand
to it when you retire saying the
following words:
Happy themes
Enter my dreams.

CYCLAMEN CHARM
TO GUARD AGAINST NIGHTMARES

PURPOSE To defend against bad dreams.

BACKGROUND Everyone has the occasional bad dream; after all, dreams act as a safety valve, so it is not surprising that bad feelings come out as nightmares. However, if nightmares are frequent and there is no underlying trauma that can be discerned, a little magic may be used to good effect.

This particular magical charm is based on an old spell to cure night frights in children and is suitable for adults and children alike. Cyclamen is noted, by those who specialize in such things, as a great defense against bad vibes. Keeping the plant in the bedroom at night is said to reduce the occurrence of nightmares, and the flowers are sometimes carried to ease grief. The cheering nature of cyclamen is perhaps reflected in the fact that it is happiest growing in shaded parts of gardens and woodland, where it brings color and brightness to the darker places of each.

You should note that the blood used in this spell should be drawn from the person for whom the spell is intended—the directions opposite are written as if for the person casting the spell.

HOW TO CAST THE SPELL

TIMING It is best to work at the dark moon to enhance protection, on any day of the week, with Saturday, ruled by Saturn the banisher, especially auspicious.

CASTING THE SPELL

1 Cast a circle in accordance with the guidelines on pages 32–35.

2 Light the charcoal, and sprinkle on incense.

3 Light the black candle, saying:
Hecate dark
Venus bright
Drive out the bad
Bring in the light.

4 Use the needle to prick your forefinger, and squeeze out a drop of blood onto the potting soil in which the cyclamen is standing, saying:
Guard what lives in this house of skin
Protected without, and held within.

5 Pass the entire length of the ribbon through the incense smoke, saying:
That which is pure
Shall aye endure.
Tie the ribbon around the plant pot, and fasten into a bow.

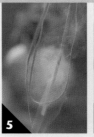

YOU WILL NEED

One charcoal disk in a fireproof dish

Matches or a lighter

Blended incense of equal parts copal gum, juniper berries, and dried cyclamen flowers

One black candle, 6–8"/15–20 cm in length

One sterile needle

One healthy cyclamen plant, any color

One 24"/60 cm length of red satin ribbon

6 Keep this potted plant in your room day and night, and nurture and care for it always if you wish to keep bad dreams at bay.

CANDLE WAX SPELL
TO BANISH UNHEALTHY HABITS

PURPOSE   To get rid of unhealthy habits once and for all.

BACKGROUND   Have you ever wanted to kick smoking, nail-biting, thumb-sucking, or hair-twisting? Look no farther—this is the spell for you! A little bit of magic and a confidence boost will go a long way toward ridding yourself of an unhealthy or unwanted habit. You will need to ask yourself, however, whether the need that is encouraging your habit is going to be answered in some other way once that habit has

gone. If it is not, you may end up back at square one, so it is worth taking time to prepare for this spell.

Begin by identifying the cause of the habit (for example, nervousness, lack of confidence, anxiety) and then working out what the consequences of banishing your unhealthy habit may be. If you are a nail-biter, you won't wish to become a smoker or a thumb-sucker instead, so ensure that what is being banished is replaced with something healthy—a new outlook, for example. Ask yourself searching questions, and answer them honestly. Then you will be ready to consign your bad habit to the garbage can!

HOW TO CAST THE SPELL

TIMING Work this spell on a waning moon to aid banishment, and on a Saturday, ruled by disciplinarian Saturn.

CASTING THE SPELL

1 Cast a circle in accordance with the guidelines on pages 32–35.

2 Light the charcoal disk, and sprinkle on incense. Light the brown candle, saying:
Saturn, witness and empower this spell.

3 Heat the point of the nail in the candle's flame; then use it to carve the name of the habit you want to banish down the side of one white candle, from the bottom to the wick.

4 Hold this candle before the candle flame, saying:
Burn it away.
Pass it through the incense smoke, saying:
Let it fly out.
Hold this candle between your palms, saying:
The habit that's in me
Fly into you
The fire burn it out.
Light the candle.

YOU WILL NEED

One charcoal disk in a fireproof dish

Matches or a lighter

Black copal incense

One brown candle, 6–8"/15–20 cm in length

One sharp 6"/15 cm iron nail

Two white household candles, approximately 6"/15 cm in length

5 Using the same method, carve into the side of the second white candle, from the wick to the bottom, "HEALTH."

6 Light the second candle, and allow both candles to burn down completely within the circle.

CELTIC STONE SPELL
TO GUARD AGAINST FREQUENT HEADACHES

PURPOSE To banish frequent tension headaches.

BACKGROUND There are many old remedies for frequent headaches; herbal remedies include the application of feverfew for migraines and good old aspirin or willow bark to kill pain. If you are plagued by frequent tension headaches, and you have checked with your doctor that there is no serious underlying condition, try this ancient cure.

HOW TO CAST THE SPELL

YOU WILL NEED

One black candle, 6–8"/15–20 cm in length

Matches or a lighter

One sharp piece of flint (or one sharp nail)

One gray or white egg-shaped stone

Pure water, 2 fl oz/50 ml

Red wine, 2 fl oz/50 ml

One salt dispenser

TIMING Cast on a waning moon to dispose of the ailment, and on any day of the week.

CASTING THE SPELL

1 Cast a circle in accordance with the guidelines on pages 32–35.

2 Light the black candle, saying:
Let this sickness shrink with this lamp
Let it shrink with the moon
Let it be cast away with this stone.

3 Using the flint or the nail, scratch onto the stone the shape of an oval; then strike it through with an X-shaped cross.

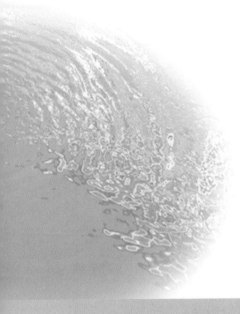

This spell relies on the transference principle of sympathetic magic—the belief that an ailment can be transferred from a person into an object, which is then symbolically acted on or placed where it cannot contaminate anyone. This spell employs a stone as the object and follows the practices of the nature-revering Celts, who often cast sacred or magical objects into deep water.

Here, the curative and concealing properties of water are brought into play to ensure that the transference of the headaches into the stone is sealed, and the headaches themselves are healed.

4 Rub the stone three times on the part of your head that gives you the most pain, saying:

Place my headache in this stone
That I may have no cause to moan
Until its flesh be shrunk to bone.

Pour the water over the stone. Hold up the wine, saying:

I name you my pain.

Pour the wine over the stone.

5 Place a circle of salt on the ground around the stone, saying:

Shrink and wither,
Come not hither.

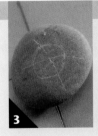
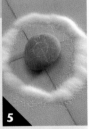

6 Cast the stone into the deepest local natural water source.

SUN SPIRIT CHARM
TO GUARD AGAINST SORROW

PURPOSE   To prevent you from falling into melancholy.

BACKGROUND   Here is a charm to help you to remember to look on the sunny side, especially if you are prone to fits of melancholy or pessimism. The power of the sun to raise our spirits is recognized in the sayings we have that refer to a generally happy person as having a "sunny" nature or always walking on the "sunny side of the street." In this spell, the spirit of the sun is called on to empower a charm that will ensure you resist the tendency to dwell on sorrow. If you are suffering from depression, do seek counseling or medical advice.

 ## HOW TO CAST THE SPELL

YOU WILL NEED

Four white candles, 6–8"/15–20 cm in length

One yellow candle, 6–8"/15–20 cm in length

One cinnamon incense stick in a holder

Matches or a lighter

One pen with brown ink

One small disk of oak wood cut from a severed branch

One can of clear varnish

One 24"/60 cm length of thong or cord

TIMING Cast this spell on a waxing moon, and on a Sunday, ruled by the sun, patron of health and happiness.

CASTING THE SPELL

1 Cast a circle in accordance with the guidelines on pages 32–35.

2 Place the candles in a row, with the yellow candle in the center.

3 Light the incense stick and all the white candles.

It is worth considering the power of the sun in dispelling gloom if you are considering casting this spell. In temperate climates, it is now generally acknowledged that the lack of sunlight during winter can cause severe depression. Even if this does not apply to you, it is worth increasing the amount of time you spend outdoors each day. If lack of sunlight can make us sick, it follows that a reasonable amount of daylight can raise our spirits. To complement this spell, engage in more outdoor activities in order to maximize the effect that the sun's many gifts will bring to you.

4 Using the pen, draw a circle in the center of the disk, surrounded by points to represent the rays of the sun. In the center of the circle, write:

SALVE

SOL.

5 Light the yellow candle, saying:
I invoke the powers of the life-giving sun
I invoke the powers of the sun's fires
That sorrow be burned away
And happiness revealed.
Allow the ink to dry in the light of the candles until all are burned down.

6 After the circle, drill a hole near the edge of the disk. Varnish it to protect the ink markings, then thread through it with the thong and wear it around your neck at all times.

RASPBERRY LEAF SACHET
FOR EASE IN CHILDBIRTH

PURPOSE To provide a tonic for late pregnancy and to work toward ease in delivery.

BACKGROUND For centuries, those with herbal and midwifery knowledge were village wisewomen whose knowledge was passed from mother to daughter. During the witchcraft persecutions of the sixteenth and seventeenth centuries, this knowledge condemned many women as "witches." Thankfully, their herbal wisdom and knowledge did not entirely die out with the witch-hunts, and many witches today still claim the historical link between witches and midwifery. It would be unthinkable, therefore, if this *Spells Bible* did not include a spell reflecting this tradition.

YOU WILL NEED

One pale blue candle, 6–8"/15–20 cm in length

Matches or a lighter

Nine dried raspberry leaves

One 6" x 3"/15 cm x 7.5 cm oblong piece of white cheesecloth

One sewing needle

One 18"/45 cm length of white thread

Scissors

One small container of dried loose raspberry leaves

Cups for drinking tea

TIMING Perform this spell at the full moon, symbolic of all things coming to fruition. Any day of the week is suitable.

CASTING THE SPELL

1 Cast a circle in accordance with the guidelines on pages 32–35.

2 Light the candle, saying:
Full moon
Fruitful womb.

3 Hold the raspberry leaves between your palms, and chant the following, at least nine times:
Mother of all
Mother of earth

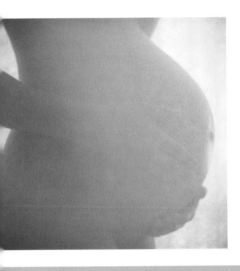

This spell, probably more than any other in this book, is as much based on the health-giving properties of the ingredients as it is on the magical nature of the spell casting. Raspberry leaf is commonly acknowledged to be helpful to women in the later stages of pregnancy. It contains an ingredient that relaxes the uterus, which is thought to aid contractions during labor.

For this spell, you can either purchase the dried leaves from a reputable herbalist or harvest and dry your own thoroughly, to ensure no toxins are present.

Grant me ease
When I give birth.

4 Place the leaves in the cheesecloth, which should be doubled over and sewn up. As you fasten off the thread, cut it with the scissors, saying:

So mote it be.

5 Keep the sachet in the container until your delivery day; then remove it to take with you into the delivery room.

6 Drink between two and four cups a day of a tea made from two teaspoons of raspberry leaf to one cup of boiling water.

WARNING Do not take raspberry leaf sachet tea if you have a history of miscarriages, or before the twenty-eighth week of pregnancy. Always consult your doctor for advice before taking any herbal remedy during pregnancy.

GOODWIFE'S TISANE SPELL
FOR GENERAL GOOD HEALTH

PURPOSE To engender good health and to indicate where health problems are likely to come from.

BACKGROUND For centuries, wisewomen's brews have bestowed cures and general good health. The brews are assembled from herbal and magical knowledge and are health-giving physically as well as spiritually. But teas—for this is what a *tisane* is— also have a reputation as divinatory tools, through the dregs, or leaves, that are left after they have been drunk. This spell combines the two functions in order to bestow good health and provide an early warning system of where health may be compromised in the future.

There is an entire science to go with tea leaf readings, and there is very little space here to explore all of the traditional meanings of all the shapes you are likely to encounter at the bottom of your cup. However, it is possible to give a few hints that will aid you if this is the first time you have "read" the tea leaves; the rest is up to you and your powers of intuition—and of research, should you need it! On the purely herbal front, you may be interested to know that the ingredients of this tisane provide plenty of vitamins, settle the digestion, and aid sleep—all basic ingredients of general good health.

HOW TO CAST THE SPELL

YOU WILL NEED

One pale blue candle, 6–8"/15–20 cm in length

Matches or a lighter

One large freshly chopped dandelion leaf

Three dried camomile flower heads, chopped

Five large freshly chopped mint leaves

One teacup and saucer

Boiling water

TIMING Work on a waxing moon, and on a Monday, day of the Moon, to honor the wisdom of the wisewoman or cunning man within!

CASTING THE SPELL

1 Cast a circle in accordance with the guidelines on pages 32–35.

2 Light the candle, saying:
By sun, wind, and rain
I bless this tisane.

3 Place the ingredients in the cup and pour on the boiling water, then place the saucer over the cup to keep the heat in. While the tisane is brewing, chant the following:
By the goodness in this brew
Sickness slay and life renew.

4 Leave it for five minutes, then uncover it, and when it is cool enough, drink it.

5 Tip the residue onto the saucer.

6 The following shapes indicate associated areas to look out for in the future:

HORSESHOE OR CUP:	*kidney or bladder*
ANIMAL:	*thighs or hips*
FACIAL FEATURES:	*the head*
LINES AND ANGLES:	*joints or arms/ hands/legs/feet*
FIGURE EIGHT:	*chest or sinuses*
WAVES:	*stomach or bowels.*

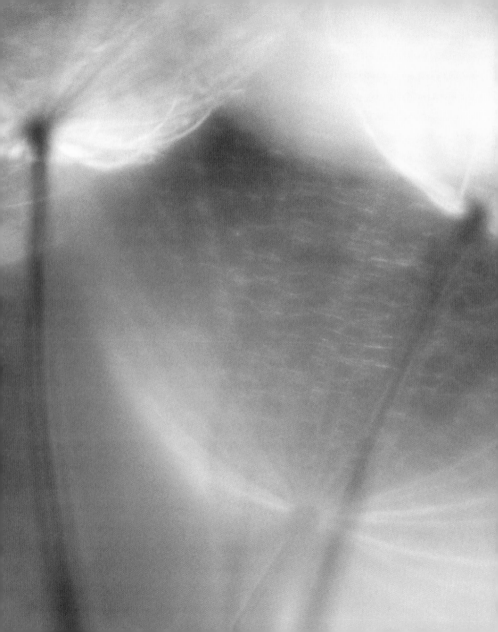

FAMILY, FRIENDS, AND HOME SPELLS

INTRODUCTION TO FAMILY, FRIENDS, AND HOME SPELLS

This section contains spells that operate close to home, focusing on family, roommates, neighbors, friends, and your home environment. Domestic harmony is so important in busy modern life; we need the peace and sanctuary of home in order to stay healthy and to go out into the world to work and socialize with ease. When the stability of our home "base" is compromised, these essential aspects of our lives are also under threat. Being happy and settled in our home space, then, is crucial to the balance of our lives and health.

The spells in this section recognize the importance of certain key elements in maintaining a happy household. Clearly, frequent disagreements are not going to add to anyone's sense of security, so keeping the peace while recognizing the justice of some complaints is crucial in keeping a balanced and restful home life. Here you will find spells to keep housemates and relatives sweet, to help mend quarrels on the home front, and to keep unwelcome relatives at arm's length. In recognition of the importance most of us place on entertaining at home, there is also

a spell to draw more welcome visitors. You could, if casting a spell to fend off disruptive relatives, follow this by casting one to attract sociable and welcome friends to prove that you are not unsociable, just choosy!

You will find in this section a number of spells that focus on the physical and emotional home environment. These include ways of protecting your living space, dispersing a bad atmosphere

following quarrels or other forms of household tension, and promoting communication within the home. Magical recipes to protect your territory and make your garden fruitful and productive are also found here.

Before considering using magic to enhance your home, you should ensure that the basic means for a nurturing and supportive home life are in place. Practical issues such as the fair division of housework and responsibilities are not resolved by magic but by negotiation, honesty, and fairness; a spell for harmony won't alter the atmosphere if there are genuine grievances to be answered! Similarly, material contributions in the way of money or equivalent input should be taken into consideration; ask yourself whether the wealth coming into the household is being distributed fairly. Consider also whether other forms of contribution, such as housework or home maintenance, are being properly recognized and appreciated. This way it is easier to identify when someone is being unreasonable or quarrelsome without fair cause, and consequently, the situation is easier to deal with, magically or otherwise! Magic works best with a practical basis.

PLANT SPELL
TO PROMOTE HARMONY WITHIN THE FAMILY

PURPOSE To bring a harmonious atmosphere to family situations.

BACKGROUND Plants are used in a number of spells in this book, and this reflects their popularity as magical ingredients generally. Often, the common name of a plant directs us toward its magical use, and nigella, the flower recommended for this spell, is no exception. *Nigella damascena,* a beautiful blue flower that nestles among delicate fronds, is commonly known as love-in-a-mist.

 HOW TO CAST THE SPELL

YOU WILL NEED

One charcoal disk in a fireproof dish

One pale green candle, 6–8"/15–20 cm in length

Matches or a lighter

One teaspoon equal parts chopped orris root and white sandalwood

One wineglass containing one packet of loose *Nigella damascena* seeds

One wineglass containing 5 fl oz/150 ml of water

TIMING This spell should be cast indoors on a new moon, in early spring, on any day of the week except Saturday, which is dedicated to stern Saturn. The first part of this spell should be undertaken indoors at sunset, and the planting should take place outdoors, preferably in your garden.

CASTING THE SPELL

1 Cast a circle in accordance with the guidelines on pages 32–35.

2 Light the charcoal disk, then the green candle, saying:

Spirit of the green earth
Make fruitful the wishes I plant in you.

Its use refers not only to romantic love but also to ties of kinship and affection.

This spell involves a bit of gardening. Planting and harvesting Nigella is particularly rewarding; this annual grows well in poor soil and is extremely reliable. When the flowering is over, attractive seed heads are left, from which seeds may be harvested and dried, then packed up as gifts or kept for next year's crop. Harvesting seeds can be fun for all the family, although it is recommended that rubber gloves be worn in case some people are sensitive to the seeds.

3 Sprinkle incense onto the charcoal disk, with a pinch of Nigella seeds, saying:

Love in a mist
Seeds in sweetness
Carried in earth
Born of richness.

4 Hold the bowl of the glass containing the seeds in both hands, and close your eyes to envisage scenes where your family members interact happily and in harmony. Take a deep breath and breathe your out-breath onto the seeds.

5 Take the seeds outside and plant them evenly in finely tilled soil; then sprinkle the water from the wineglass onto them, saying:

Blessed be!

NEW MOON SPELL
TO FIND NEW FRIENDS

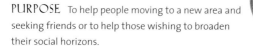

PURPOSE To help people moving to a new area and seeking friends or to help those wishing to broaden their social horizons.

BACKGROUND Wishing on a star, especially a shooting star, is a widely established custom, but the lesser-known tradition of wishing on the moon has an equally long history. There are a number of superstitions relating to the first sight of a waxing moon, including the imperative to turn over any silver coins you have in your pocket when you see the first sliver of the moon's crescent, in order to wish for money luck. Another superstition is a prohibition relating to the first sight of the waxing crescent, that one should never observe it through glass—such as a closed window.

The latter practice appears to relate to the importance of marking time according to the cycles of the moon: looking for it outdoors in order to retain a contact with the rhythms of nature—a very wise superstition indeed! The moon rules over various natural tides and cycles, including the movement of the seas and the habits of much animal life on the planet. In magic, we observe that among other things, the moon presides over matters of dreaming, psychic abilities, and mysteries. Just as the moon reflects the sun's light, magically it is a mirror of the soul and our deepest desires—therefore an appropriate celestial body on which to wish!

HOW TO CAST THE SPELL

YOU WILL NEED

One tablespoon of granulated sugar

Six cherry stones from cherries you have eaten, bleached in the sun

One small bowl

One sewing needle

One white tea-light in a jar

Matches or a lighter

TIMING This spell should be cast on or within three days of the new moon, when the moon is visible in the sky, in the open air, preferably on a hill or high place.

CASTING THE SPELL

1 Place the sugar and the stones in the bowl together.

2 Using the needle point, on the right side of the wick inscribe a waxing crescent moon, and to the left, the planetary sign for Venus (the circle with a conjoined cross at the bottom).

3 Light it, and then looking up at the moon, say:

I fire an arrow from your bow
And sweetness add that sweetness flow.

4 Place your right palm on the stones and the sugar, and say:

I cast you to the east wind, to the south
The west, the north
To summon friends and companions
forth.

5 Bow to the moon, then scatter the sugar and stones to the four directions.

HOUSE GUARDIAN SPELL
TO PROTECT YOUR HOME

PURPOSE   To create a guardian to protect your living space.

BACKGROUND   Guarding the home by magical means is a practice that goes back thousands of years in the history of human societies. Prehistoric figurines thought to be house guardians have been found all over the world. Considering the universal importance of shelter and protection, it is not really surprising that the practice of setting up magical safeguards for the home is so ancient and so widespread.

It is likely that the humanoid figures were favored as substitutes for, and replicas of, the householder, or a representation of them in a stronger and more powerful form—as a god or goddess renowned for protective abilities, for example.

Charging a magical figure with your protective intentions is very straightforward and comes from some of the very oldest traditions of magic. It can be imbued not only with our own wishes but also with the influence of any protective deities that we might wish to invoke. All the goddess names used in this spell refer to particularly fierce and protective deities.

Although the practice of making wax figures is one of the popular stereotypes associated with "curses," it is used here as a guardian and protector of your household.

HOW TO CAST THE SPELL

TIMING Work on the night of the dark moon.

CASTING THE SPELL

1 Prior to casting your circle, place the household candles in the jar. This should be placed in a pan of boiling water on a burner on the stove until the wax is liquid.

2 Cast a circle in accordance with the guidelines on pages 32–35.

3 Light the black candle, saying:
May Hecate, Black Annis, and Kali Sekhmet, and Lilith witness and empower my spell.

4 Make a human-shaped hollow, approximately 4"/10 cm tall, in the modeling clay, and place it on a heatproof plate.

5 Fill this mold with the molten wax. Place in the liquid wax the thorn, nail, bay leaf, and juniper berry, saying:
Defend this home by tooth and claw Let no evil pass my door.

6 When the figure is set hard, peel away the modeling clay, and bury your guardian outside to the front or rear of your home, close to a door.

YOU WILL NEED

Three white household candles
One empty glass jar
One pan
Boiling water
One black candle, 6–8"/15–20 cm in length
Matches or a lighter
One heatproof plate
One tennis ball-size piece of soft modeling clay
One bramble thorn
One iron nail
One dried bay leaf
One juniper berry

KNITBONE POUCH SPELL
TO MEND QUARRELS

PURPOSE To calm quarrels in homes where this pouch is hung.

BACKGROUND Comfrey, or *Symphytum officinale,* is known as knitbone partly because of its medicinal properties. Historically, its leaves have been used in poultices and leaf teas to speed the mending of sprains, breaks, and muscular pain as well as treatment for various skin complaints. Contemporary herbal use is based on its high levels of allantoin, calcium, potassium, and phosphorus, which encourage the renewal of cells in bone and muscle damage, so it certainly lives up to its folk name. In its magical usage it is renowned as an herb that soothes anger and induces peace.

 ## HOW TO CAST THE SPELL

YOU WILL NEED

One charcoal disk in a fireproof dish

Matches or a lighter

One teaspoon equal parts frankincense and cinnamon

One blue candle, 6–8"/15–20 cm in length

Two dried eucalyptus leaves

Two cloves

Root, leaves, and flowers of comfrey

One 3"/7.5 cm square red velvet pouch, sewn on three sides and attached to

a 24"/60 cm cord handle

TIMING Pick the comfrey on the waxing moon, close to full, but cast the spell at any phase thereafter.

CASTING THE SPELL

1 Cast a circle in accordance with the guidelines on pages 32–35.

2 Light the charcoal disk, and sprinkle on the incense.

3 Light the blue candle, saying:
   Let peace be amongst us now and always.

There are sometimes good reasons why people should air their views or express their disappointment or anger with each other at home, however, a prolonged bout of unpleasantness between relatives or friends should be avoided for the sake of all concerned.
This spell will help calm things down and bring a little peace to your home.

For this spell, you will need leaves, flowers, and the root of a plant, so be certain to thank the earth for its sacrifice by leaving out a small coin and a piece of bread soaked in red wine. It would be wise to replace the comfrey used, too.

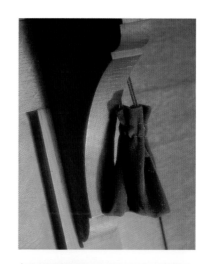

4 Place the eucalyptus leaves and cloves on the charcoal, saying:

Let healing be amongst us now and always.

5 Put the root, leaves, and flowers of the comfrey into the pouch, and sew it shut. Hold it over the incense smoke, and chant the following at least eight times,

visualizing a reconciliation after a quarrel.

May quarrels mend
And hurts amend
And each heart shall
Be whole again.

6 Hang the pouch by its strap on a wall in the heart of your home.

ELF-SHOT SPELL
TO KEEP TROUBLESOME RELATIVES AT BAY

PURPOSE To keep relatives from interfering in your life and to discourage them from dropping by unannounced.

BACKGROUND Flint arrowheads have been identified in different locations around the globe, dating back more than twenty-five thousand years. They are still found in large quantities in Britain and Europe, most of them dating from the Neolithic era. These prehistoric artifacts are still discovered on farmland after plowing, heavy rains, or floods. So common are these finds that country folk have a name for them—*elf-shot*— and a rather unusual idea about their origins.

As the country name indicates, elf-shot was deemed to be the remnants of fairy weaponry. It was thought that elf darts, or *saighead sidhe* as they are known in Scotland, were from arrows fired at humans or animals by the fairy folk when they were displeased or feeling particularly mischievous. They were also deemed to have magical qualities and were used as talismans or amulets. One of their chief virtues was that of protection—a merit used in this spell to protect you against troublesome relatives.

If you are not lucky enough to have access to a genuine Neolithic flint arrowhead, you should obtain a small, thumbnail-size piece of pointed flint, either by going out into a flinty area to pick one up or from a rock and crystal dealer.

HOW TO CAST THE SPELL

YOU WILL NEED

One charcoal disk in a fireproof dish

Matches or a lighter

One black candle, 6–8"/15–20 cm
in length

One red candle, 6–8"/15–20 cm in length

One small piece of flint

Fire tongs or tweezers

One teaspoon of dried juniper berries

One 2" x 2"/5 cm x 5 cm black drawstring
pouch

TIMING Prepare this charm on a dark or waning moon, with Tuesday, day of fiercely protective Mars, as the favorite.

CASTING THE SPELL

1 Cast a circle in accordance with the guidelines on pages 32–35.

2 Light the charcoal disk, then the black candle, saying:
   By the dark of the moon.
Light the red candle, saying:
   By the fierce light of Mars
   This spell is made.

3 Hold the flint between your palms. Close your eyes and visualize it as an arrowhead pointing at troublesome relatives who attempt to enter your home.

4 Using the tongs, hold it in the flame of the red candle, saying:
   In fire I forge thee
   My intent will harden thee.
   As I will it, so mote it be!

5 Sprinkle juniper berries onto the charcoal, and pass the flint through the smoke.

6 Place it in the pouch, and hang it above your front door.

HARMONY INCENSE SPELL
TO PROMOTE DOMESTIC HARMONY

PURPOSE To bring a sense of peace and concord to your home.

BACKGROUND Incense is put to many uses in magic. It can be used to psychically "cleanse" a space, to carry messages into the ether, and to help alter your state of consciousness. Apart from the magical vibrations it raises, its ingredients may key into systems of symbols and other psychic correspondences, such as a relationship to a deity or planetary influence. The incense used in this spell is really a mixture of many of these functions, as its ingredients are known for their powerful cleansing and calming energies as well as for their magical symbolism. Raising and releasing magical

 HOW TO CAST THE SPELL

YOU WILL NEED

One charcoal disk in a fireproof dish

One pink candle, 6–8"/15–20 cm in length

Matches or a lighter

One teaspoon of orris root powder

One teaspoon of dried lavender

One teaspoon of saffron

Mortar and pestle

Two teaspoons of finely chopped dried orange peel

One airtight jar

TIMING Work with a waxing moon to draw harmony, and on a Friday, day of peace-loving Venus.

CASTING THE SPELL

1 Cast a circle in accordance with the guidelines on pages 32–35.

2 Light the charcoal disc, then the candle, saying:
> *Star of love*
> *Star of peace*
> *Witness and empower*
> *The work of this hour.*

intentions through incense can be very powerful, so censing your entire home with this blend will have quite an impact.

The key components of this mixture are found in a variety of spells. Lavender is widely used in love, healing, and cleansing rituals and in spells for better communication—a quality that helps to bring harmony to any home. Orris root is frequently used in love magic, and dried orange peel is known to help foster amity and raise spirits. Saffron is included to enhance insight and intuition. The properties of these ingredients will "lift" the heaviest atmosphere.

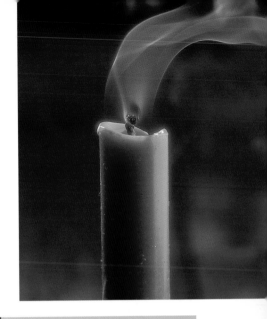

3 Place the orris root, lavender, and saffron in the mortar, and grind them thoroughly, chanting the following as you work:
May all changes come with love
May love come with all change.

4 Add the orange peel; then sprinkle some onto the charcoal, saying:
The circle is open
The spell unbroken.

5 Carry the incense clockwise around each and every room of your house, adding incense liberally when required.

6 Return to extinguish the candles, and thereby seal the spell. If sealed tightly in a jar, the incense will keep well for some time, so you might consider doubling or trebling the amounts in order to keep a store for censing the house whenever trouble is brewing!

POTATO SPELL
TO BANISH A BAD ATMOSPHERE

PURPOSE   To banish bad atmospheres, whatever their origins.

BACKGROUND   If you are scouring this book for a spell to remove a bad
atmosphere, then you probably already know the sort of situation this spell refers to.
Sometimes you may get a vague feeling of unease in a particular room in your house
or feel that a certain spot in your home has a "bad" or "cold" feeling. This is similar to
the sensation of walking into a room where an argument is taking place or where there
is hostility or tension in the company. Some people are so spooked by this sort of
experience that they become convinced that their home is "haunted."

The ability of humans to decide
whether a space feels good or bad
is a little mysterious. As a species,
we certainly can be observed to
become very attached to certain
places for no other reason than
we feel at home or peaceful when
we visit or live in them. Suffice it
to say that this same ability may
also enable us to detect a less than
pleasant atmosphere—it does not
matter whence it came—and desire
it to be removed. Once you have
banished a bad atmosphere, replace
it with a better one, for example
using the Harmony Incense mixture
found on pages 192–193.

HOW TO CAST THE SPELL

TIMING Perform the spell on a waning or dark moon, on a Saturday, sacred to Saturn the banisher.

CASTING THE SPELL

Twenty-four hours before casting the circle, cut the potato in half, and place the halves in the north and south of the affected room. Just before casting this spell, light a match in the east, south, west, and north of the same room, allowing each to burn down before extinguishing it. Bring the potato halves and burned matches to the circle, which should be cast in another room.

1 Cast a circle in accordance with the guidelines on pages 32–35.

2 Light the black candle, saying:
   I call upon Saturn the banisher
   To lend power to this spell.

3 Rejoin the potato halves by inserting several burned matches in one side and impaling the other on them.

4 Place the potato in the cheesecloth with the burned matches, and tie the corners together.

YOU WILL NEED

One large potato

One box of matches

One black candle, 6–8"/15–20 cm in length

One 12"/30 cm square piece of white cheesecloth

One teaspoon of salt in an eggcup

One wineglass of water

5 Pour the salt into the water, saying:
   Conjoined these bring forth purity.
Go into the affected room, and sprinkle the water all around it, saying:
   This room is cleansed
   May only goodness enter.

6 Bury the cheesecloth parcel away from the house.

SUGAR SPELL
TO DRAW WELCOME VISITORS TO YOUR HOME

PURPOSE To help those who enjoy entertaining at home.

BACKGROUND Many of the spells in this book have a push-me pull-you element in that they are about attracting or repelling people or influences. This is a particularly appealing one that is specifically designed for sociable souls who wish to attract a welcome flow of visitors to their home. It works by using the sometimes very literal symbolism of sympathetic magic in offering a magical sugar trail into your front door. This should entice some interesting visitors.

HOW TO CAST THE SPELL

YOU WILL NEED

One purple candle, 6–8"/15–20 cm in length

Matches or a lighter

Granulated sugar, 4 oz/115 g

One pinch of saffron

One teaspoon of ground dandelion root

Three drops of orange essential oil

One bowl

One wooden spoon

One sheet of newspaper

One airtight jar

TIMING Work on a waxing moon to attract visitors, and on a Thursday, day of fun-loving Jupiter.

CASTING THE SPELL

1 Cast a circle in accordance with the guidelines on pages 32–35.

2 Light the candle, saying:
   Mighty Jove
   Bringer of cheer
   Bring good company
   Here.

Using magical "powders" in this way is a familiar feature of very traditional magic from all around the world. Some magical powders are specifically blended to send enemies far away, whereas others are created to attract lovers or bring money or fortune. This powder is designed to draw good company toward you so that you can experience the blessings that frequent, good-humored gatherings can bring.

This spell requires a little patience to carry it out. Note that the directions recommend that the powder should be left undisturbed to dry in the sun.

3 Place the sugar, the saffron, the dandelion root, and the oil in the bowl, and mix them together, chanting the following:

Come bee to honey
Come sun to flower
Come tide to shore
Come joy to share.

4 As you are stirring, let your mind drift with the chant, and try to visualize a golden line going from your front door out into the world. Imagine lots of friends and welcome family members traveling along that line to your front door, and continue to chant and stir until the mixture is quite even.

5 Sprinkle the mixture flat on the newspaper, and place it in the sun to dry.

6 Store the mixture in the jar, and spoon in a line outside your front door whenever you have need of visitors or company.

MAGIC JAR SPELL
TO PROTECT YOU FROM TROUBLESOME NEIGHBORS

PURPOSE   To fend off spite.

BACKGROUND   Given the store that we set by a secure home life, any disruption to it can result in our health and peace of mind being compromised. When neighbors behaving badly or inconsiderately cause such disquiet, it can feel that it is out of our control and that our peace is being invaded. Such situations can seriously damage our quality of life and even our health. The business of negotiation is a tricky one, but sometimes compromises can be reached, and it is worth trying to reach a reasonable agreement with your neighbors before casting this spell.

The custom of burying containers of magical ingredients goes back centuries, and they have been used for a variety of purposes, including safeguarding those in danger and warding off evil. There are several versions of this spell in circulation at the present time, and the one used here is found in several places around the globe.

The deity that you call on to empower your spell is Annis, a goddess of the traveling people, known for her protective powers. She guards those who are being oppressed by others, so ensure that your cause is just and that you are not being unreasonable in your dealings with neighbors.

198

HOW TO CAST THE SPELL

TIMING Cast this on a waning moon, close to its dark phase. Saturday, with its saturnine associations, is favored.

CASTING THE SPELL

1 Cast a circle in accordance with the guidelines on pages 32–35.

2 Light the candle, saying:
Saturn of the stern visage
Bless this spell and bear its message
All who wish us ill are spurned
With all evil thrice returned.

3 Place the thorns inside the jar, saying:
Throw yourself upon this thorn
And only your blood shall be drawn.

4 Add the chiles, saying:
Every spite that shall be given
For each bite you shall be bitten.

YOU WILL NEED

One black candle, 6–8"/15–20 cm in length

Matches or a lighter

Nine thorns from a blackthorn tree

One airtight jar

Three red baby chiles

One teaspoon of chili powder

One square of cheesecloth to cover the jar

5 Place the chili powder inside, saying:
Fire from the south
To fly into the spiteful mouth.
Fasten the jar.

6 Pass the jar three times counterclockwise over the candle flame, saying at each pass:
I abjure thee.
Wrap the jar in the cheesecloth, and bury it close to your front door.

MERCURY SPELL
TO ENHANCE COMMUNICATION IN THE HOME

PURPOSE To help communication flow easily within your home.

BACKGROUND The ability to communicate effectively is an essential skill in all areas of our lives, but it is never so important as when it applies to our personal relationships. People who live cheek by jowl in the same living space particularly need to be able to communicate their needs and wishes to each other. Otherwise, misunderstandings among families or roommates can be terribly upsetting and disruptive to home life.

HOW TO CAST THE SPELL

YOU WILL NEED

One charcoal disk in a fireproof dish

One yellow candle, 6–8"/15–20 cm in length

Matches or a lighter

Two teaspoons equal parts lavender, pine needles, and lemongrass

One white household candle

One plastic or metal coaster

One small pine twig for inscribing wax

One 2"/5 cm square black drawstring pouch

TIMING Work on a waxing moon, and on a Wednesday, sacred to Mercury the messenger.

CASTING THE SPELL

1 Cast a circle in accordance with the guidelines on pages 32–35.

2 Light the charcoal disk, then the yellow candle, saying:

Hail Mercury
Swift messenger
Empower and bless this spell
Grant me favor in my labors.

Mercury, the planet associated strongly with communications of all sorts, is the key correspondence called on in this spell. The malleable substance mercury is also sometimes called *quicksilver*, as it was thought to be "alive." It is poisonous, so it is represented here by molten wax, into which you will imprint the symbol that stands both for Mercury, the planet, and the mercury the metal. This will form a talisman to ensure ease of communication, so that your household can function effectively and the chance of misunderstandings amongst its members is minimized.

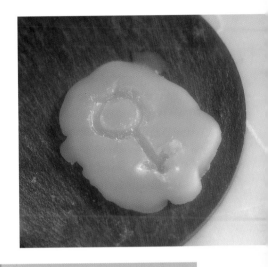

3 Sprinkle the incense onto the charcoal, and cense the circle traveling clockwise. Add more incense, and light the white candle.

4 Allow wax from this candle to drip onto the coaster to form an oval tablet about 1"/2.5 cm in diameter. While the wax is still soft, inscribe the symbol for Mercury (the circle with the conjoined cross at the bottom and "horns" at the top).

5 Allow it to cool; then remove it intact from the coaster. Place it in the pouch and seal. Breathe on the pouch, saying:

I seal you by my breath
I charge you by my desire.

6 Place the pouch over the doorway to the most frequented room of the house.

EARTH DRAGON SPELL
TO ENSURE A FERTILE AND BEAUTIFUL GARDEN

PURPOSE   To make your garden grow.

BACKGROUND   Folkways, customs, and traditions of ancient origin are replete with "superstitions" concerning the spiritual management of fields and harvests and the changing of the seasons, indicating that magic has long been used to ensure future growth. One very old custom, after the harvest was brought in, was for a couple to make love in the field, symbolically reproducing the crop in preparation for the next year. You will no doubt be reassured that this spell does not require you to follow suit in full view of the neighbors—but instead works on the principle of representing the transformation of the earth from barren to fruitful in symbol.

The key ingredient to be used here is an empty chrysalis, the universal symbol of transformation. Obtaining one should not be too difficult—particularly if you are ecology-conscious and grow plants attractive to butterflies—but in the event that none are available, contact a local butterfly conservation center to see if they can oblige.

This charm calls on the powers of the great dragon who represents the enormous natural energies of the earth. Acknowledging and respecting Earth Dragon energies enables us to step into the magical realm, where the laws of nature and the life force are all-powerful.

YOU WILL NEED

One charcoal disk in a fireproof dish

One green candle, 6–8"/15–20 cm
in length

Matches or a lighter

Sandalwood

Three drops of patchouli essential oil

One pen with green ink

1" x ½"/2 cm x 1 cm strip of paper

One empty chrysalis

One teaspoon of mustard seeds

TIMING This spell should be worked in
early spring, on the day after the new
moon, to ensure maximum growth.

CASTING THE SPELL

1 Cast a circle in accordance with the
guidelines on pages 32–35.

2 Light the charcoal, then the candle,
saying:

> *Within me and around me*
> *The power of the earth*
> *Come creature, eating fire*
> *Come through the air*
> *Come by water*
> *Make this good earth your home.*

3 Sprinkle the sandalwood and patchouli
onto the charcoal.

4 Write in green ink, on one side of the
paper strip, the following words:
> *Draco*
> *Erce*
> *Venit.*

Roll it into a tiny scroll, and insert it into
the chrysalis. Insert the mustard seeds
into the chrysalis.

5 Pass the chrysalis through the incense
smoke, chanting the words written on the
scroll three times over.

6 Bury the chrysalis and its contents
in the center of your garden.

SEASONAL SPELLS

INTRODUCTION TO SEASONAL SPELLS

All of the festivals in the sacred wheel of the year carry their own magical power and meaning, and many witches and magicians notice that different times of year are particularly auspicious for certain types of spell. Unsurprisingly, these spells are as linked to the needs of humans in given seasons as they are to the powers that prevail at that time. Thus for example, at Yule, when we are most likely to feel the need for the sun, we are able to draw on the energies of the season of sun return in order to strengthen us in the winter. Similarly, at Eostre, as we tip over into the lighter part of the year, we are likely to need physical and mental balance to carry us forward now that a new season, requiring our more outgoing energies, is upon us. Because Eostre is a time of outer balance, between light and darkness, we can draw on this to inspire inner balance.

On pages 22–31, there are explanations of the eight main festivals of the year, their main foci, and their respective traditions. These are not

exhaustive—indeed, any of the festivals could justify a whole book on their history, customs, and magical meaning—but they do provide a framework for what follows in this section of the

Spells Bible. In the following pages, you will find spells bent to purposes most suitable to the time of year with which they are associated, numbering three to a festival. By way of example, under the heading of Imbolc—the time of early seed sowing after thaw—you will find spells for new projects. As Imbolc is sacred to Brigid, a Celtic fire and healing goddess, there is also a spell for healing or to bring general good health. Imbolc is also associated with justice and change, so a spell to obtain justice is included.

This is the case for each of the spells in this section—they all have associations with the time of year or the customs that correspond with festival traditions. Accordingly, they are designed to be performed within a circle cast especially for the appropriate festival. All of the spells for Beltaine should be cast at Beltaine in a circle to celebrate May Day, and all the spells for Litha should be woven in a circle that celebrates the summer solstice, and so on. The spells appear as rituals to be performed as part of a seasonal celebration, which makes them versatile enough to use in group situations and thereby enable some powerful, collective energy raising. "Merry Meet!" (a greeting for a group), as the pagans say.

YULE – FIRE ASH SPELL
TO ENSURE PROSPERITY IN THE COMING YEAR

PURPOSE To bring prosperity in the next solar cycle.

BACKGROUND The tradition of the Yule log dates back to pagan times in northern Europe and is believed to be associated with the nature-based religions that existed for millennia before the coming of Christianity. Our ancestors held that all things contained the life force and that trees, in particular, were the abode of spirit people, gods, and goddesses. Certain trees, therefore, were regarded as especially sacred, and if felled to build a special fire—at Yule for example—the ash was thought to be particularly powerful.

 ## HOW TO CAST THE SPELL

YOU WILL NEED

An open fireplace or outdoor bonfire

One section of any branch, complete with bark

One sharp knife

Six dried holly leaves

One green candle

TIMING Cast this spell at Yule—see pages 22–31 for details.

CASTING THE SPELL

1 The night before your Yule celebrations, make a roaring fire in your fireplace or with an outdoor bonfire.

2 With the knife, carve into the side of your "Yule log" the word "PLENTY."

3 Place the log on the fire, and crumble the dried holly leaves over it. When it is reduced to ash, remove it from the fire. As part of your Yule celebrations, and in a properly cast circle, work as follows:

We know that the tradition of the Yule log originally came from Scandinavia, as did the naming of the midwinter season as *Yul* (meaning "wheel"), which took place in the early eleventh century C.E. That the winter solstice was already a well-established part of the ritual year in prehistoric Britain and Ireland is evident from the alignment of many prehistoric monuments; invaders from Denmark simply overlaid this tradition with some of their own.

The Yule log carried an especially potent magic if it was of oak, reflecting the power invested in this tree, but it is clear that other woods were used, too.

4 Carve your first name along the side of the green candle, and light it, saying:
You are named for me
That blessed you be.

5 Sprinkle half of the ash in a circle around the candle, saying:
Though storms come
None shall remove you.

6 Keep a pinch of ash to place in next year's Yule fire, and place the rest on your doorstep to ensure that prosperity finds its way to your home in the coming year.

YULE—MISTLETOE SPELL
TO LEND STRENGTH IN THE WINTER

PURPOSE To help you gather strength for the rest of the winter.

BACKGROUND The mistletoe, or *Viscum album,* has a venerable place in herb lore as the plant sacred to the Druids. Perhaps because of its semiparasitic habit, it was associated with fertility, and the Yuletide custom of kissing beneath it is a pale reminder of this. It was associated with potency for another reason—its milky berries, which surround its seed, were thought by our ancestors to resemble semen, and the life-giving properties of this fluid lent its reputation to the plant. In magic, mistletoe represents power and strength in many forms, and the one referred to in this spell comes from its association with the sacred oak—tree of the sun.

Bringing the sun back in the midst of darkness is part of the purpose of Yule celebrations; in the darkest hour we not only celebrate the prospect of the return of the sun's strength, but we positively encourage it! In short, when we celebrate, we are trying to bring the sun back. This is less a human tendency to believe that we control nature than an atavistic fear that the sun will not rise on the most important of days. It is important to acknowledge that we not only celebrate the sun's return; we *encourage* light in darkness by using a kind of latter-day sympathetic magic, otherwise known as fairy lights, tinsel, and shiny baubles. This spell draws on the potency of the sun just as the mistletoe draws on that power from the oak, the sun tree itself.

HOW TO CAST THE SPELL

YOU WILL NEED

Six white candles, 6–8"/15–20 cm in length

One bunch of hung and dried mistletoe

Mortar and pestle

Three 3"/7.5 cm square pieces of white paper

One pen with green ink

One fireproof dish

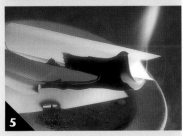

TIMING Cast this spell at Yule—see pages 22–31 for details.

CASTING THE SPELL

As part of your Yule celebrations, and in a properly cast circle, work as follows:

1 Place the candles in a circle, and light every other one, saying:
   Here in the season of sun return
   May life return and strength return.

2 Using the mortar and pestle, grind the dried mistletoe to dust.

3 Choose up to three areas in your life where you need strength, and write them as a single word on each square of paper. For example: HEALTH, ENERGY, EMOTIONS, and so on.

4 Sprinkle mistletoe dust on each one of them, then fold them and set them alight using lit candles.

5 Place them in the fireproof dish to burn, and light the remaining candles.

6 Bury the ash under an evergreen.

YULE—YULE FRUITCAKE SPELL
TO FIND THE KEY TO THE COMING YEAR

PURPOSE   To help you spot major influences for the new solar cycle.

BACKGROUND   Yule has traditionally been a time for looking back over the year, as it comes at the time of the *solstice* (literal translation: "sun stands still"). In the darkest season, it affords a pause in which to weigh up events since the last winter solstice. It is also a time for looking forward, and this spell aims to help you do just that.

In Victorian England, the custom of putting silver charms into the Christmas or "figgy" pudding was played out in middle-class households, while poorer households

HOW TO CAST THE SPELL

YOU WILL NEED

Self-rising wholewheat flour, 6 oz/175 g

Brown sugar granules, 4 oz/115 g

Butter, 4 oz/115 g

Mixed dried fruit, 2 oz/55 g

One teaspoon of allspice

Wooden spoon

Twelve baking cases

Twelve 2" x ½"/5 cm x 1 cm strips of paper

One pen

Twelve 3" x 2"/7.5 cm x 5 cm strips of aluminum foil

TIMING Cast this spell at Yule—see pages 22–31 for details.

CASTING THE SPELL

1 Mix the edible ingredients with a spoon, or by hand, until they are smooth, adding the fruit last. Spoon the mixture into the cake cases, and bake them prior to the circle at 400°F/200°C until firm and golden.

As part of your Yule celebrations, and in a properly cast circle, work as follows:

would place a coin in the pudding. This is an echo of an older tradition in which revelers dining on rich cake or bread baked at Yule hoped to draw a plum or other fruit from it—a prediction that the year ahead would be good for the lucky recipient. The older tradition seems a far safer one, given the potential for choking, cutting gums, or breaking teeth on coins or metal charms!

You will be happy to note that this version of the Yule fruitcake divination is safer by far—and also very tasty! It also honors a custom that goes back many centuries.

2 Write the following words, one to a paper strip:

HEALTH	TRAVEL
WEALTH	SPIRIT
HOME	FRIENDS
LOVE	BEGINNINGS
CHILD	ELDERS
WORK	TIME

3 Roll the strips and secure them separately in foil, then mix them up. Insert the foil "bullets" into the cakes from underneath.

4 Choose a cake and break it open to remove the message. Eat the cake; then read the message.

5 Distribute the remaining cakes to friends, explaining their purpose. Ensure that the friends remove the messages before eating the cakes.

6 The word you select provides the key to life developments in the coming year.

IMBOLC—SEED SPELL
TO GROW WISHES AND
BRING SUCCESS IN NEW PROJECTS

PURPOSE   To bless wishes and favor new projects.

BACKGROUND   Seasonally, Imbolc is linked to the appearance of the first spring flowers—snowdrops—an early sign in Europe that winter is retreating and spring is approaching. This is the time of early seeding, and in temperate climes, farmers keep their eye to the soil to see if it is warm enough to sow crops. It is a good time for sowing other "seeds" as well—ideas that you wish to come to fruition and plans and projects that you have for the coming year.

   The following spell is based on a first principle of sympathetic magic—symbolizing "like with like." The seeds you plant now represent your wishes for the coming months.

In the Imbolc circle, you enact on the seeds what you wish for these plans. In short, you plant them in good soil and promise to feed, nourish, and care for them, trusting to nature—just as we entrust our wishes to magic—to help them to grow. As you minister to these seeds, so will magic minister to the wishes they represent. For this reason, you will need to take care of them when Imbolc has passed to ensure that they yield results!

   There are plenty of seeds available at this time of year. Resourceful gardeners may have some stored from last year. The genus of the plant is immaterial. What matters most are the intentions with which you magically charge the seeds and that the seeds themselves are large enough to handle separately.

HOW TO CAST THE SPELL

YOU WILL NEED

Three white candles, 6–8"/15–20 cm in length

Matches or a lighter

Nine seeds of any variety

One pen and some paper

Good seeding soil or potting soil

One small garden trowel

One indoor planter

TIMING Cast this spell at Imbolc—see pages 22–31 for details.

CASTING THE SPELL

As part of your Imbolc celebrations, and in a properly cast circle, work as follows:

1 Light the candles, saying:
> *Triple Brigid, you are welcome*
> *Thrice you are welcome.*

2 Name each seed as a wish or project you hope will take root and grow in the next year. Write these wishes down, to be reviewed next Imbolc.

3 Place the seeds in your right hand, and cup your left hand over them, saying:
> *Now her breath is upon the earth*
> *Her warmth will bring new seeds to birth*
> *Holy Brigid, bless all that lives*
> *Between my right hand and my left.*

4 Plant the seeds in the soil or potting soil according to the directions for the seeds you are planting.

IMBOLC—BRIGID'S WELL SPELL
TO HEAL OR BRING GENERAL GOOD HEALTH

PURPOSE To ease ill health or bring well-being in the coming year.

BACKGROUND Imbolc is also known as the Feast of Brigid, a well-beloved Irish goddess renowned as a patron of healing. Many springs and rivers are sacred to her, bearing features of her name, in Brittany, England, Ireland, Scotland, and Wales, but her strongest association with the healing power of waters is with wells.

In pre-Christian times, people venerated the *genii loci*, or "spirits of place," of natural locations that were considered particularly sacred. Springs and wells, sources of water that came up from the earth, were considered very special, and healing properties, including cures for eye and skin problems, became attributed to many of those associated with Brigid. In this spell, you will be recreating Brigid's Well in symbol, in the form of a pottery or stone bowl or cup. Since Brigid's Healing Well is a spiritual symbol, this recreation is just as valid as if you had applied to the spirit of a well in Kildare, in Ireland, or a river in Wales. You may make up to three requests for healing, including one for general good health, as appropriate.

HOW TO CAST THE SPELL

YOU WILL NEED

Six white candles, 6–8"/15–20 cm in length

One stone or pottery cup or bowl

Three small beach pebbles

One small cup of salt

Spring water

Matches or a lighter

TIMING Cast this spell at Imbolc—see pages 22–31 for details.

CASTING THE SPELL

As part of your Imbolc celebrations, and in a properly cast circle, work as follows:

1 Place the candles all around the cup.

2 Name each stone as an ailment you wish healed, as appropriate, sprinkling a pinch of salt over each. Breathe onto them, saying:

By my breath.

Cover them with your hands, saying:

By my flesh.

Place them in the cup, and cover them with water, saying:

By the living waters of Brigid
May health prevail and good reside.

3 Light each candle, saying:

Hail, lady of fire.

4 Hold your palms toward the flames and close your eyes, then visualize dark stains on the stones dissolving in the water, rising to the surface to be burned away in the candle flames.

5 Chant the following until you feel the energies in the circle rise:

Earth, water, flame
Work in her name
Earth, water, fire
Work my desire.

Discharge the energy raised by raising your hands into the air and mentally releasing it.

6 Return the stones to a beach as soon as possible after Imbolc night.

IMBOLC—CLOUTIE SPELL
TO OBTAIN JUSTICE

PURPOSE To help those who have a just cause to plead.

BACKGROUND Imbolc's patron goddess, Brigid, is a famous protector of women, children, and animals and has a reputation as a firebrand for justice and equality. It is fitting that this aspect of Brigid is celebrated at this time of year; just as the growing light makes visible the dust and grime hidden by winter, Brigid's bright sun can also shine light on dark deeds. Spring cleaning with a mop and bucket can clean away dust, but answering injustices requires something special. Happily, magic pertaining to matters of justice and fairness is favored at this time.

HOW TO CAST THE SPELL

YOU WILL NEED

One charcoal disk in a fireproof dish

Matches or a lighter

One teaspoon of myrrh

One white candle, 6–8"/15–20 cm in length

One purple candle, 6–8"/15–20 cm in length

Thirteen 12" x 3"/30 cm x 7.5 cm strips of white cotton cloth

One dead branch, propped up

TIMING Cast this spell at Imbolc—see pages 22–31 for details.

CASTING THE SPELL

As part of your Imbolc celebrations, and beginning in a properly cast circle and progressing outdoors toward a tree where your spell will remain undisturbed as long as possible, work as follows:

1 Light the charcoal disk, and sprinkle on myrrh.

2 Light the white candle, saying:
Brigid is here.

3 Light the purple candle, saying:
And justice will come.

Tree dressing, the old custom of tying clouties, or "strips of cloth," to trees above sacred wells, was originally done to leave tokens of requests for healing and mercy where the spirit of that place was strongest. Here, the custom is used to send your plea for justice via the sun, wind, and earth into the great web of spirit, where all things are balanced out. Blessed by fiercely protective Brigid, your spell is not about revenge, but about redressing a grievous imbalance. Imbolc is a time for rendering all things anew. Redeeming balance is a part of this process.

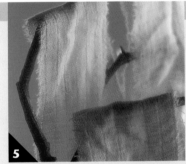

5

4 Speaking your anger, fear, or despair at the injustice you wish redressed into each strip of cloth, seal them by passing them separately through the incense smoke.

5 Hang them loosely on the dead branch, and placing your hand on the topmost twig, say:

Brigid, pity this branch
For it is as dead as my enemy's cause.

6 Go out to the tree, and as you tie each cloutie loosely to its lower branches, say:

May the earth hear me in the roots
*   of this tree*
May the air carry my cry
May the sun take up my plea
And the moon decry it
For with Brigid on my side
My cause is carried.

EOSTRE–HARE SPELL
TO AID FERTILITY

PURPOSE To help when there is no known medical reason why a pregnancy cannot succeed.

BACKGROUND The long association between hares and fertility is partly due to a fact of nature and partly to the hare's symbolic link to moon goddesses all around the world. The fertility of hares is proverbial—a doe can produce forty-two young in a single year—so it isn't surprising that they came to be associated with the fertility of the earth, and of humans. Hares are seen to race about madly in the fields at mating time, around Eostre—sacred to the Teutonic fertility deity Oestra, or Ostar.

HOW TO CAST THE SPELL

YOU WILL NEED

One green candle, 6–8"/15–20 cm in length

Matches or a lighter

One pencil

One 12"/30 cm square sheet of white tissue paper

Scissors

One 12"/30 cm square sheet of black tissue paper

One free-range egg

One 18" x 1"/45 cm x 2.5 cm length of wide yellow ribbon

TIMING Cast this spell at Eostre—see pages 22–31 for details.

CASTING THE SPELL

As part of your Eostre celebrations, and in a properly cast circle, work as follows:

1 Light the green candle, saying:
   Let Ostara come now
   Let her people drum the earth awake
   Let Ostara come.

2 Draw a circle roughly 9"/22.5 cm in circumference on the white paper, marking the outline of a hare's head in the center, and cut it out.

The association, across several cultures, and a variety of moon goddesses has a certain logic to it! One likely explanation is that lunar features seen from earth sometimes resemble a hare. As the cycles of the moon were seen to coincide with women's menstruation and reproductive cycles, the two became synonymous. Goddesses of the moon were seen as patrons of fertility, pregnancy, and childbirth. Thus the hare has become a totem of many goddesses, including Andraste in Britain, Maia in Italy, Chang O in China, Freya in Scandinavia, and Harfa in northern Europe.

3 Place the hare's head on the black paper. Put the egg in the center of the white disk; then bunch the white tissue over it, saying:

Sent from the moon.

4 Bunch the black paper up over this, then say:

Grown in the womb.

5 Fasten it with the yellow ribbon.

6 Take it outside, and place it in a hole approximately 12"/30 cm deep, saying:

When hare leaps
And moon peeps
Let us grow big together!

EOSTRE–DOORPOST SPELL
TO BALANCE YOUR PHYSICAL AND MENTAL HEALTH

PURPOSE   To aid balance in all areas of your life.

BACKGROUND   Alongside the fertility aspects of Eostre, the astronomical event of the spring equinox is also celebrated. At this point, when daylight and darkness are of equal length, we are about to spill over into the light side of the year, when light will prevail. This makes it an especially fortuitous time to ensure positive balance around and within us. Eostre is therefore a good time to look to health and consider whether our current lifestyles are supportive of mental and physical balance.

HOW TO CAST THE SPELL

YOU WILL NEED

One charcoal disk in a fireproof dish

Matches or a lighter

Incense blended from equal parts of frankincense and myrrh

One black pillar candle, 12"/30 cm high

One white pillar candle, 12"/30 cm high

Two teaspoons of almond oil in a saucer

One eggcup of salt in a dish

TIMING   Cast this spell at Eostre—see pages 22–31 for details.

CASTING THE SPELL

As part of your Eostre celebrations, and in a properly cast circle, work as follows:

1 Light the charcoal, and add incense.

2 Light the black candle, saying:
   The pillar on my left is night
   All things within it are held in potential.

3 Light the white candle, saying:
   The pillar on my right is light
   All things within it are brought to fruition.

4 Anoint your feet, knees, breast, mouth, and forehead with oil, saying:
   I make myself sacred to enter a sacred space.

The space of equilibrium, of perfect balance between light and darkness, may be represented in Eostre circles by a white and a black candle. These are the posts of a doorway through which we pass into the season of light. To stand between these posts is to enter a magical realm where neither darkness nor light rule, but both hold excess in check. In this spell, you will step into this space to find the source of that same balance within. Prior to the circle, therefore, spend some time thinking about priorities and superfluities within your life and the possibilities for balance within it.

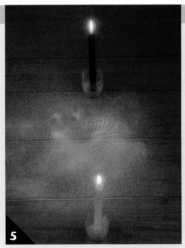

5 Throw salt onto the ground between the candles and step onto it, saying:
I make myself pure to enter a pure place.
Recite the following:
In the doorway of the year
Between the gate of night and day
I have a word to leave: BALANCE
And beg a word to take.

6 Close your eyes and wait for a word to come to you. This will provide the key to attaining balance throughout the coming year.

EOSTRE—DAFFODOWN DILLY SPELL
FOR GROWTH IN ALL AREAS OF YOUR LIFE

PURPOSE   To make wishes concerning all areas of life.

BACKGROUND   This time of year is suitable for planting wishes that will come to fruition in the summer. Using plant ingredients for magic is a well-established custom, and casting a spell using flower bulbs is simple, fun, and most of all, effective. Charging bulbs—which are life in potential—with a wish is a favorite magical method in many working circles. Staggered planting, however, is a method more usually favored by gardeners than magicians, so this spell is a little different in that respect!

 ## HOW TO CAST THE SPELL

YOU WILL NEED

One green candle, 6–8"/15–20 cm in length

One yellow candle, 6–8"/15–20 cm in length

Matches or a lighter

Summer-flowering bulbs, one to a wish

Soil or potting soil in a medium-size indoor planter

TIMING   Cast this spell at Eostre—see pages 22–31 for details.

CASTING THE SPELL

As part of your Eostre celebrations, and in a properly cast circle, work as follows:

1 Light the green candle, saying:
By the shoot.

2 Light the yellow, saying:
*By the flower
I invoke Ostara's power.*

3 Take each bulb, and separately name it after the wish you seek to achieve.

The daffodil is a spring flower that generally appears in March in England, and this spell is named for an old English term for it. The bulbs used for this spell, however, are not daffodils, as by the time Eostre comes, these are already in bloom. The idea here is to trade on the fertility of the daffodils by empowering summer-flowering bulbs and planting them close by. The summer bulbs will get the general idea from the flowering daffodown dillies and, charged with your wishes, hurry to grow and flower.

Choose from the many summer-flowering bulbs available. Choose a hardy variety, as it would not do for your "wish" to be eaten by slugs or bugs!

4 Hold them in your hands, and chant your wish into them with the following words:

As the nights shrink down
And this bulb goes underground

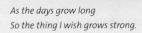

As the days grow long
So the thing I wish grows strong.

5 Bury the bulbs in the soil or potting soil. Place your hands palms down on the soil, and visualize the growth you have wished for coming to pass.

6 Keep the bulbs inside until the threat of frost is passed; then plant outside next to the spring-flowering bulbs.

BELTAINE—NUT SPELL
TO KEEP FIRM PROMISES

PURPOSE To boost your willpower by helping you keep a promise to yourself.

BACKGROUND In some pagan mythologies, Beltaine celebrates the marriage of the Green Man and the earth goddess. The time when the May blossom bursts into flower is known, for this reason, as the *Goddess's Bridal*. This marriage requires that the Lord of the Greenwood and the pregnant goddess declare their commitment to each other and to the child of their union. For this reason, Beltaine is a good time for making promises and celebrating and honoring commitments.

It is an ideal time, in fact, to make a pledge and commit to keeping faith with it for the remainder of the year—or longer, if appropriate. Prior to casting your Beltaine circle, think carefully about the implications of any promises you are considering. Ask yourself whether it is necessary or realistic; consider any sacrifices it might entail. Your promise to yourself can relate to a habit, a behavioral trait, or a desire to improve an area of your life. Whatever it is, ensure that it is genuinely required and that you are not trying to fulfill someone else's idea of health, beauty, conformist behavior, and so on.

The pledge is represented by a nut—a common fertility symbol of Maytime. Eating it seals the spell and causes you to absorb literally the promise that will nourish your life.

HOW TO CAST THE SPELL

YOU WILL NEED

One broomstick
Two green candles, 6–8"/15–20 cm in length
Matches or a lighter
One fresh almond for each promise
One nutcracker
The juice of a lemon
One saucer of sugar

TIMING Cast this spell at Beltaine—see pages 22–31 for details.

CASTING THE SPELL

As part of your Beltaine celebrations, and in a properly cast circle, work as follows:

1 Place the broomstick across your path.

2 Place the candles at either end of the broomstick, and light them, saying:

Here's to Marion in the wood
Here's to Jack so green and good.

3 Hold the nut between your palms. Envisage the promise you wish to keep, and speak your pledge to the nut.

4 Crack the nut open, and dip one end in lemon juice, saying:

Bitter though it prove
I plight my troth.

5 Dip the same end into the sugar, saying:

Sweetness to who
Holds fast and true.

6 Place the nut between your teeth, and jump over the broomstick. Eat your nut immediately, and repeat the process for each promise you wish to make.

BELTAINE – RIBBON SPELL
TO ATTRACT AN EXCITING LOVER

PURPOSE   To attract a new lover.

BACKGROUND   Beltaine rightly has the historical reputation of being an erotic time of year. Much of the sixteenth-century English church's objection to Beltaine rites was based on the nature of the entertainments and the custom of staying out all night on April 30 to "bring in the May." Given the opportunity this offered youngsters to indulge in lovemaking away from the watchful eyes of their elders and the local priests, it is little wonder that churchmen who preached against the "sin" of sex outside of marriage sought to ban it.

Happily, some rural communities have managed to hold onto the old ways and Maypoles are still seen in England.

HOW TO CAST THE SPELL

YOU WILL NEED

One oil burner with a tea-light

Two teaspoons of water

Six drops of ylang-ylang essential oil

Matches or a lighter

One green pillar candle, 12"/30 cm high

One rubber band, to fasten around candle

Two 18"/45 cm strips of red ribbon

One 18"/45 cm strip of green ribbon

TIMING Cast this spell at Beltaine—see pages 22–31 for details.

CASTING THE SPELL

In a properly cast circle, work as follows:

1 Place the oil and water in the burner and light the tea-light.

2 Press the candle in both hands, saying:
   This Maypole I endow
   With my fond vow
   He/She that would seek me
   Find me now!

A latter-day entertainment inspired by these historical fun and games is known as the Beltane love chase. This custom, which lets everybody be a little crazy, involves a form of hide-and-seek, with the men tying bells onto ribbons that they attach to their clothing and the women pursuing them into the woods. Once caught, a man surrenders a kiss to his captor, and they come back to the party to drink each other's health. Needless to say, there are variations on this for same-sex couples or groups— and it's all innocent fun! This spell uses ribbons, seen at Beltaine in the love chase and on Maypoles, to lead an as-yet-undiscovered lover toward you.

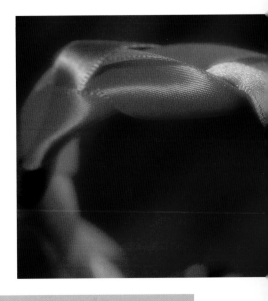

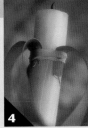

3 Place the rubber band around the candle, approximately 1"/2.5 cm from the wick.

4 Tuck the end of a red ribbon into the band, saying:

> *An he/she be kind*
> *I'll not repine.*

Repeat, using the green ribbon, saying:

> *An he/she is saucy*
> *Send him/her to me.*

5 Tuck in the remaining red ribbon, saying:

> *An he/she bring love*
> *I'll not remove.*

6 Light the candle, then remove the ribbons and weave them together to wear on your wrist until a lover appears.

BELTAINE—MAY TREE SPELL
TO COMMUNICATE WITH THE SPIRITS OF THE GREENWOOD

PURPOSE This spell is for those who wish to commune with nature and explore a new spiritual path.

BACKGROUND In the cycle of the festivals, there are two that stand face to face across the circling seasons, sharing much in common, although they have many oppositional aspects. Both Beltaine and Samhain are renowned as times when the veils between the worlds are thin. At Samhain, the worlds of the living and the dead come close together, and at Beltaine the border between the world of humans and the world of faerie is narrowed. This makes Beltaine a good time to make a spiritual link with the natural world and the spirits of the greenwood.

Many superstitions relate to this time of year, including the custom of avoiding bringing greenery and may into the house. This reflects a much older fear of the fairy folk, also known as "the sidhe," "the gentry," "the little people," "the shining ones," or "the hill folk" in parts of Europe. Modern-day pagans now consider it lucky to bring greenery and May blossom into the house for May Day, to honor the growth of greenery outdoors and to bring this natural fertility magic into our homes. Some of us even leave out a saucer of milk to show our goodwill toward the nature spirits, although I suspect many of these nature spirits take the form of grateful cats and hedgehogs.

HOW TO CAST THE SPELL

YOU WILL NEED

A private spot beneath a tree

One charcoal disk in a fireproof dish

Matches or a lighter

One tea-light

One clean jar

Two tablespoons of dried mugwort

TIMING Cast this spell at Beltaine—see pages 22–31 for details.

CASTING THE SPELL

As part of your Beltaine celebrations, work outdoors as follows:

1 Find a spot beneath a tree, and light the charcoal.

2 Sitting with your back to the tree, light the tea-light in the jar.

3 Sprinkle mugwort onto the charcoal; inhale, and say aloud:

Spirits of the greenwood
I come in love and trust to
Learn what you will teach
I wish no mischief
And ask for none.

4 Close your eyes, and meditate on the life force of the tree against which you are leaning. Allow yourself to daydream, occasionally adding mugwort to the incense.

5 When you are ready to leave, take a leaf, twig, stone, or feather from that place, to be kept under your pillow until after the next full moon.
Happy dreaming . . .

LITHA—FLAME TALISMAN SPELL
TO DRAW ENERGY AND STRENGTH FROM THE SUN

PURPOSE To gain energy that you can carry right through to the winter solstice.

BACKGROUND Litha, or the summer solstice, celebrates the sun at the height of its powers. On the longest day, we honor the strength of the sun just before the days begin to shorten again. It is generally well known that the sun has some positive physiological effects on humans: at this time of year we are generally more outgoing, happier, and healthier. This spell enables you to capture some of that sun power to carry

HOW TO CAST THE SPELL

YOU WILL NEED

One red candle, 6–8"/15–20 cm in length

One white candle, 6–8"/15–20 cm in length

Matches or a lighter

One sharp iron nail

One plain copper disk with a hole through it

One 24"/60 cm length of fine cord

One tea-light in a jar

TIMING Cast this spell at Litha—see pages 22–31 for details.

CASTING THE SPELL

As part of your Litha celebrations, work the first part of this spell indoors in a properly cast circle prior to going out overnight to await the Litha sunrise.

1 Light both candles.

2 Using the nail, inscribe on the disk a circle divided by eight lines meeting in the center and overlapping at the edge.

with you throughout the summer and all through the shorter days of the fall and early winter to the winter solstice.

The sun is fire in its most elemental form—encapsulating even a little of its energy on the magical plane can provide great strength to those who invoke it. This talisman uses the powerful symbol of the sun's rays to magically embody that power. It should be prepared just prior to going outdoors into the open overnight in order to greet the sunrise on the longest day. As dawn breaks, place the talisman on a stone or rock so that the first rays of the sun will shine down and charge it with strength.

3 Hold the disk in your left hand, then cover it with your right and close your eyes. Focus on the afterimage of the candle flames behind your eyelids. Visualize it moving through your body to your solar plexus and through your hands into the disk.

4 Thread the pendant, and take it with you to greet the sunrise.

5 Place it on a rock next to the tea-light, which should be lit as dawn breaks. As sunlight strikes the pendant, raise your arms and say:

Ignite the sacred
Fire within.

6 Wear it until the winter solstice.

LITHA—SPIRAL SPELL
TO PRODUCE OPPORTUNITIES TO TRAVEL AND MEET NEW PEOPLE

PURPOSE   To create travel options and lead the way to new friendships.

BACKGROUND   At Litha, in the center of the light half of the year, we tend to spend more time out of doors. Many of us make travel plans in the summer, either for relaxing vacations or visits to friends and family. Humans tend to be more gregarious generally in the lighter half of the year, perhaps because the outdoors offers us more flexibility in our travel and social arrangements, or because we simply have more energy when the sun is at the height of its powers. Whatever the reason, it is a good time to get out and about, and an even better time to cast a spell for travel opportunities and new friendships.

The spiral shape used here is an ancient symbol of the mysteries of life, death, and regeneration—a symbol of spirit, or connection. In this spell, we are working so that connection manifests as opportunities for travel and meeting new people. You will need a sandy beach to work on, which may not afford you a great deal of privacy from vacationers at this time of year, but you won't look out of place among fellow beach visitors if you wear a swimsuit and carry a towel!

HOW TO CAST THE SPELL

YOU WILL NEED

A sandy beach

One fallen twig at least 18"/45 cm in length

Five pebbles of equal size

TIMING Cast this spell at Litha—see pages 22–31 for details.

CASTING THE SPELL

As part of your Litha celebrations, work this spell on a sandy beach as follows:

1 Using the side of your twig, smooth a 5 ft./1.5 m square area of sand.

2 Visualize a circle of white light entirely surrounding you and this area.

3 Standing outside the smoothed area, beginning in the center, use the twig to draw a clockwise spiral of at least five parallel curves, ending at the edge of the area.

4 Walk around the spiral clockwise, depositing the five pebbles equidistant from each other.

5 Imagine a line of light emanating from each pebble and meeting in the center to make a five-legged wheel. Watch it spinning faster and faster until it rises up from the ground and disappears skyward.

6 Step into the center of the spiral, taking care not to disturb its shape, and spend a while meditating on why you wish to travel and what new friendships would mean to you.

LITHA—SEA SPELL
TO BRING GOOD HEALTH

PURPOSE   To bestow good health—and the power of healing.

BACKGROUND   This is another Litha spell to be performed on a beach next to the sea. One of the joys of the warmer days is that traveling is easier, as is getting out into nature. Many of us are drawn to seaside locations at this time of year where we can enjoy being near the element—water—that produced the cells which millions of years ago developed and evolved into life as we know it. In the magical circle, water is the element of love, balance, natural justice, and healing, and it is with this latter aspect that this spell is concerned.

As Litha celebrates the glory of the midsummer sun—a symbol of health and well-being in its own right—it is possible to combine these aspects of its fiery power with the healing energies of water in a special blessing ceremony. You should be at the waterside at sunrise on the longest day to perform this ritual, which calls on Yemana, goddess of the sea, to bestow good health—and the power of healing. To honor this much-beloved lady of the sea, carry turquoise, pearl, or mother-of-pearl, to remind you of her blessing.

236

HOW TO CAST THE SPELL

TIMING Cast this spell at Litha—see pages 22–31 for details.

CASTING THE SPELL

As part of your Litha celebrations, work this spell next to the sea as follows:

1 At dawn, walk to the water's edge and use the twig to draw a triangle measuring 6 ft x 6 ft x 6 ft/1.8 m x 1.8 m x 1.8 m in the sand.

2 Place lighted tea-lights at each corner.

3 Stand in the center holding the goblet, and facing the water, say:

Yemana, goddess of the waves
Know me as your child
And grant me the power of healing.

4 At sunrise, carry the goblet to the sea, and fill it.

5 Return to the center of the triangle, and using the shell, scoop water onto your feet, saying:

Let me walk in health.

Scoop the water over your head, saying:

Let me be healed.

Then scoop water onto both hands, saying:

As I heal myself
So might I heal others.

YOU WILL NEED

A sandy beach by the sea

One fallen twig at least 12"/30 cm in length

Three tea-lights in jars

Matches or a lighter

One wine goblet

One large watertight seashell

6 Pour the remainder of the water into the center of the triangle, and extinguish the candles, saying:

By the grace of Yemana
So mote it be!

LUGHNASADH—
WINNOWING SPELL
TO CAST OFF BAD HABITS

PURPOSE To help banish unwanted habits.

BACKGROUND Lughnasadh falls in the period of the grain harvest, and one of the activities undertaken when reaping corn is the separation of the wheat grain from the chaff—known as winnowing. This act carries over into the symbolic "harvest" of our lives, and at this time we consider all of the good things that have come to fruition, gather them to us in appreciation, and decide what needs to be cast aside. Lughnasadh is therefore a good time for getting rid of bad habits.

You will need to spend some time considering what your personal harvest has been this year in order to acknowledge and appreciate the material and spiritual features of your life that have sustained and rewarded you. It is possible to consider life events as a part of that harvest—for example, a cherished plan that blossomed into success, the attainment of good health, or a valuable experience. Your pleasure in the things that are gathered in will enable you to identify those things that need to be cast out, particularly those within your control, such as tendencies of behavior. Shedding what is no longer needed is as much a part of the harvest as the celebration of abundance.

HOW TO CAST THE SPELL

TIMING Cast this spell at Lughnasadh—
see pages 22–31 for details.

CASTING THE SPELL

As part of your Lughnasadh celebrations,
work the first part of this spell in a
properly prepared circle; then repair
outdoors to a bonfire as follows:

1 Light the candles, saying:
Come the harvest
Come the fruit
Those I need and
Those I don't
Some I'll keep and
Some I won't.

2 Write down, one to each paper strip, the
good things that have come to you and
the habits you wish to lose.

3 Light the papers bearing these bad
habits, and drop them into the fireproof
dish to reduce to ash.

4 Sprinkle the ash onto the papers
bearing the good things that have come,
and fold each one tightly.

5 Go out to the bonfire, and cast them in
one by one, saying:
Blessings and curses
Come from the harvest
Return to the earth
To nourish next year's.

YOU WILL NEED

Three orange candles, 6–8"/15–20 cm
in length

Matches or a lighter

One pen with brown ink

Sufficient 3" x 1"/7.5 cm x 2.5 cm strips
of paper for each harvest blessing and
each bad habit

One fireproof dish

LUGHNASADH–HARVEST BLESSING SPELL
TO SHARE GOOD FORTUNE AND RECEIVE A BLESSING

PURPOSE To distribute magical gifts from the harvest to friends.

BACKGROUND The custom of harvest home—a community feast at the end of the harvest—has been kept since before medieval times in Europe. Many historical customs are attached to this meal, including the crowning of the last sheaf of corn (called "wheat" in the U.K.) at the feast. In some places, the dinner was partial payment from a farmer to the harvesters, but whatever its intention, the harvest home meal ensured that at least some of the harvest was distributed among the laborers. Lughnasadh, likewise, is a time for celebrating abundance *and* a time for sharing it.

    This spell uses the principle of distribution and the custom of the last corn sheaf to magically pass blessings to friends. You will need to work with at least one other person, and the more of you there are, the more effective the spell. Prior to the circle, get everyone to think how they might sum up in one word the greatest blessing they have received this year. Those who have been helped through difficult times by a friend might put "friendship," while those who benefited from a material blessing—say, a car—might write "mobility," and so on. Remember: blessings shared are never halved!

240

HOW TO CAST THE SPELL

YOU WILL NEED

Six orange candles, 6–8"/15–20 cm in length

Matches or a lighter

Nine stems of ripe corn (wheat) per person

One 9" x 1"/22.5 cm x 2.5 cm length of wide red ribbon per person

One 3" x 1"/7.5 cm x 2.5 cm strip of paper per person

Writing pens

One large basket

TIMING Cast this spell at Lughnasadh—see pages 22–31 for details.

CASTING THE SPELL

As part of your Lughnasadh celebrations, and in a properly prepared circle, work as follows:

1 Light the candles in the center of your circle, saying:

Harvest time, harvest time, all gathered in
The labor has ceased, and the feast
*   shall begin.*

2 Distribute nine stems of ripe corn (wheat) to each participant. Each should weave these into braids and loop them, then fasten them with ribbon, chanting as they work:

We weave you and hail you
As queen of the corn
When all's gathered in and
When you are sown.

3 Each person should write the word signifying their chosen blessing (for example, FRIENDSHIP, MOBILITY) on paper, keeping it secret. Fold it, and attach it to the hoop.

4 All corn (wheat) hoops should be placed in the basket. All are then invited to close their eyes and pick one.

5 When all the papers are distributed, they may be opened and read.

6 Hang the hoop indoors until Imbolc; then burn and sprinkle the ashes in your garden.

LUGHNASADH— CORN SPIRIT SPELL
TO ENSURE BOUNTY IN YOUR LIFE DURING THE FOLLOWING YEAR

PURPOSE To keep abundance in your home all year.

BACKGROUND Corn dollies—shapes and figures woven from corn (wheat)—are nowadays sold as good luck charms. Keeping them in the home was originally a way to capture the spirit of the corn and thus ensure an abundant crop the next year. Given the importance of the harvest in cultures where wheat is a staple food, it is not surprising that the custom of the corn dolly, with all its pagan associations, has endured for so long. The corn dollies that we now see in shops are the descendants of a craft that honored the spirit of the fields, and their intricate shapes are testimony to the skill of the weavers and the importance of the task they undertook.

You may be pleased to know that this spell does not require the expertise of a seasoned corn weaver, but it does draw somewhat on the original reasons for making corn dollies. Here, you will weave a spirit cage—which is not as cruel as it sounds, incidentally— to capture your own corn spirit, which will ensure abundance in your home throughout the next year. This will enable you to mark your appreciation of the blessings that have come to you and your household and magically reserve a little of it to "seed" abundance for the coming solar cycle.

242

HOW TO CAST THE SPELL

YOU WILL NEED

One green candle, 6–8"/15–20 cm in length

Matches or a lighter

Twenty-four stems of ripened corn (wheat)

One embroidery needle

One 4" x 4" x 4"/10 cm x 10 cm x 10 cm triangle of cardboard

One 9" x ½"/22.5 cm x 1 cm length of wide green ribbon

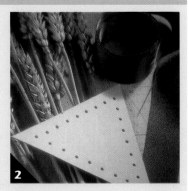

TIMING Cast this spell at Lughnasadh— see pages 22–31 for details.

CASTING THE SPELL

As part of your Lughnasadh celebrations, and in a properly prepared circle, work as follows:

1 Light the candle, saying:
  I call upon the element of earth to bless this circle.

2 Using the needle, pierce holes in the cardboard, one at each corner. Add seven along each side, between the corner holes.

3 Thread the corn (wheat) through root first, knotting it beneath the triangle and leaving 6"/15 cm of stem below the ear above the surface of the triangle.

4 Tie the stems together with ribbon just below the ears.

5 Hold up your spirit cage, saying:
  Come spirit of the corn
  Live within this home
  Stay content twixt turf and roof
  And have no cause to roam.

6 Hang it in your kitchen, and burn it at Imbolc to release your corn spirit into the fields for seedtime.

MABON—
POMEGRANATE SPELL
TO GAIN WISDOM

PURPOSE To advance spiritual development and attain wisdom.

BACKGROUND At Mabon, the hours of daylight and darkness are balanced before darkness prevails. Around this time, many trees shed leaves, fruits, and seed, and nature prepares for the deep cold of winter. There are numerous world myths to explain this seasonal change, many involving a descent into the underworld, to the land of the dead.

One such myth recorded in ancient Sumer almost four thousand years ago is the tale of Inanna's visit to the underworld. In this, Inanna's descent and eventual return account for a season of barrenness. This bears an uncanny similarity to the Greek legend of Persephone, whose disappearance from the earth causes her mother, the earth goddess Demeter, to mourn, thereby causing the first winter. Read more closely, both tales may be interpreted as adventures where both divine heroines go into the dark to gain wisdom. In fact, Inanna's slow striptease at each of the seven gates to the land of the dead is thought by anthropologists to represent the stripping away of ego in order to assume spiritual power.

In Persephone's tale, her consumption of six seeds while in the land of the dead binds her to remain there for six months out of every year. In this spell, you will eat six pomegranate seeds to help you explore the darkness of the winter and the quiet time within you, in order to gain spiritual wisdom.

244

HOW TO CAST THE SPELL

TIMING Cast this spell at Mabon—see pages 22–31 for details.

CASTING THE SPELL

As part of your Mabon celebrations, and in a properly prepared circle, work as follows:

1 Light the charcoal disk, then the candle, saying:

> I call upon Inanna, queen of heaven
> Earth, and the land of the dead
> Wise beyond reckoning
> To bless my spirit quest
> And guide my footsteps
> Through the darkness.

2 Sprinkle the dittany onto the charcoal.

3 Slice open the pomegranate, then extract six stones and eat them.

4 Close your eyes. Imagine yourself sinking into the darkness behind your eyelids, going deep into the dark, where there is nothing but silence. Remain there for as long as possible; then slowly return to the circle.

YOU WILL NEED

One charcoal disk in a fireproof dish

One purple candle, 6–8"/15–20 cm in length

Matches or a lighter

Two tablespoons of dried dittany of Crete

One whole pomegranate

One sharp knife

5 Blow out the candle, and burn it for an hour at each sunset until it is gone.

6 Bury the pomegranate deep in your garden, and keep a dream diary throughout the winter.

MABON–WILLOW BARGE SPELL
TO CAST OFF SORROW

PURPOSE To help you to stop dwelling in the past.

BACKGROUND In the wheel of the year, Mabon is in the west, the element of water. As the memories of the summer fade with the light, many of us are prone to sadness. Spiritually, we are in the time of water—a place of emotion and sometimes of sorrow. It is also a place of departures—the sun sets in the west, and for our ancestors, that was where the dead went. At Mabon, we can cast melancholy thoughts aside— and indeed, send them "across the water" to the sunset in fine style.

HOW TO CAST THE SPELL

YOU WILL NEED

Five willow switches 12"/30 cm in length

One reel of natural twine

One thin twig 8"/20 cm in length

One 4"/10 cm square piece of white paper

One 3" x 1"/7.5 cm x 2.5 cm strip of paper for each sorrow

One white candle, 6–8"/15–20 cm in length

Matches or a lighter

TIMING Cast this spell at Mabon—see pages 22–31 for details.

CASTING THE SPELL

As part of your Mabon celebrations, conduct this ritual outdoors as described above, as follows:

1 Construct a "long ship" shape by bending and fastening the switches, using two to form the rim of the hull and the others to shape the rest of it.

2 Secure the 8"/20 cm twig "mast," and thread the square paper "sail" onto it.

3 Write one sorrow per strip of paper, and fasten them to the mast.

For this spell you will need to be outdoors by a tidal river or sea in order to send your sorrows on their way. The idea here is to prepare a "Viking funeral," such as that prepared for Baldur in Nordic legend, and such as was witnessed in Rus by the Arab traveler Ibn Fadar in 920 C.E. The construction of the willow barge is very simple, and the remains will not cause any pollution or leave any dangerous rubbish at the waterside.

You will need to think about the causes of your sadness, as you must be able to identify these in order for the spell to work.

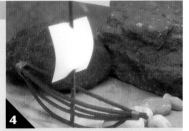

4 Place your boat next to the water. Plant the candle in the sand, and light it, saying:

Set sail into the west
Across the water
Away from my heart
All sorrows named.

5 Place your right hand on the mast, and mentally send all anguish and regrets you have named into the boat.

6 Drip candle wax onto your willow barge, and set it alight. Watch until the tide carries off the remains.

MABON—APPLE SEED SPELL
TO OBTAIN ARCANE KNOWLEDGE

PURPOSE   To improve your magical abilities.

BACKGROUND   Mabon coincides with the apple harvest, and apples and apple trees feature quite strongly in world mythologies, both in relation to gaining knowledge and to entering another realm. In the Judaic myth of Adam and Eve, consumption of a single fruit that grows on the Tree of Knowledge results in the first man and woman passing through the gates of Eden into another world. In the Arthurian legend, Avalon, sometimes called the Isle of Apples, is part of a Celtic otherworld. In this spell, you use apple seeds to travel into the realm of magic and gain arcane knowledge to aid your spiritual development and magical abilities.

There is a message hidden inside the apple; cut in half horizontally, it reveals the shape of a five-pointed star, symbol of humanity and the five sacred elements. The free-standing star, or pentagram, represents spirit; depicted in a circle, as a pentacle, it represents the planet earth. As spirit is the element that joins all things together, and many magical folk honor the earth as sacred, the pentacle is much loved by witches. If you wish to attain the knowledge of the *Wicce*, or "wise ones," create an apple seed talisman using this spell.

HOW TO CAST THE SPELL

TIMING Cast this spell at Mabon—see pages 22–31 for details.

CASTING THE SPELL

As part of your Mabon celebrations, and in a properly prepared circle, work as follows:

1 Light the candle, saying:
Old one of the apples
Waiting with your sickle
Give me the courage
To grow in your knowledge.

2 Halve the apple horizontally, then place all the seeds in the pouch and tie it around your neck.

3 Eat half of the apple, and close your eyes.

4 Imagine you are walking in an orchard of apple trees. In its center stands an ancient tree and below it, an old woman. Approach her and repeat the last two lines of the rhyme you have spoken. Mark carefully all that she does and says, and when she is finished, return from your inner journey to your circle.

5 Bury the remaining half apple outdoors.

6 Wear the apple seed talisman for one lunar cycle, keeping a dream diary, and note any "coincidences" that happen around you—it is now for you to interpret these symbols and their meaning.

YOU WILL NEED

One black candle, 6–8"/15–20 cm in length

Matches or a lighter

One seeded apple

One sharp knife

One white 2"/5 cm square drawstring pouch

One 24"/60 length of fine cord

SAMHAIN—CRONE SPELL
TO PRODUCE PSYCHIC DREAMS

PURPOSE To aid all-around psychic development.

BACKGROUND Samhain is the season of the crone—the "old woman" aspect of the goddess, the divine midwife who brings us into life and helps us cross over into death. A guardian of sacred thresholds, she also spins, weaves, and cuts our life threads. Because of this, she is sometimes depicted as a spider or represented by a web. Sometimes known as the "hag," or Cailleach, the crone is strongly connected with psychic abilities and the ability to walk between the worlds—the capacity to traverse the borderland between everyday reality and other realities such as faerie or the land of the dead.

HOW TO CAST THE SPELL

YOU WILL NEED

Two teaspoons of dried mugwort

One teaspoon of powdered elder leaves

Six drops of cypress essential oil

Mortar and pestle

One charcoal disk in a fireproof dish

One black candle, 6–8"/15–20 cm in length

Matches or a lighter

TIMING Cast this spell at Samhain—see pages 22–31 for details.

CASTING THE SPELL

As part of your Samhain celebrations, and in a properly prepared circle, work as follows:

1 Blend the mugwort, elder leaves, and cypress oil in the mortar and pestle.

2 Light the charcoal, then the black candle, saying:

> *Hecate, goddess of the crossroads,*
> *Direct me.*
> *Weaver, guide my thread into*
> *The spaces between.*

Shamans are said to walk between the worlds when they engage in magical acts, follow their intuition, or enter a lucid dreamtime in order to bring back important information or expand their spiritual understanding.

Being psychic is less about foretelling the future than it is about learning to inhabit this "between space" in order to grow. Hecate, one of the many names of the crone, as the guardian of thresholds and spinner and weaver of the great magical web, is the ideal goddess to appeal to if you wish to improve your psychic abilities. You will need to visualize the crone for this spell.

3 Sprinkle the incense onto the charcoal, and inhale the scent.

4 Close your eyes. Visualize yourself walking from the east to a crossroads at sunset and stopping to face north. From

this direction, a dark figure approaches. This is the crone. When she stops, she will beckon you to follow her. She will lead you to a gateway; do not pass through this time, but note what it looks like and any symbols that are written on it. This is the gateway through which you must pass before you can walk between the worlds— and you will need to look out for it, or its symbols, in lucid dreams during this winter.

5 Keep careful note of your dreams between now and Imbolc.

SAMHAIN— GATEWAY SPELL
TO COMMUNICATE WITH THE DEAD

PURPOSE To speak with our beloved dead.

BACKGROUND Samhain is the time of year when the veil between the realms of the living and the dead are thinnest. This is when we remember and honor our ancestors as well as the recently dead, and in many circles we build a gateway to the

west—the quarter of death—through which the dead might come and visit just for that one night.

Giving ourselves this special time to acknowledge our sorrow at being separated through death from friends or family is a healthy approach. Western society generally discourages too much contact with death, and just as the bodies of our loved ones are tended to away from home by professional funeral directors, so our feelings are filed away so as not to cause embarrassment in public.

At Samhain, we can let ourselves feel sad at departures and acknowledge the importance to us of those who have died. The Samhain circle is a safe space in which to grieve—and remember on our own terms—those we have lost.

HOW TO CAST THE SPELL

YOU WILL NEED

Two blue candles, at least 12"/30 cm in length

One white candle, at least 12"/30 cm in length

One charcoal disk in a fireproof dish

Matches or a lighter

Two teaspoons of dried Solomon's seal

Approximately 25 seaside pebbles

TIMING Cast this spell at Samhain—see pages 22–31 for details.

CASTING THE SPELL

As part of your Samhain celebrations, and in a properly prepared circle, work as follows:

1 Place the blue candles at the western quarter of the circle and place the white one to your left.

2 Light the charcoal, then the blue candles, and face the "gateway," saying:

> *Ancestors of blood, ancestors of spirit*
> *You are honored here*
> *I call my beloved dead to this gateway*
> *Only those who wish me well may enter*

Sprinkle incense onto the charcoal.

3 Name friends or relatives who have died in the last year:

> *I remember [name] who . . .*
> *I want to say this to you . . .*

4 For each person, place a pebble near the white candle. Next, remember those who have passed away before this year, and then groups of people you wish to commemorate.

5 When you have finished, and the pebbles are heaped around the white candle, light it, saying:

> *All are mourned, remembered, and honored.*

6 Say farewell, and close the gateway before the circle is closed. Return the pebbles to the sea.

SAMHAIN–THARFCAKE SPELL
TO PREDICT YOUR FORTUNE IN THE COMING YEAR

PURPOSE   To gain insight into your fortune for the next solar cycle.

BACKGROUND   There are many recipes for tharf cake, all associated with this time of the year and all including the basic ingredient of oats. Tharf cake eaten at Samhain reputedly has the special quality of foretelling the fortune of those eating it. This may be related to a much older custom in which flat cake with a little darker dough mixed in would forecast the death in the next year of the one unlucky enough to receive a slice with the fateful "shadow" on it. The purpose of this tharf cake is much less morbid; it predicts, instead, where your fortune will lie in the next twelve months.

   The methodology employed here is very similar to that of reading tea leaves, in that it involves interpreting patterns from the dregs or leavings of a drunk or eaten substance. Here, crumbs from a tharf cake are tossed into a small bowl that is overturned and removed, and the formation of crumbs is read according to the guidance below. Tharf cake (*tharf* comes from a word meaning "unleavened" in Old English) has been eaten at this time of year since before Anglo-Saxon and Viking times.

254

HOW TO CAST THE SPELL

YOU WILL NEED

One black candle, 6–8"/15–20 cm in length

Matches or a lighter

Butter, oats, and wholewheat flour, 4 oz/115 g of each

Sugar, 2 oz/50 g

One teaspoon of allspice

Chopped apple, 2 oz/50 g

One tea plate per person

One small bowl

TIMING Cast this spell at Samhain—see pages 22–31 for details. Bake your tharf cakes prior to casting the circle.

CASTING THE SPELL

1 Mix all the ingredients, adding the apple last; roll them and cut them into round cakes, and bake at 350°F/180°C until firm.

2 As part of your Samhain celebrations, and in a properly prepared circle, work with friends as follows:

3 Light the black candle, saying:
   Hail to the cake
   Hail to the baker
   Hail to the coming year.

4 Distribute one cake each. Eat half and crumble the other half onto another plate.

5 Taking turns, tip the crumbs of each person into the bowl, then pour them back onto their plate and read the crumb patterns as follows:

MAINLY TO THE EDGE:	*you will work for your bread*
MAINLY TO THE CENTER:	*necessities will come easily*
TO THE LEFT:	*fortune leaving*
TO THE RIGHT:	*fortune coming*
TO THE TOP:	*you will triumph over adversity*
TO THE BOTTOM:	*guard your health*
SPIRALS, CURVES, OR CIRCLES:	*what is owed will be repaid*
STRAIGHT LINES, ANGLES:	*a steady income*
HORSESHOES:	*a journey will bring luck*
ANIMAL SHAPES:	*guard your home.*

6 Place the crumbs outside for the birds after the circle.